DARKWOLF UNLEASHED

E. Don Harpe

Flint River Press

Ellijay, GA

E. DON HARPE

Original title: born wolf – DIE WOLF The Last Rampage of the Terrible Harpes

Second Printing - February 2014
Flint River Press - Ellijay, GA 35040
ISBN-13: 978-0615748030 (Flint River Press)
ISBN-10: 0615748031

THIS BOOK is dedicated to my wife Helen, and to my children, Shelly, Jason, Syntha, and Derek, all of whom have never wavered in their faith in me and my writing.

IT IS dedicated to Wayne Scott and Delilah Reed, who believed in me and my work, and were kind enough to read the manuscript and offer suggestions as the book progressed.

FIRST LAST AND ALWAYS, it is dedicated to my father, Birtle Odell Harp, who was the Harpe before me, and to my mother, who gave me the gift of loving to read and write. I think of them daily, and miss their wisdom and guidance.

E. DON HARPE

There is one called Harpe who walks with the Wolf as a brother. They are evil, hungry, and un-killable. Kill them today, tomorrow they return, even more evil, and hungrier. Beware the Wolf, Beware The Harpe.

Cherokee Legend of the DarkWolf

E. DON HARPE

PROLOGUE

Silas McBee and Jim Tompkins stood in the soot and ashes of the burned cabin, staring at the remains of the three people who died in the fire. Two are adults, a man and a woman, one is a small child. From marks still visible, it's plain they were dead before the fire started.

McBee is between 35 and 40, overweight and already balding near the crown of his head. He is fair skinned and the store bought broadcloth cloths he wears are dirty, covered with ash and soot and soaked with sweat. Tompkins is older, perhaps 60, much more weathered, and is as slim as McBee is heavy. He wears leather clothes, made of tanned deerskin, and they have plainly seen better days. His skin is tanned almost black from the sun and elements, and his hair is long and worn down and unfastened. He wears no hat, and carries a Kentucky long rifle in his left hand as he uses a long stick to poke about in the ashes.

They look at the three charred corpses lying just outside what is left of one of the walls, and McBee shakes his head.

"I think maybe this will be all we find of the Stegalls, Jim." McBee is clearly having trouble with the manner in which the people died.

Jim Tompkins spit a streak of brown tobacco juice from his mouth, which barely missed the corpse of the man. "Yessir, I believe yer right. But I don't think that's the body of Moses Stegall."

McBee looked at Tompkins, and back at the body. "Me neither. The woman is Mary Stegall, all right, and I think the man is Major

William Love. From the way they was killed, I spect we know who we're dealing with here."

"Yessir, I spect we do. Only two men around what cut up folks that bad. It had to be the Harpes.

I hate to think they're back, but it's them, sure enough. Stegall said he had business with Love, just a day er so ago when he was over to my place."

McBee squatted down and picked up a handful of the ashes. He sifts them through his fingers and let them blow away in the wind. "We never know, when we make plans, how they air going to turn out."

Tompkins watched the ashes drift to the ground. "Well, yer right bout that, fer shore, Squire McBee. Whar do ye reckon Moses might be? Thar hain't no more bodies in this cabin, I'll swar to thet, so he wasn't here when she burnt."

"Nosir, that's the way I see it too." McBee said.

Tompkins stared off into the distance, as if he could see something that wasn't there. "Ye don't think Moses lit out after the Harpes, do ye?"

McBee looked at Tompkins for a moment before answering. "Naw, he has more sense than that.

"Yessir, I spect he does. Probably ain't been here yet, don't know what's happened."

McBee looked down the same little worn path that Tompkins was looking at. "Reckon as how ye'd better be seein' if you kin track down John Leiper. I think we're goin' to be needin' him."

"Well, sir, I kin find Leiper, but air ye sure bout wantin' him? He knows 'em." Tompkins paused for a moment, then cut his eyes over toward Squire McBee. "Ye knows 'em too, don't ye Squire? Haint you knowed these boys a long time?"

McBee sighed, a long low sound that told of the heaviness he felt in his heart. "Reckon I have, old son, reckon I have. I met their daddy onc't, back on Kings Mountain. Back in the war."

1

It was almost sundown when John Harpe walked into the small clearing where his cabin stood. He'd been gone for more than three months, and it was good to be getting home at last.

Like many of his fellow Carolina settlers who remained loyal to England, John had been away fighting the King's war, the war the colonists called the Revolution. He didn't particularly believe in the cause of the British, but he was a Tory, like his Daddy, and his Daddy's Daddy. So in this war, he'd fight for the King. But in his heart John knew the colonies were right, freedom from England was the most important thing in the New World, and the revolutionists meant to have that freedom, no matter the price.

On his journey back toward Granville County, South Carolina, John had been thinking and had decided that if the way old Ferguson had lost the battle of King's Mountain last month was any indication of the way the tide of the war had turned, then the colonies freedom was surely close at hand. For a man who was supposed to be one of the King's leading officers, Ferguson had botched things up to a fare thee well.

Damn-nation, thought John to himself. *That fight didn't even last two hours. T'was nothin' more than pure luck that ever man-jack one of us warn't kilt. Them colony boys fought like the Devil hisself. And them new rifles we had didn't do us a lick of good.*

John had seen Colonel Furguson fall, and he had known then the battle was over. Just as soon as he had the chance, he and several of the remaining King's men had just slipped into the woods and made for home. He didn't think of it as deserting, and should it come down to explaining, it was more like they were just living to fight another day.

Almost as an afterthought, John picked up the newfangled breechloader rifle Furguson had carried in battle. It was a good weapon, and Ferguson wouldn't be needing it any longer.

He took as many back trails as he could, to throw off anyone who might happen to be following him, and headed back to his cabin, and the family he'd left behind.

John knew his neighbors wouldn't welcome him home with open arms. Most of the people around this neck of the woods were none too fond of Tories, and all of them were more than willing to share their opinion with anyone who would listen. John knew they'd make it rough on him and his family, but he thought they could weather the storm. John was not a man to let anyone drive him from his home.

He knew all too well there were men who would kill him if they got half a chance, and he'd have to watch his back every minute, but he intended to try to work his farm, stay on his own land, and not bother anyone. Perhaps in a few years, all of this would be over and forgotten.

No matter, King's Mountain was the last fight he was ever going to fight in the name of the King of England. Given the slightest chance, John would turn his coat and join his neighbors in the fight for freedom.

It had been raining for the better part of a week now, and the woods were wet and uncomfortable. Harpe was glad when he began to see familiar landmarks that told him he was getting close to home.

He wanted to see his small cabin, and just thinking about his two sons filled his heart with gladness.

But most of all, he wanted to see Amandy.

Amandy was the prettiest girl John had ever seen, and there was nothing he wouldn't do for her or his two boys.

Micajah had just turned twelve, and Wiley was ten, and both were already expert woodsmen, handy with rifle or knife. They had provided meat for the table while John was away, and kept the place up in a way that did the two of them proud.

John was a mountain man, not much given to words, but he meant to tell the boys he was mighty proud of them, just as soon as he got home.

Of course, he'd have to greet Amandy first, and he could hardly wait.

2

Although the daylight was fading, John saw the old dead tree that had stood behind the cabin had finally fallen, and was leaning against the cabin wall at the back of the house.

That's strange, he thought. *I know we cleared all the timber away from the cabin this summer.*

As he started in the direction of the log, suddenly he saw it begin to move. For no apparent reason, the log seemed to lift itself and go sailing three or four feet away from the cabin.

John was at the back of the cabin in an instant, and wasn't really surprised at what he found.

"I should have known," John said, when he saw his oldest son Micajah standing there brushing off his hands.

He grinned at his eldest son. "It either had to be ye, or two grown men to have thrown that old oak tree thataway," he said. "I swear, Micajah, I believe yore about as strong as anybody ever I seed, man or boy."

"Pa," Micajah cried, "Pa, yore home. Mama. Wiley. Come quick. Pa's come home."

At the sound of Micajah's voice, Amandy and Wiley came rushing out of the cabin.

Tears ran down Amandy's face as she threw her arms around her husband.

"John, oh John, it's really you. We were afraid you'd been killed on that old mountain. They was a rider come through last week and told us not a man was left alive, what fought for the King that day. And he told us we wouldn't be a'staying here much longer, either. He said the folks herebouts won't abide no Tories living here. Oh John, I'm so glad yore safe."

John wrapped his strong arms about his pretty wife, and looked at Wiley as the boy spoke.

"Pa, they said if'n we didn't leave, why they'd just run us off, and burn down the cabin. They won't do thet, will they Pa? Ye won't let 'em, will ye?" It was plain the boy was upset and that didn't set too well with John.

John ran his fingers through the bright red shock of his youngest son's hair. "No Wiley, not as long as I'm alive, they won't run us off. But I spect they'll make things awful hard on us. Awful hard."

"Well, they've already started, Pa," Micajah said, pointing to the tree he'd just moved. "They chopped down that old tree and throwed her up agin the cabin jist today. I don't know what fer. Me and Ma and Wiley was at the spring, and Ma was washing clothes, and me and Little Wiley was taking care of her, jist like you told us to do. If'n I'd been here at the house, I'd a taken me a shot at the rascals. I'll get me one o' them rascals one 'o these days, wait and see."

"Ye did real good boys," John said. "Ye got to take care o' `yer Ma first, always remember that. Ye can always find the time to settle a debt later. I jist want ye to know I'm mighty proud o' both of my boys. I think ye'r a lot closer to being men, and I'm proud of ye."

As the weeks passed and the days turned colder, there were more attempts to try to force Harpe and his family to leave the South Carolina country. His small lean-to of a barn was burned down, and one of his horses, a little red mare, was stolen. Harpe, although not a wealthy man, had managed to purchase two horses. He used them to work his small farm, and the boys dearly loved to ride them about the meadow. Wiley was turning into a first rate horseman, and even at his young age, there were few men around who could out ride him.

But now one of the horses was gone.

Even though John had a good idea of the identity of the neighbor who had taken it, he had no idea at all how to go about getting it back, short of violence. He knew he already had too many hands turned against him to provoke them any more than was absolutely necessary. He needed the horse, true enough, and it went against his nature to let a man steal from him, but he waited, thinking that silence was the best course he could take right now.

Just last week, when John went into the settlement to buy some meal and a little salt, five men set upon him and beat him severely, telling him if he didn't leave the country, he was as good as dead. John knew he could have beaten the men, especially if he'd turned the Wolf loose, but he knew if he still had a chance to live in this country, he couldn't afford to injure or possibly kill four or five men. He took the beating silently, and smiled to himself, thinking perhaps this was best.

He knew only too well the Wolf wouldn't have been satisfied unless blood was shed, and for the Wolf, the more blood, the better.

John made up a story about the horse being spooked by a snake to explain his bruises to Amandy and the boys. There was no use in frightening them any more than they were now. Of course, John didn't think Micajah was frightened at all. He was mad, and ready to strike out at something, or someone, but he didn't seem to be frightened. Not like you'd expect a twelve-year-old boy to be. And John Harpe was sure he knew why.

It had to be the Wolf.

May God help us all if the Wolf is already taking control of the boy, he thought.

3

Winter turned to spring, and spring to summer, without any further actions from Harpe's neighbors. Still, he knew they hadn't forgotten. It had been a long cold winter, and there was a lot of work to be done now that the weather had turned warm. But Harpe knew as soon as the men of the settlement had finished planting their crops, and repairing the damage the harsh winter had left behind, they'd get back to the business of trying to drive him and his family out. John knew they would use any means to make him leave, and if he wouldn't leave, then they'd just kill him.

Well, they'll try to kill me anyway, he thought. "That might not be as easy as they think."

Sure enough, it would be no easy job to kill John Harpe. He was a large man, known for his great strength and fighting skill, and was among the best marksmen in the country. Harpe wasn't afraid of anything in the world. He'd fight one man, or five, if the need arose, and more often than not he'd win. The beating he'd taken in town had been from ambush. They'd jumped him in the dark, used a club to knock him down, then hit him as many times as they could as fast as they could. And of course, Harpe hadn't called upon the power of the Wolf.

Well, let 'em come, he thought. *They'll not find easy pickings in John Harpe.*

Come they did. Late in the night, when Harpe and his family were fast asleep. To the door of the cabin the men came slipping, with drawn weapons and burning torches. Men who had once been friends of Harpe, but were now set against him.

Men who, in other times, had helped raise the very cabin they now intended to burn. Men who had helped clear a patch for his corn, and drunk his whiskey and danced to his lively fiddle tunes in celebration of the cabin, or the crop.

There were men out there he'd given a helping hand to. More than once, if the truth were told.

Yet, none of that mattered anymore. Harpe had fought as a Tory, and that was too much for the men of the new America to forget.

Of course, they didn't want to come in the daylight, when they knew they would be recognized. The deeds they were about were not deeds a man could be proud of, but rather they were deeds of such a cowardly nature they would forever be ashamed should any find out who they were.

So it was at night they came, but even though Harpe was sleeping, he had prepared for just such an attack as this.

John had been busier than most of his neighbors during the spring months. He'd repaired the winter's damage around his homestead as quickly as possible, and had made his fields ready and planted his corn crop. Knowing his neighbors would be coming to visit him when they had a little time on their hands spurred Harpe to make some unusual preparations.

He instructed Amandy to make a strong, thin rope of rawhide, upon which he tied the rattles of several large rattlesnakes. He had also journeyed to the village of one of his Indian friends and there he had traded for four very large, very mean dogs. He'd tied one dog to each corner of his cabin with a piece of the rope Amandy had made. The dogs would be quiet unless something, or someone, disturbed them, then they would make such a racket as to raise the dead, or the soundest sleeping man.

It was sometime after midnight, when the men came creeping to the cabin. Not noticing the thin rope in the darkness, two of the men tripped upon it, setting the rattles to shaking. Thinking they must have stepped directly upon a big rattlesnake, both men jumped back, causing a loud ruckus. It was this noise that awakened Harpe and his family. Being careful to make very little noise of his own, John picked up his freshly charged rifle and knelt by the small window in the front of the cabin. Sure enough, he was able to make out the outline of a figure skulking around in the dark. Drawing a fine bead on the leg of the intruder, Harpe squeezed off a round. Seeing the shadow tumble to the ground, and hearing a cry of pain, he knew he had scored a hit.

At the same time, the dogs at the rear of the cabin began to loudly bark, and he could hear them straining at their ropes. Knowing there were several men about the cabin, Harpe called to Amandy and the boys to gather in the front room, where he had placed ammunition and some meager supplies, for just such an attack as this. Should the men decide to remain for a siege, Harpe could hold out for at least a week, maybe longer. But he didn't think they would stay past daylight, and he was right. He heard excited whispers and a few low grunts of pain as the other men helped their wounded comrade out of the yard and off into the woods.

The next attempt came less than three weeks later. This time a burning torch was thrown out of the forest, landing on the roof of the cabin. Wiley was sleeping directly under the spot where the torch landed, and was awakened immediately. Springing out of his bed, he ran into his father's room, calling; "Pa! Pa! Come quick. The cabin is on fire."

Running out of the cabin in haste, John was almost hit by a shot fired by someone hiding in the edge of the woods. Falling to the ground, he grabbed at the chopping axe lying by the cabin wall. Hacking at the rope that held the big dog, John cried; "Go git 'em boy, sic 'em. Eat the bloody bastards alive. Go get 'em boy."

The big dog was in the woods almost before the commands were out of his master's mouth. Almost immediately out of the forest there came the sound of someone running at full speed, not minding the brush or the undergrowth.

Getting to his feet, John saw Micajah was already on the roof; beating at the small flames the torch had started. Amandy was standing in the door of the cabin, not hurt, but there was a scared look about her features, and she seemed extremely worried.

"I jist don't know, Mister Harpe," she cried. "I jist don't know what we air going to do. They ain't never going to leave us be. I'm afeered fer the boys, John, I don't want my young'uns hurt none."

"Hush now, Mandy." Harpe said. "Long as they be breath in my body, they won't hurt nary a hair on the head o' none o' my family."

John Harpe meant every word he spoke. He was not afraid of man nor beast, and he'd surely kill to protect what was his.

4

Like most of the women of her time, Amandy Harpe was made of stern stuff. She suffered heat and cold, joy and pain, and the many ups and downs of life with a cheerful outlook. She was happy most of the time, though she didn't have a lot of worldly possessions. She had her husband and children, and a strong faith in God that served her well.

Amandy was only concerned when the safety of her children was threatened.

Her cabin, with its flowers and small vegetable garden, was all she needed and all she wanted in the way of a home. When she was forced to endure the many hardships living in the wilderness brought, she gave thanks for the good things she had. When the pain of childbirth ripped through her body, she said a small prayer her children would be born healthy and strong.

When it seemed as if every hand in the Carolina country was set against her family, she gritted her teeth and vowed they'd not find the Harpes easy targets, nor quick to run.

Through good times and bad, Amandy took things one at a time. And without fail, she hummed the little song she had learned so long ago.

The melody floated down on soft butterfly wings from Amandy's earliest memories, and the words had been sung to her even when she was at her own mother's breast.

Whenever her boys heard her little song, they knew all was well with the world, and sometimes they even sang along.

Amandy was humming the tune as she and little Wiley walked along the path back toward their cabin. They'd been into the settlement to buy some much-needed supplies, and were returning home, and Amandy had not given much thought to danger. She had not reckoned with the three men that came up behind them on the path. The three men beset Amandy and Wiley as they drew closer on the narrow path, calling them names and making rude gestures to them.

"Ye air mighty brave folk, when hit comes to fighting women and little children," Amandy said angrily, as she turned to look at her tormentors.

"Do ye think ye'd be this brave if'n my husband were standing here? I think not. Thar ain't a one o' ye who would face John Harpe straight on, and all 'o ye know it. We've been friends and good neighbors to ye people, and now ye set upon us in this manner. Whar's all the Sunday preachin' talk yer always sayin'? Ye think because my man fit fer the King God has deserted us. Well, it's the likes o' ye that God has deserted, and not the Harpe's."

"Hold on thar, Missus Harpe, jist a minute," she heard someone call, and turned to see the speaker was none other than Mister Homer Biggs, the community's only blacksmith.

"I've been a friend to John Harpe, nigh on to ten year now, but I cannot hold fer any man whut fights agin his neighbors. The King is in England, and the colonies must have their freedom. Yore husband had the chance to fight with the rest o' us, but he chose to folly in the footsteps o' his father, and fight as a Tory. He should have known the rest o' the men in these mountains would be dead set agin him. We got no truck with ye and yer child, but we want yore family out o' this community, and we mean to run ye off. If'n ye won't leave without a scuffle, then a fight is what ye'll get. None o' us kin go hand to hand with yer husband, right enough, but we kin burn ye out, and if'n we has to, we kin go farther than that. Tell John Harpe he no longer has a place in these mountains, and we mean to see to it he leaves."

Knowing there could be no reasoning with the angry people, Amandy again turned to leave. As an afterthought, she said over her shoulder.

"Ye air right, Mister Biggs, my man fit fer the King. But it tweren't so long ago that ever last one o' ye was loyal subjects too. Mister Harpe jist still has a lot o' feelin's in his heart fer the way that he, and all o' ye were raised. Don't forget that. And if'n ye come skulkin' round our cabin, then ye jist might find yerself face to face with the Harpe, and which one o' ye desires that?"

While his mother had been talking, little Wiley had spotted a smooth round stone, nearly as big as his fist, lying by the side of the path. Quickly scooping it up, he concealed it in his hand as they started down the trail.

Sneaking a look back over his shoulder, Wiley saw the men had turned back toward town. Drawing a dead bead on the back of Homer Biggs, he let the stone fly. Wiley felt a touch of satisfaction when he heard the solid "thunk" the stone made as it struck the prominent rear end of the man. He quickly picked up a large tree limb from the side of the path, and turned to see if Biggs was going to come after them.

Not really being hurt, Biggs decided not to pursue the matter, and continued on towards town. This was a smart, although unknowing, move on the part of Biggs. Young Wiley had made up his mind he would not be further abused by this man. He intended to use the tree limb to smash in the man's head should he come at them again.

Catching Wiley up by the hair on the back of his neck, Amandy spoke to her upset son.

"Little Wiley, t'was a foolish thing ye did, and ye need yer hide tanned fer it. But I'm not of a mind to take a rod to ye. Ye must always protect yer family above all others, and thet's whut ye were doin' today when ye hurled thet rock at thet old scoundrel. Ye air a Harpe, boy, and don't ye forget it. Nobody can run over a Harpe and get by with it. Yore Pa will be proud o' the way ye stood up fer us today. And don't fret yer head none either, yore Pa will take care o' the likes o' them people, should they gather e'nuff courage to come out to the cabin."

With a little smile, Wiley dropped the tree limb and took his mother's hand as they continued on down the long path to the cabin. Both mother and son hummed the little song of Amandy's, and it seemed as if the forest itself joined in.

5

John Harpe was a man of his word, but even the most diligent of men wear down with time. The attacks continued, on an average of one every three or four months, throughout the summer and winter of 1781. The boys were growing stronger, and every attack helped them to hone their fighting skills, and also served to make them bitterer.

Micajah killed his first man on a hot day in July 1782.

Several men rode into the yard of Harpe's cabin a little before dark that afternoon, their faces concealed by masks of course cloth, with slits cut for them to see through. John was at the spring when he heard the dogs set up a big commotion. Dropping the oaken bucket, he started up the path as fast as he could run. He hadn't gone a hundred yards when he heard a rifle fire. Praying one of his family hadn't been hurt, he ran even harder.

When Harpe reached the cabin, he found five men surrounding Micajah. Another man lay on the ground at his son's feet, his neck twisted at an odd angle. One of the men held a still smoking rifle, while the other four all had their guns trained on the boy.

As had been his habit for the past two years, John had two pistols at his belt. Drawing one, he ran into the yard and leveled it at the nearest man.

"I'll kill the next man that fires a shot," he shouted. "Whut do ye mean, coming upon my home in this manner? Have ye no common decency left a'tall?" Harpe was not bluffing about shooting one of them, and the masked men knew it.

"Harpe, yore boy kilt one o' us, with no provocation. We come out here fer to talk with ye, and to ask ye one more time to leave the country. We is tard o' fighting, and we don't really want to kill a man what has been a friend o' our'n, but ye be leaving us little choice." Although the speaker wore a mask, Harpe recognized Homer Biggs.

"Homer Biggs, yore a liar and a scoundrel, and a coward as well, to ride in here behind a mask, telling me to leave property which is rightfully mine. And if'n ye ever had any honor, ye've not showed any of it to me or mine. Didn't my Mandy midwife two o' yore children? Didn't I brang ye meat, when ye were down with the fever and couldn't hunt? And didn't I dig the grave, whenst we laid yore wife to rest? How kin ye turn agin a man what's shown ye more kindness than a brother?"

John spoke low, and the men on horseback knew he was sincere. He had been a good friend to each of them, and a better neighbor than most of them. But still they couldn't forgive him for the side he took in the war. The revolution had a strong hold on them, and nothing else meant half as much. They were fighting for what they saw as the noblest cause of their lives, and they would stop at nothing to win for the colonies. Nothing could stand in the way of freedom. Not friendship, not decency, and not even the killing of an entire family, should it come to that.

"Yore right, Harpe," the man behind the mask said. "Ye have been a friend to many o' us, and a good neighbor, but ye picked up yore rifle and fit with the wrong man on the mountain. Ferguson was a Tory, and a foe to all men who want freedom from the King above all else. We wants nothing to do with a man what fit fer the Brits, and they is nowhere in this country for ye, nor that murdering whelp o' yourn either. Why don't ye jist leave this country, afore they is more blood shed? Ye have two pistols in yer hand right now, and they ain't a one o' us what wants to die this afternoon. But ye know we'll be back. Yore boy cain't get by with breakin' Isham's neck, and ye should know that."

"Had ye not rid in here, raisin' cane and threatnin' harm to my family, Isham would still be alive. His death is on yore hands, Biggs, and the hands o' yore masked friends, not the hands o' an innocent fourteen-year-old boy. My boy was protectin' his Ma and his little brother from six armed riders, all wearing masks, and all meaning harm to his family. Hell's bells, Biggs, they ain't a court in the land what wouldn't see what happened here, and ye know it. Pick up yore dead, and leave my home. If'n ye return, and if'n it ain't as friends and neighbors, then they is apt to be more killing. I told ye, the days of my fighting fer the King is long over, and I desires freedom fer this country as much as any man among ye. Why don't ye jist accept it, and leave my family be?"

"We're sorry Harpe, we truly air, but they is no turning yore coat now. It's leave the country, or suffer the fate o' the other Tories what tried to stay. And ye know whut I mean," the masked Biggs said, as the other men draped the body of Isham Cannon across his horse, and prepared to leave.

"Leave the country, John Harpe, and this is yore last warnin'." With these parting words, the men rode away, leading the horse upon which rested their dead comrade.

John looked at Amandy, standing by the door of the cabin, and at Micajah, still silently standing where he had stood throughout the confrontation. Looking around, John noticed the muzzle of a rifle gun sticking through a firing hole in the cabin wall.

"Lay down yore rifle, Wiley," he called, "and come on out here. I need to have a talk with you and yore brother."

"Once't agin, boys, I want ye to know I'm mighty proud o' the both o' ye. Wiley, I seed that gun ye had poked out, and I know ye war fixin' to shoot one o' them fellers. It's only right and proper, fer ye to protect yer Ma. Now Micajah, it war wrong fer ye to break old Isham's neck, but it war even more wrong fer him to come ridin' in here like that. Ye did what ye had to do, and standin' up fer yerself and yer family is a thing a man has got to do. If'n ye don't take care o' what's yers, then ye won't have nothing. But boys, I'm telling ye both that what happened here today is shore to set everbody in these hills agin us, even them what has paid us no never mind up till now. They's already run off ever other man what fit fer the King, ceptin' me, and I reckon we will have to leave too, sooner or later. Maybe not tomorry, ner the next day, but one o' these days we'll have to pack up and go. They won't never let us rest as long as a one o' them remembers Kings Mountain. Now boys, I ain't afeerd fer me, but I am fer ye and yer Ma. We'll try to make it through one more winter here, but when spring comes, well, I reckon we'll be moving on."

Micajah's strange blue eyes seemed to be on fire. He was rock steady, in spite of just killing a man, and with a seriousness that belied his years, he solemnly asked his father.

"Pa," Micajah began, "why must we allow these men to make us leave our home? We cleared this land, and we planted these crops, and it war our sweat and blood what raised this cabin. They ain't got no right to tell us to go nowhere, Pa, they jist ain't got no right. I killed old Isham Cannon today with my bare hands, and I'll kill any man what sets a foot on this property agin. This is Harpe property, and they can't run us off. Why don't we jist get some o' them red Injuns what fit with ye in the war, and go on into town and kill the lot o' them, Pa. Why don't we jist do that?"

"Boys, one thang ye need always remember. We Harpe's fight er own battles. We don't need the red Injuns. Though they be our friends, it would not be right ner fitting to turn 'em loose on the folks in these hills. No boy, we is Harpes, and we will stand or fall on our own. Family, boys, family. That's all ye will ever have in this world. Ask no man fer nothing, and depend on no one cept yore brother. Harpes don't quit, boy. Not even should it mean the death o' us. Death holds no fear, boy, fer them that do not fear life." John was not sure the boys would understand much of what he was trying to teach them, but he hoped his words would stay with them. He knew in the years to come, probably sooner than later, the meaning of his words would become clear.

"Now boys, they might kill me, and they might even kill yer Ma, but the two o' ye has to remain alive. Someone must keep the name o' Harpe from dying.

"Yer Ma and me, we has had a good life together. If'n it comes to pass we must be buried afore another year goes by, then bury us on Harpe land. Up on the hillside, next to whar yore baby sister lies sleeping. Thet is a peaceful place, thet hillside, and a good place it will be to rest, whilst we wait to meet our dear Savior." John was not a religious man, but he had a deep faith, and believed in the Bible, though he was not sure there was anything in the good book that covered the Wolf that lived inside him.

He had never spoken to his sons in this manner before, admitting the fact he might be killed. Yet he knew his neighbors would not let him and his family simply pack up and leave, especially not after Micajah had killed Isham Cannon here today. They would demand blood for blood, and in the end, they would win. There were just too many for him to fight, even with the power of the Wolf. He'd fight, of course, but it was a losing battle.

Even if he really did leave the country now, he knew the people would just follow him. No, he would make his stand on his own land.

Mandy and me will surely die right here, he thought. *No help fer it a'tall. But I must make the boys understand they must leave when the fightin' begins. T'will do no good fer my sons to die here in these hills, fer something their Pa did.*

John walked over to an old stump at one corner of the cabin. He'd been planning on burning the stump out, but with all the feuding and fussing going on, he hadn't been able to spare the time. He sat down on the stump and called the boys over to him.

"Boys, here is the way of it," he began.

31

"The riders will return. Most likely they'll come at night, and they'll have torches. And they won't jist be five er six o' them this time either. They'll brang enough men to finish the job, and they'll burn us out. I'll fight, ye know thet, but they may be too many o' 'em fer me to win. If'n I can't beat 'em, then I'll try fer to get yer Ma and the two o' ye to safety. If by chance they happen to get the best of me, then I want yore solemn promise thet both o' ye will sneak out through the trap door and hide in the woods. Ye knows these woods better'n anybody, and they'll never find ye onc't ye get out of the cabin. After they leave, if'n they be anything left, I want ye to pack up whut ye kin and head on down towards the Tennessee country. They's fine land down thar, and two smart lads like yerselves will make it well and good." John paused for a minute to collect himself, and took a long look at his boys. *They'll make fine men,* he thought. *But they have the Harpe danger about them, sure enough.*

With a deep breath, he continued.

"Now Micajah, I'm leavin' ye as the head of the Harpe family. Take good ker o' yer Ma and yer brother. Yer already the size of a grown man, and stronger than any two men ever I seed, so ye'll be understanding why I'm giving Wiley the long gun. When I come running into the yard today, I seed the fire in yore eyes, and I didn't even have to look to know you'd killed a man. I seed that same fire in my Pa's eyes, and they tell me it shines in my own eyes at times. Whut I'm tellin' ye boy, is thet killing comes natural to some Harpe men. It's a thang what comes from inside them, and it is terrible to behold. Tis a Wolf inside ye, a wild rage ye must larn to control. He's a wild and vicious animal, the Wolf is, and onct he tastes blood, he's almost impossible to stop. The Wolf is as much a part o' ye as it has been o' me, and ye must ever be on guard thet it not be turned loose."

It was plain John was more than a little disturbed by what he was telling the boys, and it was just as plain the boys had no idea what he was talking about. He was not sure they would even believe what he was about to tell them, but he had no choice anymore.

"Anyway, Micajah," John continued, "I'm a'givin the long gun to Wiley. And I'm a'givin ye this."

John Harpe took a leather thong from around his own neck, and with great care handed it to Micajah. Securely attached to the thong was beautiful oval medallion. Made from pure silver, the medallion bore the ancient sign of the Harpe family. A gleaming, four pointed silver star, set against a background of blood red crimson. It was bordered by a hand worked design that was almost like a twisted rope. The medallion was a little larger than a silver dollar, and the four points of the star were thin and sharp and slightly raised.

As Micajah took the amulet from his Father's hand, it seemed to come to life. The silver was warm to his touch, and no sooner had he touched it than it began to pulse in time with his heartbeat. Touching one of the star's points to his finger, Micajah was surprised to find it was sharp enough to cut him. Micajah watched as his blood spread about the face of the medallion, mixing and mingling and becoming as one with the dark background of the piece. He instantly knew how the Amulet got its color. Holding it, Micajah had never felt such raw power before in his young life.

"This amulet is yore heritage, Micajah. Ye are my oldest son, and a true Harpe, and from this day forth ye shall have the honor and bear the pain of wearing the ancient silver star, the symbol of the Harpes for untold ages. Tis a blessing, boy, and a curse. From Old Erin crost the water it came, on the neck of my Grandfather. My father wore the Amulet, and wore it with pride. He handed it down to me, and now tis yores to wear. Yore blood has now mixed with the blood of many generations of Harpes, and they watch o'er ye now, even as they have watched o'er the others who have worn it. Tis an awesome responsibility, Micajah, to bear the name Harpe, and to wear the amulet. It has powers, son, of which ye shall learn as ye grow older. Though it seems but warm silver, in truth it is a living thang, and it offers the one who wears it certain things. It gives its owner a certain amount of protection against danger, which is why I'm passing it on to ye today. I think perhaps you will have need of it in the days to come, more so than I will. Onct the amulet is around yore neck, t'would take a lucky shot indeed to brang ye down, and hurts and sickness will almost be thangs of the past. But its power carries a price. A powerful price ye'll not be wantin' to pay anymore than you absolutely have to. There is a Wolf inside the amulet, son, and it must be fed. It craves blood and its hunger is ravenous. You will soon find it is almost impossible to keep from listenin' to the voice of the Wolf when he demands you kill for him. That's why I say ye must larn to control the Wolf. The amulet grows stronger when the Wolf feeds, hence it wishes for the Wolf to remain free at all times." Once again John paused and looked at the boy at his side.

"I pass this on to ye, knowing full well thet ye will have need of its powers soon. Wear it with pride son, but with caution. I have managed to control it, but may God have mercy on us all, should it ever be given full rein. Its appetite is strong. I have never known a time when it didn't hunger, and ye should know if'n ever it breaks loose entirely, it may well feed upon ye as well as yore enemy."

The two boys sat spellbound by their father's words. They knew nothing of the amulet, and while they had seen it around their father's neck, they had placed no significance upon it.

Micajah slowly raised the leather thong to the top of his head, and slowly lowered in into position around his own neck. As the amulet settled into place, the boy stiffened, and his eyes closed. For a second he trembled as though he were being shaken by the hand of God himself, or by the hand of whatever power controlled the silver star.

When at last his eyes opened, he was no longer the boy that had sat down on the stump beside his father. He had grown older looking, and the glowing blue eyes seemed strangely devoid of emotion, though they shone with an even more savage intensity than before. Wiley looked at his brother, and for the first time in his life, the boy knew fear. He knew a terrible change had taken place in Micajah, and he could feel the stirrings of something evil deep inside himself.

Micajah turned to look at Wiley, and his eyes burned his brother's soul. He reached out and took his brothers hand and brought it slowly towards the amulet.

"Ye be a Harpe too, Wiley, even as I am, and yer blood belongs as much as mine on this silver star."

So saying, he brought one of the stars points forward and drew it across the middle fingertip of Wiley's right hand. Wiley shuddered with a depth of raw emotion such as he had never known. His eyes stared straight ahead, unblinking, as his blood flowed across the medallion and mixed with that of his brothers and of the many Harpes before him. Deep, deep inside, he felt something tightly grip his very being, and he knew from this day forth there would never be any true peace for him. His eyes touched Micajah's face, and as they stared into each other's soul, there was a bond forged that would last till the very end of time itself. They were caught in the force of the Harpe amulet, and their souls would forever be as one with the wild and terrible demon that their father had called the Wolf.

Wiley's blood mixed with that of his brother on the star of the amulet and had not even had to time dry when the boys heard the savage whisper as the Wolf spoke to them for the very first time.

Harrrrrpe, the voice whispered in their minds, *Harrrrrpe, soooooon shall we hunt.*

They both smiled as they heard the raspy whisper of the Wolf, somehow knowing that his power was now theirs.

As they walked back to the cabin, the boys hummed the tune they had learned from their mother. Whatever happened, they were ready. They were Harpes.

6

It was late May of the next year before the night riders once again returned to visit John Harpe and his family.

John heard the dogs set up an awful barking, and came awake at once. He leaped from his bed and ran into the front room of the small cabin.

"Get up, Mandy, get up," he shouted.

"Micajah, Wiley, get up. They're here, the riders have come back." He picked up the loaded rifle from its place in the corner, poked it through a firing hole in the wall, and squeezed off a shot. A grim smile caused his lips to curl back from his teeth as he heard a cry of pain, and saw one of the milling shadows pitch from his horse.

The clearing around the cabin was aglow from the light of a dozen torches, and the wild cries of the riders could be heard as they rode round and round in the yard. The barking of the big dogs added to the din, and when the men saw one of their number was down, they began to fire their weapons at the cabin.

Amandy was standing by the fireplace, an anguished look upon her face. Micajah and Wiley had climbed down from their sleeping loft, and were clutching their Mother tightly. John gave the boys a quick look and hastily said; "Remember boys, if'n I fall, ye must run into the woods. Go to yore secret hidin' place and wait till the danger's past. Don't try to fight the riders. They is too many fer ye, and I've told ye the two o' ye must live. The Harpe name must live. Swear to thet boys, swear to thet right now."

But even as the boys began to speak, John saw Amandy thrown backwards, as though hit by a giant fist. She was jerked from the grasp of her son's arms, and before they knew what had happened, she lay slumped against the wall, warm blood spurting from a hole in her breast.

Without a word, Amandy Harpe was dead. Her blood was streaming down the face of Micajah, and there was a look of shock on his boyish features.

John leaped to her side and lifted her body up and held her for a long moment. With a last look at his sons, John lifted his face and screamed his rage to the heavens. He then gently lay down her down on the floor and shoved the rifle into Wiley's hands. Grabbing Micajah with an unholy strength, he literally flung him towards the secret opening in the rear of the cabin.

"Go boy, go now," he grunted. The voice was a guttural animal sound, almost a growl, and not one the boys had ever heard before. Silently they began to crawl out the small opening. The last sight the boys remembered of their father was the unholy blue fire that burned in his eyes.

John Harpe watched as his boys left the cabin, then looked down upon the body of the woman he loved, and for the first time in his life, he released his inner control completely. All the mental shackles were thrown off and the chains that had held the demon in check for so many years fell away like so much rusted metal. Harpe walked over and opened the front door of the cabin, and his grim smile turned into a full snarl as he bounded out of the cabin and among the men who rode about his front yard. He paused for a moment to vent his rage in another scream, and leaped full force into the arms of destruction.

7

The wild Wolf was loose. It was completely unfettered, and terrible was its rage. Never before had John Harpe dared to so completely give in to the raging hunger. Never had he once dreamed such savagery existed within him.

To his right he bounded first, and grabbing two men by their heads, he bashed them together and felt brains and tissue squish between his fingers. His mighty fist came around and caught yet another man full in the face. Bone splintered and gave way, and his eyes popped from his head.

The Harpe felt a mighty blow to his back, and turned to see a man behind him with a tomahawk, preparing to strike him again. With an oath, he wrenched the hatchet from the hand of the man with enough force that two fingers were pulled from the man's hand, and he didn't even watch as they fell into the dirt. With a full roundhouse swing, he struck the man on the neck with the tomahawk with such a blow that his head was severed from his body. The man fell from his horse and lay on the ground threshing about, not realizing he was already dead.

Looking about and not seeing anyone close enough to strike, Harpe threw the tomahawk and saw the jagged edged blade bury itself deep into the head of a man twenty feet across the clearing.

Harpe's attack had been so swift and so ferocious the men at first had been unable to stop him. But now they were composing themselves, and beginning to fire their rifles at the berserking Harpe. Once, twice, three times he was struck by a well-aimed shot. Another shot rang out and once again he was hit.

John Harpe stopped in his tracks, and with fists clenched, he raised both mighty arms skyward. His arms were outspread and trembling, the muscles corded and knotted like rope. For a moment he stood still in the clearing, his head raised and his eyes closed. Another volley rang out as the men hastened to fire as quickly and as many times as possible. The heavy lead slugs struck Harpe full in the head and body, and still the men continued to fire. A full twenty rounds punched into the mighty frame, until at last Harpe sank to his knees. With a last defiant snarl, he turned his fearful, burning gaze upon each man in the throng.

"Goddamn ye. Goddamn ye all for cowards and murderers. Shoot on, and may ye all be damned to eternal hellfire. But remember this, and mark it well. I am the Harpe. In this life or the next, I will be yore destruction."

With those words, the fire went out in the raging blue eyes of John Harpe, and a son of the Wolf died.

In the deep woods, at the same time as the fire was extinguished in John's eyes, two boys turned into men. Deep in the eyes of the Harpe child Micajah, a cold blue flame was kindled, and again a voice whispered…

I am the Wolf, Micajah, and I hungerrrr.

The voice in Micajah's mind was low and seemed far away.

Today you become the Harpe. We shall hunt, young one, together you and I shall hunt. The Wolf is dead, Micajah Harpe, long live the Wolf, long live the Harpe.

And the world screamed.

8

Every instinct inside Micajah and Wiley was telling them to stand and fight, but they had no choice but to obey the words of their father and leave the cabin. They had seen their mother fall, and both boys had seen the awful fire that burned in the eyes of their father, and they knew the end was near.

Even as they crept through the woods, they heard the terrifying sounds of battle coming from the front of the cabin, and over and above the other sounds, came the mighty roaring of a wild animal. In its rage, it sounded as if it were defying the Devil himself.

On it went, for several minutes, and then there came the sound of many rifles firing. After that there was a sudden and awful silence. Even the trees seemed to be holding their breath. The boys stopped in their tracks and strained their ears for the sound of anyone moving through the forest, but the silence was complete. The boys looked at each other in the darkness, and knew in their hearts their father was dead. He would never quit fighting, so long as he lived, and also the roaring of the animal had ceased. Somehow the boys had connected that wild sound with their father, and when that voice became silent, they knew the worst had happened. They understood the roaring battle cry of the animal had actually come from what their father had called the Wolf, and that he had set it loose upon the men who had attacked their home and killed their mother.

"Our day will come, Wiley," Micajah said, in a hushed yet harsh whisper. "We won't hide out in these woods ferever. We'll go back and kill ever last one o' the bastards. They'll pay fer whut they've done to the Harpes this night. They'll pay in blood, and it'll be me and you thet collects the debt."

Although the pain was evident on their faces, not a single tear was shed between the two of them.

They made their way deeper into the forest; to a place only the two of them knew. A small cave they had found several years before, which would offer protection from the weather, and a hiding place that would not be likely to be found. Wise beyond their years, and also acting upon the advice of their father, the boys had taken a small supply of food to the cave, along with water and a supply of firewood. They could live in the cave for weeks if need be, without having to come out for any reason. By then, the townspeople would think they had fled the country, or else had perished by wild animals or a roving band of Indians.

They didn't know it, but life in a cave would come to be a second part of their nature, and in later years, they would take refuge within the darkness of Mother Earth on many occasions.

The boys were adept at living off the land, and could find more than enough small game and roots and berries to live on. They were quite satisfied with an occasional squirrel or a tasty rabbit, and now and then they managed to kill a fat groundhog, but hardly a day passed they did not miss their mothers home baked bread. Not a single day passed they did not sit in the cave and plan their revenge on the men who killed their parents.

"It can't be an open attack, Micajah," Wiley said more than once. He knew his brother wanted to kill every one of the raiders with his bare hands, but Wiley knew they needed to be a cleverer than that. "No open attack. They are too many and too powerful. We must slip up on their cabins as they did our'n, in the pitch darkness of night. And we must be kerful o' their dogs, too, lest the sniff us out and betray us."

"We won't have to worry bout the dogs, Wiley," Micajah said. "I got a plan. We'll take along some fresh squirrel meat, and slip up right quiet and feed the hounds. Whilst they is eatin' we'll light our torches, set the cabins on far, and fade back into the woods. We has plenty o' time. They ain't a man jack among 'em what kin find us here in the woods."

"When they come a runnin' out of the burning cabin, then I'm jist naturally gonna shoot a hole plum through ever one o' the bastards." Wiley liked that part. He wanted nothing more than to spill the blood of every man that took part in the raid.

"An I'll tell ye something else, brother," Micajah exclaimed one day. "Do ye remember thet little red horse they stole from us? We is going to get it back, I swear thet. And maybe even more."

The days passed, and the boys remained hidden in the woods, and soon the townspeople forgot about them. As the brothers had supposed, they were considered dead, or the people thought they had left the country. There had been no efforts made to catch them after the first few attempts had failed to turn them up. The boys exercised a great amount of patience, doing little save living in the cave, and awaiting their opportunity.

Over two months passed before the boys felt it was safe to venture back to their burned cabin. Traveling silently through the forest, they kept to animal trails, or trails used only by Indians, and no one even suspected they were anywhere around.

It was a hot day in August when they at last stood beside the charred timbers of what was once their home. Some well meaning person had buried their parent's bodies, but had done so at the wrong place. The boys set out to dig up the remains, intending to follow their father's final instructions about where he wanted to be buried. Using sharpened sticks and an old knife they found in the ashes, they slowly dug two graves on the hillside overlooking the farm, close beside the tiny grave that was already there.

When they had moved the remains of their parents to their new resting places, and had finished replacing the dirt into the graves, Micajah sent Wiley back to the site of the cabin to pick a handful of the yellow flowers their mother had planted. Even among the signs of death and destruction, the blossoms had flourished and were beautiful to behold.

Micajah carefully placed the flowers on the graves, and both boys knelt down in the fresh dirt. Micajah took Wiley by the hand, and for the first time since their parents had been killed, the boys allowed the hot angry tears to fall from their eyes. It was among the few times they ever allowed themselves to cry, and was one of the last times in their lives that they felt any kind of remorse for anyone or anything.

Kneeling by the graves, Micajah removed the Harpe amulet from his neck. He held fast to one point of the star, and bade Wiley to hold to another.

"Father and Mother," Micajah said, his voice low and throaty. "We swear by the ancient silver star of the Harpe clan, thet yore deaths shall not go unpunished. They war wrong, the men who did this to ye, and they'll answer to the two o' us. Harpes we air, and Harpes take ker o' their own. The men who war at the cabin thet night will know the fury o' the Wolf. They will feel his fangs, and he will devour their hearts. They will be destroyed, even as they destroyed us. On this amulet we swear."

"And Pa," Micajah said as an afterthought, "When this be over, the Wolf shall never be set loose again."

High above the boys, unseen by all, an eagle circled majestically in the sky.

Only one sound disturbed the silence that hung over the hillside. The soft, sad sound of the little tune of Amandy Harpe, being hummed by her first born son as he knelt in the grass by her grave.

9

George Robert Turpin had not thought about the Harpe boys now for a couple of months, but for some reason tonight his thoughts had returned to them, and to the night the men killed John and Amandy Harpe. Turpin had been one of the masked men who rode on the Harpes that night, but he wasn't proud of it. Harpe had been a friend to every man in the raiding party, and Turpin couldn't bring himself to believe what they did that night was right. Amandy Harpe had mid-wifed both of Turpin's children as well as the Biggs's sons, and it was hard for him to think it may have been one of his bullets that took her life that night. He didn't think it was, but he couldn't be sure. He hadn't fired a single shot in the direction of the cabin, but the facts were plain. Someone had fired into the cabin, and Missus Harpe was dead. It didn't make a lot of difference which of them had fired the fatal shot; they were guilty to a man.

Turpin was glad he hadn't been among those closest to Harpe when he went on the rampage. It was a terrible sight to behold. Harpe came roaring out of the cabin, and began killing men left and right. He was like a wild animal, with no thought of his own safety nor of anything else. The blood lust was on him, sure enough, and more than one of the raiders met their maker that night. Why, he must have taken twenty or twenty-five bullets before he finally went to the ground, and even then he lived long enough to put a curse on every man who heard his voice.

No, Turpin wasn't proud of his part in the events of that crazy night, and he knew there was nothing he could do to make up for it.

Turpin's wife and oldest son had gone back to the cabin and buried the remains of Harpe and his wife. It was the only decent thing they could do, and it should count for something, come judgment day. He would have liked to have found John Harpe's boys, and looked out for them until they were a few years older, but he found it impossible to do.

The boys were more than likely dead by now, killed by some beast of the forest, or by one of the bands of red Indians who roamed the countryside.

Even as Turpin dug deep inside his own torment, outside his cabin two shadows silently slipped out of the trees, one shadow moving to each corner of the wall. Two hands gently placed a generous helping of freshly killed squirrel meat down before the dogs that slept there. The dogs cocked their heads and eyed the shadows, but instead of barking, they began to feed on the squirrel. The shadows once again blended into the darkness, and as the dogs fed, the shadows became very busy.

One crawled to the front of the cabin, and carefully peeked in the single window. Turpin was sitting in an old cane rocker, an open Bible on his lap, bathed in the faded, flickering light of an oil lantern that sat on the rough mantelpiece.

The small shadow slipped away from the front of the cabin as silently as it came, and joined the other in the back.

"He seems to be asleep, Micajah," Wiley whispered. "He's a sittin' in his chair, but his eyes is closed."

Micajah quickly struck a spark to the tinder on the torch he held, and in less than a minute from the time Wiley had made his way back around the cabin, the boys had two torches roaring with flame.

Micajah held his torch against the cabin, and gave thanks there had been no rain for the last few days. Turpin's cabin was old, and dry as corn shucks. The walls caught fire almost as easily as the torches had, and the cabin was burning wildly in a very short time.

Wiley had thrown his torch to the roof, and the boys smiled when they saw the fire there was no less bright than the one on the walls.

George Turpin came awake with a jolt. He felt the heat of the flames, and saw the orange and red flickers as they danced through the cabin. Knowing the thick black smoke that was rolling along the ceiling would soon overcome him, he didn't even try to save any of his meager belongings. He jumped to the front door, determined to at least make his own escape.

But when he threw open the door, he was startled to be met by a wild apparition, a strange boy swinging an axe handle toward Turpin's head. The last thing Turpin ever saw in this life was the eerie glow of Micajah's blue eyes. Turpin reeled backward from the blow, and as he lost consciousness, he heard a harsh voice call;

"I send ye to eternal hell-fire, George Turpin. I am the Harpe, the wild Wolf, and I am yore death and destruction."

George Turpin became the first to feed the ravenous Wolf that now lived inside the boy. But only the first. From this day forward, the Wolf would feed well indeed.

The boys took absolutely nothing that belonged to Turpin. They went to his cabin with the sole intent of killing one of the men who had mistreated their family. They burned the cabin to make it look like an accident, so no one would suspect they were about. When they left, they even carried with them a short stub that was left from one of the torches, and ate the remaining squirrel meat as they traveled through the woods. As they walked, both boys subconsciously hummed the haunting little melody.

It was now the second week of November, and the mountain folk were readying themselves for winter. The nights were already freezing cold, and the days had a numbing chill in the early morning and in the afternoon.

The boys were also preparing for winter. They had laid in a good bit more firewood, and had stolen several heavy quilts. They had gathered enough soft dry moss to make comfortable beds, and had a supply of dried meat, salt, meal, and corn. They could winter in the comfort of their cave, with no fear of being discovered. No one, save a few Indians, knew they were in the territory; therefore no one was looking for them.

They passed their time in solitude, neither boy being given much to playing games, and they waited for the right time to go after their next target.

10

As the winter grew colder, day-by-day Henry Potter's supply of firewood was growing smaller. It was the middle of February 1784, and the winter had been the coldest anyone could remember. Cows and hogs had frozen to death, not thirty yards from the cabins of their owners. There had been a heavy blanket of snow for the better part of six weeks now, and showed no signs of melting. The mountain air was crystal clear, and so cold it hurt your teeth to breathe it. On many days, the sun shone brightly, but offered no warmth, and more than one man lost his life that winter.

It was on just such a day that Henry Potter went into the woods for firewood, and never came back.

Neighbors found his frozen body lying half under the ice in a small creek about two hundred yards from his cabin. From the sign in the snow's crust, it was plain to tell he had slipped on the icy bank and hit his head on a large rock when he fell. Whether it killed him instantly or not was hard to tell, but was of no consequence anyway. He never opened his eyes again. The cold water drained the life from his body, and when he was found, ice had frozen the features of his face into their final grimace.

The men who found Potter read the signs plainly, but quickly, and didn't bother to look around the scene for further clues as to how the man had really died.

Of course, they wouldn't have found any clues, had they looked. The two boys had used a tree branch to wipe away all traces their feet had left in the snow and ice along the creek bank. The rock

Henry Potter had struck his head upon was huge and heavy, and no one would have believed a boy such as Micajah could have smashed in the man's head with a rock that weighed so much.

No one wondered, if at all anyone even noticed, why there was a mark shaped like a four pointed star imbedded deeply into the flesh of Potters forehead. The outline of the star was blood red, and the lines it left were raw and angry looking.

Even as wild Wolf drank the icy red blood of Henry Potter, Potter's soul warmed the cold silver star. A voice echoed from the depths of the forest, out across the snow in the meadow, and was colder even than the ice itself.

I am the Wolf...I am the Harpe.

No one thought it strange that both Turpin and Potter had met accidental deaths. Life in the mountains was harsh. Men perished, but life went on.

Sam Duncan had been accused of stealing a hog from the farm of Thomas Barr, and when Duncan faced Barr and denied the accusation, Barr had shot him squarely between the eyes, killing him instantly. Duncan's brother, fearing Barr would next come for him, left his cabin in the dark of night and quit the country, never to be seen again. That left only two of the original nightriders alive. Jeremiah Massie, and the leader of the riders, Mister Homer Biggs.

11

Jeremiah Massie was a large man, weighing in excess of four hundred and fifty pounds, and standing three inches over six feet tall. He was not a man to be trifled with, and had killed his share of men, both white and red. He was as mean as they come, and feared neither man nor devil.

It was late May of 1784, a full year after the riders had killed John and Amandy Harpe, and tonight, as he had done almost every night since the raid, Jeremiah Massie re-lived the incident for his own satisfaction. Massie had been the first to fire into the cabin, and was certain beyond a shadow of a doubt it was his bullet that had killed Amandy Harpe.

"Twas all she deserved," Massie often remarked, "To remain true to that Tory brigand." Massie didn't regret his part in the raid on the cabin, and had repeated to others he would do the same thing again, and enjoy every minute of it. He cared not that Harpe had killed several men that night, and scoffed at the idea that the man had cursed them even as he died.

Massie, like Biggs, believed in freedom for the colonies at any cost, and held only hate in his heart for each and every man who had fought on the side of the British. It was Massie, more than anyone else, who would not hear of Harpe turning his coat. Massie had lost two brothers fighting against the King, and he himself had been wounded in the same battle John Harpe had walked away from. Massie would not hear of any Tory remaining in the settlement, and swore he would kill every man-jack of them himself, should it come to that. He felt it was his destiny, and he relished the death of every British sympathizer.

Jeremiah Massie didn't know it, but tonight was the night when his true destiny would come calling.

Blue-eyed Destiny called Micajah and Wiley Harpe.

Although they waited until almost midnight to creep up on the cabin of Jeremiah Massie, Micajah and Wiley found the man still awake, and drinking heavily. To their surprise, two young girls sat at the feet of the huge man. One looked to be perhaps thirteen; the other a little older, and both had a haggard look of fright about them.

Every so often the man would reach down and fondle one or the other of the girls, slapping their faces if they showed the slightest sign of resistance. The eyes of the youngest girl were bruised deep purple and black, and swelled almost completely together. The other girl was in even worse shape.

A heavy set, ugly woman roamed about the room like a restless animal, all the time encouraging Massie as he molested the children.

Micajah and Wiley peeped through a crack in the wall of the run down cabin, and stared in disbelief at what they witnessed inside. Micajah laid his hand on his brother's shoulder, and they came to a silent understanding. This time they would turn away from their carefully made plans. This man needed a plain, open killing, and not a death dignified by making it look like a simple accident

Micajah would turn sixteen in less than a month, and already he towered five inches above six feet, and weighted almost two hundred and forty pounds. He strength was proportional to his size, and he used every bit of it in kicking down the door to Massie's cabin. He rushed inside the small room and didn't stop until he was standing full before Massie. Wiley was close on his brother's heels, the rifle in his hands primed and ready to fire.

Micajah stood staring at the slovenly Massie in the thin lamplight. "What manner o' man be ye," he asked, the words grating from between his teeth and sounding low and menacing in the smoky confines of the cabin? "Have ye stooped so low as to commit atrocities agin the likes o' these two innocent and helpless girls? We came here tonight to kill ye fer the wrong ye did agin our family, but it were to be a merciful death. A quick slash o' my knife and it would be all over. But now, I think not. It's not to be a quick death, nor will it appear to be accidental. Slow will yore death be, Jeremiah Massie, and painful as a man like ye deserves."

The huge man looked at Micajah, his beady little eyes bored into the boy, and the words he spoke only fanned the rage in Micajah's heart.

"Ah, whut have we here. I believe it be the whelp o' that infamous Tory scoundrel, John Harpe. Well boy, I helped kill yore Daddy, and it were my lead what took the life o' yer Ma. I enjoyed it too, I did. And I'll enjoy pinching off yore fine head. Come on over a mite closer, boy, so old Massie kin get his hands on ye. Ye won't sing sich a fine tune then. Jist a mite closer, thet's all I ask."

Suddenly, and with a speed that belied his size, he made a lunge for Micajah, and succeeded in catching the boy by the hair. He swung Micajah against the wall, also sending both of the girls flying across the room. Micajah hit the wall a jarring blow, but the big man didn't turn loose of his grip in his hair.

"Now sing me a purty tune, boy," he laughed, and jerked Micajah back across to the other side of the room, banging the boy's head into an oaken bucket that was lying in the corner.

Shaking his gigantic hands about, he handled Micajah's considerable weight as though it were nothing.

Micajah shook his head to clear it, and realized he had to do something, and do it fast. The man was too big, too strong, and too experienced in fighting. If Micajah didn't gain control of the fight quickly, the man would do just exactly what he'd said he would do.

He reached up and caught both of Massie's wrists, one in each hand, and slowly began to exert pressure. He squeezed on the bones in Massie's hands, and allowed himself a little grin when he felt the vise like grip began to loosen. With a mighty effort, he ripped the man's hands loose from his hair, and felt a lot of hair give way as he did so. Throwing his own head forward, he struck Massie a mighty blow in the forehead, and saw the man's eyes glaze over. Before Massie could react Micajah kicked him between the legs as hard as he could, and fell backward away from him.

Micajah took a quick moment to catch his breath, and saw the ugly woman had come back into the room with an even uglier pistol in her hands. She was making every effort to bring the weapon to bear on Micajah, but the huge body of Massie was between them.

"Wiley," Micajah shouted, knowing his brother was ready for whatever he needed to do. "Wiley, shoot the woman, shoot her now."

Almost before the words were out of his mouth, he heard Wiley's rifle speak and the woman's head exploded into a thousand bloody bits. There was a large hole where her nose had been, and the back of her head was completely gone, most of it splattered all over the walls of the cabin.

"Wiley, take the girls. I want to be alone with Mister Massie."

"Air ye shore bout this one, brother," Wiley asked? "Massie is a mean man, and not afeered to put up a fight. Let me jist shoot the bastard."

"No brother, I'm shore alright. Git the girls and wait fer me outside." Micajah's voice sounded strange to Wiley.

Then he turned for a second and looked at Wiley.

It was the first time Wiley had seen the Wolf flame dancing in his brother's eyes. The blue eyes burned brighter than Wiley had ever seen them, and a change came across Micajah's face. His face turned darker, and his jaws tensed, and his lips pulled away from his teeth in a savage snarl. From his mouth came a low sound, almost a growl, and Wiley felt chill bumps on his arms and on the back of his neck. Wiley knew without a doubt Micajah had loosed the Wolf, and without another word he hastily and roughly grabbed the girls and hurried through the open door, into the coolness of the night.

For the first time a trace of fear showed in Massie's eyes. It was no longer a young boy standing in front of him, but a wild, ferocious animal.

An animal that had every intention of tearing him apart bit by bit.

"Well, damn ye, whelp," Massie screamed. "Have at ye."

With an oath he jumped forward once again, straight for Micajah. But this time Micajah wasn't caught by surprise. The Wolf was loose, and ready for battle.

The boy was all muscle and motion as he sidestepped the giant's lunge. Micajah's big fist hit the man in the back of the head as he drove past. Massie hit the fireplace with a crash, where he grabbed a sharpened metal rod he had used as a poker. He lurched to his feet, wildly swinging the poker, and came at Micajah again. The poker whistled in the air above Micajah's head as he ducked underneath the attack. Such was the force of the blow the poker hit the cabin wall and was torn from the grip of the big man. It hit the floor with a racket, and had not stopped bouncing when Micajah caught it in his own right hand. Lunging forward at Massie, Micajah caught him trying to recover from the speed of his attack. Thrusting with all his great strength, Micajah drove the poker into the open mouth of the grunting Massie. The poker pierced the roof of Massie's mouth and entered his brain, and was driven completely out of the back of his head. Such was the force of Micajah's blow the poker was buried three inches deep into the wall of the cabin. With all his strength, Micajah pushed on the poker, driving it deeper and deeper into the wall. When he finally turned it loose, it supported the weight of the big man, and held him pinned against the rough logs of the wall. Panting for breath, Micajah moved close to the dead man, and with a grim smile, he pressed the silver amulet deep into the forehead of Massie, and left the mark of the Harpe clan.

The Wolf drank deeply of Massie's blood, and the Harpe walked away from the cabin without a single word or a backward glance.

The first time Susan Roberts ever saw Micajah Harpe was when he bounded through the door of the cabin and confronted Jeremiah Massie. From that day forward there existed a bond between the two of them nothing would ever breech. Neither time nor distance mattered. Though they were separated more than once in the years that followed, Susan always found her way back to Micajah. She knew he would return for her, should they be parted, no matter what else happened. If Micajah said go, Susan went, if he said stay, she stayed, and if he said he'd be back for her, then he'd be back.

When she looked up from the feet of the monster that had so cruelly used her and her sister for six years and saw Micajah standing there, she didn't see a killer come to commit murder on a decent man. No indeed. She saw a savior. A handsome young man come to rescue her from a demon. The strange fire in Micajah's blue eyes didn't frighten Susan. It was the fire of righteous anger, unleashed against those who deserved it. His words of wrath were music to her ears. He was a savior who killed a monster Susan herself had wished a thousand times to kill. Love was born with the first look that passed between them, and it was a love that would never die.

Susan had been almost nine, and her sister Betsy barely seven when their mother had passed away. For a year, their stepfather had used them to work his farm in the daytime, and to sleep in his bed at night.

Then one day, in a drunken stupor, he sold the young girls to Jeremiah Massie for twenty dollars in gold, a small hog, and four chickens. The girls soon found out that even as cruel as their stepfather had been to them, he couldn't hold a light to Massie.

For six years, Massie treated the girls as little more than animals. He worked them without mercy, performed unspeakable acts upon them, and beat them constantly. During the first year, the girls had tried several times to escape from the monster, but each time they were caught, and each time the punishment became more severe. Finally the girls gave up on running away, and resigned themselves to living with whatever perversions the man would place upon them. They agreed that when the opportunity came, they would kill themselves rather than suffer anymore at the hands of the man who owned them.

So it was that this was the way they were living the night Micajah and Wiley came to call.

When Micajah walked out of the cabin after killing their tormentor, Susan and Betsy saw him as a knight in shining armor, a hero, and placed the remainder of their lives in his strong hands. Over the next few years, the feeling came to be much more than love. It was undivided devotion and complete trust they placed in this strong youth, and not once in their lives did he ever betray them.

After his own fashion, he fed and clothed the girls, and provided them shelter, and eventually he came to take Susan as his wife. In reality, Betsy was as much a wife to Micajah as was Susan, and loved the man every bit as much as her sister. Each bore him children, and each followed him without question. They came to know the meaning of the terrible fire that burned in his eyes, and sometimes knew fear of the man. Micajah was not given to beating the women, but when the Wolf was upon him, and the black rage was in control, he could easily kill both of them without even knowing it had happened until it was too late.

The Roberts sisters knew there was a feeling that beat in his heart for them. Call it love, or call it something else, still he protected them and cared for them, and they were family. Above all, family meant everything to Micajah.

The Name was all.

Harpe.

They were Harpes, and to Micajah that was the way of it.

Susan and Betsy never again ventured far from the man they worshipped, and never wanted to.

As they rode away from the cabin of Jeremiah Massie, Susan heard Micajah humming a lonely little tune almost to himself. She later learned he hummed the tune at times of great stress, and sometimes when he found something that made him happy. When she asked about the song, he told her it was one of his most precious memories of his mother. It was the song she hummed to Wiley and him when they were babies, and it brought comfort to him, and set his mind at peace. It calmed his mind, and filled his heart with the only light in a dark and sad world.

Susan learned the tune, and found herself humming it at times. It seemed to bring comfort to her also, and became a small thing only the two of them shared. Not even Betsy knew the song. Susan determined she would teach it to her own daughter someday, when she and Micajah had children of their own.

12

Homer Biggs was worried. They had summoned him to the cabin of Jeremiah Massie early this morning to view the bodies of Massie and his woman. Biggs found it hard to believe anyone had been able to beat the man in such a fashion. On more than one occasion Massie had been known to fight two or three men at a time and whip them all. What kind of man could have beaten him this badly, and then killed him with his own poker? The fight had taken place at least three days ago, judging from the stench and the rot already setting in. The huge bloated body was still pinned to the wall, and the woman still lay where she had fallen. There was blood everywhere, and the cabin stank to high heaven from the filth.

The strangest thing of all was there didn't seem to be anything missing, though this was a clear case of murder. There were a couple of gold pieces lying on the table, and more were found in Massie's pockets. His fine rifle, of which he'd been so proud, had been smashed against the fireplace, and lay in fragments on the floor.

And of course, the Roberts sisters were gone. That was no surprise, as they had tried to run away before.

Tis no wonder they've left, Biggs thought, *the way the man treated them."*

But even though he didn't agree with the man's treatment of the two sisters, it was Massie's business. Homer Biggs was not a man to interfere with the private doings of another.

Biggs's mind was on the night they raided John Harpe. Thinking of the men who were there that night, he knew all too well he was the only one still alive.

There was the Duncan boy, but he'd left the country. The rest were dead. Turpin had burned in his cabin, Trotter had frozen to death, and now Massie had been brutally murdered, in his own cabin. Biggs wondered if there might be a connection, but dismissed the thought because he could think of no one who would want revenge for what they'd done to the Harpes. Of course, they'd never found the Harpe boys, but the two of them were too young and inexperienced to be able to kill this many men without being caught. It would have taken a full-grown man, and a very strong and experienced one at that, to have murdered Jeremiah Massie in the fashion in which he had died. There was no way two young boys could have done that. Besides, even though it was apparent Massie had been brutally murdered, everyone knew Turpin and Trotter's deaths had been accidents.

Biggs heard a sound at the cabin door, but he knew the other men who had been with him were already gone. He had bid them farewell, saying he would stay and bury the two bodies, as they had been friends of his.

Maybe one of them has returned to help with the digging, he thought.

Biggs turned to the cabin door and was surprised to see the two Harpe boys standing there, silently staring at him.

Homer looked at the boys and said; "What kin I be doin' fer ye, boys? Ye air the sons of John Harpe, ain't ye? I knowed yore Pa well, and was a friend o' his'n, back afore his untimely death."

"Aye, Mister Biggs," the smaller of the two boys replied, "We be the sons o' John Harpe, and we air aware ye' knowed our Pa. We air also aware thet ye war in the party what raided our farm, the night our Ma and Pa was kilt." Wiley was mad at this man, and he paused for a second to clear his throat before going on.

60

"I also rec'clect thet onc't ye told me and my Ma thet ye would kill our family if'n we didn't leave the territory. Do ye rec'clect speakin' them words, Mister Biggs?"

"Well, boys, I can't rightly say thet I do. Course, it's been more'n three year since yore Pa fit fer the Tories, up on the mountain, and back then why I jist might have said anything." Biggs recalled the incident on the road as clearly as if it had happened yesterday, but he knew better than to let on.

"Well, let me refresh yore memory fer ye," Wiley said. "Ye told us all them things, then I throwed a rock and hit ye square on yore fat behind. If'n I'da used a tree limb and kilt ye thet day as I intended, my Ma and Pa might still be alive. But I didn't. I let ye go back into town. Well, thar ain't a thang I kin do 'bout it now, I can't brang 'em back no ways a'tall. But I kin finish what I started thet day on the trail, Mister Biggs."

Without another word, Wiley raised the rifle his Pa had given him and shot Homer Biggs directly between the eyes, killing him instantly.

"Well done, brother, well done," Micajah said. "Now we has one more piece o' unfinished business to attend to, and then we can quit this Godforsaken country."

The boys left the cabin of Jeremiah Massie, leaving the dead where they'd fallen, their deadly handiwork a grim indication of what the years ahead held for them.

13

Walking the two miles from Massie's place to the farm of Royland Instone, the boys seemed almost happy. Their job was about over. They had avenged the death of their parents, and there was little to hold them here anymore. They intended to move on down into the Tennessee country, as John as told them to do, and stake out a home of their home.

Once again, Micajah hummed his song as he walked.

The boys found Royland Instone working his garden on the side of his big house. Instone was the most prosperous farmer in the territory, and yet was not above helping himself to the belongings of someone else if there seemed to be little chance of getting caught.

"Howdy, Mister Instone," Micajah began, "Do ye perhaps know who we air?"

Instone stared at the two boys for a long minute.

"I know who ye air alright boy. Yer the son of that Tory bastard, John Harpe." Instone replied. "I don't want ye coming round here begging to me, jist cause someone kilt yore Pa. He fit fer the King, and met the end he deserved. Now git out 'o here. They ain't nothing fer ye here. Nothin' but trouble."

"They's trouble here, right enough, Mister Instone," Micajah said, a smile playing at the corners of his lips, "but it ain't the Harpe boys that's in it. We ain't come a'beggin, we come to claim what is rightfully our'n. We know thet it war ye who took our little red mare, nigh three year ago. They ain't nobody cept the three o' us, so it won't do ye no good to deny it. Ye know tis the God's truth, and so do we. Now Mister Instone, if ye'll be so kind as to fetch her fer us, they won't be no trouble a'tall. We know ye still has her, fer we seen her in yore pasture as we walked up."

"They ain't a chance in hell o' me givin' ye one o' my horses, boys," Instone said with a harsh laugh. "Maybe yore right, and I did take her from yore Pa, but he war a Tory, and an enemy to everbody in these hills. Takin' one o' his mares warn't no crime boys, it war jist another act agin the King. Nah, I don't think I'll be a'givin' ye none o' my horses. Now, git off'n my land afore I take a stick to the both o' ye." Instone was mad, and it was clear he wasn't going to give up the mare without a tussle.

Micajah was just as determined as Instone. He wanted his mare back, and didn't really care what he had to do to get it back.

Instone turned back to his garden, expecting the brash youngsters to leave as he had told them to do. He was surprised when he felt a hard hand gather up the shirt at the back of his neck, not sparing the hair in the process. He was roughly lifted off his feet, and spun about in the air as if he were made of feathers.

"Let me make my position a mite more clear, Mister Instone," Micajah said, and Instone heard the raspy edge that had suddenly crept into the boys voice.

"I mean to take our mare. She don't belong to ye, and it's not right ye should keep her. Ye have more than anyone in this country, Instone, so why do ye insist on keepin' our little red mare. She ain't worth mor'n a few dollars at most. And ye know full well she's not your'n."

"She's mine, boy, she's mine all right," Instone said. "And I'll keep her till hell freezes over. I got mor'n anybody else in this country, and that's a fact, and I mean to keep everthang I got. Why don't ye jist go on down and tell the constable about yore horse, and see if'n it helps any. Ha. Naw, boys, I'll be a'keepin' the little red mare. Now git on with ye. Git on or I swear I'll make ye wish ye'd never set foot on my place."

Micajah slowly began to exert pressure on the back of Instone's neck.

"Let me explain it one more time," he said, and squeezed a little harder. The bones in Instone's neck began to rub together and pop, and the man could feel the pressure building in his ears. Micajah squeezed a little harder, and said; "I can pinch of'n yore head, Instone, and it would pleasure me a lot. And if'n I do, then I'll still take my mare with me when I leave. Now, I don't know as how I have to kill ye, but it shore don't make me no difference a'tall. Would ye like to reconsider givin' me back my horse, afore it's too late?"

Instone yowled in pain, as his eyes threatened to pop from his skull. The pressure didn't let up a bit. He collapsed to his knees, but the boy's grasp became even stronger. Instone's head was roaring, and the edges of his vision were growing black. He became violently ill, and was at the point of choking on his own vomit, and still the pressure increased.

"Stop it boy, stop it," he cried. "I can't stand it no more. I'll fetch yore horse fer ye. Turn me a'loose, afore ye kill me." Instone was close to passing out, and he knew if he lost consciousness, he would never wake up.

But the pressure didn't stop. Instone felt the last bit of air cut off, as the boy's huge hand clasped even tighter. His vision turned from black to blood red, and spots swam before his eyes. He felt himself passing out, and just as he knew he would never breathe again, Micajah turned him loose. Instone slumped to the ground and lay there taking in mighty gulps of air. His ears were popping, and his head was swimming, and the sudden intake of oxygen made him dizzy. He lay face down in the dirt in the middle of his tomato plants, and tears ran from his eyes. His hands clawed at the ground in involuntary spasms.

"If'n ye'll be so kind as to git up, we'll be takin' our horse and goin' now," Micajah said.

Instone slowly rose to his feet, gingerly rubbing his neck with both hands. Each breath was an agony, but the air was the sweetest he ever remembered tasting. His lungs were on fire, and his windpipe was almost swelled closed, and he counted himself lucky to still be breathing. Silently, for talking hurt too much, he turned and looked at the boys, and motioned for them to follow him.

Instone began walking toward the pasture where he kept the mare, and his thoughts were already on how to make the boys pay for this humiliation. He'd considered trying to grab the rifle, but he was hurting too bad, and the boy was too fast. He'd decided to let the law handle the matter as soon as the boys left his farm.

Aye, take the mare, an see if'n ye live to enjoy her. Horse thieves hang in these mountains, even boys like ye air. He thought to himself.

He watched as the younger of the boys caught the mare and led her back toward the house. He even allowed himself a little smile, content with the knowledge these two boys would pay dearly for their actions today.

Suddenly he felt the hand close about his neck again. Again he fell to his knees from the awful pressure. The pain was intensified this time because his neck was already bruised and hurting. He felt himself lifted to his feet, and the boy shook him as though he were a child. But just when Instone thought he must surely be dying, the boy threw him to the ground. He felt a rib snap, and the air was forced out of his body in a great whoosh. His head hit the ground so hard he heard a loud ringing sound in his ears.

Before he had even stopped moving from the throw, he felt the strong hands once again grab him, this time by the shoulders, and lift him into a sitting position.

Royland Instone opened his eyes very slowly, and there, about a foot in front of him, he saw the devil. Wild black hair framed the face, the lips were curled into an animal snarl, and the breath was hot and heavy. Worst of all, though, were the eyes. The devil's eyes glowed with an un-holy blue flame that threatened to set Instone's soul ablaze. Lurking inside those eyes he saw death and destruction, and he felt more fear than he had ever thought it was possible to feel. At that instant he knew he would rather die than to look into those eyes for another moment, for a moment seemed to last a lifetime.

It was not the devil Royland Instone had gazed upon, but he had gotten a fleeting look into the face of Hell itself. A fleeting look at the savage features of the Wolf. Instone would never forget that single moment when he stared full into the fires of hell, and he would hear the voice in his nightmares for the rest of his life.

"Royland Instone," the voice of the demon growled, "I let ye live today. I am only taking that which is rightfully mine. Should ye be so foolish as to go to the constable, know that I shall return. I am the Wolf, Instone, and I will feed on yore mortal soul. As shore as my name is Harpe, I'll come back. Mark my word, Instone. Drop this matter here and now. And I'll only tell ye the one time."

When Instone next opened his eyes, the boys were gone, and so was the little red mare. In later years, Royland Instone told how he had returned the mare to her rightful owners, but never once did he reveal to anyone what had happened in his garden that day. Instone was a strong and hard man, but the Wolf child had made a believer out of him.

The Harpe brothers returned to their cave, gathered their few belongings, and together with Susan and Betsy Roberts, they set out for the Tennessee country. It was the beginning of summer, 1784.

14

Joseph *"Devil Joe"* Ballenger was a man who could not abide anything he considered a crime, or anyone he considered a criminal. He was a man with the courage of his convictions, willing to act on his beliefs, strong in his resolve that wrong should not go unnoticed and wrong doers should be punished.

Although he had not yet reached his twenty-fifth birthday, Ballenger had already acquired a reputation that called him a hard man, and a man one did not want as an enemy. He was known as a fair man, a man who lived by the letter of the law, and a man who expected as much of others as he did of himself.

Ballenger had been in the Carolina Territory since the battle of King's Mountain, having fought with the colonists. Like many of the men in the area, he also had no love for Tories, but at the same time, Ballenger didn't believe in running a man off of his own land, or killing him simply because he fought for the British. That battle was over, and it was time to get back to the business of everyday life. God knows, everyday life was hard enough for the folks that lived in these hills.

For a couple of years Ballenger had known some of the men were trying to drive out as many of the remaining Tories as possible, and one family in particular wasn't driving all that easy.

Ballenger saw John Harpe as a stubborn man, and a deadly one when he set his mind to it. He wouldn't be run off his land, and he'd made it plain what the consequences would be should any raise a hand against him or his family. Ballenger knew Harpe stood a good chance of getting killed if he didn't leave, but he was afraid Harpe would take several with him if it came down to a fight. Harpe had a wife and two sons to care for, and that made him even more dangerous.

Ballenger had met Harpe on more than one occasion and found him to be a witty, hardworking man, but not a man to be taken lightly. There was something about John Harpe that made even the tough Ballenger think twice before he would confront him, and John's oldest boy had that same menacing air about him.

In 1783, Ballenger got his first job as a deputy sheriff, the occupation he was destined to follow for the rest of his life. It was also in 1783 the nightriders finally raided the family of John Harpe, killing him and his wife, and driving the boys away forever. As Ballenger had feared, Harpe fought as though he were a man possessed, and the night riders paid dearly for what they did that night. But the end result was the same. John Harpe and his wife were dead. Like everyone in the settlement Joe Ballenger figured that was the end of it.

Ballenger spent quite a few days exploring the forests, looking for the Harpe boys, but it was as though the very trees had swallowed them up. They had vanished without a trace. Like the rest of the townspeople, Ballenger finally gave up looking for them. He thought they had either left the country, or had been killed in some way. Anyway, they were gone, and Ballenger had no reason to think he'd ever come in contact with them again.

He didn't know the sons of John Harpe would grow up to be men he would devote the rest of his life to bringing to justice.

Ballenger knew George Turpin, and knew him to be a good man. He was saddened when Turpin was killed in his burning cabin. He knew Turpin was one of the men who took part in the raid on John Harpe, but again, like everyone else, he placed no significance on that fact.

In February of the next year, when Henry Potter was found frozen, Ballenger had no reason to connect the two deaths. The frontier was harsh, and men lost their lives everyday. Though many deaths were violent, most were accidental or natural, and Ballenger believed both Turpin and Potter had met their end in an accidental manner.

Ballenger began to suspect there was something out of the ordinary going on when Jeremiah Massie and his woman were found murdered in their cabin. There was nothing strange about the death of the woman. She'd been shot through the head with a rifle, from very close range, killing her instantly. But there was evidence Massie himself had put up a ferocious struggle, which ended when someone drove a poker through his open mouth and into his brain.

Ballenger himself noticed the strange mark on Massie's forehead. It was a perfect oval, with the outline of a four-pointed star inside. Ballenger had no idea what it meant, but he was sure it didn't get there accidentally. He filed away the information in his mind, sure he would come upon it again.

Ballenger was the one who had sent word to Homer Biggs to come to the cabin to look at Massie's body, and had left the man alone when he was requested to. When he returned to the cabin, he found the body of Homer Biggs himself, lying in a pool of his own blood on the floor beside the rotting corpse of Massie.

Later Ballenger had sat down and made a list of the men who had taken part in the raid on John Harpe. Every one of them was dead, with the exception of the Duncan boy, and no one knew where he was. He might even be dead also, for all Ballenger knew. Every one of them had met a terrible and painful death, and there was not a single clue to suggest the identity of the killer. Joe Ballenger swore he'd never rest until he found the person or persons responsible, and brought them to justice. Even if it took forever.

15

Moses Stegall was in hot water sure enough.

In the two years since he'd come down out of the hills of Virginia, he'd never been in a fix quite like this one. He'd spent his time wandering the wilderness along the Kentucky Tennessee border, and had run ins with both settlers and Indians, but this was the first time he'd been this careless.

Yesterday, he'd come across a flock of chickens out behind a small, vacant cabin, and seeing no one about, he'd just naturally grabbed a couple of the slower hens. He'd gone back into the woods, built a fire, roasted the chicks, and was in the process of licking his fingers clean when four of the biggest, meanest looking men he'd ever seen walked into his camp. Before he could move, they had him surrounded.

"Howdy, feller," the biggest one said. "See ye been a'cookin up a few chickens out here."

"Yessir, I have," Stegall responded. "And they's right tasty little critters at thet. I'm shore sorry they ain't none left fer me to offer the four o' ye. I know whar ye might ketch a few more, though. The cabin ain't fur from here." Stegall had decided he'd make an attempt at being friendly, till he found out what the men were up to.

"We know whar the cabin is stranger. Hit belongs to us. And them is our chickens ye is so fond of. Don't recall ye askin fer 'em either."

The big man spoke with deliberation, emphasizing the fact the chickens were stolen.

"I purely didn't see nobody about the place when I taken these chickens, Mister," Stegall said. "Had they been someone round thar, I would have offered to buy the birds. But they warn't and I war hungry, and so here I set, caught red handed. Though not hungry anymore. However, if'n these birds belong to ye, as ye say, then I'll gladly pay ye twenty-five cents fer the two o' 'em."

"Thet's a right good offer, feller," one of the men said, "But them chickens warn't fer sale. They was fer us to eat, and not fer any stranger to hide out in the woods and roast. We'll take the twenty-five cents, fer shore, and maybe more, but I'm afeered yore gonna have to come along with us. Chicken stealin' is frowned upon in these parts, and we'uns don't take lightly to it." Without another word he hustled Stegall to his feet.

The men had tied him up and thrown him into a little lean-to on one side of the cabin, and throughout the remainder of the day and night he lay there, trussed up like a sack of meal. He managed to get a few fitful hours of sleep, but being tied in the position he was in made it impossible for him to get comfortable at all. He awoke the next morning stiff and sore, but managed to squirm around until he could see into the front yard of the cabin. There were two horses tied at the front post, and a couple of packs lying against the cabin wall.

What the hell have I stumbled into here, Stegall thought, as he saw two more men come riding into view.

There seemed to be some kind of gathering going on at the cabin. Stegall could hear loud talking every now and then, but was unable to do anything else. He settled back for a long wait, curious as to what might be happening.

Being new to this part of the country, Stegall had no way of knowing the settlers were up in arms over a small band of Indians who had been attacking some of the more isolated cabins during the past few months. A farmer had been killed outside his cabin two months ago, and just last week an entire family had been murdered.

Simon Carneal, his wife Jane, and their three children had been surprised one day while they were working their garden. The Indians had brutally murdered the man and his wife, even scalping the children, and it had the whole community in an uproar.

The men had been scouring the woods for six days, with no luck. They were angry, and every day without finding the Indians caused them to become more irritated.

They had gathered back here today at the cabin of Robert Holder to re-group. Two of the men had jugs of peach brandy, and Holder had a good supply of homemade whiskey, and some of the men were already well on their way to getting drunk, though it was still early in the morning.

The frustrations they were feeling, along with the strong drink, made it seem likely they would take out their feelings on a common chicken thief.

As the day wore on, talk got around to maybe hanging the thief, and as the men got more intoxicated, the more it looked like the hanging might really happen.

Stegall watched the men getting drunker all day, and had managed to piece together part of what was going on from little snatches of conversation he had overheard. The men were getting louder all the time, and Stegall was beginning to get worried. He'd tried and tried to loosen the ropes that held him, to no avail, and he was also weak from no food. This could get out of hand, unless something happened to stop it.

It was about four o'clock in the afternoon, judging from the sun, when Stegall saw two more men walk into the clearing. They were younger than most of the rest, but they seemed to be cut from the same cloth. They wore buckskin leathers, Indian moccasins, and were hatless. The larger one wore a dangerous looking long knife low on his belt at his left side, and an equally dangerous looking

E. DON HARPE

pistol on his right. He stood well over six feet tall, weighed close to two hundred and fifty pounds, and had course dark black curly hair, worn long.

The smaller of the two carried a rifle, and even from his vantage point Stegall could tell it was a fine weapon. Although he was not as big as the other, he was still over six feet tall and weighed over two hundred pounds. He had the same long hair as the larger one, although of a wile bright reddish hue, and Stegall decided they must be brothers.

Once, when the bigger of the men looked in his direction, Stegall got a glimpse of the strangest blue eyes he'd ever seen. *Now, thar's a pair fer ye,* he thought.

Micajah carefully looked at the eight men gathered in the clearing, then spoke softly to Wiley.

"Wiley, I reckon it's best thet we ain't met up with no Indians, not with sich a company as these fellers. Why, any self-respectin' redskin would have us kilt afore these men could draw their blades, or charge their rifles. And to top it all off, now they is gettin' drunk."

"They is a sorry bunch at thet, Micajah," Wiley agreed. "And unless I miss my guess, they is fixin' to hang thet feller they got tied up over thar."

"I reckon yore right bout thet, little brother," Micajah said. "Although I myself don't hold with stealin' chickens, I shore don't hold with hangin' a man fer cookin' one when he's hungry. Whether it be his'n er someone else's. Had these fellers not been a mite upset over the Injuns, and lookin' fer someone to have some sport with, they wouldn't a' bothered bout the chickens neither. Maybe we ought to ease over thet way, and set thet feller loose. What say ye to thet?"

"Sounds jist fine with me brother," Wiley said. "But ye know if'n we cut the ropes on the chicken thief, we stand to have to fight the whole lot of them. I don't want to have to kill none o' them, but

76

ye know how tis. They's got enough trouble with the red Injuns, much less if'n we has to turn the Wolf loose on 'em."

Micajah considered his brother's word for a moment before speaking, then replied.

"Yes, Wiley, I spect we will have to fight em. And I know what ye er worried about. But I have the Wolf under control. He has not been loose in over six months, and ye know it."

But even as he spoke, Micajah nervously fingered the silver Amulet that hung around his neck. There were times when he could swear the star was alive. Sometimes it would begin to burn, and he could hear the Wolf whisper to him, and at those times he was not always able to control the power within it. It was especially apt to try to control him wherever he had to defend himself or if he got into any kind of fight at all. The Wolf seemed to be asleep most of the time, but it always woke up when Micajah was in trouble. Micajah was glad it had been quiet for a while now, and if he could, he meant to keep it that way.

"Well brother, one o' us has to worry bout the Wolf," Wiley said. "The power is mostly too strong fer us, and ye know it. When the Dark power is upon us, they is no stopping until its hunger is satisfied. Course the power has been good to us this past year. We would be dead had ye not been able to rely upon the Wolf. But we know fer shore thet the pull o' the Amulet is strong, and not a thing to be taken lightly." The Wolf was also in Wiley, but not nearly as dominant as it was in his brother. He had turned it loose himself on occasion, and it was a terrible thing. But in Micajah it was different. He was the eldest son, and wore the Amulet, and the power was stronger by several fold. It consumed him with a passion no other man could ever know, not even Wiley. Although Wiley's blood was also part of the Amulet, and he felt compelled at times to feed the Wolf, still it never controlled him as it did Micajah. Micajah was in truth the chosen one. The firstborn son. The Harpe. And at times, he even scared Wiley. No, Wiley didn't want the Wolf loose, unless it became a matter of life and death.

However, the matter of life and death was not the Harpes today, but was Moses Stegall's. The drunken woodsmen grew wilder by the minute, and the time was quickly approaching when they would take out their rage on the prisoner.

Micajah walked over to the group of men in the clearing, while Wiley slowly began to move toward the lean-to where Stegall lay tied. Wiley made no quick moves, so as not to alert the men, but all the same he didn't waste any time either. He had to be close enough to cut the prisoner's ropes when Micajah made his move.

Stegall saw the young man approaching, and watched as he drew the long knife at his belt.

This is it, Stegall thought. *Of all the fool things I've done, from stealin' horse to killin' men, I never thought I'd meet my maker fer cookin' a few chickens. And by the hand of a boy, at thet. Tis a sorry end I've come to.*

Wiley crept closer, the long gleaming blade in his hand, and softly placed his other hand over Stegall's mouth.

"Not a whisper, feller, not if'n ye want to live to see another sunrise."

Micajah walked out into the crowd of men and looked at each of them in turn. Although he never drank, he weaved from side to side as though he were drunk.

"And which one o' ye lads be the strongest," he bellowed, getting their attention, "who's the fighter here?"

"Look at me, boys," Micajah cried. "I'm a he bar, and the king o' the woods. I'm a horse allygator, and they call me Sudden Death. I drink a barr'l o' whiskey fer breakfast, and I'll fight any two o' ye, one at a time, er both together. Step up boys, don't be afeered. I'm jist a half growed boy, the identical infant that whupped the bar with a willer switch, but surely mor'n the match fer the likes o' any o' ye. I could stand a good tussle from any o' ye who is man enough. Which one, lads, which one will it be?"

Rueben Bell looked at the youngster standing in the middle of the clearing. Rueben was a grizzled old mountain man who had seen many a knock down, drag out fight, and was considered to be one of the best brawlers in the hills. He'd had a couple of swigs of the peach brandy, and was in a mean mood. Bell should have been able to find and either capture or kill the Indians long before now, but had not been able to find a single trace. He was downright disgusted with himself, and needed a way to work it off. Whipping this brash young man just might be what he needed.

"Ye need to larn a lesson, boy, and old Rueben Bell's jist the man to teach hit to ye. Step right on over here, and I'll be glad to oblige ye, if'n hit's a fight yore a'lookin' fer."

Micajah sized up the huge mountain man, and knew he was in for a mighty battle. The old boy had been around for years, and knew every trick of scuffling a man could know. Still, there was no way he could be as strong as Micajah. It would be a contest of age and skill against youth and strength. Micajah decided to try to make the man as mad as he could, hoping to gain an advantage if he got the least bit careless.

"All I want to know about this fight, is air we a'fightin' fer the fun o' it, er air we a'fightin fer to hurt one another. If'n this is only in fun, then I surely don't want to gauge out no eyes ner pull off no ears. On t'other hand, I've got no scruples bout killin' this gentleman, should any o' ye be willin' to make a small wager on the outcome. I have, in my possession, the goodly amount o' thutty dollar in gold, which amount I am willin' to wager thet I kin beat this wore out old feller in less than five minutes. Well, boys, ye got any sportin' blood?"

The remark caused the desired reaction from Rueben Bell. With a roar of outright rage, he shouted at Micajah;

"Wore out old feller, am I? I'll show ye who's wore out, ye young scoundrel. I'll twist off'n yore head like t'were one o' them chickens thet feller stole. I'll splatter ye like a ripe punkin, I'll tear ye limb from limb, I'll..."

Micajah was on him before he finished the sentence. His big right hand struck swifter than the eye could follow, coming around with an audible rush of air. It caught Bell just below the left ear, and sent the mountain man reeling backward some ten feet across the clearing, before he finally came to rest against the trunk of an oak tree. He hit the tree with enough force that several leaves fell from its branches and fluttered about his head as he sank to the ground.

Knowing the other men might not take to the idea of him finishing off their best fighter with only one blow, Micajah spun around in a circle, eyeing each man in turn.

"Which one o' ye is next?" he cried. "Come on boys, whar's yore sportin' blood? Ye kin see thet this old boy warn't much of a fighter. Step right up now, don't be shy. I still got the thutty dollar."

The men stood looking at Harpe for a minute, not believing he had beaten Rueben Bell with only one blow. Bell was one of the most feared men in the woods. He had built his reputation in Natchez-under-the-Hill, fighting flatboat men on the river and Indians in the tangled wilderness, and had been known to beat three men at a time when he was liquored up. Bell was more than a match for any one of them there, and everyone knew it, so that put some doubt in their minds about stepping up to the youth who had beaten him so soundly.

As they stood there staring at him, they realized they didn't know the young man or his brother. The two had joined the men in their search a few days ago, and they seemed like likeable young fellers. They had helped scour the woods, and seemed as upset as the others when no trace was found of the Indians. Still, the men didn't know who the youngsters were, and had no reason to trust them. It would be better if they would both would just leave, and stay away. The men weren't afraid of the boy, but they had reason to respect his right hand, after the blow he'd delivered to Rueben Bell.

Robert Holder, being as he was the one who owned the cabin, spoke up;

"Well boy, we don't know ye, but we do know old Bell here. He has been in many a fight, and I don't think he has ever been bested like this afore. Ye is a strong man, sure enough, and might be able to beat ever one o' us, one at a time. But ye surely know ye can't beat us all at onct. Now if'n ye boys want to jist got on bout yore business, well, I reckon we'll jist be a'lettin ye leave. If'n ye don't want to go peaceably, then we'll jist shoot the two o' ye. Hit's yore choice."

"Tain't much o' a choice, feller," Micajah said. "I kin whup ye, sure enough, but it's true ye kin shoot me. But tisn't whut neither o' us wants I guess. I was jist lookin' fer a little sport, and if'n ye ain't in the mind fer it, then I reckon we'll jist leave. My brother is a'standin' out yonder in the woods with his rifle pointed right over here, jist to be shore ye don't decide to shoot me as I walk away. Hope ye understand thet. I wish ye all the best luck in runnin' down them killin' red Injuns. Good day to ye, sirs."

Micajah looked at the fallen Rueben Bell, and gave a little laugh. "Give Mister Bell my warmest regards when he comes to, and tell him his ears will quit ringin' in about three days, at least thet's what the last feller I hit that hard told me, when he finally come to. Onct agin, good day to ye." Micajah turned and walked out of the clearing.

As soon as Micajah had offered his challenge to the men in the clearing, Wiley had bent down and cut Stegall's ropes, whispering in the man's ear.

"Get up slow, feller," he said, "and move to the edge of the trees. We want to be all the way to the other side of the clearing when Kiga finishes his business."

"Who air ye' feller," Stegall wanted to know. But he kept his voice as quiet as possible.

"Shhh," Wiley said. "They'll be time enough fer innerductions onct we is clear o' this mess."

Wiley and the man made their way to the other side of the clearing, even as Micajah was getting ready to take his leave of the mountain men who had been holding Stegall prisoner.

When Micajah joined the two men in the woods, he paid Stegall not the slightest bit of notice. Excitedly he spoke to Wiley; "I did it, little brother, I did it. I fought the big bastard, and knocked him clean out, and I faced the other men, and I didn't turn the Wolf loose. Not even a little bit. I controlled it. I told ye I could do it Wiley, I told ye."

"I'm proud o' ye brother, ye know I am, but ye shouldn't be a'talkin' bout the Wolf in front o' this here feller. Ye knows how superstitious some folk air, and he might not understand what yore talkin' bout." Wiley said.

For the first time, Micajah seemed to notice the stranger.

"Howdy feller," he said. "My name is Micajah Harpe, and this is my brother Wiley. What might yore name be?"

"My name is Moses Stegall," the man replied, "and I am more'n happy to make the acquaintance o' the Harpe brothers."

Moses Stegall knew from the first time he laid eyes on Micajah and Wiley he'd never be able to live down the fact they had saved his life, and they knew he was a chicken thief. Stegall was a proud and vain man, a few years older than Micajah, and he was not a man to be beholden to anyone. Even though the brothers never mentioned the incident again, Stegall never forgot it. He held the hatred inside and for years claimed to be the best friend the Harpes had, but he knew one day he'd have the chance to make them suffer for the blow they'd delivered to his ego. He didn't care if they had saved his life, the day would come when he'd make them pay.

"Well Mister Stegall, I am pleased thet ye air alive, though I don't know what in tarnation we'll do with a chicken thief." Part of the happiness had left Micajah as he addressed the man they had rescued.

"I have been hungry myself, and I know the felling well, so I can't hold a few chickens agin ye. I must warn ye though, anything o' ourn comes up missin', ye'll think what happened back yonder was one o' her Majesty's tea parties." That had been a favorite saying of his Pa's, and Micajah smiled as the familiar words rolled out of his mouth. "And Stegall, I'll only tell ye the one time."

"I ain't a thief feller," Stegall hotly denied. "Well, leastways I ain't never stole nothing big. A few chickens here and thar, and some roastnears maybe, but I ain't never stole nothin' important. And I ain't never stole from no friends neither. And never from no people whut rescued me from a sure death. Although to tell the truth, ye be the fust people whut has had to rescue me from anything. I don't normally git myself into anything I can't git myself out of."

"Ye didn't seem to doin sich a hot job o' gettin out o' thet little mess back thar, as I recall," Micajah said, with a little spirit coming back into his voice, as he remembered the fight.

"Well, I was workin on it, I was, and about to git free from them dang ropes when ye showed up. Course, I know thet ye war a big help, and without ye I might be a'swingin' by now. And I shorely want to thank ye fer it. But I do believe I was beginnin' to feel them ropes startin' to loosen jist a mite."

Now that Stegall was safe, he was trying to convince himself he hadn't been in nearly as much trouble as he was really in. Stegall, like almost every other man in the country, didn't want to be indebted to anyone. And the more he talked, the more he was becoming convinced he had been in control of the situation back at the cabin.

Stegall was eight or ten years older than Micajah Harpe, and had been on his own for as long as he could remember. He was a rough customer, and was well known throughout Virginia and in cities and towns in the East. He had only been in the West for a short time, having to leave his home a few jumps ahead of the local Sheriff. He had a disagreement with the law over a horse Stegall claimed he borrowed, but whose rightful owner swore had been stolen. Stegall left in the middle of the night, astride the borrowed horse. That had been about three months ago. He had sold the horse, bought a few supplies, and headed west.

Wiley spat on the ground, looked at Stegall, and spoke in his most serious tone of voice.

"Well," he said, "I spect if'n we hand ye back over to them fellers, ye'll have no further need of us a'helpin ye out. Is thet right?"

"Well now, I wouldn't go so fur as to say I relish bein' handed back over to a bunch of wild, drunken brutes, who is of a mind to be strecthin' my neck fer me." Stegall replied. "I got a mite more sense than that. In fact, lookin back, maybe ye did git me outn a real tight spot, at thet. It's jist thet a man hates to admit thet he's about to hang fer stealin two chickens. Even when he is hungry. Aw, hells bells boys, ye saved my bacon back thar, and I must admit thet I'm muchly beholden to ye."

The brothers looked at each other and without a word turned and walked into the woods. Wiley made a motion for Stegall to follow them if he wished to, and the three of them set off together.

Moses Stegall was a good looking man, standing just under six feet tall and weighing about one hundred and seventy pounds. He had a full head of thick, straight brown hair, and had flashing brown eyes that sparkled when he laughed, which he did quite often. He preferred clothes made of cloth, rather than the buckskins the Harpes wore, and Stegall almost always wore a hat. In the style of the day, he wore a hat made of raccoon skins, with the big bushy tail hanging down in the back. Moses was not a man given to being sad, and could seldom be found with a frown on his face. Although he was almost thirty when the Harpes first met him, he didn't look much older than either of the brothers.

His boyish charms and ready smile told little of the man inside, however.

Stegall was a mean man, often killing animals for the fun of it, and not just for food, as was the habit of most men on the frontier. He was always ready for a fight, and seldom did anyone get the best of him. Contrary to what he said, the man was a thief, and a liar to boot. Although from the first, something inside him kept him from stealing from the Harpes. Moses Stegall had never met a man he was afraid of, but Micajah Harpe was different from any man Moses had ever run into before.

Stegall had heard the boys speak of the "Wolf," and although he didn't understand exactly what that meant, he recognized there was a force inside the big Harpe that was beyond anything he had ever seen. When he looked deep into Harpe's eyes, the chill bumps played about his spine, and his heart beat just a little faster. Stegall would not admit it, even to himself, but he was deathly afraid of Micajah, and had been from the first day they met. He believed Harpe would kill him, should he decide to, and there was nothing he could do to prevent it. Yet even under these strange circumstances, still Stegall enjoyed the company of the boys. They made quite a little band, the five of them. Stegall knew the women didn't like him very much, nor trust him, but that didn't really matter. They would never go against the big Harpe in anything, and as long as Micajah wanted Stegall's company, the women would not say a word against him.

16

When Micajah and Wiley Harpe, the two Roberts sisters, and Moses Stegall left the territory of North Carolina in the summer of 1784, they had no idea where they were going, other than they were headed for the Tennessee country, as John Harpe had suggested. The five of them had very few possessions with which to start a new life. The girls had three or four dresses between them, two pots and an old iron skillet. Betsy had a tiny ring her mother had given her when she was a small child that she had managed to somehow hide from Jeremiah Massie. The Harpe brothers had, as their only possessions, the red mare they had taken back from Instone, the rifle John had given Wiley, a meager assortment of clothes, and the pistol and knife each wore at his belt. Stegall had the clothes on his back, a pistol he had managed to pick up in a trade, and a pouch filled with black powder. They had only a small amount of money between them, but needed very little. They could hunt their food, trade with the Indians for salt, and they could find suitable lodging in a rock house, or build a rough lean-to in the forest.

In this manner, they passed the summer and winter of 1784. By April of 1785 they had made their way westward into the land the Indians called Tennessee.

The land was wild and untamed, with a savage beauty unparalleled anywhere. There were crystal clear streams, teaming with fish, the woods were filled with wildlife, and strawberries grew wild in the lush green meadows. It was a beautiful and bountiful land, where a man might build a cabin, put in a few rows of corn, and maybe raise a few hogs. Settlers were scarce, and for the most part the Indians were friendly and helpful to the white men. There were minor disputes at times, but seldom any real violence. That would come later.

The Harpes had little friction with the Indians; indeed they lived among them in an atmosphere of friendliness and respect. They lived solitary lives, and didn't bother the Indians, and in return were not bothered by the Indians.

It was in early September of 1785 that Susan discovered she was expecting a child. Micajah seemed pleased at the prospect of becoming a father, and Betsy was every bit as happy as her sister, and couldn't wait to become pregnant herself. Both girls planned on large families, and the sooner they got started the better. After all, Susan was already past seventeen, and Betsy past sixteen. Most mountain women gave birth to their first born by the time they were this old. In fact, many women already had several children by the time they were as old as the Roberts sisters. Having children was a natural part of life in the mountains, and it was expected of the womenfolk to stay pregnant much of the time. Many children died in the harsh mountain winters, or from the deadly epidemics that sometimes plagued the hills, and these things made a large family almost a necessity. More children meant more hands to work the fields, and a better chance of the family surviving.

The Harpes were no different than the other people of the country. They wanted to settle down in the Tennessee territory, and build themselves a good life. With several acres of land, some good crops, and a few head of horses and cattle, they could put the past behind them and forget the things that had happened to their families.

They had no way on knowing their feet had already been set upon the path of destruction.

17

In the late fall of that year, the red mare they had recovered from Royland Instone had been seen and recognized by a settler who was him self from the same North Carolina country they had just left. The man, one Phillip Lumkin, recognized the horse as one that once belonged to Mister Instone, and recalled the tale of the murders of Massie and Biggs back in Carolina. Putting two and two together, and being a curious sort by nature, one afternoon Lumkin went to visit the Harpes, intending to find out how and where and how the brothers had come by the horse.

Lumkin rode into the small clearing where the Harpes had started working on a cabin, and, after the customary greetings were exchanged, got to the reason for his visit.

"Boys," he began, "Not being the nosy kind, I still feel it is my duty to inquire as to whar ye came upon thet fine red mare ye have. I know fer a fact thet it were onct the property of a Mister Royland Instone, back in the Caroliny country. Though Mister Instone would never say so, I heerd the mare had been stolen by the same persons responsible fer the murders o' two other respected men in the country, a Mister Biggs and a Mister Massie. Now I ain't accusing the two o' ye boys o' nothin', ye understand, but afore I go to the constable, I thought it would be the right and proper thang fer me to do to let ye know what I was about. I ain't one fer a'stirrin up the pot, but them fellers back in Caroliny were acquaintances o' mine, and I feel it is my duty to find out what I kin."

Lumkin was plainly a man who could not rest as long as he perceived something to be wrong, and, despite his protestations, he was in fact a very nosy man, with a very bad habit of entering into things that were no concern of his. But this time, however unknowingly, Lumkin was treading on very thin ice in this conversation with the Harpe brothers. Micajah and Wiley had very strong feelings on what had happened to them back in Carolina, and would brook no interference whatsoever in what they considered their business. Being men that kept to themselves, they expected the same courtesy from others, and would accept no man coming into their home and inquiring as to the nature of anything they did.

"What might yore name be, Mister," Micajah asked, in a voice which barely masked his anger?

Deep inside of Micajah, the eyes of the Wolf snapped open, and looked at Lumkin: *Sssshall we hunt, Haaaarpe? I am hungry.*

"My name is Phillip Lumkin, young man," Lumkin replied. "Recently of the Caroliny territory. I came to the Tennessee country to seek my fortune. And who might ye young people be?" Lumkin was determined to find out as much about the boys as he could, and was not trying to hide his curiosity.

"I am Micajah Harpe, and this is my brother Wiley. We er the sons o' John Harpe, and we too recently come from Caroliny. Yore right about the mare, she did indeed onct belong to Mister Instone. He acquired her from our Pa, and afore we left the territory, we war lucky enough to persuade him to sell her back to us." Micajah intended to avoid trouble with Lumkin if it was at all possible.

Lumkin was almost beside himself with joy in being right about the mare. He looked at Micajah, and in a very self righteous tone said; "Well young feller, if'n yore story be true then ye'll have no problem with the constable. Ye know, I seem to recollect a man named Harpe, back in Caroliny. Whut was it I heerd bout thet man? Got hisself kilt, didn't he? Why, yore Pappy war the same Harpe whut fit fer the King, and raised sich a ruckus when the folk tried to git him to leave the country, warn't he?"

"Yessir, thet war our Pa," Micajah exclaimed, through lips that were now compressed into a thin line. Although Lumkin didn't know it, he was hunting a grizzly bear with a willow switch, and his very first swipe would likely be his last. Micajah would only go so far to avoid a serious problem with this man. If it became apparent the man was going to the authorities, regardless of what Micajah said, then the Harpe would find another solution to the problem. He didn't particularly want to kill the man, but he had no intention of being brought to answer for taking a horse that was rightfully his.

Micajah stared for a long angry moment at Lumkin before continuing. "Now Mister, if'n ye recollect anything a'tall bout the Harpes, then ye'll be knowin' we ain't people to hold with no man making accusations agin us. Our Pa kilt a passel o' the men what rode on our cabin thet night. Kindly like the way ye rode in here, wouldn't ye say? I ain't one fer makin' threats, but I kin tell ye thet if'n ye goes to the constable and tells him we is horse thieves, er if'n ye causes the law to come about us in any manner, then ye best be headed back to Caroliny on yer fastest horse. The Tennessee country won't be safe fer ye a'tall. We ain't done nothin wrong, and we will take it harshly if'n ye brang any trouble upon us. And Mister Lumkin, I'll only be tellin' ye the one time."

Phillip Lumkin turned white as the blood drained away from his face. In his mind, the story of how John Harpe had killed the party of men that day came back to him. He looked at the face of the boy standing in front of him, and saw his own destruction. A fire had begun to burn, deep inside the boy's eyes, and Phillip Lumkin felt the terrible heat. The blue fire caused a cold lump to form in the pit of Lumkin's stomach, and he knew beyond the shadow of a doubt the boy meant every word he'd said. If Lumkin went to the constable this afternoon, Micajah Harpe would make sure he didn't see the sunrise tomorrow morning. The boy would kill him as surely as he breathed.

"Yore right young feller," Lumkin said, in a voice that sounded much too loud to his ears. "Yore jist as right as rain. T'would not be a good idée to go a'spreadin nasty rumors. I seem to recall Mister

Instone sayin as to how he had sold that red mare, now thet ye brang it up. Hit had jist slipped my mind fer an instant. Ye kin rest easy knowin' thet old Phillip Lumkin won't be a'carryin no tales bout ye boys away from this clearing. Now if'n ye don't mind, I'll be a'gittin back to my own place. I'm surely glad we got this matter resolved. Good day to ye boys. I hope to see ye agin in the future." Lumkin turned his horse and rode out of the clearing.

Wiley was silent as he watched Lumkin ride away. When the man was completely out of sight, he spoke to Micajah.

"What do ye think Kiga," he asked? "Do ye think the man will run to the constable with his tale?"

"Naw, I don't think he will Wiley," Micajah answered. "However, I believe we should make preparations to leave this part o' the Tennessee country. Next spring we'll be a'movin on."

On May 22, 1786, Susan gave birth to an eight pound, seven ounce baby girl. They named her Elizabeth Jane Harpe, and from the very first they called her Betty.

On June 19, four weeks from the day Betty was born, the Harpes again packed their belongings and moved a little deeper into the Tennessee territory. They never heard another word from Phillip Lumkin.

After the birth of Elizabeth, Susan noticed Micajah humming the little song they had shared. Micajah would find many occasions to hum the tune over the next few years, but not always in happiness.

It was in this fashion they spent the next three years. Wandering about the woods, never staying in one place more than a few months except to winter, all the time learning more about themselves and each other.

On September 19, 1788, Betsy Roberts gave birth to her first child. Also a baby girl, she weighed seven pounds, five ounces, and was named Rebecca America Harpe.

Baby Rebecca became the first of the Harpe family to die. In the bitter January cold of 1789, the tiny child came down with the fever, and died in her mother's arms on the second day of February. On the fourteenth of March, that same year, little Elizabeth Jane was also lost, to the same raging fever that claimed the life of Rebecca.

Susan and Betsy wept in each other's arms, and from that day forward, Micajah Harpe seldom smiled.

In the spring of 1789, Moses Stegall took his leave of the Harpes, saying he wished to explore southward. In reality, Stegall was becoming more and more afraid of Micajah. The big Harpe was becoming crueler with each passing day, and Stegall didn't want to be the target of one of his vicious rages. Micajah was being consumed by the amulet, and the fire burned brighter in his eyes with each new discovery concerning the silver star. Stegall could not long restrain the boyish side of his nature, and lately found little of joy about the small band he traveled with.

Saying goodbye was no problem for Stegall. One morning in May, he put the things he required into a small pack, and told the other four it was time for him to leave. Should their travels bring them to the South, he was sure they would meet again.

"Old friend," Stegall said to Micajah, as he prepared to leave. "Old friend, I know ye too well. I see the Wolf in yore eyes more and more everyday, and I know it must be fed. Ye must take care, Kage, fer the Amulet holds the Devil himself, and the Devil is slave to no man. Ever time ye feed the Wolf, Micajah, the Devil grows stronger. Ye air the best friend ever I had, old son, but they is times when ye frighten even me. I want ye to know I am always at yer service. If'n ye need me, al ye has to do is call, and I'll come a'runnin. This ain't goodbye, tis jist farewell."

With those few words, Moses Stegall walked away without once looking back. He felt a kinship with the Harpes that would last forever, and he respected them as fighting men, but he never forgot they had rescued him when he'd stolen the chickens, and this imagined humiliation would travel with him always. In his heart, he never forgave them for seeing him at his worst moment.

18

Laughing Bird was sitting in front of her wigwam weaving a new cane mat, and was not exactly sure when she first felt someone watching her. She had become very engrossed with the pattern she was weaving into the mat, and so she didn't realize there was anyone about. She was softly humming to herself, when suddenly she became aware she was not alone.

It was the middle of the afternoon and the sun was bright, but still it took the girl a few minutes to notice the four people standing by the tree line. When she finally did see them, they were standing perfectly still, none of the four moving so much as a finger. Silently, they stood just outside the trees and stared at her. There were two men and two women, all dressed in buckskins, and all hatless.

These strangers are not like most whites, was her first thought upon seeing the four of them standing there, *They stand too quiet and wear no hats.*

For a moment Laughing Bird sat still, returning the strangers stare, and then slowly rose to her feet. Not taking her eyes off the strangers, she began to whistle the call of the Bobwhite quail. She knew it would not be long before the men of the village came to investigate. The Bobwhite whistle was used to warn the village of danger, and its call would not long go un-answered. She knew the strangers heard the whistle, and they probably knew what it meant, but still they didn't move. They might have been statues, for all the motion they were making. It seemed to the girl that even the leaves in the trees where they were standing had stopped moving, and the wind had died down.

Again the girl whistled, and this time she heard the call returned. The men were coming. They would see what the strange whites wanted. If they were not friendly, the men would be very harsh with them.

With a sudden cry, five young Cherokee men leaped from the other side of the wigwam where Laughing Bird lived with her parents and brothers and sisters. Their cries rang through the air as they bounded across the clearing and surrounded the four whites, which still had not moved nor made a sound.

The five Indians danced about the whites, sounding their fiercest war cries for several moments, then the larger of the two white men slowly raised his empty hand, palm up, in the sign of peace.

"We wish ye no harm," the man said. "We come to your village as travelers, and want only to pass through your land in peace."

"No one owns the land, white man, but the Cherokee do dwell here," one of the braves answered. He looked to be a little older than the other four, and seemed to speak for them all. "Do you think so little of your hair that you would come to a village of the People and try to pass?"

Micajah looked at the unsmiling brave for a moment, being careful to maintain direct with his eyes, and then answered. "Redskin, I reckon I think as much of my hair as the next man, but this trail be the fastest way South. We only wish to pass, and will cause no trouble for your tribe."

The white man spoke slowly, not speaking much of the Cherokee language, and not wishing to be misunderstood.

"My brother and me and my women be tard and hungry, and wish to rest fer awhile by the stream. Tell me redskin, air ye the Chief of this village?"

"No, not Chief. Chief named Running Canoe. Greatest Chief of the People. My name is Job." It was plain the Indian wasn't quite sure how to handle the situation. He had faced white men before, but always with a knife or a tomahawk in his hand. This white spoke without anger, and looked him in the eye, and said words of peace. He decided to send John One Feather into the village to get instructions, while the other four remained to watch the whites.

Still, with the exception of the few words and the peace gesture, none of the whites had moved at all. The smaller white man stood balanced on the balls of his feet, ready to move quickly in any direction. The two women, each armed with a long knife at her belt, seemed unafraid, and like the men they were calm and motionless. Their eyes were steady, and they showed no fear in the presence of the Indians.

The largest of the white men had about him an energy, a vibrancy the Indians could almost see. *There is power in this man,* thought Job. *He would make a fine friend, or a terrible enemy.*

The Indians believed there was power in all living things. Animals, plants, the heavenly bodies, even the mountains, all possessed power. Now and then a man would come along in whom they also saw the same forces of nature. Job thought this big stranger must be such a man. He could see the fire burning deep inside the man's eyes, and feel the waves of energy as they poured from his body.

Scarcely five minutes had passed before John One Feather had returned from the village.

"Running Canoe say bring whites to village." He said.

Job looked at the whites, "You come with us," he exclaimed. It was not a question.

The party moved off towards the village, two Indians leading the way, the four whites next, and three Indians bringing up the rear. Laughing Bird followed along some ten or fifteen yards behind.

The Indians, born to the woods, walked silently, doing very little to betray their passage through the forest. The whites, also born to the woods, moved with equal grace and silence.

For all of his great size, the big white man was the most graceful of them all. He moved like an animal, his feet making almost no noise, and hardly disturbing the forest floor at all. He reminded Job of one of the great hunting animals, roaming the forest, always watchful, always hunting, never letting down his guard.

He has been visited by the spirit of the Wolf, thought Job. *No other animal spirit could bestow upon his such mighty medicine. He is young in the way of the Wolf as yet, but one day, one day...* Job let the thought slip out of his mind as the entered the village.

Chief Running Canoe was one of the most powerful of the Cherokee chieftains in the territory. He was an imposing man, large for a Cherokee, standing one inch over six feet tall, and weighing almost two hundred pounds. He had the piercing black eyes, the straight black hair, and the hawkish nose of the true Cherokee. He was a wise and fearless leader, known for keeping his head under any circumstance. He was one of only a handful of Indians in the territory who realized the true meaning of what the white settlers would mean in the future. He knew their numbers were many, and they would keep coming until they covered the entire land. In his councils, he attempted to teach his brothers these things, yet they scoffed, and still thought the settlers might be driven away from their territory by occasional raids and the taking of a few scalps. Running Canoe knew this was not true, but his brothers persisted in their age-old customs.

Now, here among his people, had come four whites, and one of them was such a man as Running Canoe had never seen before. Big and powerful, and filled with much medicine. Running Canoe knew his people might wish to kill the whites, but he could tell from the power he saw living inside the big man this would be no easy thing to do. Many braves would meet their ancestors before the man fell, if indeed they could kill him at all.

In his wisdom, Running Canoe made a decision that would affect the life of every settler in the territory for years to come.

The small band of whites stood before Running Canoe, and waited for him to speak.

"In a dream," the Chief began, "I saw a great Eagle overhead. With a wing tip, he bade me follow him, and we crossed over the River of Death, and climbed the Mountain of the Sun. There, on the highest peak, the Eagle landed, and waited for me, only a slow man, to reach the place where he stood. When I at last stood before the great Eagle, and asked him how I might serve, he commanded me to fast, and to purify myself, and paint my body, and dance for him. These things I did, for to disobey the Eagle would bring much evil upon our people."

"For six days I fasted, and then I built a smoke lodge to rid my body of its impurities. Then did I remove my breechcloth and stripped myself naked. The hair I shaved from my head, save the scalp lock, and I adorned my neck with the medicine necklace handed down to me by my father. My whole body I painted, in colors I hoped would please the Eagle. And when all my preparations were complete, I danced for the Eagle."

"I danced a dance of Joy, for great was my pleasure at being chosen to be so honored by the Eagle. Then I danced a dance of offering, promising whatever it was in my lowly power to offer. I danced a dance of Wisdom, and asked that the Eagle, wisest of all Spirits, show me the truth of his visit. Lastly, I danced a dance of Obedience, and placed my trust and confidence in the Eagle himself, and swore to use the wisdom of the Eagle to benefit my people at all times."

The Chief's eyes were closed, and he spoke as if in a trance, and all present knew he was reliving the dream, and was again standing in the presence of the great Eagle spirit. All of the ones listening stood spellbound and in awe, and hung on the Chief's every word.

"The Eagle was pleased with my dancing, and he spread his mighty wings and hopped about on the pinnacle of the mountain, performing his Eagle dance for me. And when he had finished, he again folded his wings and spoke to me.

"Running Canoe," the Eagle spirit said, "Running Canoe, great Chief of the over-hill Cherokee, I have tales to tell you. As I fly over the land of the People, I see that which has been, that which is, and that which is to come. You know what has been, and you know what is now, and so I will tell you a tiny portion of that which is to come."

"Your hunters will find an abundance of game, and their arrows will fly true, and you will have much meat this season. Your warriors will have success on three raids, but three raids only. Two in the heat of the summer, and the third when the leaves have turned to gold. But only three, Running Canoe, this year only three. Should you raid for a fourth time, many of the People shall perish."

"And more of the whites shall come. As surely as I speak to you, as surely as the wind blows and the sun rises, the white-eyes shall come. They cannot be stopped, Running Canoe, and you and your people shall have to move. South shall you go. South. And after that you shall go West. But that will be later. Not all of your warriors will go to the South with you. Some will remain, and continue to try to drive the whites from the mountains. But as many of the white-eyes as your warriors kill or drive out, one hundred times that many will come, and one thousand times that many, till there is no forest left for the People. But you will move first. When green next comes to the trees, so it will be then that you must go."

"Now heed my next words, Running Canoe, and heed them well. Before the sun sets tomorrow, there will come four whites to your village. But not whites such as the People have ever seen before. Four of them, two men and two women they will be. Dressed in the leather of the woods."

100

"This is the reason I have appeared to you Running Canoe, to tell you of their coming, and to tell you of the power they carry. Old is this power, and of the spirit world itself. My ancient enemy, the Wolf, has spoken with me about these whites, and has told me he has pledged his allegiance to the power. Even as I am the most powerful spirit of the Air, the Wolf is the most powerful spirit of the land. Cunning and strong, ferocious and savage the Wolf is. And his hunger is never satisfied."

"The leader of the whites will be a big man, and possess strange blue eyes that will chill your heart. He will hold all of the power of the Wolf himself and will also be filled with a power even older than any we know. The man will be young, and will not know the extent of his power, and the People will have to guide him as he learns. He will be a terrible enemy, should you bring his anger to bear on the People. But treat him as you would treat your brother, and he will become as one with the People, and be a friend and a trusted ally."

As Running Canoe finished his story, his eyes remained closed, and he swayed from side to side. Then without opening his eyes, he settled to the ground on crossed legs, and sat as though he were meditating. He made not a sound, and such was the quiet that the breathing of those around him could be heard.

At long last, Running Canoe opened his eyes. He looked about him as though unsure of where he was. As his eyes began to focus once again, and he seemed to be returning to his senses, he fixed his eyes upon the big white man standing in front of him.

"You are the man," he said to Micajah, "you are the Wolf. Him that I saw in my dream. The man the Eagle said would come. You have the eyes, and I would have you know you are welcome in the village of Running Canoe."

Rising to his feet, Running Canoe said to his assembled people; "This man is our friend, and is to be treated as a brother. He will stand beside us in this time of trouble."

With a small show of ceremony, Running Canoe then removed a medicine pouch from a small basket that rested on the ground at his feet. He opened the pouch to reveal the sacred paints used to prepare the warriors for battle. Dipping his finger into a small patch of silver paint, he once again turned to Harpe.

"Remove your shirt, Wolf, I would paint upon your chest a symbol of great power."

Harpe pulled his shirt up over his neck and handed it backward to Susan. His chest muscles rippled as he stood bare before the chief.

The chief closed his eyes and extended his hand toward Micajah. He began a slow, halting dance step, every now and then touching the paint to the chest of Harpe. Dipping his fingers once again into the paint, he held the second color aloft for all to see. His finger was now the dark scarlet of fresh blood. Dancing and chanting, Chief Running Canoe dabbed the red on Harpe's chest, his eyes still closed, and suddenly finished with a flourish. Standing before Harpe, the chief opened his eyes to look at his handiwork.

On Harpe's chest, the Chief had painted a four-pointed silver star, framed against a background of dripping scarlet. With one look, he sank to the ground into his position of meditation.

"Leave me," he commanded.

Micajah, Wiley and the women didn't know what to think when they first stepped out of the woods and saw the Indian girl. They stood as quietly as possible, thinking they may have a chance to slip back into the trees before she noticed them. But when the girl looked up and saw them, they had no choice but to remain where they were and try to bluff it out. But they couldn't fight an entire Indian village, and they knew it.

What happened during the next two hours was as mystifying to them as it was to Job and the other Cherokees. Micajah didn't know how to account for the knowledge the chief had of them. He knew he and Wiley called the power "The Wolf," but when the old Indian also called it by that name, they were stunned.

How could he have known about the Wolf? Micajah wondered. *How could he have drawn the silver star on my chest without looking at the Amulet?*

The fact was, the Chief knew, and it didn't matter how he knew. There was nothing the Harpes could do about it. Perhaps they might even learn more about the power if they lived with the Indians for a while.

"Well," Micajah told the others, "This is as good a place as any to stay, and better'n most."

It was May 1790. It had been a year since the Harpes and Stegall had parted company, and fifteen months since the death of the two babies. They had been with the Indians for ten months, and they had been ten good months, overall. Not only had they been accepted as friends, they had become members of the village, living their everyday lives as the rest of the Cherokee. And both women were once again pregnant, with Betsy ready to give birth any day now. Susan's second child should be born sometime in July, and if everything went as the wise women of the tribe said, this child would be a boy. They weren't so sure of Betsy's child, however. She had had quite a lot of problems carrying the baby. Betsy was not as big nor as strong as her sister, and the people had moved several times during the year, putting her under even more of a strain.

The day the first baby was born, the men were out on a rabbit drive. The rabbits were young and tender, and very delicious when roasted over an open fire, or boiled in the big cooking pot. The men had stretched a woven net between two rocks in a small gully, and then proceeded to beat the underbrush with sticks, chasing the rabbits into the gully, and into the net. This method was much better and faster than shooting them with arrows, and would give the men time during the afternoon for a game of dice, while the women prepared the feast.

As the men returned to the village that afternoon, Micajah saw several of the old women of the village standing outside his wigwam. Each woman had a smile upon her face, and then he saw Susan, holding a small bundle in her arms. As he approached, he knew Betsy's time had come, and she had delivered his child while he was gone.

"Be it a boy er girl, Susan?" Micajah inquired. "An be Bet alright?" He was concerned for the health of the beautiful Betsy, for she had not been well since tiny Rebecca had died.

"Tis a beautiful girl, Micajah," Susan replied, "and Bet is resting tolerable well. She wanted another girl, ye know. Losing her precious Rebecca was all she ever thought about lately."

"Aye, Susan, I know," Micajah said. "Tis on my mind quite a lot also. As is losin' our darlin' Elizabeth. I loved that girl dearly, Susan, ye know I did. She war our first born, and meant the world to me."

"And to me, Micajah. We shall never replace her, and she will not be forgotten. But the women say I'm to give ye a son this time, and ye'll be proud o' him as well." Susan held her grief better than Betsy, but it was plain her heart was still broken over the loss of her first little girl.

"Micajah, I think ye should know, me and Betsy has named this baby already. We had decided on a name fer her, and our minds is made up. Tis a beautiful name, and one we think ye'll like, and will be in agreement with." Susan said this as though she were ready to defend the fact they had named the baby while he was not there, should Micajah voice any objections.

Micajah could not help but notice the difference in Susan's tone. It was something he had not heard before, and it surprised him. Seeing the fire in her eyes though told Micajah the women felt strongly about this name, and he wisely held his tongue. He well knew the sorrow the women felt, and if the name of this babe brought them comfort from that sorrow, then that name would have his complete blessing.

"What might the name be, woman," he asked, silently vowing not to say one word regardless of what name the women had chosen.

"We have named her 'Mourning'," Susan said. "With this name she will always remind us of our lost children, and each new day with her will be counted as a blessing."

"I truly believe ye have named her well, Susan. Tis a beautiful name, right enough. And ye air right. Each new day with little Mourning will indeed be a blessing." Micajah took the babe from Susan, his large hands displaying all the tenderness to the tiny body found in the hands of any new father.

Micajah's hands were anything but tender toward the body they were holding at this moment, however. It was three weeks to the day since the baby had been born, and Micajah had joined the warriors in a raid on a small village, some twenty miles from their own. Micajah had his hands around the neck of one of the braves, and was in the process of squeezing the life from his body. His knife had made short work of several of the enemy, and he had broken the back of another. The one he was strangling was among the last left alive. The raid had been a complete surprise. They had moved into position just before dark, with not a sound to betray them. With the dark of the moon, they had slipped up on the sleeping men and begun their slaughter. With bodies painted with their strongest medicine, and with the fiercest war cries they could scream, they had leaped from their concealment and were upon the men before they could react. The small band hadn't had a chance. Micajah knew he had killed at least five of the men, and was proud that not one of his red brothers could match that number.

Micajah enjoyed the raids, and with each one he added to the legend of Wolf Spirit. In a short time, he had become known as the most feared killer in the territory. But so far, he was only known among the Indians. They had raided only a few small camps of white men, and killed them all, and no one save the little band of warriors knew of it.

On these small raids, Micajah and Wiley could feed the Wolf, and not worry about the white man's law. But the power of the Wolf grew stronger with each raid, and it became harder and harder to control the Wolf. Once or twice, Micajah had been on the verge of losing control completely, but had managed to regain his senses just in time.

Wiley had better control of the Wolf than Micajah, perhaps because he did not wear the Amulet. He was a part of the power, and his blood was mingled on the Amulet, but he had very little actual physical contact with the Amulet, and so was not held quite so strongly by it's strange powers. But he could feel the power of the Wolf as it surged through his veins, and had to remain on constant guard, lest it become stronger than he.

They both knew that during one of the raids, when the blood lust ran strong, it would be so easy to give in to the rage, and turn the Wolf loose completely, and let it feed as it saw fit.

Yet Wiley was afraid that if that should ever happen, the Wolf would feed on friend as well as foe, and perhaps even family. Although it was hard, he knew he must never, even for an instant, turn the Wolf loose all the way.

Micajah was different from Wiley. As the first-born son, Micajah wore the ancient Amulet about his neck, and felt the terrible urges much stronger than his brother. He could use more of the unholy power of the talisman than Wiley, but it asked much more in return. The feeling that came over him when the Wolf fed was indescribable, but with each new raid, it became harder and harder to refrain from turning the Wolf completely loose, and losing himself in the blackness and sweetness of the monster's hunger.

With each new kill, the blue flame in Micajah's eyes grew brighter and brighter, and stronger and stronger grew the power of the Wolf.

On July 4th, 1790, the fourteenth anniversary of America's independence from England, Susan Roberts Harpe gave birth to their firstborn son. He weighed nine pounds, five ounces, had thick, black hair, and flame blue eyes. They named him James Burton Harpe, and the Overhill Cherokee of Running Canoe called him Wolf Son.

As the great chief Running Canoe had been instructed to do in his dream of the Eagle, he moved the village southward when the leaves began turning green. They followed the rolling waters of the Tennessee River out of the Knoxville hills and toward the lower five cities around the town of Chattanooga. Though the journey was not a particularly long one, the Indians still moved slowly, for they were in no hurry at all. They passed the summer and fall of 1790 in a leisurely fashion, moving slowly but steadily southward. All of the lands of the Cherokee were fruitful, and they killed much game as they traveled. The clear, cold streams were teaming with fish, and it was an easy matter to spear enough for the entire village to feast upon.

The Harpe babies were secured to their cradleboards and carried safely along on the backs of the women. They were healthy and good-natured children, neither being given to crying a lot. Betsy was in much better spirit since the birth of tiny Mourning, and Susan spent every minute possible with baby James. It was plain Micajah loved the little girl, but that his first-born son was the apple of his eye.

The Cherokee, feeling the Harpes and their women were now members of the tribe, accepted the children as if they were true Indians. The Cherokee women helped mind the babies, and the

Harpe women helped with the work of the village. It was a good arrangement for both sides, and the next two years were relatively peaceful. There were occasional raids, to be sure, both on other Indian bands and on small settlements of white men, but no serious warfare was waged by Running Canoe's small band.

In this way the Harpes spent the years from 1789 through 1792, learning as much as they could from the Cherokee, both good as well as bad. Their skill as woodsmen became honed to a fine edge, and even among the Indians they were unsurpassed as hunters and trackers. The power of the Amulet aided their natural powers and made them almost invisible in the woods, giving them an uncanny ability to escape detection. They could be in plain sight, walking along the trail with their red brothers, and with no warning would almost seem to disappear. They seemed to be a part of the very fabric of the forest, and it seemed as if the trees and brush, and even the animals themselves helped them to escape discovery.

But if the Harpes had become excellent woodsmen from their association with the red man, their skill as killers had increased tenfold. By the summer of 1792 Micajah had become the most feared killer of men the forests had ever seen. Wiley, called Wolf Brother by the tribe, was second only to Micajah in his ferocity and blood lust. Together, they were so fearsome even the bravest of the Indians were cautious around them.

The Cherokee sometimes tortured their victims, especially those who showed little or no bravery, and the Harpes soon learned every method of torture the Indians knew. And made up a few of their own. The Wolf seemed to delight in the screams and cries of the captives as their eyes were poked out, or their ears were torn off, of the skin was slowly peeled from their bodies an inch at a time. It was during this time the Harpes devised the method of slitting open the bellies of their victims and replacing their entrails with rocks or sand. In this way, they could dispose of the bodies in the lakes or rivers and they would not float to the top. The Harpes also learned if no one is left alive after a raid, there is no one to point a finger of blame.

The hunger of the Wolf knew no end, and with every vicious act the Harpes committed, the Wolf fed and grew stronger.

The summer of 1792 also brought about two other significant developments in the life of the Harpe clan. It was during their wanderings up into Kentucky that summer they found the rock house they would use as a safe haven over the course of the next few years, and that was the summer Micajah acquired the mighty tomahawk from Dancing Hawk, the most powerful of the Cherokee medicine men.

19

Running Canoe's Cherokee had set up their village on the south bank of the Little Hiwassee River, at a point a little more than halfway between Knoxville and Chattanooga. With the mountains to their backs and the river bordering one side of the village, the Cherokee used the land to its fullest extent.

There was abundant game and fish, and the fertile land would grow whatever the Indians chose to plant. Some of the women planted sunflowers, and used the seeds for cakes, and the oil to make their hair soft and shiny.

There on the banks the village prospered for two years, making occasional raids on other Indian villages, as well as on the few white settlers that were foolish enough to build a cabin within striking distance of the village.

On the fifth of August 1792, trouble came to Running Canoe's little village.

The trouble was in the form of two warriors and a medicine man from the Cherokee town of Nickajack. They came to the village of Running Canoe seeking the white Indian known as Wolf Spirit.

Running Canoe rose from his position in front of his wigwam where he had been idly tossing his dice about, and greeted the three strangers who entered his village.

"I am Running Canoe," he said, "Chief of the Overhill Cherokee. What are your names, and what brings you to my village?"

One of the men stepped forward.

"I am called Ravenwing," he said, "and these two are the mighty warrior Bearkiller and Dancing Hawk, the wisest and most powerful of the Cherokee medicine men. We are from the lower town of Nickajack, and we seek among you the one called Wolf Spirit. It is said he is the greatest warrior ever to come to the five towns, and we would speak with him, if it pleases the mighty Chief Running Canoe."

"There is one among us known as Wolf Spirit, and it is true he is a mighty and fearless warrior. What would the great Ravenwing, war chief of Nickajack, wish with Wolf Spirit?" Running Canoe wanted Ravenwing to know he knew who he was, and that he knew he was a war chief.

"Even in Nickajack we have heard of this warrior, this Wolf Spirit, and it is said that you, Running Canoe, claim the man is truly kin to the Wolf. It is said you had a dream and foretold the coming of the Wolf, and that this white man is he." He paused, and then looked at the men standing around him before continuing.

"Dancing Hawk is the son of Red Hawk, the greatest medicine chief the People have ever known, and Dancing Hawk too has had a dream and a vision. In his vision, the Wolf's lair was in the spirit cave, in Nickajack town, and there did the Wolf live with the other animal spirits of the Cherokee. In his dream, Dancing Hawk was told to craft a great, magical tomahawk and bring it to the cave. There he was to build a fire and purify the blade, turning it into the most awesome, fearful weapon of its kind ever made. The tomahawk was to be used by the mightiest warrior of the Cherokee to help drive the white man forever from our lands. When the elders of Nickajack learned of the tomahawk, they sent for the warrior known as Bearkiller, as he was thought to be the mightiest of the many great fighters of the People. At the council, I told of hearing the story of the warrior called Wolf Spirit, and it was decided to bring the tomahawk here to the village of Running Canoe, to find out if the tales are true. I will tell you now, Running Canoe,

Bearkiller believes not the tales of this warrior, and wishes the tomahawk for himself. He has said if Wolf Spirit makes any claim to be the greatest warrior among the People, then he must prove that claim in combat. This is truly a serious event in the history of the People, Running Canoe. We all agree the white man must be driven out, and this weapon may help us do that. But it is important that only the mightiest warrior use it. So it is the elders sent us here to lay a challenge at the feet of Wolf Spirit. If he will use the tomahawk to aid us in our fight against the white man, he must first fight and defeat Bearkiller. If he wishes not to fight, then he can return to the world of the whites, and we shall return to Nickajack and Bearkiller will lead the warriors against our white enemies."

Ravenwing stopped and smiled at the thought of a fight between the two men. He had seen the giant Bearkiller in action many times, and was sure there was no man in the small village of Running Canoe who could best him.

Bearkiller was a big man, and wore a belt heavy with scalps, both white man and Indian. Ravenwing, himself a mighty warrior, would not have wanted to fight Bearkiller if it could be avoided. The man had never been beaten, and wore an air of confidence about himself everyone in the gathering could see.

"Well do I know of Bearkiller," Running Canoe said.

"I have heard of his feats in battle for years. It is said that once, though unarmed and severely wounded, still he single handedly defeated four white men. This is a mighty deed, and will be sung about for as long as the People gather. Still, you should know one thing, Ravenwing, before you allow Bearkiller to challenge Wolf Spirit."

Running Canoe had decided to tell a tale, and then when Wolf Spirit defeated the mighty warrior Bearkiller, as he surely would, forevermore all the People would know of the wisdom of Running Canoe, and respect his dreams and visions.

"Know this, Ravenwing," Running Canoe said.

"Three years have passed since the brothers called Harpe came among the People. Only boys they were, and yet already they were fearsome fighters. In a dream, the Eagle came to Running Canoe, and told me the Wolf lived in the boys, and that the biggest boy had all of the Wolf's fearsome powers. The Eagle told me the Wolf could not be beaten by a mortal man, and would stand against all challengers. I named the boy Wolf Spirit, and it is a fitting name. He is truly the Wolf, and there has never been a more awesome warrior among any tribe of the People." Turning to face the giant warrior, Running Canoe spoke softly but with great emotion.

"Know this, Bearkiller. If you fight today with Wolf Spirit, he will kill you, and feed your blood and soul to the thing that lives inside him. We call the thing the Wolf, for that is the strongest of the earth spirits, but it may well be something older, something even more terrible. It may well be the thing inside Wolf Spirit is an ancient demon, sent among us to feed. Know, Bearkiller, if you challenge Wolf Spirit, this night shall your family weep and mourn." He paused dramatically.

"So speaks Running Canoe, Chief of the Overhill Cherokee."

"Wolf or Spirit, man or demon," Bearkiller thundered, "today I will leave him lying on the ground in a pool of his own hot blood. So speaks Bearkiller, mightiest warrior of Nickajack."

With those words the warrior glared at both Running Canoe and Ravenwing. "Bring out this timid Wolf Spirit, so I might spit upon him before I kill him."

Behind the three men of Nickajack, as silently as his namesake, Wolf Spirit had appeared. He stood with his arms folded across his chest, listening to the words of Bearkiller. He made not a single move, until at last the three felt the intensity of his gaze upon their backs and at last turned to face him.

Dancing Hawk looked into the eyes of Wolf Spirit and quickly lowered his eyes and turned away. With that one glance he had seen the demon, and waves of fear washed across him relentlessly. With the precognition many Indians seem to possess, Dancing Hawk knew he would be bound to Wolf Spirit throughout time. He knew Bearkiller would surely die today, and the brave Indian who thought himself to be the mightiest warrior of the Nickajack would be nothing more than food for the Wolf.

Ravenwing had seen the blue flame that burned within Wolf Spirits eyes, and knew this day would live forever in the history of the People.

Bearkiller recognized in the big warrior a kindred spirit, and at that moment he also understood he could not stand against this man, or rather against the thing that lived within him. He was not afraid, and he meant to fight Wolf Spirit, but he knew today he would die.

Dancing Hawk slowly sat down his pack, and slowly withdrew an object from it. The object was wrapped in the softest deerskin, and covered with the mightiest symbols known to his family. As he unwrapped the object, the very air seemed to shimmer, and all there could feel it's magical vibrations. Drawing aside the last covering, the great tomahawk was finally revealed. The blade was razor sharp, and measured seven inches from top to bottom. It was over an inch thick at it's middle, tapering back into a point, and was almost nine inches long overall. Its handle was made of cured hickory wood, and carved with many symbols of magic and power, and its grip was tightly wrapped with sinew, so it would not slip in the grasp of whoever used it. There was an awesome feeling of power about the tomahawk, and it was plain it was a great weapon of destruction.

Dancing Hawk removed the tomahawk from its deerskin wrappings and held it aloft for all to see. He held it with both hands, palms up, slightly above his forehead, and began a slow shuffling dance step. As he danced he presented the higher above his head, raising it up to the spirits, and chanted for them to bless the weapon.

Bearkiller watched the medicine man's dance with reverence, never taking his eyes from the tomahawk.

All the while, Wolf Spirit watched Bearkiller, with the same amount of intensity, never taking his eyes from the warrior.

When Dancing Hawk finished his dance, he laid the tomahawk back on its deerskin wrap and placed it at the edge of the clearing. He then took a step backward, and turned to watch Wolf Spirit and Bearkiller. Every man in the clearing was doing the same thing.

Bearkiller looked at Wolf Spirit and spoke, his voice choked with hatred;

"It is said Wolf Spirit is a mighty warrior, and is as one with the Wolf himself. Bearkiller says Wolf Spirit is only a white man, and not worthy to live among the People, nor to possess the mighty tomahawk. The white man has brought nothing to the Cherokee except death and destruction. He rapes our women and kills our children, and takes for himself land that no man owns. Today Bearkiller will kill the Wolf. Here in this clearing shall the legend of the white warrior known as Wolf Spirit come to an end. Bearkiller will return to Nickajack with the tomahawk, and with the scalp of the Wolf at my belt."

Micajah looked at the giant Indian and saw the hatred in his eyes. Looking about him, he saw the hatred reflected in the eyes of many of the Indians around the clearing, and realized that to many of them he was indeed nothing more than a white man, and not worthy to be called Cherokee. He knew beating Bearkiller would only be half the battle he must fight here today. He must win in such a manner that none here would ever doubt him again. Returning his attention to his adversary, the Big Harpe spoke for the first time since entering the clearing.

"By my white father I was named Harpe, and I am proud to be called by the name of my ancestors. When I came to live among the People, Running Canoe gave me the name Wolf Spirit, and accepted me as brother to the Indian. He says I am the Wolf, and the Wolf is me, and perhaps he is right. I know I have fought in many battles along side my red brothers, and brought honor to the name I have been given. Bearkiller now calls me a white man, and in truth,

Micajah Harpe is a white man. But Wolf Spirit is Cherokee. Know, Bearkiller, today you will die at the hands of two men. The Indian named Wolf Spirit, and the white man called Harpe. The Wolf will feed upon your spirit tonight, and the Harpe will laugh as he watches. Your soul will never rest, Bearkiller, but will roam the barren world of the wild Wolf for eternity, and your everlasting torment will give me pleasure for eternity. So speaks Harpe. So speaks Wolf Spirit. So speaks the Wolf."

For the first time in so very long, Harpe heard a low, deep growl inside himself.

I hungerrrrr Harrrrpe, I hungerrrr...

The Big Harpe heard and understood the inner voice. He smiled a little smile, softly hummed the haunting melody of his mother and stood quietly, waiting for the Indian to make his move.

Bearkiller's move was not long in coming.

With a great bellow, the big Indian leaped across the ten feet that separated the two of them. From his belt he drew a long knife, and held it poised in his right hand for a killing stroke. Thinking his war cry would un-nerve his opponent, Bearkiller hoped to use the knife before Wolf Spirit could react.

But in a motion that was a blur of blinding speed, Wolf Spirit dropped to his right knee, and a grim smile crossed his lips as he heard the savage blade of Bearkiller pass over his head. Then in a savage thrusting blow, he sank his huge right fist deep into the belly of Bearkiller, just below the heart, and felt cartilage give way. He was sure he felt a rib break. He quickly regained his feet and brought both hands crashing down into the middle of Bearkiller's back, sending him sprawling face down in the dirt. He knew Bearkiller was a mighty opponent and he should end this fight as quickly as possible, and yet he also felt he must prove to the Indians that Wolf Spirit was invincible. Stepping back away from his downed foe, he growled out a few words.

"The Wolf is hungry, Bearkiller, he would feed. On yer feet with ye, so that he might feast on yer bright red blood."

Bearkiller had dropped his knife when he fell to the ground, and didn't bother to look for it. Still full of fury, he jumped to his feet and let out another wild war cry. Once again he leaped for Wolf Spirit, his hands clawing the air in front of him, hoping to close about the throat of his opponent. But this time Wolf Spirit also leaped forward, rapidly closing the distance between them and as they met, Wolf Spirit grabbed Bearkiller's head with his big right hand. Using the Indians own momentum, he threw Bearkiller past him and into a group of warriors that stood watching. As the braves caught him, Bearkiller screamed in pain and fury, and clutched the side of his head where Wolf Spirit had held him. Droplets of bright red blood seeped from between his fingers.

Wolf Spirit stood with his right hand raised in the air, shaking it at the man on the ground. Looking closely, the warriors could see that between his thumb and forefinger Wolf Spirit held the right ear of Bearkiller.

Wolf Spirit let his eyes touch every warrior gathered there so each of them would see the full fury of the raging Wolf. When every eye in the clearing was on him, he slowly brought the ear to his mouth and bit it in half. Resting his gaze on the face of Bearkiller, he walked across to where the Indian sat on the ground, and spit the half ear in his face.

"Is this warriors blood I taste?" he asked.

"No, it cannot be. It tastes like woman's blood to me. Lie down Bearkiller, and spread yer legs that we might get a better look."

The Wolf fire was blazing in Harpe's eyes now, and the black killing rage was very close to taking control.

He opened his arms wide and raised his face to the sky, and the roar that escaped from his lips ran through the souls of the Indians, and each of them knew without a doubt they were in the presence of a demon. Even the mightiest among them trembled in fear, and all there fingered their strongest medicine tokens.

Yessss, Harrpe, killll...I hungerrrr. I hungerrrr Harrrpe...

Bearkiller dropped his hand from his mutilated face and a strange look came across his features. He drew himself up to his full height and slowly stepped back into the arena where Wolf Spirit stood waiting. He too turned his face to the sky and gave a mighty roar. "I am Bearkiller," he shouted, "Mightiest warrior of the Nickajack."

Once again he leaped at Wolf Spirit.

This time he managed to get his hands around the waist of Harpe and lifted him clear of the ground. He ran across the clearing with Harpe on his shoulder and using every ounce of his strength slammed his enemy into the trunk of a huge tree. Again and again he crushed his shoulder into Harpe's midsection, and let out a great laugh as he also felt ribs break. The white man shuddered and every muscle in his body grew taut.

Bearkiller raised his head, expecting to find his enemy battered and almost unconscious. Instead, he looked into the eyes of a monster.

The Wolf was in full control now, and the eyes were wild blue flames that seared their way directly into the brain of Bearkiller. Trance like, the Indian was held by the icy stare, and at that moment he knew the fight was finished.

Wolf Spirit turned his back on Bearkiller and walked across the clearing to where the tomahawk lay on its bed of deerskin. Bearkiller followed, beating on Wolf Spirit's back every step of the way, but his mightiest blows didn't even make the man turn.

Micajah Harpe, the Wolf, picked up the mighty tomahawk. With the weapon in hand, he then turned to once again face Bearkiller. His flaming blue eyes raked across the clearing, once again touching every man there, and in a voice filled with doom, he said;

"Let the tomahawk be baptized in the hot fresh blood of Bearkiller, so says the Wolf."

Without another word, he brought the tomahawk crashing down upon the skull of Bearkiller with such force that the man's head was split open almost to the bridge of his nose. Blood and bones and bits of brain were splattered over those in the clearing, and many fell to their knees, and the high keening of their anguished cries filled the air.

Wolf Spirit raised the tomahawk high and began a slow dance around the clearing. He danced around the body of Bearkiller and over to where Ravenwing sat with Dancing Hawk. Holding the dripping weapon over the heads of the two men, he shook it several times, watching as hot drops of blood spattered in their faces. Without missing a step in his dance, he softly intoned;

"The mightiest warrior of Nickajack is no more. The tomahawk belongs to the Wolf. Leave the village of Running Canoe, and know the Wolf will soon some to visit Nickajack. Go and make ready."

He continued his dance along the clearing until he came to the edge of the forest, and with one last brandishing of the tomahawk, he turned and vanished into the shadows of the trees.

Running Canoe looked at the fallen warrior and then at the place where the Wolf had disappeared in the forest. Turning to the men from Nickajack, he said;

"Go now, lest he return while the demon rages. The time of the Wolf in the village of Running Canoe is over, and I feel he will soon come to live in the spirit cave in Nickajack. Go now, leave at once. Even the Eagle cannot long protect you from the rage of the Wolf."

In August 1792, Micajah and Wiley Harpe, along with Susan and Betsy Roberts and the two children, Mourning and James Burton Harpe, came to live in the spirit cave at the Cherokee town of Nickajack.

20

Nickajack Cave was dark and damp, home to nothing save bats, spiders, and the occasional scurrying salamander. According to the Cherokee, it was also home to many evil spirits, and the Indians avoided the cave at all times. They called it the Spirit Cave, and believed it would bring certain doom upon the town of Nickajack should the spirits become angered for any reason.

The town of Nickajack was close to the banks of the river, and the cave itself was some three hundred yards from the village. That distance was as close as most of the Indians cared to come. The Indians living in Nickajack were among the fiercest warriors of the Cherokee, fearing none of the natural dangers that lived in the forest, yet all were deathly afraid of the spirits that lived deep within the darkness of the mighty cave.

As war chief of the Nickajack, Ravenwing had led many raids against the white men, and had taken many scalps. It was his dearest wish that the whites be driven forever from the land of the Cherokee, but in his heart he was afraid it was not to be. It made little difference how many of the white settlers the People killed, twice that many came to take their place.

So it was that Nickajack Town seemed to be in a constant state of war, waging an almost daily fight against the whites.

This was the way Harpe found Nickajack the night the Wolf came to take up residence inside the Spirit Cave.

Ravenwing woke from a deep slumber. Something was not right. He stepped outside his wigwam and looked up at the dark clouds rolling wildly across the night sky. The storm clouds rolled, and the thunder boomed, and yet the wind was still. Not a leaf stirred on any tree. Dancing Hawk, who had also been awakened, joined Ravenwing almost immediately.

"What strange magic visits the world tonight, Dancing Hawk?" Ravenwing asked. "Are the spirits angry with Nickajack for some reason?"

"I am not sure, Ravenwing," the medicine replied. "But it is for certain something strange prowls about tonight."

At that moment, Ravenwing's eyes were torn from the rolling clouds and jerked in the direction of the spirit cave. "Look, Dancing Hawk, look," Ravenwing cried. "Look at the cave."

His cries caused other Indians to emerge from their wigwams and look toward the cave also.

The mighty cave seemed to be on fire. Flickering tongues of red, yellow and orange lit up the inside of the cave, and caused a glow to shine down toward the village, as though the very air itself was ablaze. Deep in the heart of the glow there could be seen an eerie blue light, a light that grew brighter until it engulfed the enthralled Indians. Worst of all was that even though the dancing flames looked to be red hot with hell-fire, the blue glow was cold, and caused a chill to pass across the heart of Ravenwing as he stood watching. He had seen a portion of that eerie glow before, and he was very much in fear of it.

"Look, Ravenwing," one of his warriors called, "Look in the mouth of the cave."

Suddenly, starkly outlined against the flames and the blue glow from within the cave, there stood a mighty figure of a man. He was huge, and even as the Indians watched in awe, he took on step forward and stood looking down upon them. His great legs were widespread, and slowly he lifted his arms from his sides and raised them to the night sky. In his right hand was a mighty tomahawk, it's faceted blade dully reflecting the blue glow, and his left hand was clinched in a fist. Even from this distance, and in the dark, the muscles in his arms were almost visible. As his face turned upward, from his mouth came a massive roar such as the Cherokee had never heard before. Seemingly more animal than human, the roar caused the Indians to drop to their knees and to cover their heads, for they were sure the figure was one of the cave spirits come to destroy them. Once again the roar sounded, and then the great face was turned from the skies and back toward the Indians below him. They could tell the icy blue glow was coming from the eyes of the creature, and the fear became worse and spread to the center of their beings as they felt those eyes touch them.

Suddenly, the Demon spoke.

"I am Harpe," the Demon said, "the Wolf. He who is called Wolf Spirit by the People. I would live in the spirit cave of the Nickajack. Disturb me not, and I will be a brother to the Nickajack warriors. Bother me or my family, and the Wolf will be turned loose among you."

With those words the apparition roared again, and as suddenly as it had appeared, it disappeared within the cave, and within moments the blue glow had started to fade, leaving only slim fingers of dancing flame. As the flames flickered and died, the storm clouds rolled across the face of the moon, and were swept away to the East.

Dancing Hawk was the first to recover his tongue. "It is the Wolf, Ravenwing. He has come to Nickajack even as Running Canoe said he would. His power is great and in a dream I have foreseen that he shall lead us into a mighty battle. But his power is evil, and my heart fills with dread with I think of what may come with this man living in our village."

"I too worry, old friend," Ravenwing said. "For I have also looked into the blue eyes of the Wolf. Let us hope what we have turned loose shall feast upon the hearts of the whites, and not the souls of the people."

"I fear once the Wolf is loose, it will feed whenever it hungers, and will care little if it is feeding upon foe, or friend. The Wolf is not of the people, even though it came here from our own ancient spirit world, and yet neither is it of the white man; even though the man who is the Wolf is white himself. The Wolf is of the Demon World, and is one unto itself. The Harpe is one and the same as the Wolf, and neither can long control the terrible hunger that lives within them. There is no magic Dancing Hawk knows of strong enough to calm the beast once it starts to hunt."

It was over a week before the people of Nickajack again saw Wolf Spirit. He walked into the village one day, wearing a large smile upon his face, with a small naked boy perched upon his shoulder. The blue eyes were friendly, and did not seem at all strange in the bright sunshine.

He walked up to the warrior named Fivekiller and spoke in a deep, not unpleasant voice;

"Howdy feller. I am called Wolf Spirit, and I seek counsel with your war chief Ravenwing."

Fivekiller looked at the friendly giant with the smiling face and the boy on his shoulder and thought to himself, *Can this be the mighty Wolf Spirit we are all so afraid of? This is only a man, not some demon Wolf that can cause us to tuck our tails and slink away. Fivekiller could easily take this white's hair.*

Aloud he said, "I am called Fivekiller, and if you wish to follow me I will take you to Ravenwing."

"Lead on Fivekiller," the man said, "I'll be right behind ye. And could ye get a message to Chief Cornstalk, tellin' him that Wolf Spirit and Ravenwing wish to speak with him?"

"Does Fivekiller look like a messenger for the white man?" the proud Indian stopped and snapped angrily at Wolf Spirit.

Wolf Spirit stopped dead in his tracks. Fivekiller quickly turned; hoping for a chance to prove himself against the man the whole village was terrified of.

The smile was still on Wolf Spirit's face, frozen rigid by the foolish taunt of Fivekiller, but the eyes were no longer friendly. He took the boy from his shoulder and sat him on the ground, and didn't turn to watch as the youngster ran into the trees. A tiny blue spark burned within each eye, and he focused his gaze upon the face of Fivekiller.

"Yes, Injun," the voice was now cold and harsh, "yes, ye look like a messenger to me. But it's yore choice. Ye kin be a live messenger to yore Chief Cornstalk, er ye kin be a dead messenger to the Devil. Wolf Spirit has no feelin's either way. But ye don't' have long to decide. And I'll only tell ye the one time."

The cold blue flame seared itself into Fivekiller's eyes, and suddenly he knew why Ravenwing and Dancing Hawk were scared of this man. He was human in form only. There was absolutely no emotion in his voice when he spoke of killing the Indian and Fivekiller knew he was closer to death than he'd ever been before.

"I'll take your message to Chief Cornstalk," Fivekiller said, and in his heart he was ashamed of the taste of fear that now filled his mouth.

Ravenwing walked up to Harpe even as Fivekiller started away. He'd heard enough of the conversation to figure out what had happened.

"He is young, Wolf Spirit, and does not yet fully understand the way of warriors. He believes a sharp knife and a strong right arm are all it takes to make a man. He is a good fighter, and the thought perhaps entered his mind to see if Wolf Spirit is as mighty as he had been told. He means well."

"Aye, Ravenwing, he is a good man, and still young. For that reason I gave him a choice. Still, it be best ye have a word with him." Wolf Spirit was telling Ravenwing, in his own way, that if the young Fivekiller should speak to him in this manner again, he would not live to be an old Fivekiller.

"Speak with him I will," Ravenwing said. "What does Wolf Spirit want with the war chief of Nickajack this day?"

"I wanted to tell ye it be my wish to live in the Spirit Cave fer a spell, and I wanted to tell Chief Cornstalk I mean no harm to him ner to any o' his people. Nickajack cave holds many secrets I must learn, and only by fastin' and meditatin' will they be revealed to me."

As they spoke, the two men came to the wigwam of Chief Cornstalk, son of Little Corn, one of the greatest of the Cherokee chiefs. Cornstalk had come out of his wigwam, and stood waiting the coming of the two men. Fivekiller had wasted no time in taking the message to the Chief, and the Chief eager to talk to Wolf Spirit.

"Greetings, great Chief Cornstalk," Ravenwing began. "I bring a mighty visitor who wishes a word with you."

Chief Cornstalk bowed to Wolf Spirit, and very formally asked; "Are you come a friend in the name of the Great Spirit?"

Wolf Spirit replied, also very formally;

"The Great Spirit is with me. I am come a friend in his name."

Cornstalk then settled to the ground, in a cross-legged fashion, so their conversation might begin.

"Cornstalk, great Chief of Nickajack, I am he who is called Wolf Spirit, and I come as a brother to the People. I was trusted by the mighty Chief Running Canoe to live as one with the Cherokee. I come before you a friend, seeking to live at Nickajack so I may learn from the spirits who dwell within the cave. My coming has been foretold by the mighty medicine man of the Nickajack, Dancing Hawk, who dreamed a dream of Wauh-yauh, and who made for me this magical tomahawk." Harpe took the tomahawk from his belt and presented it so Chief Cornstalk might inspect it.

Taking the tomahawk from Harpe's hand, Cornstalk said; "I know of you, Wolf Spirit, and I know of your coming to Nickajack.

I know also the medicine of Dancing Hawk, and of his dreams of the Wolf, Wauh-yauh. I will tell you it was I who sent Bearkiller to test you in battle, and was more than a little surprised you bested him. Ravenwing and Dancing Hawk said you would come, and now you are here."

Cornstalk was trying everything he could think of to show Wolf Spirit who was in control here in Nickajack. He wanted Wolf Spirit to understand he knew everything that went on in his town, and had a say so in every decision made that affected Nickajack in any way.

"That you have come as a friend is good," Cornstalk continued. "I will listen to you, and treat you as a brother. Running Canoe is a wise chief, and he has judged you worthy to live with the people. Can Cornstalk do any less? Speak, Wolf Spirit, tell me more of what you would do here in Nickajack."

"Wise is the judgment of Cornstalk," Wolf Spirit began. "Dancing Hawk has told me of the spirits who dwell in the cave, and of his dream that the Wolf also lives within the darkness there. I would have permission from Cornstalk to live in the cave for a period of time, so I might learn how to better serve the spirits. It has been said I am as one with Wauh-yauh, the Wolf. Only by living in the cave can I come face to face with myself, and know if it is true that I am the Wolf himself. I also desire my family be protected from harm while I dwell in the world of the Wolf. If I wander deep into that spirit world, I might not be able to return quick enough to save them from danger should someone wish them harm. I ask that Cornstalk provide that protection. If no harm comes to my loved ones while I am gone, the Wolf shall then become the protector, and Cornstalk will be known as the greatest of Chiefs among the People. But know this also, Cornstalk," and Wolf Spirit lowered his voice and his eyes began to softly glow, "If my family suffers harm from anyone while I am away, when I return the Wolf shall feed upon the town of Nickajack. Not a man, woman, nor child shall be spared the fury of the Wolf."

The suggestion that the Wolf might serve Nickajack seemed to please Cornstalk, and the possibility that the Wolf might be turned loose upon the village brought an even greater amount of fear to his heart. Combined, there was little to say but to agree to Harpe's request.

"Go to the cave, Wolf Spirit. With my blessing you may live there, and learn what you can from those who dwell within. Your family will be as one with the family of Cornstalk while you are gone, and no man shall raise a hand against them. I would have the Wolf be a friend to Nickajack."

Both men rose and left the wigwam, only to find a large crowd of warriors had gathered to learn the outcome of their meeting.

"Our brother, Wolf Spirit, has come among us to dwell in the spirit cave and gather wisdom from those mighty ones who live deep inside. Chief Cornstalk has seen this is good, and believes the People will learn much from Wolf Spirit. I have given my word Wolf Spirit may live in the cave, and his family will be treated as part of my own family from this day forth."

Cornstalk knew his decision would be honored by all the People, even though there were some who disagreed with him. The word of a Cherokee, particularly a Chief, could not be broken. Not even when given to a white man.

Standing at the edge of the gathering, listening to every word the Chief spoke, were the family members the Chief was speaking of. This was the first time the people of Nickajack had seen them, and they looked them over with great curiosity.

There was Susan Roberts Harpe and her child, James Burton, first born son of Micajah. Also there was Betsy Roberts Harpe and her daughter Mourning. And last there was Wiley Joshua Harpe, known as Wolf Brother among the People. Wiley was only a shade less savage looking than his brother, and glowered back at the Indians as they stood there in the clearing.

The truth was, Wiley was more than capable of protecting the family while Micajah was living in the cave. However, Micajah didn't want his brother to get into any trouble with the people of Nickajack while he wasn't around. There was just too big a chance Wiley would turn the Wolf loose and not be able to control it at all. Neither of them wanted that to happen.

Micajah and Wiley agreed they needed to try to contact the spirit world and learn as much as he could about the powers of the being they knew as the Wolf, and of the Harpe amulet. They knew much of their power seemed to be derived from the amulet, but they weren't sure what that power was, nor how much of it they had, not when it might be used up.

After the fight with Bearkiller, they had sat in the forest for several hours trying to understand all that was happening to them. They knew their father had called the power inside the amulet "The Wolf," but he'd never had a chance to explain it to them. They were very surprised to hear Running Canoe also refer to the power as "The Wolf" and speak of it as though it were a natural thing. They had lived with Running Canoe's people over three years, and though the power grew stronger during that time, still they learned little about it.

The fight with Bearkiller had shown Micajah another power of the amulet. He had suspected it for sometime, but now he was sure the power of the amulet had helped him to heal much faster than was humanly possible. When Bearkiller had slammed him against the tree, he was certain he felt at least one rib break, and maybe two. Yet within an hour of the fight, there was hardly a bruise, and almost no soreness in his ribs at all. The amulet had grown warmer and as the heat spread throughout his body, the pain just seemed to fade away. He was equally as certain the amulet had many other powers as well, and he'd like to know as much as he could about them.

When Ravenwing told of the dream of Dancing Hawk, and said the Wolf lived within the cave at Nickajack, the brothers decided they must look for answers there. As it was Micajah who wore the amulet, it would be Micajah that would go alone into the cave, there to try to make contact with the Wolf himself, if indeed he truly did live inside the cave. Micajah knew well that the People's animal spirits were the keepers of great powers, and also that they allowed certain warriors to use those powers at times.

Micajah had no way of knowing the power of the Harpe amulet would prove to be greater than even the mightiest of the animal spirits, and much more fearsome.

So, to the lower town of Nickajack came the Harpes with their women and children, to seek knowledge in the great cave. The power that would be unleashed during the next few months would be the most ravaging force the world had ever seen, and might ever see in the future. The power of the ancient Harpe amulet, once combined with the hunger of the Wolf, would be too terrible even for the Harpes to control and certainly too evil for the many inhabitants of the wilderness.

Deep in the heart of the spirit cave the blue spark in the eyes of the Wolf grew ever brighter.

21

Micajah sat cross-legged on the floor of the cave, with a small fire burning in front of him. He was in one of the deepest chambers of the cave, completely out of touch with the outside world. He was in a semi-conscious state and neither saw the tiny flames which danced On the floor, nor felt the heat from them. During his first three days of fasting and meditation he had been visited by several of the lesser spirits that lived in the cave.

He had purified his body by fire and water before he entered the cave, and cleansed his mind of all impure thoughts. He made his way to this small chamber and here he built a shrine of stone, and started his fire. He had stripped himself naked and painted upon his body the greatest of the magical symbols he had learned in his years of living with the People. In the center of his forehead, and again on his chest, he had painted the awesome four pointed silver star of the amulet, set against it's own field of blood red crimson. Directly above his heart he had painted the savage sign of the Wolf, and on his right biceps was the sign for thunder, and on his left biceps the sign of the lightning. Surrounding his eyes he had painted the sign of the Hawk, to aid his vision, and his ears were painted red with the blood of bats so that even in the darkness he could find his way. His legs held the signs of the deer and the fox, to signify speed and stealth, and on his genitals was the symbol of the he-goat, showing great stamina and re-productive powers.

The only piece of jewelry he wore was the Harpe amulet itself, and it hung about his neck upon its leather thong. Now and then the silver of the star would catch the light of the dancing fire and cast a darting sliver of brightness about the walls of the cave. In contrast to the star, the deep red of the Amulet's background seemed to absorb whatever light came upon it, and most of the time seemed more black than red.

Harpe had chanted the prayers he had learned from the People, first to the Great Spirit, and then to the Wolf Spirit, asking each in turn for wisdom and guidance, and soon found himself sinking into a deep state of meditation, where he could be visited by the spirits as they wished.

On the fourth day of his meditation, there came to him the Spirit of the Bear, symbol of strength and endurance. On its hind legs the Bear walked out of the darkness and stood bathed in the dancing yellow light of the fire. Without hesitation, Micajah spoke to the animal spirit.

"Oh Great Bear Spirit, strongest of all animals, share with this un-deserving one the secret of your strength".

Suddenly, even before the Bear could speak, out of the darkness of the cave came a large paw, with razor sharp claws, and with one mighty swipe felled the Bear Spirit, rendering it into a thousand small bloody pieces. The pieces faded quickly away, save for one of its front paws.

With this, Harpe realized he needed not the Bear Spirit for strength, for even the mighty Bear fell before the fury of the Wolf.

On the fifth day of his meditation, there came to the cave the Owl Spirit.

Out of the pitch black darkness of the roof of the cave, where not even one single shaft of the light from the fire had penetrated, came the sound of mighty wings beating against the dank, damp still air. For a second the great Owl hovered in mid-air above the fire before descending and alighting before the man.

"Oh Great Owl", Micajah intoned, "Wisest are ye among the Animal Spirits. Mighty are ye that soars on the wind and sees all things. Sit with me and teach me, for I have much to learn".

Yet before the Owl Spirit could speak, once again came the sweep of the black furry paw. Without a sound it came out of the darkness, and struck the Owl a single savage blow.

Even as the Bear had fallen, so too fell the wisest of the animals, the Owl. All that was left of the visitor were seven small feathers from his tail. A sudden gust of chill wind blew from deep in the cave, gathering the feathers into a small pile, and depositing them softly at the feet of the man seated there.

Once again, Harpe understood. Just as he didn't need the strength of the Bear, so also he didn't need the wisdom of the Owl. Wise though he may be, still the Owl could not stand before the Wolf. The wisdom Harpe would find from following the way of the Wolf would more than suffice to fill all of his needs.

Then, in a flurry of excitement, on the morning of the sixth day came the Eagle. It's great wings beat the air and brought the fire to a full roaring life, until it's flames lit up the shadows of the cave until it was almost as bright as the outside world. Harpe understood the Eagle would not chance the darkness, as had the Bear and the Owl. The eyes of the Eagle searched the cave from floor to cavern roof, and only when it was satisfied that the Wolf was not present did the Eagle land. Once the Eagle's talons were at rest on the smooth rock floor of the cave, it spoke to Micajah;

"Listen carefully Man-child, for it is very important you understand fully what it is I teach you this day. Your being here is not by chance. Far from it. Long and long ago were you chosen to serve the Wolf. For in truth, you and he are of the same family. For generations have your fathers been preparing the way for the coming of the Wolf. It is in you that the Wolf shall become full grown, and once again stalk the ancient hunting grounds of the People."

"Once in all the World there was only us," the mighty Eagle spirit continued. "The Eagle and the Wolf and the Bear and the other animal spirits, and we lived as one with the Air and the Water and the Land. Each of us ruled our own domain, and each was content in that respect. None wanted that which was not his to have. All was peace and harmony."

"Then came Man.'

With his black piercing eyes fixed upon Micajah's face, the Eagle went on.

"Peace and harmony was no more, for man wanted all, and would not stop until all was his. Slowly were the spirits pushed back across the boundary into the realm of half-life. Where once we soared on the clouds, and walked the forests, now were our wings clipped and our legs hobbled. We sought refuge on the mountaintop, and in the deep forest, and in the darkness of the great caves, and showed ourselves only in dreams from that time on. And only then to certain wise men who understood the forces we are must come first, and must not be cast aside."

Almost sadly, the Eagle kept speaking.

"As the years passed, our visits to the People became fewer and fewer. We came to believe the time would come when man would vanish once again from our lands, and so we waited, thinking to one day reclaim what is rightfully ours. Desiring that man not destroy the lands we love, we visited some among you and offered wisdom and vision. We could guide those men, and they in turn could safeguard the fabric of the World."

"Patient have we been for these countless ages, and none of us have had direct intervention in the affairs of man. None of us, with the exception of the Wolf."

'Once, long ago, the Wolf stole from his den deep here inside the mighty Spirit Cave, and took for himself a human woman as his mate. In a green land on the other side of the World he found a suitable one, a woman strong enough to bear his cub, and he carried her back to the depths of his Kingdom in the Spirit World, and there they raised the he-cub, and taught it the Way, and when it was grown and well versed in the way of the Wolf, he sent it once again to the world of Man, there to hunt and feed the soul of the Wolf. Around the cub's neck the Wolf placed a sacred amulet that bore a four pointed silver star. The four points of the star stand for Air, Water, Earth, and Fire, and the background is red with the blood of each firstborn male child, binding that child forever to the Spirit World and to the wishes of the Wolf. The powers of the amulet are many and wondrous strange, for it is of our World, and holds much of our strengths. Beware, for even as it holds our strengths, so too it holds our weakness. These powers shall be soon be explained to you, and by the Wolf himself. But heed ye this warning. Within the hour the Wolf shall come to you, and show you many strange and wonderful things. Listen to the Wolf, even as ye have listened to me, but do not answer the Wolf in haste. Think hard on his every word, and make no pledge to the Wolf without much consideration."

"For I shall reveal to you at this time the He-cub born to the Wolf and his mate and returned to the World of man was named Harpe, and the Talisman you wear is the self same Talisman that was placed around the He-cubs neck, and is now called by you the Harpe amulet."

Taking a breath, the Eagle went on. "The Talisman holds not only the power of the Wolf, but of the other animal spirits as well. You are one with the Wolf, young Harpe, and upon your pledge shall ye remain with the Wolf in all respects, but think hard before you agree to unleash the awful power of the Amulet upon your world, for the Wolf is ever hungry, and it will feed upon the living souls of those you kill for it. Know also that even though ye be one with the Wolf, still it is the Wolf who is stronger between the two of you. Forever and always will the Wolf control the man, and not even the strongest first born can stand before the Wolf's fury. Neither foe nor friend, stranger nor family will be safe should you unleash the full power of the Wolf."

"So, fare thee well, Harpe who is the Wolf, fare thee well. May your mind be as strong as it needs to be to use the gift you have been given."

Once again the mighty wings beat the air of the cave, and with a final piercing look from his eyes, the Great Eagle was gone.

Without a word Micajah collapsed on the floor of the cave into a deep and dreamless sleep.

How long he slept, he knew not, but he did know what it was that awakened him. A great wet tongue licking his face was what brought him back to his senses. As Harpe's strange blue eyes opened, he found himself staring into the equally strange blue eyes of the being called the Wolf.

It seemed forever the two of them, Wolf and Man, sat staring into each other's eyes. Harpe was breathless and spellbound for a moment, not knowing what to say, when suddenly the Wolf moved. It walked slowly to the other side of the fire, which had by now died down, and then, turning to Harpe, the Wolf spoke.

"Harpe, man-cub of the Wolf. You are one with my family, and I am one with yours. One we are, and one shall we be, always and always".

Try though he may, Harpe could not answer. His heart beat as if it would tear itself from his chest, and his mouth was so dry that even should he be able to form words, he would not be able to mouth them aloud. His mind was reeling from the contact with first the Eagle and now the Wolf. He was filled with dread of this creature that stood before him, and realized that even while part of him feared the Wolf, another part was completely fascinated by the creature.

Again the Wolf spoke.

"Ask what you would of me, Harpe. What troubles you the most?"

Micajah sat silent for a moment, staring at the strange creature and now and then touching the amulet.

"Who am I?" he asked. "Why am I called the Wolf? And what does this amulet have to do with me and mine?"

"Good questions, one and all," the Wolf replied, "and ones I will be happy to answer. Listen closely, for this is of the greatest importance to you and your world, as well as to the world I currently abide in."

The Wolf then began to relate the wondrous history of the association of the Wolf with the Harpe family, and Micajah marveled as he heard the words.

22

Wiley and the two women had just about given up hope that Micajah was still alive. He had been in the spirit cave now for over four weeks with no food nor drink, and although Wiley had ventured inside the cave in search of Micajah many times he had found no traces whatsoever of his brother, save for the ashes of a small campfire deep inside one of the caverns.

It had been mid August 1792, when Micajah had brought the family to Nickajack, and he had entered the cave in late April of 1793. It was now the end of the first week of May, and there had been no sign of Micajah since he had entered the cave. For the first few days they had left food and water at the entrance to the cave every day, but none had ever been touched. After a few weeks they had stopped leaving the food, thinking something must have happened to Micajah. Everyone in the village had seen the bright light that had issued forth from the cave on the sixth night, and all of the Indians thought Harpe had been consumed by the brightness.

But Wiley knew better. Perhaps something had indeed happened to his brother, but he had not been vanquished by anything so harmless as a glowing light, no matter its brightness. No. Wiley was afraid Micajah had somehow slipped into a crevice or fell into some bottomless pit in the ink black darkness. Perhaps striking his head and maybe even dying from the fall, or from hunger after he could not be found.

In any event, Wiley and the women and children were making plans to take their leave of Nickajack. With Micajah gone, the three of them were beginning to want the company of someone other than Indians. They had also noticed that the Indians, thinking now that Wolf Spirit may not return, were becoming resentful of the whites and of the status they had enjoyed among the family of Chief Cornstalk.

Another event took place in the first week of May that had some bearing upon Wiley's decision to leave the Cherokee town.

Moses Stegall had shown up in Nickajack.

Several days ago Moses had come walking out of the woods as big as life, and told the Indians he was blood brother to Wolf Spirit. Moses always spelled trouble, and what with Micajah gone and the Indians beginning to act up, Wiley decided it was about time to leave. They would stay perhaps another three or four weeks, but that was about all they would remain here.

Wiley had also heard the rumors that John Watts, the greatest war chief of the Cherokee, was trying to rally the People into making another raid on the whites, in one last attempt to drive them forever from the land. Wiley didn't mind participating in the raid at all, but like Chief Running Canoe and many other of the more realistic thinking Indians, Wiley thought the raid futile, and doomed to failure. The white man was here, and here he would stay. If anyone left the land over the next several years, it would be the Indian. There were too many whites already here, and each new day saw more of them moving into the region. The land was already so crowded you could scarcely walk for two or three days in any direction without coming upon a white settler, or, even worse, and entire white settlement.

No, Wiley could see what lay ahead. The future of this land lay in the hands of the white man, and if Wiley wanted to survive in this country, then it must be as a white man. The time of the Indian was drawing to a close.

Late in the afternoon of May 11, dark storm clouds began to roll in from the West, and the temperature in Nickajack began to rapidly cool. By six that evening the winds were raging, and thunder and lightning crashed from the skies. In a sudden torrential downpour the rains came, almost as if the clouds had been violently burst open.

At the very height of the storm, when all the People had found shelter from the elements, there came such a roaring as none had ever head before. Many in the village thought the spirits were angry, and it must be the end of the world, and many rushed outside to try and discover the origin of the sound.

Suddenly as it had started, the rain stopped. The wind died away and the clouds passed from the face of the moon. It seemed as if the entire world had grown deathly silent, even the animals of the forest seemed to know there was something out of place with the universe. Then, in the midst of the strange stillness, the mighty roaring came once again.

Leaving the women and children inside for safety, the rest of the men of the People rushed out to see what was happening. Wiley and Stegall stalked about in the night, seeking the cause of the sound. It was only when the entire village had turned out that the roaring came for the third time.

Suddenly from the spirit cave there came a light, brighter even than the lightning of the storm. Painful to look upon, the light hurt the eyes of each person who stared into it. But so impelling was the light the People found itn impossible not to look. And all that looked saw the silhouette of a man framed in the light, standing at the entrance of the cave. And all that saw the figure had no doubt the Harpe had returned.

It was almost the same as when he had first appeared in the mouth of the cave, the day the brothers came to Nickajack. He stood, bathed in the light at the entrance of the cave, and roared his dominance over all who heard. But this time the light was brighter, the man was bigger, almost a giant, and the roar this time was louder, more menacing, and deadlier by a thousand fold. The sound struck terror into the hearts of all that heard it, and echoed throughout the land, and the world trembled.

The Wolf was alive, and returned from the depths of the spirit cave, and the town of Nickajack was doomed.

23

When Micajah appeared in the mouth of the cave, Wiley could hardly believe his eyes. He'd had no doubt his brother was dead, and when he saw him come walking out of the cave, he ran toward the cave as fast as he could. Hard on his heels came Susan and Betsy, and close behind and catching up ran Moses Stegall. It took them less than a minute to run the three hundred yards to the cave, but by the time they arrived, the bright light was already beginning to fade.

Up on the rocks Wiley jumped, and to the mouth of the cave, only to be stopped dead at what he found waiting there. It was Micajah, rightly enough, but not the same man who had ventured into the cave so many months ago.

This man who stood before them had a dark beard, and hair down over his ears. He was leaner than when he had entered the cave, yet his muscles were larger and more defined. However, even with all the changes, there was no mistaking the eerie blue eyes, nor the Amulet he wore around his neck.

"Micajah. Kage, it's you," Wiley exclaimed. "We thought ye dead. Whar have ye been, brother, and how came ye to look so different?" Wiley was finding the strange new appearance of his brother a little hard to get used to.

"Time fer all thet later, Wiley" Micajah said, sending an inquiring glance in the direction of Moses Stegall.

"We've matters of much more importance to discuss first. All o' ye, including you, Moses, step inside the cave fer a moment."

143

Micajah turned his attention to the Indians who were slowly beginning to approach the ledge when the small party stood.

"Oh great Chief Cornstalk," he began. "Ravenwing and Dancing Hawk, the Wolf has returned. I would speak with my family tonight, after so long away from them, and on the morrow I would meet in council with my red brothers. I have many wondrous things to tell ye of the Spirit world, fer thet is whar I have spent my recent past. The Eagle I saw, and the Hawk, and many others of the animal brothers of the people. There, among the spirits, the Wolf is greatest of all. Leave me now to sit with my family, and come the dawn I will tell ye many things of great interest."

Micajah didn't wait for the Indians to withdraw, knowing full well they wouldn't come into the cave. He turned his back on them and entered the spirit cave alone to greet his family.

Micajah slapped Stegall heartily on the back, and then embraced his younger brother in a great bear hug.

"My God, Wiley, more often than not lately I thought I'd never see ye again."

"Aye brother, and we were sure ye had met an untimely end. But come, tell us of your adventures." Wiley was not going to get off the subject until he had a satisfactory answer, and so far he had no answers at all.

"I'll be gittin' to thet, Wiley, in jist a minute. First give me a minute to speak with me two beautiful darlin's."

Micajah turned to Susan and Betsy and opened his arms wide for them. With hardly any effort at all he swept them both from their feet and swung them around in the cool air of the cave. "I've missed the two o' ye, how much I could not tell ye. How be the children, James and beautiful little Mourning? Though I be not good with the honeyed words, ye know I place them two young'uns above life itself." Setting the women down, he twirled around and around a couple of times himself.

"So ye believe Micajah's changed, do ye?" he almost shouted.

"Ye be changed, sure enough," Wiley exclaimed.

"Aye tis so," Micajah admitted. "Now, if ye'll answer a few questions fer me, I'll git on with the story of how I changed so much. First, tell me, be thar a man in Nickajack lately who calls himself by the name of John Watts?"

"John Watts? Fer shore he's been here brother. John Watts is the greatest War Chief the Cherrykee has ever seen, and they mean to folly him to the West in a few weeks on the biggest raid they has ever been on. We was thinkin' o' jinein' up with them, and onct it were over, we was plannin' on headin crost the wilderness. But when ye never come back from the cave, we all jist kindy decided to leave the Cherrykee fer good, and go of somewhar and live with er own people fer awhile." Wiley decided to tell Micajah they had planned to leave without him, and see how he took the news.

"Without me here, t'would have been wise fer ye to leave the People. Ye have a good head on yer shoulders, Wiley, that's fer shore. But now thet I have returned, thangs will change jist a mite, with all due respect to yore plans. I still be head o' the Harpe clan, and I will decide when we will leave the Cherrykee."   That was all there was to that. The eldest son was the head of the family, and there was no disputing that.

"Aye Micajah, thet ye be, and we all be thankful thet ye has been returned to us in good health, and not a'tall dead, as we supposed." The tone in Wiley's voice left no doubt he was sincere in what he said.

"I'll be thankin' ye fer the kind words, brother, and now, if'n ye'll all settle down on a comfortable spot, I'll spin a tale fer ye o' the spirit world, and the wonders I encountered thar." Without further ado, Micajah began relating the events that had transpired in his journey inside the spirit cave of the Wolf.

So it was the Harpe family, along with Moses Stegall, were re-united, and spent the rest of the night listening to the wondrous tales of the Wolf and the Eagle, the Bear and the Owl, as Micajah told of one adventure after another, each one more exciting than the one before.

Along towards morning, Micajah first spoke of his dream encounter with the Wolf; on the faraway grass of a world unlike any he had ever known.

"I'll tell ye now of my dream, and what I larned when the Wolf spoke to me. I know not of the truth of the dream, nor how wise t'would be fer us to act upon what I larned, but here is the gist of it, and I tell ye thet as I lived it, so do I believe it."

With words filled with awe and in a voice not quite his own, Micajah related the story of his visit to the strange and wonderful visit with the demon spirit known as the Wolf.

24

The Wolf was on a rampage. Everywhere he turned, he found an enemy, and every enemy he found, he killed. Since leaving Nickajack and following John Watts West into the middle country of Tennessee, the Wolf had fed with great regularity and even greater ferocity. At least two people a day met their death at the hands of Micajah Harpe, and most days there were even more. Harpe had lost count of the lives he had taken, but he could feel the Wolf grow stronger with each passing day, and with each new kill the Wolf gained a little more control over the man.

This was the sixth day of the great raid, and the Harpe brothers, along with Moses Stegall, had proven to be wilder and deadlier than almost any of the Indians. John Watts was a great leader, and had planned the raid well, and so far all had gone as expected. Right from the very first day.

They had not been more than twenty miles from Nickajack before the raid had claimed it's first victim. Around noon of the first day, they had come upon a small cabin, and the raiders had wasted no time in killing the man and woman they found inside, and setting the cabin afire. They took the two horses they found there and added them to their own stock, and resumed their march. In the days that followed, this scene was repeated many times.

John Watts truly believed this raid would let the white men know the Indians were serious about keeping their land. The Indians had lived on this land for many generations, and were determined the white settlers would have to leave. Watts, the greatest War Chief of the Cherokee, thought if he killed enough whites on this raid, it would cause the others to leave the Cherokee country, and no more would come. He had no way of knowing this raid would mark the beginning of the end of the Cherokee way of life.

John Watts sat on his pony overlooking a settlement outside Buchanan's Station, the site that would later become Nashville. Several women were tending the crops, and ten or twelve young children played on the edge of the field. But everywhere he looked, John Watts saw men with rifles close at hand. The big man who sat on the horse next to John Watts also saw the rifles, and it was plain to both men the settlers were prepared for trouble.

After surveying the situation for several minutes, John Watts turned to his companion and said; "What think you, Wolf Spirit? This is the largest settlement we have come across, and the men are well armed and seem ready for a fight. We have many warriors, but I fear in this battle we will lose many of them. What says the Wolf? Shall we pass this settlement by, or attack and suffer the losses?" John Watts valued the word and council of the big white man more than any other, especially in the ways of war.

"The Wolf is hungry, Chief," growled Big Harpe. "Let any warrior who wishes to ride around this settlement do so, the Wolf will ride through the middle of it."

Harpe uttered the words with such a quiet ferocity that even Watts was taken aback. For a moment, the war chief of the Cherokee studied the man called Wolf Spirit. He saw a big, strongly muscled man with a full black beard and wild blue eyes. His breech was spotted with dried blood, and at his belt hung seven fresh scalps. In his right hand was the fearsome tomahawk, and with his left hand he fingered the silver amulet that hung from a leather thong around his neck. About the man there hung an air of brutal, wild savagery, and in his eyes John Watts could see a complete disregard for anything or anyone.

This man is more savage than any red man I have ever known, thought John Watts, *and knows nothing save that the infernal Wolf must constantly feed. Well, so be it.*

With a wild war whoop, the war chief urged his pony down off the hill and into the midst of the white settlers. From all sides came answering cries from his warriors as they leaped into the fight with full force. But John Watts was right about the cost of this fight. He had not advanced half way down the hill before he saw his followers begin to fall from the hastily aimed shots of the whites. The settlers were more ready than it had seemed, and fired at the Indians as fast as their rifles could be recharged.

It was not long before the first wave of Indians reached the outermost cabins, and the deadly business of massacre began. John Watts felt a bullet strike his leg, and could feel the hot blood as it flowed down his calf and filled his moccasin. Hastily looking at the wound, he saw it had only creased the skin, and was not crippling. With another fierce war cry, he swung his own axe at the head of the closest white, and felt satisfaction as it splintered bone and splattered brains across his arm. To his right he heard the mighty roar of Harpe, and knew the Wolf was feeding well this day.

The Wolf was feasting. With reckless abandon Harpe rode through the settlement, his tomahawk cutting a swath of crimson. He had suffered several minor cuts, and at least one rifle wound, but they seemed to have no affect at all on the big man. In fact, the blood of the first few cuts had already begun to dry, and the hole made by the rifle ball had begun to close. His great roars filled the air, making white man and red man alike shudder. His eyes almost glowed with the wolf fire. The wild blue flames were flashing hotter and hotter as each victim fell, and all that looked upon him saw a man more animal than human.

On Wolf Spirit's right rode his brother, and he was caught up in the same killing lust and killing fever as Big Harpe. Armed with a great long knife in his right hand and a stout club in his left, he slashed throats and bashed in heads almost as quickly as did Wolf

Spirit, and his battle cry was the same wild, frenzied shout. His eyes glowed with the same blue flame, and there was not doubt he was the brother of the Wolf.

Moses Stegall was almost as bad as the Harpes. He slashed about with little regard as to who or what he struck. Even some of the Indians would pass over the body of a fallen foe and leave it lying, but not Stegall. He stood out on the field of battle as he knelt beside the body of every wounded person, man woman or child, and viciously cut the exposed throats with his razor sharp blade. Even when it was clear the battle was over, Stegall hunted the field for any living person, killing all he found. He was as caught up in the killing rage as any Indian, and more so than most, and when the last victim had been dispatched, he stood in the middle of the clearing, and shouted his rage at the skies. He beat upon his chest, and tears ran down his cheeks, so caught up was he in the emotion of the killing. When at last it was over, Moses Stegall sank to his knees, his head in his hands, and remained that way for several long minutes. Finally, he arose, and stood looking about the settlement as though seeing it for the first time.

"My God," he screamed at whoever was listening. "My God, what have we done here? Are we men or animals? Am I Moses Stegall, a white man, or some renegade killer, and a traitor to my own people? Micajah, Wiley, what have we done? What have we done?"

The Harpe brothers looked at each other, and then at the man sitting on the ground, once again holding his head in his hands. They dismounted their horses and took their friend by his arms, and lifted him to his feet.

"We did what we had to do, Moses," Wiley said. "We have lived with the People, and took their ways as our own, and we can have no regrets about the battle here today. John Watts would have killed each person here as surely as we did, even had we not been here. Perhaps with even more pain and suffering. There will never be lasting peace between the Indian and the white man as long as they try to share the same land. One or the other must go. If Watts be right, and this raid does drive the white man from the land, then we will all live in peace. If not, then the time of the red man is over, and the whites will rule this land as they do much of the country already."

Wiley paused and looked around one more time at the dead in the clearing, both red and white.

"Either way, my friend, I fear our time with our red brothers is also almost finished."

Micajah had stood and listened as his brother spoke, and thought Wiley's words made a lot of sense.

"We will winter at the Nickajack Town, and with the greening be gone," he said.

He had made up his mind, and all that was left to do was finish the raid and return to the cave.

But something happened that prevented the Harpes from leaving Nickajack when spring came. After they had returned from the raid, and the nights had begun to turn chilly, Micajah learned both women were once again pregnant. The babies would be born in mid-summer, so Micajah decided to put off leaving the shelter of the cave, and the protection of the village, until after the babies were a little stronger. But still, they would leave before winter, and if all went well they would return to the world of the white man once again.

The winter of 1793 was harsh and cold in Nickajack Town, and many of the People came down sick, and many died. Thinking to cleanse the fever from their bodies, the People would go into the sweat lodge and steam themselves until they were sweating profusely. They would become hotter and hotter, until the moisture poured from their bodies, and at the height of the sweating they would run from the sweat lodge and throw themselves into the frigid waters of the river. Many died thinking this would drive the sickness from them.

Both Susan and Betsy gave birth in April, and both had large, healthy baby boys. William Joseph Harpe was born to Betsy on the sixth day of April 1794, and eight days later, on April fourteenth, Susan gave birth to Joshua Benjamin Harpe.

25

As Joseph Ballenger rode through the carnage and destruction left behind by the rampaging Indians, tears came to his eyes. Though he was a seasoned fighting man and had witnessed more than one brutal slaying, the battle site left behind by the rampaging Cherokee was almost more than he could look at. Everywhere he turned there were bodies. Men, women and children lay scattered on ground darkened by blood. White and Indian lay side by side, blood mingling in the dirt that each side wanted to claim for their own.

Ballenger knelt and scooped up a handful of the bloodied dirt and sifted it through his hands, and knew why so many were so willing to die for it. In the land lay the life of the people. In its woods and waters, and its fruits and grains. Ballenger knew also the land had not seen its last violent death. As so many had fallen in this senseless raid, so to would the coming days and years see the land bring many other similar battles, and many more lives lost. Blood would flow like a mighty river through the land of the People before the fight with the white man was finished, and Ballenger knew a terrible grief deep in his heart. He wished he had an answer, a means to prevent the coming slaughter. Some way he could make everyone, both white man and red, see the only way to survive was together. There was room for all, but Joseph Ballenger knew in his heart the men of both sides could not see that as the truth.

Here and there Ballenger came upon a man or woman still half alive, and each of them swore they had seen several white men fighting alongside the Indians. That was why he was here. If indeed

153

there were white renegades, Ballenger meant to either kill them or bring them in to face a white mans jury.

Ballenger met with Major James Ore in June of 1794, and they discussed the plans for an upcoming raid on the lower towns of the Cherokee, down toward Chattanooga. Ballenger told Major Ore he didn't believe any good would come from such a raid, but wished him and his men Godspeed. It they intended to carry the fight to the Indians, then Ballenger hoped one mighty sweep would be all that was required to end the terrible wars. In the meantime, he would continue searching for the mysterious white men said to be fighting with the Cherokee.

MOSES STEGALL

Moses Stegall now had one more thing to blame on the Harpe brothers. He never would have taken part in the raid had not Micajah urged him to do so. Stegall had much rather see the Indian driven out, and the white man settle the land. In that way, a man such as himself might claim a few choice acres and build himself a good home.

The thing that bothered him the most, however, was the knowledge that if the Harpes ever got caught and were made to talk, they could tell too many things about Moses Stegall. Things that not only could keep him from living a decent and respectful life, but things that could easily get him hung. For instance, if word ever got around the territory about his part in the big raid, he'd be wanted by every lawman in five hundred miles. And he'd not allow that to happen, regardless of what he had to do. At some point Moses was sure there'd be a showdown between himself and the big Harpe. He was just as sure that before that day came he'd find a way to stack the odds in his own favor. Friends were friends, but Stegall wouldn't hesitate to take advantage of whatever opportunity came along to shut the brother's mouths forever. He'd bide his time, and when his chance came along, he'd do what he had to do.

MICAJAH AND WILEY

Micajah and Wiley had a lot of misgivings about their friend Moses Stegall after the John Watts raid. Stegall had lost control of himself and the most brutal side of his nature had come to the surface. Micajah suspected Stegall had gone farther than he had intended during the raid. He had relished the slaughter and blood letting as much or more than any of the others, and now that it was over he was afraid someone would find out he'd taken part in it. Micajah knew the truth about Stegall could never be forced from either himself or his brother, but he was equally certain Moses would never believe it.

From this day forward, Micajah would never completely trust Stegall again. Though they were friends, and had been for years, the friendship would wither under the strain of Stegall's traitorous nature.

26

On September 7th, 1794, Major James Ore left Nashville with over five hundred men and began a march towards the five lower towns of the Cherokee. They intended to storm all of the towns, but Nickajack was the primary target. Many of Major Ore's men had lost family and friends in John Watts's great raids, and they were anxious for revenge. With their scout, a young lad named Joseph Brown in the lead, the army made good time. Camping at such places as Black Fox spring, and the Old Stone Fort, the army crossed Monteagle Mountain and on the afternoon of September 12th, 1794, they reached the Tennessee River.

That night, under cover of darkness, the men crossed the river and made their way to Nickajack. They lay in ambush around the town until dawn was breaking in the east, and with full daylight the army fell upon the town.

Major Ore led his men forward toward the first two small cabins they came upon. With wild shouts and much shooting, they chased the Indians from the cabins and killed every one of them as they fled across the clearing. These shots somewhat alerted the rest of the town, but it was already much too late for anyone to escape.

Many women and children were killed as they ran from their cabins, and others as they tried to hide in the midst of the cornfields. Major Ore was surprised to find most of the men in the village were not there, but he had no idea where they were. They had no way of knowing the men of Nickajack were some miles away, in another of the Cherokee towns, attending a council of the Chiefs.

A lot of the Indians made it to the river and jumped in, thinking to swim to safety on the other bank, but Major Orr and his men made short work of the swimmers. Standing on the bank and firing at the Indians in the water was great sport for the army. Not one Indian safely climbed out of the water on the opposite side, and the river ran red with the blood of the dying. The soldiers checked every cabin, and made sure there was not a single person left alive when they were through. Only when they were sure all the Indians were dead did the army pause in their effort.

It was not even mid-morning when scout Joseph Brown rode up to Major Ore and reported; "Major Ore, Sir. I believe we have killed all of the enemy. There looked to be some three or four that got past us through the cornfield, but they will be all we missed. Will we continue our march on the other towns Sir? We have not killed many men here today, only women and children for the most part."

"Oh yes, Brown, we'll continue our march all right," the Major said. "We have to find the men. I won't rest until the last of the red devils are dead and in hell."

The Major had been one of the first men to arrive at the sight of the John Watts massacre last year. He had seen men and women with their throats slashed, and small children with their heads bashed in. Today was his first sampling of revenge, and the taste upon his tongue was sweet indeed. Yes. They would sure as hell continue their march upon the other Cherokee towns.

The Harpes heard the sound of gunfire from where they lived in the spirit cave. Micajah and Wiley rushed to the mouth of the cave and cautiously looked out. They saw the town was overrun with soldiers, and the sound of rifles firing was like nearby thunder.

"Whut is tarnation is going on, brother?" Wiley quietly asked. "They must be three or four hunnerd men down thar."

"At least thet many, Wiley. My guess is it's the white men gettin' back at us fer the big raid last year. I don't reckon thar's no use fer us to go down thar. We cain't change a damn thing, and won't do us no good to git ourselves kilt."

Micajah was speaking out of common sense, and not fear, for the raging Wolf inside him desperately wanted to charge down the hill and feed.

"Stegall is down thar, Micajah," Wiley stated.

"Aye, I know. Thar be nothin' we kin do," Micajah answered. "Gettin' ourselves kilt will not keep Moses alive, nor bring him back if'n he be already dead. No, we'll be holdin' 'er ground right here. If'n they come up to the cave, then we'll do whatever be necessary."

For hours the Harpe brothers lay in the mouth of the cave and watched as the Indians were slaughtered. The big Harpe's eyes were glowing, and it was all he could do to keep the Wolf under control. After awhile the shootings stopped, and the town was still, save for the sound of the army as they milled around, looking for any who might have escaped their guns. They watched as one man rode up the officer and speak with him, and then the man rode out and began bringing the troops into formation. In less than an hour, the town was empty of the soldiers, and the only movement to be seen was the graceful turns of the large birds that slowly circled overhead.

Micajah and Wiley stood and walked back into the cave. They hastily began to gather his personal belongings, and told the women to do the same. They must be out of the cave, and well on their way before noon.

27

The Harpes found another large cave on the banks of the Wolf River where they spent the winter of 1794, and in the spring of 1795 the family made their way to the town of Knoxville, in the upper Tennessee country. They had decided to settle down on a small farm and live in peace with the white men, and they had made up their minds that whatever happened in the years that followed, they would never turn the Wolf loose again.

"Well, little brother," Micajah said, "Knoxville town shore air not much like the village. Thar's more people here than I've ever seen at one place a'fore."

"Yore right about thet, brother," Wiley replied, "but I believe we'll come to like it onct we get used to it. Thar's a heap of opportunity here bouts, and I'm thinkin' we'll fit right it."

"I hope so, Wiley, I dearly hope so. Them red Injuns was good people, and they was good to us, but I been cravin' the company of white folks fer awhile. The women folk been a'wantin' fer us to build 'em another cabin, and this is as good a time as any. They're hankerin' fer a good home fer the chillun, so's I reckon as how tis time we settled down." He looked at Wiley for a moment and smiled. "They tell me they's some o' the best horse racin' in the country right here in Knoxville. Thet should tickle yore fancy."

"Thet's a fact fer shore, Kiga. I bet ye I kin out ride any man jack white man in the whole town of Knoxville. If'n ye ask me, I think we got the fastest horse in the territory. Them Injuns stole thet horse over in Nashville, and he has outrun everthang we matched him agin so far. Seeing as how you won it fair and square from old Running Canoe, I don't see no harm in racing it here in Knoxville. I 'spect as how we'll be winnin' a few dollars here and thar. What say ye to thet?"

"Well, nobody in this part of the country has seen this horse afore," Micajah said, "so I reckon we'll be safe to run him agin the folks around here. But the first thing we got to do, little brother, is find us a piece of land we kin work. Let's ride around a bit and see what's available."

Knoxville was a young town in 1795. Laid out on the south branch of the Wilderness road, close to where the Holston and French Broad rivers met, it was a booming frontier settlement. It's population was increasing daily, changing overnight as travelers stopped for a day or so to buy supplies before they headed west again. The shops in town prospered from the great westward immigration, and catered to the wild and rough ways of the men and women as they passed through.

To be sure, there were schools and churches aplenty. The people who settled in Knoxville, not intending to move on, wanted to make their town an ideal place for people of a like mind. They were good, law abiding citizens, and for the most part avoided the rum shops and groggeries that also abounded in the thriving town.

On the frontier, people were more than glad to lend a helping hand to settlers who wanted to put down roots. Helping others build cabins and clear small patches from the thick undergrowth was a community affair, and all the neighbors turned out and pitched in to help. The men worked felling trees and chopping, and splitting the logs for the cabin walls, and the women stayed busy helping with the gardens or making a find quilt for their neighbor.

When the day's work was done, often a whiskey jug would be passed around, and someone would start sawing on an old fiddle, and the people would gather round and dance a reel. All in all it was a time when neighbors welcomed neighbors, and worked together for the common good of all. And they each knew they could all be called on whenever the need arose.

Micajah and Wiley Harpe, along with Susan and Betsy, found an ideal home site down on Beaver Creek, just a few miles west of town. It was a beautiful level plot of ground, and had very little of the dense undergrowth that was so plentiful in the area. There were plenty of big trees for the cabin, and the land was rich and black, and would grow beautiful corn. There was a small spot by the woods, about fifty yards from the house, where they could raise their hogs. Micajah and Wiley were good hog farmers, and the meat brought a good price when sold. The money they got from raiseing and selling the hogs would more than buy whatever supplies they'd need.

Susan and Betsy were making plans for a flower garden, and had already cleared a path to the nearby creek. They knew they'd need plenty of water for such a large family, and Beaver Creek was clean and clear, the water so cold it made your teeth ache when you drank it. And the water had the pure sweet taste so common in these mountain streams. The Harpes were going to enjoy living in Knoxville, and God willing they would remain there for the rest of their lives.

"Hand me thet ax, Wiley," Micajah said, "and I'll go chop down a few more trees. I've about felled enough fer the pig pen already, and I'd like to get enough fer the smoke house afore nightfall."

There were a good many men and women about the clearing, working on the cabin and the corn patch. It looked as if they might finish the cabin before nightfall.

Wiley wiped the sweat from his eyes with the back of his shirtsleeves. Picking up the great broad ax, he held it out to his brother.

"You know, brother," he began, "thar ain't no place on God's green earth purttier than right here in this spot. But I've got a feeling in my bones thet it won't last forever. Go ahead and chop down yore trees, brother, but keep the ax handy. We might be a'needin' it fer more than jist the lumber."

"You know me, little brother, I always keep my weapons close at hand." Micajah answered. To emphasize the point, he pulled a bright razor sharp long knife from a scabbard tied around his waist, and held the blade up for Wiley to see.

"I feel a little more at ease when I kin git to this in a hurry. I was down in the town yesterday getting supplies, and I run acrost a little blacksmith shop where the smithy had made some of the finest blades ever I seed anywhar. I plan on goin' back down thar and gettin' me one o' them." Micajah paused for a moment, then looked at Wiley.

"I'm beginnin' to like this town, little brother, and I'd like to settle here for a good long spell. So I'm hopin' yore wrong bout thet feelin' you got in yore gut. This is now Harpe land, and I don't plan on leavin' it. Heaven help the man what tries to take it from us."

So saying, Micajah took the ax from his brother's hand and started walking over toward the tree line.

Wiley saw Betsy coming round with a wooden bucket of water and called to her; "Woman, bring thet water bucket round. I've worked up a powerful thirst, and I'm needin' a drink."

Betsy brought the bucket over and sat it down and Wiley's feet. Filling the gourd dipper with the cold sweet water, she handed it to Wiley.

"I heerd whut ye said to Micajah, Wiley. Ye don't think we'll be a'runnin' into trouble here in Knoxville, do ye? Ye know how the Big Harpe gets when the Wolf comes upon him. If'n these people rile him, these woods will run red with blood. These people ain't nothin' ceptin' sheep and lambs, Wiley, and if'n Micajah turns the Wolf loose, he won't rest till he's slaughtered 'em all. Them red injuns thought they could tame the Wolf, and look at whut happened to them. The Big Harpe kilt nearly all of 'em."

"Hush up woman," Wiley said. "Do ye want all of our new Knoxville neighbors to know we spent time a'runnin with them red savages? Hush yore mouth, afore I hush it fer ye. Micajah and me, we plan to be good law-abiding citizens of Knoxville town, and we don't want nuthin' a'messin' it up. If'n they hear ye, they'll be tryin' to make us move on, afore the cabin is even finished. Ye know Micajah won't stand still fer thet. If'n ye really want to raise yer family in this here town, ye'd best be hushin' up."

Betsy picked up the bucket, turned and began to walk away. "Ye know me and Susan's got our heart's set on stayin' here fer a spell," she said over her shoulder. "Ye jist skeered me a mite with yer talk bout a bad feelin' down in yer bones. Thet's all."

She walked across the clearing to join her sister, where she sat quilting with some of the other women. Motioning for Susan to follow, Betsy started down the path toward the creek.

Catching up with Betsy after a few hurried paces, Susan touched her sister on the arm and asked, "What's wrong with ye Bet? Ye seem a might upset at a time when ye should be a'grinnin' and a'laughin' and gettin' ready to dance a jig. The raisein' will soon be finished, and this old clearin' will ring with the fiddle. I know how ye dearly love a good reel, so it must be somethin' mighty bad to get ye in such a dither."

"Thar's shore enuff somethin' bad wrong," Betsy replied. "Wiley's a'talkin' about havin' bad feelin's here in this territory, and if'n he git's Micajah stirred up, ye know thar's no tellin' whut might happen. I jist wish Wiley would mind his tongue. Maybe ye could have a word with him, sister?"

Susan looked directly at her sister, thinking a minute before she spoke. "Little Wiley's jist not a'wantin' to settle down, thet's all, Bet," Susan said. "Don't ye fret about it. I'll speak to him myself. Lord knows we don't want the Big Harpe to turn the Wolf loose nowhere's near Knoxville town. Why, nobody would be safe. Not man, woman, nor child. The Harpe would be a hunnert times worse than them red injuns everbody is so worried about."

Susan turned and looked around the clearing at the many neighbors pitching in to help raise the cabin, and knew their lives wouldn't be worth a half cent if Micajah should fall back under the control of the Wolf. She spotted Wiley standing at the corner of the brand new cabin, and headed over to have a few words with him.

"Wiley, I don't want ye settin' yore brother off on these good people," she exclaimed. "They's been decent to us, and don't deserve what would happen. Ye jist mind yore tongue fer awhile, and let Micajah live in peace with these people."

"Woman, ye got no call to speak to me like thet." Wiley was more than a little upset with Susan. "I jist told Kiga I had a bad feelin' bout Knoxville town, thet's all. Thet ain't nothin' fer ye to be frettin' bout. We air goin' to be livin' round these parts fer quite some time, ye'll see."

Wiley walked over to the edge of the clearing and motioned for Betsy to join him. "See thet purty little gal over thar," he said, pointing to a very pretty young girl standing beside an older man. "Well, I aim to marry thet gal. I plan to court her proper, and ask her daddy fer her hand. So ye know I don't want Kiga to get all fired up here any more than ye and Betsy do."

Turning to where Wiley was pointing, Susan saw a slender, very beautiful girl with dark eyes and thick black hair standing with a man who was obviously her father. Susan took her time walking over to where the pair was standing.

"Hello," she said. "My name is Susan Harpe. I shore do feel kindly thet ye folks seen fit to come down and help us raise our cabin. It seems like the folks hereabouts air the neighborliest people ever we run into. We'uns have been travelin' all over the territory fer several years, and right here is whar we has decided to settle down fer good. I jist want ye to know we'uns is in yore debt, and we stand

166

ready to help ye in any way we kin. Wiley Harpe over thar is my husband's brother, and is lookin' fer a good woman to take fer a wife. Why, he jist now mentioned to me thet he would dearly love to meet the both of ye."

As she finished her sentence, Susan motioned for Wiley to come over to where she was standing with the couple.

As Wiley started over, the young girl said; "I'm right pleased to make your acquaintance, Missus Harpe. My name is Sarah Rice, and this is my father, the Reverend John Rice. We're happy to welcome your family to the territory, and we hope to be good neighbors to you."

Just as she finished speaking, Wiley joined the group.

"Howdy to ye, folks," Wiley began. "My name is Wiley Harpe, and this cabin ye've helped raise today is to be the home of me and my brother Micajah and his family. We is good, God fearin' men who came out of the Caroliny's to make our way in the Tennessee country. And a good choice it was, if all the people here bouts be like ye folks."

"Thank ye kindly, Mister Harpe," John Rice said, joining the conversation. "I am a preacher of God's holy word, and this is my daughter, Miss Sarah Rice. My name is John Rice, and I would be most thankful to say a prayer for your little farm as soon as the day's work is finished. My farm is down the road a piece, and you'd be welcome to come a'callin' as soon as you get settled in properly."

"Why thet's a most kindly invitation, sir," Wiley said, "and one I plan on acceptin' afore the end of the week. I'd surely like to have your permission to speak to yore lovely daughter, if I might."

"Well, Mister Harpe, my daughter is a turnin' twenty within the month, and I see no reason why ye wouldn't be welcome to come a'callin'."

Wiley didn't miss the Reverend's remark about the age of his daughter. Twenty years old and still single meant a woman stood a good chance of becoming an old maid. Frontier life was harsh, and women tended to grow old more quickly than men. It was not unusual for a father to arrange for an eligible man to court his daughter.

It was high time Sarah started a family of her own, and her father would like nothing better than for some young man to come along and marry her. John Rice had more than enough other children at home to work his small farm. Sarah would make a good wife to the right man, and would bear many strong healthy children. So, no, John Rice had no objection to Wiley Harpe coming to call on his daughter. After all, the Harpes had a promising farm, a few head of hogs, and even two mighty fine horses. Yes sir, Sarah could do a lot worse to marry up with Mister Wiley Harpe.

John Rice had no way of knowing what hell the next few years would hold for the Harpes and everyone connected with them.

The cabin had been finished for almost two months now, and the Harpes had been living peaceful lives. Their hogs were getting fatter, and the corn patch was turning out pretty good. They had helped a few other settlers raise a cabin and clear a patch, and all in all were finding life in Knoxville town was just what they had been looking for. Susan and Betsy were busy raising Mourning and baby James, and keeping up with the two babies, Will and Josh. Wiley had gotten very deep into his courtship of Sarah Rice, and it wasn't uncommon to find him hanging around the Rice's farm two or three days week. Sarah was growing fonder of Wiley every day and everyone knew it was only a matter of time before they would be wed.

Micajah had been a different man since coming to Knoxville. He had not been in one of his wild rages for the entire time they had lived in the new territory. It seemed as if he were using all his energy raising the hogs and tending to the corn. He seemed to like his new life style, and had so far made no signs of the little habits he had picked up when they were living in Cherokee town of Nickajack.

Then one day a little of the old Micajah turned up.

The sun was directly overhead when Micajah came walking in from the cornfield and called to Wiley.

"Brother. Hey little brother. Come out here and have a word with me."

Wiley walked out of the house and saw Micajah standing at the corner of the cabin, staring intently into the forest, some hundred feet away.

"Whut's out thar, brother?" Wiley asked.

"Don't rightly know, Wiley," Micajah replied. "I was comin' along the path from the creek when I heerd some strange sounds out in the woods. Grab yore rifle and let's go take a look see."

Reaching inside the cabin and picking up the rifle, Wiley asked;

"Whut kind of sounds were they, brother? Animal er human?"

"Not shore, Wiley. It sounded sorty like a wounded animal, maybe a bear, but I got the feelin' it jist might be a few two legged animals. The red kind. Anyway, I want to have a good look in the woods, jist to ease my mind."

"Well, whatever's in thar, it's wish it'd never seen the day it come on Harpe's property," said Wiley, as they started off across the yard.

"Whut I wants to know, big brother, is why ye come after me? They shorely can't be nothin' in them woods ye'll be needin' my help to handle."

"True enuff, Wiley, true enuff," Micajah answered. "I started to go on out thar and take care of it directly, but then I got to thinkin'. We been livin' in Knoxville fer several months now, and I ain't had nairy a fight in all thet time. I need to git a little exercise, and lately the Wolf's been growin' hungry. I might be able to kill two birds with the single stone, if you know what I mean."

"Thet I do, Micajah, thet I do."

Parting the underbrush carefully, Micajah and Wiley slowly made their way deeper into the forest. Wiley was none too happy with the look on his brother's face, nor the blue glow that was stirring in his eyes, but he'd rather he take out the rage of the Wolf on whatever was in the woods than their new neighbors in Knoxville.

Coming to a halt behind the trunk of a large oak tree, Micajah touched Wiley softly on the arm. "Be real still, little brother," he whispered, "ain't no bear we're on the trail of."

Micajah pointed to a small hill and motioned for Wiley to circle around and come upon it from the other side, while he moved in from here.

As Wiley faded out of sight in the forest, Micajah moved to a position where he could see the other side of the little rise. Sure enough, there was a small band of Indians lying in wait behind a fallen log.

Not today, little red brothers, Micajah thought. Moving quietly and quickly, he took a position where he could count the Indians, and see how they were grouped. He counted seven, and figured there'd be at least one more hidden in the woods, covering the little renegade hunting party's back. He'd also be the one who'd made the sounds to try and lure Micajah into the ambush.

Taking the mighty tomahawk of Dancing Hawk from its resting place on his belt, the big Harpe suddenly jumped up and with a great leap landed in the midst of the Indians. The tomahawk had crushed two skulls like eggshells before the red men could react at all, and a third went down with part of his nose bone driven through his brain when Micajah kicked him in the face. Another fell to the tomahawk before he knew what had hit him, and now there were only three. Not even a full minute had elapsed since the big Harpe had leaped from the woods, and for all practical purposes, the fight was over. The remaining three Indians were terrified by the monstrous apparition that had attacked them, and were screaming and shouting as they tried to escape into the forest. Harpe's mighty left hand curled around the neck of the closest of the Indians, as he threw the tomahawk with his right hand and watched as it buried itself into the skull of one of the other two. The tomahawk had no sooner left his hand than he drew the long knife from its scabbard and hurled it through the air at the last man. Not even looking to see if the knife struck home, Micajah turned his attention to the struggling man he was holding in his left hand. Taking the top of the man's head in his right hand, Micajah made a savage twisting motion and smiled as he felt the bones in the man's neck give way. With a loud pop, the man's neck was twisted loose from his spine, and he died even as his arms and legs were still trying to escape. At the same instant, he heard Wiley's rifle fire, and he knew his brother had found the last of the raiding party. This was one band of killers who wouldn't hide in the woods and try to ambush innocent people anymore.

Walking to where the sixth Indian had fell, Harpe pulled his knife from where it was sticking in the man's back. Flipping the Indian over, Micajah drew the razor sharp blade across the man's exposed Adams apple, and watched as the warm blood gushed out onto the grass.

Seven men were dead by Harpe's hand in less than two minutes, and he hadn't even worked up a sweat.

A small, almost inaudible sound from the woods caused Micajah to speak; "C'mon out Wiley," he said. "T'wern't much of a fight. These fellers needed to get a few injun lessons from old Ravenwing, back in Nickajack. They didn't know very much a'tall bout killin'. I'd guess they was more used to murderin' women and chillun than they was to fightin' grown men. Anyway, they war only seven of the red bastards, so it ain't like it were no big battle. I heerd ye shoot, so I reckon thet takes care of this little chore."

"I reckon it does at thet, big brother," Wiley said. He was relieved to see the blue fire in Micajah's eyes had already begun to die down. "I guess we'd better be gittin' on back to the house. Don't want to worry the women folk none. They'll have heerd the shot, and be wonderin' whut happened.

Without another word, the brothers walked out of the woods toward the cabin, leaving the Indians where they fell. They knew the wild animals would make good use of the bodies.

28

The days seemed to fly by, and it was winter before they knew it. Micajah and Wiley kept busy with the day-to-day farm work, although from their days with the Indians they believed the women should tend the garden. They had raised six hogs, and had already sold one of them to the butcher in town.

Wiley had become serious in his pursuit of Sarah, and most days he would visit with her and her family for a while. He planned to marry her just as soon as he could, and he and Micajah had already discussed building another room on the cabin.

Winter came and went with few serious problems for the Harpes. They were making a name for themselves as honest hard working people who minded their business and liked to be left alone. They raised a fine garden in the summer of 1796, and now had over a dozen hogs. They even went out on a couple of expeditions with some of the men from the town to try and track down a small band of renegade Cherokee that had been raising cain in the territory, but failed to catch up with them.

The children were growing like weeds. Mourning was a beautiful child, with eyes the color of the summer sky, and hair the same corn silk blonde as her mothers. She turned six in May of 96, and was the apple of Micajah's eye. James Thornton also turned six that summer. It wasn't hard to tell the boy was Micajah's son. Wild, thick black hair framed his handsome face, and he had the same dark, ruddy complexion as his father. But the surest way to tell was by looking at the boy's eyes.

James had the Harpe eyes. The eyes of the Wolf. Wild and strange they were, and that shade of blue peculiar to the firstborn Harpe sons. James was destined to wear the Amulet one day, and even though he was barely six years old, he had already begun to learn the way of the forest. He would probably never be quite as large as his father, and perhaps not as strong, but he would have the same fierce loyalty to the name of Harpe as all of the other sons before him. The loyalty was born into him, it sang in his veins the day he was brought forth, and would never be extinguished. He was born knowing the way of the Wolf, and would one day know the same hunger as the others who had worn the Amulet.

Little Will and Ben were now both two years old, but both were walking and saying several words, and already they were making their first few adventures around the clearing. As it has ever been with mothers, Susan and Betsy had their hands full keeping up with the children, for it was unthinkable they should be left alone for more than a few minutes. The danger from wild animals and Indians was too great for a chance to be taken.

Susan and Betsy also kept their eyes on Micajah. It had been a long time since the Wolf had been turned loose, and both women held their breath every time some little thing came along to upset him. They never knew what might disturb the delicate balance he maintained between the Harpe and the Wolf.

But 1796 passed without one of the furious rages, and as winter turned to spring the future looked very rosy for the small family.

The first few months of 1797 were very cold, and no one remembered a winter that had made the people of Knoxville so look forward to spring.

March turned to April, and April to May, and the snow had all finally melted, when one day Wiley came rushing into the cabin with some very good, although completely expected, news.

He and Sarah Rice had set a wedding day. June 1st, 1797.

29

Wiley Harpe was the happiest man in Knoxville Town. After a courtship that spanned almost two years, Sarah Rice had consented to be his wife. A date was set and Sarah's father had said he would gladly perform the ceremony.

"This calls fer a celebration, little brother," Micajah roared, when Wiley told him of Sarah's decision. He brought forth a jug of peach brandy, recently purchased in Knoxville, and poured four glasses.

Raising his glass, Micajah toasted his brother and his bride to be. "We'll take a drink to yer health, brother, and to the health of the purty Miss Sarah Rice, soon to be Mrs. Joshua Wiley Harpe. And to the Reverend Rice, Miss Rice's father, soon to be Wiley's father-in-law. And we'll take a drink to Knoxville town as well. May the Harpes live here in peace and happiness fer a long and prosperous spell."

"Amen to thet, brother," Wiley said, and downed the glass of brandy. "Knoxville will be home to the Harpes fer many years to come, and Sarah Rice will make a good and fitting wife for a Harpe. If'n our chillun be as purty as their mother, we'll shorely have the most handsome brood in the country."

The days before the wedding were filled with preparations of every kind. The women stuffed a bed tick with dried moss, and the men started clearing another patch where more corn could be planted come next spring. Micajah went to the smoke house and marked several of last years hams for the feast, and Susan and Betsy talked about how many chickens would have to be killed.

The wedding day dawned bright and clear, although a trifle cool, and a fine mist hung around the tops of the mountains. Wiley was more than a little nervous, but seemed to calm down a bit when Sarah and her family arrived at the clearing.

Dressed for the wedding, Wiley Harpe cut a handsome and dashing figure. His clothes had been fresh washed in Beaver Creek yesterday, and so had he. He had slicked down his unruly red hair and brushed it till it shone. His boyish good looks gave no sign of the many cruelties he had undergone in the past, and the light in his eyes was for Sarah Rice alone. It was not the same as the savage killing light that would shine in his eyes so often in the next few years. No one who attended the wedding of Wiley Harpe and Sarah Rice could have forecast the happy couple would soon become part of the most homicidal band of killers the world had ever seen.

Susan and Betsy had on their best homespun cotton dresses, and Micajah had replaced his worn buckskins with breeches and a shirt of broadcloth. The Reverend Rice looked very upright and dignified in his freshly cleaned black suit, and his large black hat.

Then, with his well-worn Bible opened to the Scripture he planned to read, Reverend Rich called for Sarah and Wiley to stand before him.

Wiley stood before the preacher, with Sarah on one side and Micajah on the other, and still found it hard to believe a woman such as she would soon be his wife. He hardly heard the words her father said, until he reached the part where Wiley had to say 'I Do'.

As he heard Sarah say the words that made her his wife, Wiley looked at the people gathered in the small room for the ceremony. There was Susan Roberts and her sister Betsy, both of whom called themselves wives of Micajah Harpe. There was H.L. White, one of their neighbors, who had consented to witness the marriage, and he stood with the wedding party, dressed in store bought clothes and looking very much like the successful Knoxville business man that he was. Of course there was the Reverend John Rice, Sarah's father, and several other neighbors and friends. Beside his brother, his presence overshadowing the room, stood Micajah.

Standing over six and a half feet tall, and weighing close to three hundred pounds, Micajah stood out in any crowd. His raven black hair and dark good looks brought a flutter to the ladies hearts, while at the same time sending a message of un-ease and perhaps fear into the hearts and minds of brave men.

Micajah had inherited much of his physical appearance from his father, John Harpe, although he was two or three inches taller and about forty pounds heavier. He had the same coal black hair and ruddy skin, and like his father had the strange, wild blue eyes of the Harpe men. They were a bright, almost green blue, and seemed to burn with an inner fire. But there was no warmth in their gaze. It was not the fire of life that burned in their eyes, but the fire of death and damnation. It was as though they had gazed at upon hell itself, and the fiery nether regions were reflected in each glance.

At a later time, a Methodist minister, who was one of the few people who ever encountered the Harpes and lived to tell about it, described that fiery gaze.

"When the monster turned his fearsome gaze upon me, the glowing blue eyes were icy cold, and a chill crossed my soul, as if a wind blowing out of hell had caressed me. I am a stout man, and unafraid, yet I felt fear rise up bitter in my mouth when I looked full in the eyes of the Wolf."

At times, especially while they lived in Knoxville, the decentness of John Harpe could be found in the actions of both Micajah and Wiley, but later that decentness disappeared, only to be replaced by a ruthlessness unparalleled in his day.

In his dream deep in the spirit cave at Nickajack, Micajah had learned it was best to call upon the powers of the amulet only in times of dire need, or extreme danger. It had been almost a full year since the encounter with the Indians in the forest had allowed Micajah to feed the Wolf, and he knew from experience the fasting of the demon would not last much longer. Even now, he could sense the Wolf looking over the wedding party.

All this, and more, was on Micajah's mind as he stood beside his brother on the beautiful June day, and it was with a great effort he pushed the thoughts into a back corner of his mind, controlling the Wolf, and bringing his own thoughts back to the ceremony.

The Reverend Rice finished reading the wedding ceremony, and the party stepped out into the front of the cabin, to be met by other friends and neighbors, come to wish the newlyweds well. A man struck up a lively fiddle tune, and Wiley took his new bride by the hand and waltzed her off across the yard. Others joined in, and the clearing rang with the sounds of merriment.

Susan walked across the yard to where her sister stood. Betsy had little William on one hip and was watching Ben as he played on the ground. Mourning and James were all over the place, running and skipping through the crowd, now and then pretending to dance with Wiley and Sarah.

"Well, Bet," Susan said, "with Sarah bein' a Harpe now, I spect thar'll be another child er two afore this time next year."

"I truly believe yore right, sister," Betsy replied. "Purty little Sarah had already been right friendly to Wiley, if'n I'm any judge."

"Well, thet's alright with me, Bet. The bigger the family, the better chance we has of makin' a livin' on the farm. I shore wish one of us would have another little girl though. Mourning needs a little company, other than brothers."

"Me too, sister," Betsy agreed. "A little girl t'would be mighty fine around here with all these boys up to their mischief."

"Ye know, Betsy," Susan began, "I've been thinkin', and I be gittin' a little worried about the big Harpe. Tis not like him to be so peaceful fer so long. You and me, we both seed him when the Wolf was on the loose, and we know what a terrible man he kin be. If'n he goes much longer without sheddin' blood, I'm thinkin' all hell might break loose. Perhaps we should encourage him to go with the others when next they try to capture another renegade injun band."

"Could be yore right, sister," Betsy agreed. "I've been some worried myself. This ain't like Nickajack. If'n he kills some people here bouts, thar could be real trouble."

As the two of them stood talking they were constantly watching the children with one eye, and doing their best to keep Micajah in sight at the same time. The big Harpe was standing at the edge of the clearing, talking to a man they didn't at first recognize. Both were worried, and with good reason. If the big Harpe should go into one of his rages, not a soul in the clearing would be safe. Both women knew when the Wolf had been hungry for this long a time, Micajah wouldn't need much of a reason.

Suddenly Betsy grabbed Susan by the arm. "Who is thet the Harpes speaking with?" she asked, with urgency in her voice.

"Why, I can't tell, sister, who do ye reckon it be?"

At that moment, Micajah stepped to one side and the women got a clear look at the man he was talking to.

"Lordy, lordy," Betsy cried. "It's Moses Stegall." She looked as if she'd seen a ghost. "We thought he was kilt at Nickajack."

"Yore right, Betsy, shore nuff. Thet is Stegall all right. I don't know how he kept from gettin' hisself kilt. He war right down thar among all the injuns when the soldiers started shootin'. But it looks like somehow he got away. Old Moses always were a slippery cuss."

Moses Stegall was indeed a 'slippery cuss' as Susan said. He had been in and out of trouble on the frontier for years. Stegall, like Micajah, was a large man, and was known to be a mean customer. He'd killed his share of men during his travels, and those that knew him knew he was not a man to aggravate. He had dark brown hair, and small close set brown eyes that never seemed to meet another man's eyes full on. He still preferred broadcloth to buckskin, but did wear a hat made of the skin of a coon, with the tail hanging down his back. He never appeared quite clean, a feature which was enhanced by his dark and swarthy complexion.

Stegall was a good sized man who possessed a great amount of physical strength who carried a pistol and rifle upon him at all times, and never went anywhere without his long knife.

The Harpes and Stegall had spent several years wandering the countryside as companions, and more often than not Stegall had been the instigator in whatever trouble they had gotten into. Stegall had never been completely honest, and some said he could be counted among those thieves and robbers who roamed the forests, preying on innocent travelers. In any event, trouble was always hot on the heels of Moses Stegall, and Susan and Betsy wanted none of his antics here in Knoxville.

Betsy started walking across the clearing toward where Micajah stood talking to Stegall, as Susan tried to attract Wiley's attention. But Wiley couldn't hear or see anything other than his new bride, and didn't at first notice Susan waving at him. Betsy had almost reached the two men, when they suddenly turned and began to walk into the forest.

"Micajah, wait fer me. Kiga," she called, but the Harpe couldn't hear her above the noise of the music and the dancers.

Susan had finally succeeded in gaining Wiley's attention, and was standing at the edge of the clearing speaking to him in low whisper.

"Wiley, I know I saw the Harpe talking to Moses Stegall. The man was not kilt in Nickajack, as we thought. Tis a fact thet whenever Stegall comes a'callin', trouble be not fur behind. I want ye to find 'em right now, and send Stegall a'skiddlin'. We is tryin' to live in peace here in Knoxville, and me and Betsy don't want no scoundrel sich as Moses Stegall to be a'messin' things up."

"Stegall," Wiley answered, his voice incredulous. "How could he have survived Nickajack? Well, if'n yore right, woman, and it truly is Moses Stegall, ye know we'll jist have to make him welcome in our home. Moses had been a friend to us since the day we rescued him from them mountain men who were fixin' to hang him. We weren't no more than pups back then, and many's the time since thet Stegall has fit on our side. Agin white man and red, many's the time he's stood back to back with Kiga and me. Naw, woman, Stegall be as welcome in our home as we be in his'n."

However, in spite of all his talk, Wiley hoped Susan was mistaken. If Stegall were truly alive, he'd come here wanting something. Stegall was a mean man, and the Harpes knew that better than anyone else in the territory. They had seen him do his killing at the John Watt's raid on Nashville, and many times other than that. Wiley placed Stegall high on his list of dangerous men, and Wiley, like the women, knew anything was apt to happen when Moses Stegall came calling.

He couldn't tell Stegall he was not welcome in their home, but by God he could find out what the man was up to, and why he had traced the Harpes to Knoxville.

That's exactly what he'd do, when Micajah and Moses returned to the cabin.

Micajah and Stegall had only walked a short distance into the woods when Stegall stopped and looked at the big Harpe,

"Now Micajah," he began, "ye know thet thar ain't no one in Knoxville town what knows Moses Stegall, so thar won't be no trouble in passin' myself off as a law abidin' man. I kin live in the town and set up horse races fer thet big black horse of yourn. They ain't a horse in the territory whut kin hold a light to the black, and I've got money enuff to back him. Ye know thet with Wiley ridin' the animal, we'll fleece these Knoxville sheep any way we please."

"I don't know Moses," Micajah replied. "We've lived here in Knoxville almost two years, and the people have treated us kindly. I know my horse is as fast as any animal here bouts, but tempers sometimes git out of hand when men wager on horses. I don't want the Wolf runnin' loose anymore. I've had enuff of thet kind of life."

"Ye wouldn't have to turn the Wolf loose, would ye Micajah? I'll make the bets and collect the money, and ye won't have to harm a soul. Whut could be the harm in thet?"

"It's like I told ye, Moses. These people has treated us fairly since we've been here, and if'n the Wolf gits out of control ye know what'll happen. Thet's the harm I kin see in racin' my horse."

"Won't be no trouble, Micajah, I promise ye thet. I jist want to have a mite of fun, and maybe make a dollar er two, afore I head south," Stegall said.

"I been meanin' on askin' ye, Moses, how ye escaped down in Nickajack. Me and Wiley, we seed ye plain as day, right thar in the thick of the killin'. They must have been three hunnert of them soldiers, so we knew it was useless fer us to come out of the cave till the last of them rode out. They wasn't no time to be lookin' fer bodies, but we shorely thought ye war dead."

Moses lifted his shirt, turned, and showed Micajah a large scar on his back. "Take a look at thet thar hole, Micajah. I taken a ball square in the back. It knocked me plumb out, and when I come to, the soldier boys were long gone. I had bled a passel, and I spect when they seed me a'lyin' so still and all covered with blood, thet they thunk I was completely dead, and they jist passed my on by. But the shot didn't hit no vitals, and I lived right through it. Ye know how lucky I always was, boy. Don't ye remember the time old Laughing Turtle hit me in the head with his tommyhawk? Cut off'n a little piece of my ear, and didn't do no more damage. Ye remember thet, don't ye?"

Micajah laughed at the memory. "Yes sir, I shorely do remember thet. And I remember ye poked out old Laughing Turtle's right eye with yore finger afore ye slit his throat. Course he wasn't the best-liked injun ever I seed. His wife didn't even like him, and neither did his old dog. He was better off bein' kilt, I reckon."

"We has had us some good times, all right Micajah," Moses said. "Me and you and little Wiley. And they's more to come. Let's get on back to the party now, and I want ye to think over whut I said bout racin' the horse. We kin make us a little money, and have a passel of fun at the same time. I swear to ye, they won't be no killin'. Or my name ain't Moses Stegall."

By the time they reached the clearing, Micajah had pretty much decided to go into Knoxville the next Sunday and check out the local horse owners.

Wiley met Micajah and Stegall as they walked out of the woods. "Howdy Moses," he smiled. "Pleased thet ye could jine me on my wedding day, Moses, but we shore thought ye war kilt down in Nickajack."

"Well sir, I'm alive, shore nuff," Moses replied to Wiley. "Ye'll have to git Micajah to tell ye the story though. Right now I want a drink of good whiskey and a dance with the purty new Mrs. Harpe." So saying, Moses walked across the yard and picked up the jug.

"Micajah, thet man is trouble, shore as I'm born. Whut kind of deal has he got in mind this time?" Wiley asked.

"Nothin' bad this time," Micajah answered. "He jist wants to do little horse racin'. He promised thar wouldn't be no hard words and no killin' here in Knoxville."

"Ye shorely don't believe thet scoundrel, do ye?" Wiley asked. "He's done told us more lies than any red injun ever did. Why, he'd walk thirty miles in the dead 'o winter to tell a lie, when the truth would serve him better, and he could stay at home to tell it. Ye know his word ain't worth the salt it'd take to cook it in."

"I know Wiley, I know," Micajah said. "But we still owe the old rascal a debt. I don't reckon we'll have no trouble handlin' whatever comes along. Sides thet, ye been sayin' yerself as to how ye'd like to do a little racin'. Nother thing is, Stegall has money to bet, and I don't see the harm in wagerin' a little of our own. If'n we kin win a race er two, we'll be able to buy one er two more hogs afore winter sets in. The meat will come in mighty handy when the babies get here."

"Yore right about thet, brother, and ye air shore enuff right about me a'wantin' to do some horse racin'. It'd tickle my fancy a right smart to run off and leave the Knoxville gents like they was standin' still."

"Then it's settled, Wiley," Micajah said. "Next week we'll go into town and see if'n we can't find us a horse race."

With the horse race question decided, the brothers turned back to the wedding party and watched Moses Stegall laughing as he whirled Sarah out across the clearing.

30

Knoxville was a wide-open, brawling, booming young town in 1797. It was called the "Gateway to the West" because of the large amount of immigrants passing through each day on their way into Kentucky or further on into Tennessee. The frontier was slowly pushing westward, and Knoxville found itself one of the major stop over towns in the population push.

The town was rough and rowdy, but for the most part the frontiersmen were peaceful, honorable people. Mutual feelings of neighborliness and helpfulness were among the common traits of the townspeople. Desiring to attract other settlers to the area, they were willing to help in most any way required of them.

The settlers worked long, hard days, and most believed in attending Church services on Sunday. To off set the hard, backbreaking farm work, and to take their minds off their daily routine, the people found many ways to pass what little leisure time they had.

There were community social events, such as cabin raisings and patch clearings, but by far the most popular pastime was when they got together for a horse race. Many of the men set great store in their horses, and most were willing to wager a few dollars on the outcome of one of the frequent races.

When the weather permitted, Sunday afternoons would find the men gathered at a long stretch of bottom land just on the outside of town. The ground was flat and they had cleared away the trees and underbrush to provide a good place to run the horses, and a good place for the people who came to watch them run. Two enterprising citizens had even set up small rum shops where a thirsty man could buy a little something to wet his whistle while he watched the races, and each race day they did a thriving business.

Not all the men in Knoxville owned horses they thought were fast enough to race, but almost to a man they loved to go out and watch the horses run. And they were seldom disappointed with the afternoon's activities.

Moses Stegall got to the bottom before noon one Sunday and found several others already there. Dismounting and tying his horse to a small bush, Stegall stood watching the men prepare their horses to race. Moses was a shrewd judge of horseflesh, and after watching the men for a few minutes, he walked over to speak with them.

"Howdy friends," Stegall said, as he approached the small group of men standing holding their horses. "It 'pear's to me as if'n they is gonna be a horse race round here dreckly."

"Reckon thar is at thet, friend," one of the men replied.

"I guess thar be no objection of a man watchin' yer animals run," Moses said.

"No objection a'tall from any of us, feller. Do ye have in mind to run thet little mare yer ridin'?" the man asked.

"Oh lordy naw," Stegall answered. "Though she be tolerably fast, my little Belle jist ain't the same class with them fine animals whut yore fixin' to run here today. But I might be obliged to make a small wager, should one of ye boys see fit to allow it."

"Why, we'll allow it, shore enuff, old son," the man replied. "But jist how do ye intend to pick out which horse to bet on, seein' as how we've never seed ye around here before?"

"Well, it's true I be a stranger to Knoxville town, but I sure ain't no stranger to fast horses ner the racin' of fast horses," Stegall said. "I've seed horses run all over the territory, and I've got a friend whut's got a horse on which I've won many a dollar. In fact, thet's whut I'm a'doin' in Knoxville. I've come to visit my friend, and now thet I see ye folks are so agreeable, I plan on seein' if he be interested in bringin' his horse on down here and maybe doin' a little racin' hisself. Ye do welcome other horses here don't ye?"

"We do at thet, feller. We is happy to have all our neighbors come on down and see whut their horses kin do agin ourn." He looked at his companion and smiled, "That is, as long as they bring a few dollars with them."

"I'll be tellin' him this very day," Stegall said. "I plan on visitin' with him and his family on my way home. In the meantime, however, I believe I'll jist place a dollar on thet horse ye be a'tendin'. He looks to be a fine animal."

"Your makin' a wise choice fer shore, placin' yore money on Old Red here. He has run agin' many of the fastest horses in the territory, and has never lost but once. He's faster than greased lightnin', and runs like the devil hisself is a'chasin' him. Woodrow over thar has some fast animals, but ain't a one of em kin hold a candle to Red."

"Then it'll be a pleasure winnin' a few dollars by bettin' on yore horse, friend," Stegall said. "My name be Oxford Brown, and I'll be settlin' here in Knoxville myself I reckon, seein' as how everbody here bouts is so friendly and the land is so hospitable."

"Yes sir, Mister Brown, yer right bout thet. The land is the best ever I seed anywhar, and the people is second to none. My name is George Teil, and I been here in Knoxville fer a spell now. One thing ye should know, if ye er yer friend be plannin' on runnin' a horse here. The animals here in Knoxville are considered among the best in the land, and they ain't no easy pickin's. Now whut might yer friends name be, in case I should meet up with him."

"My friend's name is Harpe," Stegall said, "Micajah Harpe. Him and his brother and their families has got a little farm down on the Beaver Creek, and both is lookin' forward to meetin' the sportin' gentry here bouts."

"I believe I know the men yer speakin' of, Mister Brown. Has they recently sold a hog er two down at Miller's market?"

"Yes sir, thet be them. They is fine hog farmers, and decent men. But I must tell ye right now, the Harpes has got a mighty fast horse. I'll wager his big black would out run anything I seed here today."

"Well, we'd be obliged to see sich a fine horse, Mister Brown. Tell yore friend Harpe thet we'll make him and his brother welcome here whenever he decides to come down."

"Why, I thank ye fer yore kind words, Mister Teil, and I'll pass em along to the Harpes. Now let's go watch some racin'."

Walking across the meadow, Stegall watched as a small Indian pony outdistanced two larger horses across the bottom. The pony was a small pinto, and Stegall could tell he was exceptionally fast. He led the way from start to finish, without once faltering.

That'll be a pony to watch, Stegall thought, as he approached another small group of men.

"Which one of ye fellers owns thet little paint?" Stegall asked.

"He belongs to me, stranger," a small red haired man said, "an I be right proud of him."

"Rightly so, Mister, rightly so," Stegall answered. "He's a fine little animal. Might he be fer sale?"

"No sir, he ain't. I plan on racin' him a few more years, then puttin' him out to stud. I got one er two other head ye might be interested in, if'n ye ker to look 'em over."

"Yes sir, I'd be interested in lookin' at yer ponies. I intend to buy me a few head onct I git settled in the territory, and if'n ye got any more as good as thet 'un, you and me jist might strike us up a deal. Let me introduce myself, friend. My name is Oxford Brown, and I rode up this way from out in Kaintuck."

"Pleased to make yore acquaintance, Mister Brown," the man said. "My name is Jack Edwards, and I been livin' here nigh on to three year. Ye kin ask anybody here bouts about my horses, and ye'll find thet I got some of the best stock in the territory. Ain't no better animals around, with the possible exception of the stock owned by Mister Teil. Course, I got several head thet is as good as any of hisn."

"I don't doubt thet a lick, Mister Edwards," Stegall said, "but would ye allow me to ask yer opinion as to who might have the very fastest horse in the territory? All of these animals gathered here today appear to be fine, spirited horses, but is there any better? I shore would hate fer someone to run in a ringer on me, onct I had my money on the line."

"Well, Sir, we is honorable men here in Knoxville, and not a one of us would do a thing like thet," Jack Edwards replied, his dander up just a little bit at Stegall's statement.

"No sir, Mister Edwards, now don't take me wrong. I never allowed as to how ye might. I only likes to protect my interests, as any bettin' man does. We will tell ye folks straight up thet we has a very fast horse which we think kin outrun these horses I've seed here today. If'n ye got a faster animal, well then, I'd jist like to know. Truthfully, however, it don't matter a whit in hell if'n ye has er if'n ye ain't got a faster horse." Now Stegall was beginning to get angry. "We kin beat any fleabag in Knoxville, and we has the money to back up er words."

"Now, now, Mister Brown. I didn't intend to upset ye. Mister Teil has a big roan stallion he brangs out sometimes to race, when the stakes is right. Truth to tell, none of us will run agin him. Ain't never been beat, and I doubt if'n ye er yore friends got a horse whut kin do the job. And Mister Teil and me has got the money to back up our words as well. Jist when do ye think ye kin gin Harpes horse ready to run."

"We kin run whenever ye'd like, old son. But why don't we go over and see if Mister Teil is agreeable to yore bargain?" Stegall had

189

the man hooked, and knew he'd help him hook George Teil into the race.

As Stegall walked across the bottom toward the other men, he stole a glance at Jack Edwards walking along beside him.

"They's geese, jist waitin' to be plucked," he laughed to himself.

The smile was still playing at the corners of Moses Stegall's mouth as they stopped before the group of men where George Teil was standing.

"Howdy again, Mister Teil," Stegall said. "Mister Edwards here tells me thet ye has a mighty fast horse thet ye only brang down here occasionally, and thet he has never been beat. He also tells me thet the bunch of ye might be willing to make a considerable bet on yore animal, fer he thinks he can't be beat."

Teil cut his eyes at Jack Edwards. "Is that a fact? Edwards said that? Well, sir, if Jack Edwards said thet, then it must be the truth." George Teil took his eyes off Jack Edwards, and turned his full attention back to Stegall.

"Well, if'n it be the truth, I was thinkin' maybe ye'd consider a race agin my friend Mister Harpe's horse. Sight unseen. Which makes it jist as fair fer ye and yer friends here as it does fer me and mine."

"No sir, thet ain't the way we do things here. We'll jist set up a race fer next Sunday so thet ye kin watch our horse run, and we kin watch yores. I'll run agin Mister Edward's little paint pony, and ye kin run Harpe's animal agin my red stallion. If'n we kin come to terms after thet, why then we'll have us a race between yer horse and mine. Thet fair enuff?"

"Sounds fair enuff to me, Mister Teil, but I has got to talk it over with Mister Harpe. I'll ride over thar right now, and be back afore sunset, if'n ye kin wait thet long."

Of course Moses knew whatever arrangement he could set up would be fine with Micajah and Wiley. But he had to keep playing the game for these men.

"We'll be here when ye gits back, Mister Brown, and tell Mister Harpe we is lookin' forward to seein' this mighty horse he owns."

The next Sunday dawned bright and clear in the mountains, and held the promise of being a beautiful summer day.

Moses Stegall rode into Harpe's place early that morning, his appetite already whetted for a day of horse racing.

"Hallo, the house," he called when he was about thirty feet from the front door. "Anybody to home this fine day."

Susan walked out into the yard, followed closely by Micajah and two of the children. Recognizing Stegall, she didn't stop, but walked on around the cabin, giving Moses a hard look as she disappeared around the corner.

Micajah was much more cordial.

"Howdy, Stegall," the Harpe said. "I trust ye had a good nights sleep, and air ready to see my horse skin these Knoxville beauties?"

"Ready and a'waitin' Micajah. They air geese, jist ripe fer the pluckin'. How bout little Wiley? Be he in good shape?"

Wiley walked out the door about that time and answered the question himself. "I be in the best shape of my life, Moses, and they ain't one man in Knoxville whut kin beat me today. I been workin' the horse all week, and he's a'rarin' to go. Them fellers down thar won't see nothin' but our dust."

"Well, we don't want to make it look too easy Wiley. Teil's big red horse is strong and tolerable fast, and has a good deal of bottom to him. I reckon we kin beat him all right, but he air a fine animal. Whut we wants to do today is to beat 'em, but not to beat 'em too bad. Thet way, they'll be apt to make a larger wager on Teil's other horse."

"Ye kin count on me, Moses. I know how to bait a trap. This ain't the first time I been in a horse race. I'll jist tickle 'em a bit, and beat 'em by a nose."

"Thet'll do the trick, son. Ye jist don't git excited and out run 'em by a mile, ye hear," Stegall said.

The little spotted pony of Jack Edwards didn't stand a chance against the big stallion of George Teil. From gate to finish line, the stallion was never even pressed. Teil laughed as the jockeys brought the horses back to where the men were standing. "What'd I tell ye, Brown, have ever ye seed a horse like this one?"

"Not often, Mister Teil, not often. But ye still got to watch Wiley run their horse. And then we'll discuss the wager."

"If'n Harpe kin beat my red stallion, thet is. He ain't done it yet," Teil replied.

"True enuff, Mister Teil, true enuff. But jist keep yer eye on the finish line."

George Teil's big red stallion was everything Moses had told the Harpes she'd be. High spirited and ready to run, the jockey lined the horse up along side the black stallion Wiley was astride.

"Good luck to ye, feller," Wiley said.

"And the same to ye, friend," the other rider replied.

But if was no more a contest than Wiley wanted it to be. He let Teil's roan stay about half a head in front until they were about fifty feet from the finish line, and then gave his own big black stallion his head. Leaning over the neck of his horse, he patted it and pressed forward with his knees. Feeling the urgency of his rider, the horse responded with a burst of speed that propelled it across the finish line almost half a length ahead of George Teil's roan.

Moses slapped his thigh and hollered, and turned to George Teil. "Thet were a close race, Mister Teil, but I believe we beat ye. If ye'd be so kind... he held out his hand, palm up, for Teil to pay the bet.

"No sir, I don't mind payin' up fer a fair wager," George Teil said, and laid the agreed amount in Stegall's hand. "However, beatin' this horse is one thing, and beatin' my stallion is another. Yore horse ran a good race today, and thar's no doubt about it bein' a fast animal, but I seed nothin' thet might change my mind. I still believe my black stallion is the faster animal, and I spect next Sunday we'll be findin' out fer shore. Don't spend all yore winnin's from today's race, Mister Brown, I'd shorely like to win thet money back."

"Well, sir, ye'll have the chance, come next Sunday," Stegall laughed.

He was still laughing when he reached the spot where Micajah stood waiting for Wiley to bring around the horse.

"Old son, I think the sheep er bout ready to sheer," Stegall said to the Harpes. "Come next Sunday we'll all three have full pockets. Courtesy of George Teil and his friends. Whut say ye, Micajah?"

"I reckon yore right, Moses," Micajah answered, "but let's don't count er chickens jist yet. Teil has a mighty fine animal thar, almost as fast as our horse. I think we kin outrun him, but it'll be a close race."

"Now Micajah, don't ye be a'gittin' no cold feet..."

Before the last syllable was out of Stegall's mouth, Micajah's huge fist had landed squarely against the side of his head, knocking him sharply to the ground.

"Nobody accuses the Harpe of gittin' cold feet," Micajah said in a strangely soft and flat voice. "I thought ye knew thet. Don't ever do it again, and I'll only tell ye the one time." Micajah's ice blue eyes had begun to catch on fire.

Stegall only lay on the ground for a moment. Bouncing to his feet, he grabbed the knife at his belt and stood as if he meant to attack Harpe. One look in Micajah's eyes caused Stegall to take a second thought. *God in Heaven,* he thought. *He'll kill me fer shore, and not even blink one of them damned eyes when he does it. This ain't the boy I used to know.* Moses Stegall felt a feeling come over him that he'd seldom felt before. Fear. Pure, stark naked fear. Stegall was a mean and vicious man, but the giant standing before him was a demon right out of hell.

Keeping his eyes on Harpe, Stegall slowly removed his hand from his knife. "Now Micajah, ye know I never meant nothin' by thet remark. I been knowin' ye since ye war jist a boy, and I ain't never seed ye back down from nothin'. Thet weren't whut I meant a'tall. I was talkin' bout bettin' yore money, not bout ye being afeerd of nothin'. Hell far and damnation, Micajah, I know fer a fact thet ye ain't even scart of the devil hisself. It war jist a mite of misunderstandin', thet's all it war. I didn't mean a damn thing."

The fire in Micajah's eyes began to dim, and he turned and stood waiting for Wiley to reach them.

Wiley had seen Micajah strike Moses, and knowing Stegall for a mean man Wiley was hurrying toward them at a dead run. He got there just as Micajah turned away from Moses.

"Whut happened, brother, why'd ye strike Stegall?"

"Jist a mite of misunderstanding Wiley, thet's all it war," Micajah said, and by now the fire had completely died away.

The only thought that ran through Wiley's mind as he stood looking at his brother was; "Thank God. He managed to keep the Wolf locked away." Wiley knew all too well the bottom would have run red with blood had Micajah succumbed to the inner hunger. Once the Wolf was loose, there would be no stopping it until it had satisfied it's awful desires. And even though Wiley himself craved the violence almost as much as his brother, he knew they had built a good life in Knoxville, and wasn't ready to give it all up.

The voice of Moses Stegall caused Wiley to bring his attention back to the business at hand.

"Let's head fer home, boys. Next Sunday will soon enuff to worry bout the next race."

The three men left the bottom with money in their pockets, and as they passed through town Micajah decided to stop by the blacksmith's shop. He wanted Wiley to see the twin knives he'd told him about.

The knives were truly works of art. Made of the finest metal and sharp enough to shave with, the knives had beautifully worked bone handles and leather scabbards. They were close to seventeen inches long, and perfectly balanced, and seemed almost as if they were made for Micajah's big hand. He picked one up and lightly drew his thumb across its razor sharp edge, and grinned when the softest touch brought a single drop of blood.

"Thar ain't never been a better pair of blades than these, Mister," the blacksmith said, as he saw the look in Micajah's eyes as he handled the knives. "They air two of a kind. The only two I ever made like thet. They'll hold an edge, and they're made to last fer the rest of yer life, and then some. They'll be around when the likes of you and me is dead and gone, I'll tell ye thet. I'll make ye a fair price fer the pair of 'em."

"I plan on owning these knives, Smithy, come this time next Sunday afternoon. I got four good hogs to sell, and a horse race comin' up on which I plan to win a fair amount of money. I'll be back then, and I expect these two blades to still be here. Don't be a'sellin' them to anybody afore then, and I'll only tell ye the one time."

Micajah turned to leave, but found Wiley staring at a rifle sitting in the corner of the smith's shop.

"This shore is a fine gun, mister, is she fer sale?" Wiley asked.

"No sir, she ain't," the blacksmith replied. "She don't belong to me a'tall. I jist fixed the sights fer old Colonel Morgan. Thet's one of them new fangled guns Ferguson had up on Kings Mountain, back in Caroliny. It's a beauty, all right, but not one I kin sell."

Wiley reluctantly set the rifle back down, and then asked the smith another question.

"I have a gun exactly like this one myself mister. My daddy was also on the mountain fer thet fight, and he brought home one of the guns too. The stock on mine is stained pure black, and I'd like to keep her thet way, but whut I want to know is kin ye inlay a silver star on both sides of the stock. Like the one on the talisman my brother has around his neck? I'll pay ye well fer yore work, if'n ye kin do it."

The smith took a close look at the four pointed star Micajah wore, and then said, "Somethin' as simple as thet ought not to be no trouble. When kin ye brang yore gun in fer me to start?"

"I got the gun with me right now. If'n I leave her today, when do ye think ye might have her ready?"

"Next week fer shore, young feller. I ain't too busy right now, so's I kin git right on it. Ye leave her, I'll put two of the purtiest stars in her ever ye laid yore eyes on."

"Ye got yerself a deal, mister," Wiley said, then walked outside and returned with his rifle. "Like I said, I got this gun from my daddy. If'n ye let anything happen to her, I'll jist probably kill ye dead. And like my brother always says, I'll only tell ye the one time."

Micajah and Wiley saw very little of Moses Stegall during the next week. They had to take the four hogs to the butcher, and Wiley spent quite a lot of time working the horse in preparation for the upcoming race. The days passed quickly, and it was Thursday afternoon when Stegall finally put in an appearance at the cabin.

Micajah was splitting logs and Wiley was walking the horse back and forth across the front yard. Susan and Betsy were at the spring getting water, and Sarah was preparing a freshly killed groundhog for supper that night.

Stegall walked into the yard and stood watching Micajah swing the heavy axe.

"Ye handle thet thar axe like she war made of feathers, Micajah, ye shorely do," Stegall said. "But then agin, ye always war a strong 'un. Do ye remember the time I bet all our money thet ye could whup them four fellers all by yerself? T'wer up thar in the Gap, right afore ye jined up with the Cherrykee."

"I reclect, all right, Moses, fer shore. jist as I reclect beatin' the stuffin' out'n the four of 'em. Course it really weren't a fair fight, seein' as how ye told 'em they could each hit me onct first, afore I got to start a'fightin'." Micajah had a small, thin smile playing around the corners of his lips as he spoke. It was obvious he took pride in his strength, as well as in his fighting ability.

"Hell's bells, Micajah," Stegall retorted. "It tweren't fair to the four of them maybe. Ye could have taken twict thet many blows and never felt 'em. No sir, it tweren't fair, and thet's a fact. I ain't never seed ye git whupped in the many years I been knowin' ye. Not even when ye war jist a youngun. I don't reckon as how they's a man in Knoxville town whut could best ye. Thet's what I feel we needs to speak about."

"How so, Moses?" Micajah said.

"Well, ye know if'n we beat 'em in the race Sunday they's a chanct ye might have to knock some heads together?"

Harpe looked at Stegall, and then turned his gaze to the distant hills. "I reckon as how yer right bout thet, Moses. Folks don't take to losin' all thet well. Well, my horse is faster, and it'll be a fair race. If'n they want to start a ruckus, I'll jist be obliged to take ker of my own. But I believe they is honorable men, Stegall, and honorable men do not behave in sich a fashion."

"I believe they is honorable too, Micajah, but they put a lot of faith in thet animal, and when ye beats him, they jist might not want to pay up," Stegall said.

"They'll pay up, Moses, they'll pay up. Ye kin count on thet." Micajah spoke with conviction, as though he had faced this same situation before.

"Now Micajah, I need to ask ye a question, and I don't want ye a'knockin' me down no more. I don't mean anything personal a'tall, but this is somethin' we must talk about. Can ye promise not to go takin' a poke at me this time?" Stegall was hesitant, but it was plain he was also disturbed, and badly needed to discuss this with Micajah.

"Moses, ye've known me longer than most, and ye know the things I don't hold with. Now ask yer question, and I'll not knock ye down. Not this time."

"Whut I must know, Micajah, is if'n things do come down to a fight, kin ye knock their heads together in a kindly fashion, er do ye think they is a chance ye'll turn loose the Wolf?" Stegall was the only man besides the Harpes themselves that referred to the rage that sometimes came over them as "turning loose the Wolf," but not even Stegall knew the full story of the true Wolf that lived inside Micajah. However, he knew Micajah might not take to the idea of him saying it right out in the open like this, but he had to know. If the Harpes did indeed "turn loose the Wolf," the bottom would run red with blood, and Stegall didn't want any of it to be his.

"I kin control the Wolf, Moses," Micajah said. "Tis not like the old days. I kin control the Wolf, and I swear it shall not feed in Knoxville."

Micajah's lips were drawn into a thin line, and his jaw was locked, and Moses could tell there was a battle raging inside him.

"It's not like the old days, when we was with the Cherrykee down in Nickajack. We run wild back then, and the Wolf fed well, and thet was our way of life. The Wolf is a demon thing, Moses, and as real as you and me. But since we have been in Knoxville, I have had the demon under control." It was plain Micajah was very upset over Stegall's question. "T'would take a great act of treachery fer me to ever lose control over the beast agin, and I have thought long and hard on it. I fear thet if the Wolf should ever agin be turned loose, thet I would not be able to contain it anymore. Ye don't understand the power of the Wolf, Moses, but I'll tell ye thet it is forever hungry, and forever trying to break the chains I have placed upon it. So, no, to answer yore question. I'll not turn the Wolf loose on

Knoxville town. I would prefer thet ye not brang up the subject agin, if'n ye don't mind."

Micajah stopped speaking for a moment and Moses could see he was slowly regaining his composure. He turned his fierce gaze full on Stegall, and in a voice as cold as the spring water on the mountain, he said;

"And, Moses, I'll only tell ye the one time."

Stegall drew a deep breath, glad this part of the conversation was over. He was deathly afraid of Micajah at times like this, never knowing when a word or a gesture might set the big man into one of his terrible rages.

"I'll be a'takin' ye at yer word Micajah," Stegall replied. "And I don't mind tellin' ye thet it be a load off'n my mind. Now come on, I'll help ye tote the wood into the cabin." And he picked up a load of the split firewood and walked away.

Micajah swung the heavy axe one last time, with a force strong enough to split the largest log in the pile. He once again turned his gaze to the distant hills, and deep within the icy stare, a small flame flickered. *I wish I was as sure as I made out to be,* he thought. But Harpe knew, and so did Moses Stegall, there was really no leash strong enough to restrain the Wolf. Like Micajah said, the Wolf was forever hungry, and it had not fed in a long, long time.

There was a light shower Saturday night, just enough that the grass was still damp when the Harpe brothers and Moses Stegall arrived at the bottom about ten-thirty Sunday morning. The race wouldn't be run until the afternoon, but they arrived early because Stegall said he had business to take care of before anyone else got there. Sure enough, there was a man already there, and Stegall went off to have a few words with him.

"Whut do ye think he's up to, brother?" Wiley asked. "We know him well enuff to know thar's somethin' goin' on."

"Yore right about thet, Wiley," Micajah answered. "But if'n it's no good he's up to, he'd best not be plannin' on us takin' the blame. I plan on racin' them fellers fair and square, and if'n we win, then takin' our winnin's and goin' on home. With a little stop off in town to pick up them knives and yore rifle." As an afterthought, he added; "Brother, whatever happens in this bottom today, we must remain in control. Should we ever agin turn the Wolf loose, I fear they'll be no turnin' back. If'n Stegall works some foul deed, then we'll settle with him at a later date. As fer today, though, the Wolf shall go back home as hungry as he was when he come down here."

Jack Edwards and his party arrived shortly before noon, and were waiting when George Teil rode into the bottom a little after twelve. Micajah and Wiley watched as one of Teil's men led the big beautiful black stallion over toward Jack Edwards and his small party. The horse was one of the finest animals either of the Harpes had ever seen. He was every bit as big as Harpe's own black stallion, and had a blazing white star on his forehead. Built for speed, with a large rib cage that showed the extent of his endurance, the horse pranced about as if he knew all eyes in the field were on him.

Wiley knew in his heart this would not be an easy race. He knew the caliber of George Teil's horse, and at first was not sure he could win against an animal such as this one. But when he walked over for a closer look, he saw evidence someone had applied a whip to his hindquarters at some point in time. He knew then his own horse had the edge in spirit. When Wiley called upon his horse to run, he ran not because of a whip, but from the pure joy he got from running full speed across a meadow. Wiley knew the great heart inside his horse would not let Mister Teil's stallion outrun him.

"Ye kin bet whatever ye want to, brother," Wiley told Micajah. "I've looked over Mister Teil's animal, and though he be good, we be better. It'll be close at the line, but we'll finish in front."

Stegall walked over to Jack Edwards to make the final arrangements of the wager. "Have ye arranged the bet with Mister Teil, Edwards," he asked. "The Harpes has gathered up quite a tidy little sum, and they desires to wager it all. I have heard thet ye are the only man in these parts George Teil trusts to handle a bet of this size. Seems he trusts you more'n most."

"Thet's true, Mister Brown, he does. And in answer to yore question, yes I have made the arrangements fer the wager. Mister Teil believes his horse is superior to the Harpe's animal, and has agreed to place an amount of money equal to what ye have. Of course, you and me has our own little side bet, which no one else knows about. I kin only assume you have the money to cover it as well." Mister Edwards rubbed his hands together briskly, in anticipation of his expected winnings.

"I surely do, Mister Edwards," Stegall said. "And I want to tell ye onct again this bet is secret. I seed that big horse o' Teil's run, and I ain't so sure the Harpe's stallion can win. Nevertheless, if'n they was to find out that I laid a side bet agin 'em, they'd be mighty upset with me. I jist want to try and cover my own interests a bit, and they ain't no harm in thet, but they wouldn't understand it. It is jist between the two o' us, ain't it?"

"Yes sir, it is. I'm a man of my word, Mister Brown, and I'm only trying to do the same thing you are. I'll make a side wager on Harpe's horse, and then I'll be covered regardless of which one wins. Course, I'm like you, and I don't want anyone else to know about this either."

"I jist want to be sure I can collect my money regardless of whether the Harpes win er lose, Mister Edwards."

"They's no need to worry bout thet, Mister Brown," Edwards said. "We er honorable men, and take our word as set in stone. The only worry we had in comin' here today was thet Mister Teil don't like to carry such a large sum of money on his person. While it would be most unlikely, many a robber would be tempted if'n they knew how much was here in this bottom today."

"If'n a robber should show his face around this bottom today, he would be in a sorry fix. My friend Mister Harpe would take it as a personal insult should a body try to steal from anyone present here.

Take it as the gospel truth, Mister Edwards, a man does not want to be on the bad side of Micajah Harpe."

Edwards looked over to where Micajah stood talking with Wiley, and it was plain to see the big Harpe was not a man to take lightly.

Leaving Jack Edwards, Stegall next walked over to where George Teil stood beside his big black horse. "Good day to ye, Mister Teil, fine day fer a bit of horse racin' ain't it," he said.

"Yes sir, it is at thet," Teil answered. "Is the Harpes about ready to run their horse?"

"I'm on my way over thar right now, Mister Teil, to see about thet. This is a fine animal, Mister Teil," Stegall exclaimed. "I understand Mister Edwards has discussed the terms of the bet with ye, and ye air agreeable?"

"You understand correctly, Mister Brown," Teil said. "I have agreed to bring this large amount of money because of the great faith I have in my horse, and the assurance by Mister Edwards thet I would not be robbed here today."

George Teil was obviously a worried man, and also a man that would speak his mind.

"Ye have only one thing to worry bout here today, Mister Teil," Stegall said, in an effort to put the man's mind at ease. "And thet's whether or not yore horse kin out run ourn. I don't believe it kin, and thet's why I'm willin' to wager ever cent I have in this world. No sir, ye don't have to worry bout being robbed, but I'm bettin' ye'll lose yer money, jist the same."

"If'n I lose it in a fair and square way, then so be it," Teil said. "I'm jist a cautious man by nature." George Teil was a shrewd and careful man, but in Moses Stegall he was up against a master.

Moses walked over to where Micajah and Wiley stood. He gently rubbed the horse's nose as he spoke to Micajah.

"I think we kin beat old Teil's horse, Kiga, but onct again, let me plead with ye thet should we lose, not to turn the Wolf loose on these folks."

Even as they spoke, Stegall continued to let Micajah's horse nuzzle his hand. The Indian he'd met earlier in the day had brought him a paste made of a little weed that affected animals in strange ways, and Stegall was rubbing the paste into the nostrils and mouth of the horse as the two men stood talking. The paste was odorless and colorless, and caused horses to momentarily lose their senses and become a little disoriented. Stegall knew the slightest distraction of the Harpe's horse would assure a victory for Teil's big stallion.

He was especially careful as he rubbed the horse's nose. If Micajah had any idea Stegall was planning on the Harpe's losing, then this little meadow would likely be the last place on earth Stegall ever saw.

His plan was to use the paste from the jimson weed to make the Harpe's horse lose, and then to secretly collect his own money from Mister Edwards. He thought it was only fair. Micajah never should have hit him, and this little plan was just Stegall's way of paying the Harpes back.

His plan worked to perfection.

The Harpe's horse ran well, but twice he jerked his head up, his eyes wild, not knowing what was happening to him, and that was all it took. Teil's big stallion finished a full half-length in front.

Micajah's horse was still acting a little strange as Wiley walked it back across the bottom to where Micajah and Moses stood waiting.

"What happened, Wiley?" was all Micajah had to say.

Wiley hung his head for a moment. "I don't know Kiga. I thought I had it won, then he pulled his head up a mite, and Teil's horse jist run right past me."

"Well, let's tell Teil goodbye, and we'll be getting' on home.

They walked over to where Teil stood, and Micajah stuck out his hand.

"Yore horse ran a fine race, Mister Teil, and he beat us fair and square. We'll be headin' o home now. Good day to ye sir."

"Yes sir, we did beat the tar out of yer horse, now didn't we" Teil crowed. "I told your Mister Brown there is not a horse in these parts that can beat mine. Too bad, boys, too bad. Hope it don't set ye back too far." Teil was all smiles as he talked.

Stegall glanced at Micajah and saw a tiny spark flare to life deep within his eyes.

"If'n ye please, Mister Teil, I think it's best thet we jist get on home."

Wiley was still standing at the horse's head, rubbing his nose and trying to settle the big animal down. His fingers passed down across the horse's mouth and wiped away a trace of foam from his lips. Wiley raised the foam to his nostrils and smelled deeply, and a strange, puzzled look came over his face.

"Damnation, Kiga. This horse has been eatin' jimson weed. Whar in the world do ye suppose he got into this stuff?"

"What's thet?" Micajah said. "What did ye say? Jimson weed? Thet explains things, don't it?"

"I reckon it does," Wiley said. "They is a little patch of the weed down by the trees yonder. I don't reclect the horse gittin' into it, but I guess he could have."

Stegall stood with Micajah and Wiley and watched George Teil gleefully counting his winnings. Moses knew he had to get the Harpes away before anything could happen. He shook his head and started walking toward the side of the meadow, and the trail back to the Harpe's cabin. Micajah and Wiley stood there for another minute, then headed in that direction also.

Stegall was delighted to see there was no flame burning in the eyes of Micajah Harpe as they left the bottomland.

They parted company not far from the meadow. Stegall had secretly collected his money from Edwards, and he wanted to stay in town and celebrate his little victory over the Harpes with a jug of peach brandy. Micajah and Wiley stopped by the blacksmith's shop to pick up Wiley's rifle, only to find a padlock on the door and the smith nowhere to be found.

Going into a rum shop next door, Micajah inquired as to the whereabouts of the smith and was told the old man had gone down on the Holston River to help take care of his daughter who was about to give birth to his fourth grandchild. The smith's wife had passed away last year and there was no one except the old man himself to help see his daughter through. He was expected to be back in another few days, and would re-open his shop at that time.

Micajah still wanted the twin blades, and now he had to sell even more pork in order to have them.

They headed back for the cabin, disappointed at their loss, and not knowing in the near future the lost race would be seen as a turning point in their lives.

31

Activities around the Harpe's farm got back to normal very quickly after the race. The corn was coming along nicely, and they had two more hogs almost ready to take to the butcher. The children were healthy and growing like weeds, and the women were kept busy making new quilts for the coming winter.

Micajah and Wiley were building an extra room onto the back of the cabin, and other than still smarting a bit from the lost race, all in all the family was peaceful and happy.

Moses Stegall hadn't been seen since the day of the race, but the Harpes had a pretty good idea where he was spending his time. The rum shops and groggeries in Knoxville were good places for a man such as Stegall to visit regularly. As far as they knew, Stegall had also lost a lot of money on the race, and was drowning his sorrows in peach brandy. They didn't know about his secret winnings, or that he was quickly acquiring a reputation around Knoxville as a big spender. He was also acquiring a reputation as a man who talked too much when he was drinking.

Of course, his favorite subject of conversation was the Harpes.

Stegall, or Brown as he was known in Knoxville, loved to tell of the years when he and the Harpes roamed the territory, and of the many things they did. As it is with talk that comes with strong drink, with each telling each tall tale grew even taller.

One night, after Stegall had been drinking peach brandy for several hours, his story telling got out of hand, and the entire countryside paid for his loose lips with red blood.

In the middle of one of his tales, he let it slip he and the Harpes had lived in the Cherokee town of Nickajack for over a year, and in fact were there when the town was destroyed by the soldiers of Major Ore. Much of what he said would have been passed over as simple drunken rambling, but on this particular night there happened to be in the rum shop a man who had fought with Major Ore in Nickajack, and knew all of the actual circumstances first hand.

The man stood up from his straight-backed chair and staggered over to where Stegall sat.

"Tell me friend," he said, "if'n ye war really thar, how did all the fightin' git started?"

"Why the rascals swum the river at night, and rushed the town at the crack of dawn," Stegall answered. "Caught us all a'sleepin'. Twas a bloody mess all round. Folks was dyin' as they tried to swim the river, and women and little chillun shot as they lay a'sleepin'. Hit war a massacre shore enuff."

"Jist what might have been yore business in Nickajack?" the man wanted to know next.

"Why, I was a'visitin' my good friends, the Harpes," Stegall said. He was too drunk to really know what he was saying, and his next sentence marked the beginning of the end of the Harpe's peaceful stay in Knoxville. It also sealed Stegall's fate for all eternity.

"Yes sir," Stegall bragged, "I am a personal friend to the greatest Cherrykee warrior of all time. None other than the mighty Wolf Spirit hisself, and also to the one called Wolf Brother."

"What has them two murderin' redskins got to do with the Harpe boys," the man wanted to know, and several other ears had perked up at the mention of the two killers.

"Why hell fire and damnation, man," Stegall exclaimed, in a loud boisterous voice. "Wolf Spirit and Wolf Brother ain't no more red skins than you and me. They is white men. In fact, Micajah Harpe is the warrior the Cherrykee call Wolf Spirit, and his brother Wiley the one they call Wolf Brother. I has knowed the both of them fer years, and I know fer a fact that whut I'm tellin' ye it the God's truth.

"Good God man, ye can't mean thet," the man almost shouted, and several of the others stood up and came over to stand around the two of them. "If thet's true, whut be the Harpes doin' in Knoxville?" he asked next.

"Yeah, why ain't they still a'livin' with them bloody red savages," another man spoke up.

"We was all gittin' a mite tard of livin' with the injuns," Stegall answered. "I didn't git to Nickajack till well after the Harpe boys, but I had my fill of the red devils up towards Buchanan's Station. Anyway, after Major Ore's raid, we jist decided it war time to take our leave of the injuns."

"Ye mean ye and the Harpes took part in the raid with John Watts? Agin yer own people? Whut kind of men air ye? I'll tell ye one thang, Knoxville ain't got no room fer the likes of ye and the Harpes. And if'n what ye say is true about Micajah bein' the man called Wolf Spirit, then we will shorely have to do somethin' bout thet."

"We oughta string em up, the lot of em," another man shouted. He pointed at Stegall. "And we oughta start with this scoundrel right here."

By this time Stegall had realized he had said too much, and the hostility in the crowd was quickly bringing him around to his senses.

Damn it old son, ye've done it now, Stegall thought. *Even if'n ye manage to git away from this bunch, one er the other of the Harpes will surely kill ye.*

Not wanting to let the men know he was coming out of his drunken state, Stegall let his head droop until it was almost touching the table top. His left hand wrapped around the bottle from which he'd been drinking, and under the table his right hand slowly closed about the grip of the long knife he wore at his waist. He slowly raised his head until he was looking at the angry men standing in front of him. With a little grin, he shook his head and said, "Fellers, I believe I have already said too much to ye. Tis time I took my leave."

Before anyone could move, Stegall smashed the bottle into the face of the man who had been doing the questioning, and jumped up, overturning the table into the others with all his strength. As his right hand came out from under the table with the knife in it, he stabbed the man closest to him on his right in the leg.

With several of the men sprawled on the floor, and the one he had stabbed screaming in pain, Stegall quickly ran out the door. His horse was just outside and he mounted in a running jump and rode out of town as fast as the animal could run. Without hesitation, he headed toward Beaver Creek and the Harpe's cabin. Before he left the territory, he had to let Micajah and Wiley know the men in town knew about them. He'd make up some story so as not to tell them about his part in what had happened, and then he'd hightail it back to Kentucky.

Micajah heard the sound of a running horse coming toward the cabin, and was already up by the time Stegall raced full tilt into the yard.

"Whut in the thunderation is goin' on, Micajah?" Wiley whispered, as he came out of his room and joined his brother at the front door.

"I'm not fer shore, Wiley, but ye kin bet it won't be good news." He slowly opened the door and stepped out into the deep shadows of the front yard. He was standing unseen by the corner of the house when Stegall leaped from his horse and shouted at the cabin.

"Micajah. Wiley. Get up boys," he yelled, and began beating on the door with his fist.

Suddenly he felt a massive arm slip around his upper body from the back, and a huge hand covered his mouth. He violently twisted to one side, but couldn't shake himself free from whoever was holding him.

With all his strength, Stegall was twisting and jerking and trying to get loose when he heard a soft voice whisper in his ear.

"Hush, Moses," the voice whispered. "Stand still and hush."

"Good God, Micajah," Moses cried, "don't grip my neck so tight."

"What's going on Stegall," Micajah asked, in only a slightly louder voice. "Tis not like ye to come ridin' up in the middle of the night, screamin' like a wild injun." Without another word he turned the man loose.

Stegall turned to face Micajah before he answered.

"I was at Hughes Tavern tonight, Micajah, jist a while ago, when I heerd some men a'talkin'. I heerd one of 'em mention Nickajack so naturally my ears pricked up jist a mite. One of the men said he was with Major Ore when they raided the town, and swore thet they was a few men who escaped gittin' killed. He claimed he knowed some of the men had come here to Knoxville, and dad blamed if'n he didn't mention the name of Wolf Spirit."

Micajah didn't blink at all when Stegall spoke his Indian name, and didn't speak a word, but he seemed to become more alert.

"Anyway," Stegall continued, "I jumped into the conversation and asked the man whut he knew about Wolf Spirit. He said he had also been in the battle at Buchanan's Station, and had got a good look at the warrior. So I told him then, 'Hogwash,' I said, 'I don't believe ye know a thang bout thet red devil.'"

"Well sir," he said to me, "Wolf Spirit ain't no red devil, he's as white as you er me."

Taking a breath, Stegall continued. "Then the man claimed to have been following Wolf Spirit for many months, and thet the trail led him right here to Knoxville town."

Stegall breathed a heavy sigh as he paused for a moment.

"Well sir," Stegall went on after a minute. "I told him then, I jist don't know as how I kin believe this wild tale of yourn. How come nobody round these parts has seen this ferocious killer?"

"Because he don't look like no injun, he don't dress like no injun, and he don't live like no injun, thet's why," he said. "He has a farm whar he raises hogs and a patch of corn, and him and his brother has got wives and chillun."

Moses paused for a moment to get his breath, and then continued. "I swar thet's whut he said, Micajah."

"So I asked him then and thar plain out, I said, well then jist who is this killer, and whar does he live here in Knoxville?"

"The feller looked me full in the face and he said,"

'The man's name is Harpe, and he lives down on the Beaver Creek. Thar is him and his brother, and three women and a passel of chillun. The good people of Knoxville oughta rid the country of a man sich as him.'

"Why feller," I said, "I know the Harpes, and they ain't no better people livin' in this territory than them. They wouldn't harm a flea. They is good, upstandin' farm people."

'They might be farmers right now,' the man said, 'but only two year ago they war savage killers, ridin' with John Watts and a'killin' their own kind. They was at Buchanan's Station, feller, I know because I was thar myself and I seed 'em.'

"I warn't the onliest one whut heerd whut the man said, Micajah," Stegall said. "They were several people in the tavern, and

I heerd one say somethin' bout ridin' out here and askin' ye bout whut the man had said. I don't know if they will come er not, but I wanted ye to know whut the man had said."

"Thank ye, Moses, fer ridin' out here with the word," Micajah said.

"Whut do ye think of Stegall's tale, little brother," Micajah asked Wiley, who had stood by the door and listened.

"Well, I don't know, Micajah," Wiley said. "But if'n it be true, then we best be gittin' out of Knoxville town, and the sooner the better." Wiley knew if the story was believed, there were a great many people in Knoxville who would want the Harpes dead.

"Git yore britches on and tell the womenfolk we air goin' out fer a spell," Micajah said. He wanted to check out Stegall's story as quickly as possible. Him and Wiley would ride toward town and see if they could find out what was going on. He knew it would be safe for him and Wiley to leave the women at home alone, for even the wildest mob wouldn't harm a female.

"Stegall, ye'd best be goin' on yer way. If'n the town folk do come out here, they won't take kindly to ye bein' here. We'll handle the situation, and thank ye onct agin."

The look in Micajah's eyes told Stegall he'd better get as much distance between himself and the Harpes as he could before they found out the real truth. With a smile and a quick handgrip, Stegall jumped back on his horse and thundered away into the night, leaving Micajah and Wiley preparing to go into town.

Micajah and Wiley took their time riding into Knoxville. If what Stegall had said was true, they didn't want to run headlong into an angry lynch party in the dark.

Just as Micajah and Wiley came in sight of Hughes Tavern, they saw a large group of men come boiling out of the door. The men looked to be in various stages of drunkenness, and were unruly and wild. They were shouting and jostling each other, and it was plain to see they were in a mean state of mind.

The Harpes sat their horses under the trees at the edge of the clearing and waited until the men had passed. Dismounting, they walked to the door of the tavern and quietly entered.

As the men finally cleared out of his saloon, old man Hughes breathed a sigh of relief. Thank God they had left before they did any damage to his establishment. The only one's left inside were himself, two brother's named Morgan, a stranger named Johnson, and Hughes friend John Metcalf, who was slumped face first on a table, lost in drunken slumber.

Johnson was drunk and was demanding still another bottle, but Hughes was ready to close down for the night. The wild bunch that had just left was all Hughes felt like listening to tonight. He was having a little trouble getting Johnson to leave and was about to ask the Metcalf boys for help, when all at once he noticed two men were standing just inside his doorway.

"Sorry boys," he called, "but I be closing fer the night. Jist as soon as I kin git this feller here to leave," nodding in the direction of Johnson.

The two men walked on into the flickering yellow glow of the interior of the small tavern and stood in the deeper shadows by the wall as the largest one said;

"Don't want none of yer rotgut whiskey mister, jist want a bit of information, if'n ye don't mind." The voice was soft, yet very easy to understand.

"Whut might thet be, mister?" Hughes queried.

"Need to know whut was goin' on with them men we seed leavin' here jist now, thet's all." The big man said.

"Well sir, I'll tell ye. It come to our attention tonight thet a savage killer is a'livin' right here in Knoxville, and the men has gone to fetch him and his no-good family and put 'em whar they belong. Either in jail, er in hell, whichever way the man wants it. He's a no-good bastard of a injun lover, who has kilt many a white man."

214

"Jist who might this feared killer be feller?" the man wanted to know. He and his companion were still standing in the shadows, and Hughes had not gotten a good look at them yet.

"Why, the bloody bastard in none other than the man the injuns call Wolf Spirit. A white man who is a traitor to his own kind." Hughes was excited, and it was plain from his words he thought the company of men should hang the two brothers first, and verify the story later.

"Jist who might this white man be?" The voice was still soft, but had an edge that would have sliced through cast iron.

"None other than the man named Micajah Harpe, down on the Beaver Creek," Hughes cackled.

As Hughes turned his head to get a little better look at the two men he was talking to, Micajah stepped out of the shadows where the tavern owner could see his face.

Hughes's complexion paled considerably when he recognized the big Harpe standing there. Even in the dim light, Micajah saw the man's eyes widen, and heard his sharp intake of breath.

"Now Mister Harpe, wait jist a second. Don't do nothin' to me. I am jist repeatin' whut I've heerd in here tonight, and don't know none of it to be the truth. They was a feller in here tonight claimed he knowed ye, and was tellin' about ye bein' a killer and all, and when the rest of them men got drunk enuff they headed out toward yore place." Hughes was scared out of his wits, and didn't know what to do.

"Who was this feller thet claimed to know me, and made these accusations?" Micajah asked Hughes.

"Why, it were the feller named Brown," Hughes said. "Claimed he knowed ye and thet ye lived together down in Nickajack fer a spell. And thet's the truth, Mister Harpe, I swar it is."

"I'll take yore word fer it feller," Harpe said. "Brown always did have a big mouth when he took to drinkin'. We'll be takin' our leave of yore establishment now Mister Hughes, and thank ye fer the information."

"Mister Harpe," Hughes said. "It ain't true is it? Bout ye bein' thet Wolf Spirit?"

Micajah turned and looked at the man and was about to speak when suddenly the man named Johnson jumped up from his table and fired his pistol point blank into Micajah's chest.

"I'll kill ye, ye murderin' bastard, I will," he shouted. "I had family at Buchanan's Station. Ye kilt my brother." He began fumbling with the pistol, trying to reload, hoping to get off another shot. When he saw he couldn't reload fast enough, he leaped toward the door, and slammed out of it and into the dark woods at a full run.

Micajah was twisting even as the man fired, and the movement caused the ball strike him high in the right side of his chest, hitting him in the heavily muscled breast area and exiting underneath his right arm, doing very little damage.

Seeing the shooter run through the door, Micajah paid him very little attention. No need to. Johnson sprinted through the door, only to run full into the waiting arms of Wiley Harpe.

Wiley grabbed Johnson, spun him around and through the door and slit his throat before the man knew what had happened. When Wiley turned him loose, Johnson sank to the ground gasping for air, and was dead in less than two minutes.

Wiley silently dragged the body to the banks of the nearby Holston River and laid it down on a gravel bar. Working quickly and without expression, Wiley cut open the body and withdrew the entrails, throwing them into the muddy water. He scooped up handful after handful of gravel and stuffed it into the body cavity, and when he was satisfied, he lifted the corpse and threw it into the deepest part of the river. He stood on the bank and watched as the body quickly sank. *Nobody won't be findin' this body fer a spell,* Wiley thought, knowing they might need a little time before the folks in town realized the story about them was true. Without a backward glance at the ripples in the water, Wiley walked back toward where Micajah waited inside Hughes tavern.

After Micajah had watched Johnson run out of the tavern, he sat down in a chair at one of the small tables in the room. He asked Hughes to wet a cloth so he could clean the wound, and when Hughes left the room, Micajah grasped the Harpe Amulet with his right hand.

For a second he stared at the Amulet, then closed his eyes and brought the talisman up to his forehead. A soft red glow emanated from between his fingers, bathing his face and his upper body. He felt the warmth penetrate the wound and knew it had already stopped bleeding. He heard Hughes as he came back into the room and opened his eyes, taking the dampened cloth from the man's hand. By the time he had finished washing off the blood, most of the soreness had vanished, and the entry and exit wounds were starting to heal. He sat back and closed his eyes once again, allowing the amulet a few more minutes to work its wonders.

After about thirty minutes, Wiley came back into the tavern and sat at the table with Micajah. Neither spoke, but Wiley knew Micajah was not badly injured, and Micajah knew Johnson was no longer among the living.

A few more minutes passed and Micajah opened his eyes and looked first at Wiley and then at Hughes. The innkeeper saw a flame flicker in Harpe's wild blue eyes, and though the night was hot a chill ran down his spine.

Still without speaking a word, the brothers rose from the table and walked out of the rum shop.

On weak and shaking legs Hughes stood up and walked behind the bar, taking up a bottle of his strongest peach brandy. Although not a drinking man, Hughes thought perhaps a little nip might help chase away the coldness he felt lingering in the air from the look the big Harpe had given him. He knew without being told this was not a night he would ever talk about.

He looked at the door as he heard the horses gallop off into the night.

"God help us all," he whispered, and the words were carried away on a breeze that slithered out the open door to be lost in the pitch-black darkness of the night.

John Metcalf had not stirred throughout the entire incident, and was still asleep at the table, perhaps dreaming of better days.

Micajah was right about the angry men not bothering the women. Nine men had ridden out from town, but when they got there and found neither of the men at home, they milled around for about thirty minutes and then left. A couple of the men made threats against the brothers, and told the women what would happen the next time the men came to town, but there was no real trouble.

Of course the women were glad Micajah and Wiley weren't at home, but not for a reason the group of vigilantes would understand, or probably even believe.

The women knew for a certainty that every man in the posse would have been killed had they arrived unexpectedly and come up against the fury of the Harpe. None of the men from town would have believed how terrible it would have been had the Wolf been turned loose among them. The women wanted to keep it that way, although both Susan and Betsy knew their stay in Knoxville was quickly coming to an end. Sarah had not seen the blue flame burn out of control in the eyes of her husband, but after the incident tonight, it was only a matter of time.

It was a little after three A.M. when Wiley rode back into the yard alone. He went inside and found Susan and Sarah at the eating table. Betsy had not been feeling well, and once the men had ridden toward town, she'd lain back down on her bed.

"Whar is the big Harpe, Wiley?" Susan asked. "Didn't nothin' happen to him did it?"

"Lord naw, Susie," Wiley responded. "Kiga took a bullet, but it didn't bother him much. He's gone down the road a piece to see if'n he kin pick up the trail of er friend, Moses Stegall. We found out in town thet it war Moses hisself who got drunked up and told the townspeople thet Micajah and me used to ride with the injuns. Mayhap this time he has let the drink loosen his tongue a mite too much. I believe he has talked hisself into a pine box. Kiga is mighty upset with old Stegall, and friend or no friend, the Harpe ain't a man to cross."

As Wiley finished his sentence, they heard the sound of another horse approaching the cabin. Picking up his rifle Wiley made a sound for the women to be quiet. He blew out the small oil lamp and moved softly over to the door. Very quietly he opened the door and stepped out into the front yard. If this war some of the men from town coming back, he'd make them wish they had minded their own business a little closer. The Harpes had been good citizens and good neighbors since they'd come to Knoxville, and that should have been all that concerned the townspeople. Their past had nothing to do with the way they were living today.

Wiley stepped out of the shadow as the lone rider brought his horse to a stop.

"Who goes thar?" he called. "State yore business afore I blow of'n yore head."

"Hold on, Mister Harpe, hold on. I don't mean ye no harm. My name is James Morgan, and me and my brother was in the tavern tonight when ye and yer brother come in. I seed how ye handled thet old Johnson feller, and I rode out here to tell ye we appreciated it. Tonight was not the first time he has caused trouble in town. He was all primed and ready to kill somebody, and my brother and me was the onliest one's in the place. One of us would have got him, but the chances er thet he would have got on of us all the same. So we thank ye fer whut ye did. I also want to tell ye thet thar was only one man in the tavern tonight thet might cause ye and yore brother some real trouble."

219

Morgan was only about twenty-one or two, and was a little scared of the Harpe brothers, but he really did appreciate what they'd done tonight, and felt he had an obligation to return the favor.

"Which one might thet be," Wiley asked, "and how kin he cause us any trouble?"

"Well sir, one of the men is named Joseph Ballenger, and he be a lawman out near the wilderness in Kaintuck. He is a mean and tough man, and a fearsome fighter, and he said tonight he was also up near Nashville after the Cherrykee raid. He may not fully believe the story of Mister Brown, and the chanct is he'll be on his way out of Knoxville tomorry, but I jist thought ye should know. If'n he comes snoopin' round, he is a man to be kerful of. As a law dog, he may come out here to question you and yer brother."

"Mister Morgan, I want ye to know thet I think ye is an honorable man, and I thank ye fer yore trouble. My brother would thank ye also, but he is not home at the present time." Wiley stopped for a minute as if considering his next words, then continued. "Now, if'n ye really wants to return the favor, when ye next sees the men whut was thar tonight, then jist tell 'em thet Mister Brown was onct er friend, and thet he crossed us and my brother knocked him down fer it. Twas down at the racetrack, and several people saw it, and will swear it happened. The man has vowed to git back at us in some manner. Tell 'em also thet stuff bout us livin' with the injuns is all jist pure hogwash. Tis nothin' but a pack of lies, and thet's the truth. And ye kin tell yer Mister Ballenger thet it war not the Harpes whut killed no people around Buchanan's Station. If'n they want proof, tell Mister Ballenger and his friends the Harpes has run thet scoundrel Brown clean out of town. He was afeerd to face us, for fear we'd show him up to be the rascal thet he truly is."

"I'll tell 'em fer shore, Mister Harpe, and would ye tell yore brother thet we hopes he recovers quickly from Johnson's gunshot." Morgan turned his horse and rode away from the cabin, and as soon as he had disappeared along the trail, Micajah led his horse into the front yard.

"Did ye hear whut the boy said, Micajah?" Wiley asked.

"Most of it, brother, and ye did well to tell him whut ye did."

"Did ye find any sign of Stegall's trail?" Wiley wanted to know.

"I found his trail alright," Micajah said. "'Tis hard to miss the tracks of that little pony he's been ridin'. Looks as if he be headin' out toward the Kaintuck Wilderness, though fer the life of me I don't know why."

Susan stepped out on the front porch just in time to hear what Micajah said.

"Why, Stegall has a wife over thar," she said. "Purty little thing she is too. He's done went and married thet little Fowler girl, Micajah. The one he had with him thet time we seen him at the Gap, back afore we went to Nickajack."

"Then ye reckon he has gone back to his old home place, Susan? Member we visited thar onct?"

"I'd say thet were it," Susan said.

Picking up the conversation, Wiley said; "Do ye be wantin' us to pack er things and ride the bastard down?" It was easy to see that was what Wiley wanted to do.

"Naw, not jist yit," Micajah replied. "Let's see whut happens around here first. Them men'll be back, jist as shore as I'm a'standin' here. If not tomorry, then next week, er next month. They ain't gonna let us git no rest here no more."

"Do ye think they might try to run us out'n the territory, brother?" Wiley asked.

"I spect they'll try, brother, I spect they will. And in the end they might succeed. But they'll pay a dear cost. I don't mean to be kilt in my own front yard as our pappy was," Micajah said. Even in the paleness of the pre-dawn the expression on his face was plain.

Susan looked at the brothers standing before her, and made a single statement that would hold true for as long as time itself endured.

"Ye men has been good husbands to us, and good fathers to the chillun. I want ye to know thet we all feel the same way. We women folk will folly anywhar ye leads us. Our place is at yore sides." With these words she turned and walked back into the house.

Sarah and Betsy were standing just inside the door and had heard the conversation. "Do ye think we'll be a'leavin' Knoxville, Susan?" Betsy asked.

"I wouldn't be none surprised sister, if'n we do. We has had over two years of peaceful livin' here, and I reckon we ought to be thankful fer thet. If'n them men comes back out here a'tryin' to run us off, the Harpes goin' to kill a passel of 'em. Yes, I reckon we ought to pack er essentials. Thar is a chanct we'll be a'leavin' Knoxville in a hurry."

Susan knew better than the other two this incident would be all it would take to give her husband a reason to go back to living the life of the savage Wolf, and she was afraid that their world would never be the same.

Susan was right. But this time when the big Harpe lost control, he lost control completely. He turned the Wolf loose on Knoxville, and it fed, and fed.

32

The peace and tranquility they had known for over two years was shattered less than two weeks later. It died a sudden and violent death, and a permanent one.

It started about four in the afternoon, when the Morgan boy came riding up to the Harpe's cabin again. He jumped off his horse before it had even stopped, and began yelling for Wiley.

"Mister Harpe, Mister Harpe, come out quick," the boy yelled. "I has some news for ye."

Wiley ran out the door, followed closely by Micajah. "Whut is it, boy?" he asked. "Whut's wrong?"

"They's talkin' bout ye in town. Sayin' bad things. They say they air comin' back out here, and this time they won't leave till the job is finished, and the two of ye air dead." The boy was breathing hard, and shaking all over.

"Whut has stirred 'em back up boy?" Micajah asked.

"Well sir, they has found the body of old Johnson, floating in the river. He was all cut up, and they said it was a bad sight to see. Well, some of the men got to drinkin' agin down at Hughes place, and one of them remembered thet Johnson was in thar the night they rode out to yer place. They kept on a'talkin' till finally one of 'em arrested old Hughes and Metcalf and accused them o' killin' Johnson. Well, it warn't long afore Hughes started to talking about the two of ye, and how ye was in his place thet night. He said he thought ye kilt Johnson and throwed his body in the river fer no

223

reason a'tall. I tried to tell 'em thet Johnson shot ye, and thet was why ye kilt him, but they wouldn't listen to the likes of me. They is tryin' to git together a big bunch of men to ride out here and take ker of ye. I jist thought ye ought'n to know." The boy rode away from the cabin as quickly as he'd ridden in, without waiting to hear the men say thank you.

"Git yer rifle, Wiley," Micajah said.

"Whut do ye plan to do Micajah?" Susan asked.

"We air goin' into town and try to stop them fools afore they do somethin' plumb crazy," Micajah replied. "I reckon it's best thet ye women git the chillun ready to go. If'n I have to kill a bunch of them fellers we'll have to be a'leavin'. But Susan, I want ye and Betsy and Sarah to know this is not what I intended. I hold Stegall responsible, and it's him who will pay. If'n I kin calm 'em down, I will, and if'n not, then so be it."

Micajah and Wiley rode the two miles into Knoxville in silence, each man lost in his own thoughts. Both knew they were probably going to have to fight the men in town, and there were a lot of them. The odds were against the brothers in this fight and they also knew they might be killed before the night was over. But at least if they fought in town, the women and children would be safe.

Micajah touched the Harpe Amulet, and no sooner had his fingers touched the silver star than the hunger inside began to gnaw on his soul. He glanced over at Wiley and in a moment of togetherness he knew exactly how his brother felt.

Micajah softly began to hum the little song of his mother, and for the rest of the way into town, it seemed as if the song were the only sound in the universe.

They dismounted in the woods behind Hughes tavern and silently stole up to the back of the building. Micajah started around the right side of the building and Wiley the left, so anyone who came out would be between them. Micajah peered around the corner of the building and saw a brief outline of Wiley on the other side. He motioned for Wiley to stay put and then softly stepped up on the rough plank porch. With no noise at all, Micajah slipped to the door and eased it open the barest crack. Risking a quick look inside, he was surprised to find the tavern empty. There wasn't a soul inside, not even Hughes himself. Micajah motioned for Wiley to join him at the door and together they walked inside for a better look.

They found no one inside the tavern at all.

"I don't like the looks of this, Wiley," Micajah said. "They's only one thing they could have done, and thet's to have gone somewhar's and gotten some more men. If'n thet's whut they did, then we must have missed them as we rode in. I reckon we better git on home Wiley. They ain't no tellin' whut this bunch will do this time. They's liable to take out their anger on the women and chillun, and if'n they do hell ain't gonna be big enuff to hold 'em all."

They spared neither themselves nor their horses as they rode back toward the cabin, fearful of what they might find once they reached home. And their worst fears were realized. They were still a good distance from the cabin when they saw black smoke rolling into the afternoon sky.

"The sons-a-bitches er burnin' the cabin," Wiley yelled, and then saw Micajah hastily pull his horse to a sliding stop.

"Come over here Wiley," Micajah commanded, and quickly began pulling his left shirtsleeve up above his wrist. Wiley knew what Micajah was about to do, and had his own left arm bare by the time he reached his brother.

Micajah laid his left arm against Wiley's, and with a savage slashing movement he brought the sharp edge of the amulet across both arms, slicing the flesh as though it were paper. The dark red blood of both men once again mingled with the scarlet background of the amulet, and the silver points of the star gleamed in the lazy afternoon sunlight.

Hunnnngerrrrr...Harpe...I hunnngerrr...must feed...

225

Micajah looked at Wiley and saw the wild blue flame burning in his eyes. "When we git thar, brother, turn the Wolf loose," he said in a course voice.

Turn the Wolf loose they did.

Micajah and Wily turned off the narrow trail and stopped their horses in the edge of the trees. Sure enough the cabin was on fire and there were twelve or fifteen men milling about the front yard, shouting and cursing as they watched the rolling flames and thick, blackish smoke. There was no sight of either the women or the children in the clearing. Micajah removed the great tomahawk from his belt, looked at his brother, and without hesitation screamed the fierce war cry that had heralded the death of so many people.

Their horses bounded out of the trees and into the midst of the angry men before they knew what was going on. With another mighty roar, Micajah swung the tomahawk and his eyes flashed as it smashed through the head of the closest man, spilling his brains onto the grass. The second blow of the tomahawk caught another of the men in the head, peeling his scalp back like a ripe orange, and popping his eyes out of their sockets. Micajah was dimly aware of hearing Wiley's rifle bark, but was too caught up in his own killing frenzy to stop and look for his brother. The men from town were still too shocked by the suddenness of the attack to understand what was going on, but several of them realized they had to fight back it they hoped to survive.

Micajah leaped from his horse and caught one of the men around the neck, bulldogging him to the ground. As they hit the hard earth, Harpe twisted the man's neck and heard a loud pop as the bone shattered. Just as Harpe gained his feet, one of the men pulled a nearby axe handle from it's resting place in a chopping block, leaving the blade of the axe stuck in place, and struck Harpe savagely across the back with it. The force of the blow drove Harpe to his knees and with a satisfied grunt the man swung the club a second time, and laughed as it caught the big man low in the back.

"Ye ain't so tough now air ye, ye bloody bastard," the man grated, and swiftly gave the Harpe another vicious blow. This time it landed a little higher on his back with enough force to drive him down on all fours. The fight might have ended then and there if the man had only clubbed Harpe a few times on the head. But another of the men, assuming Harpe was hurt worse than he actually was, gave a bellow like a wild bull then jumped on Micajah's back and grabbed him around the neck. This action only served to shield Harpe's exposed back and head from any further blows from the axe handle, and to give him a few moments to regain the breath he'd lost when he'd been hit.

Thinking to do the same thing to Harpe that Harpe had done to his friend, the man wrapped his arms tight around Harpe's neck and twisted with all his might. He thought he could break his neck or at least choke him to death, but he didn't reckon on the great strength of the man on the ground.

The man with the axe handle danced around the two men, but couldn't take another swing for fear of hitting his companion. He could only watch as Harpe grabbed the man's right arm and slowly pulled it away from his neck. When he had the arm in position, Micajah locked his mouth on the wrist and bit down as hard as he could. He tasted the salty blood, and heard bones give way between his teeth. The man screamed and Harpe spat out blood and flesh and began to climb to his feet, the man still on his back. Seeing the chopping block with the double-edged axe blade still securely stuck in place gave him an idea. He reached over his head with both hands, grabbed the man on his back by his arms, and then bent forward with a huge lunge and threw the man over his shoulder. He flew forehead first into the sharp edge of the axe, splitting his skull almost to his jawbone, killing him instantly.

Counting the man holding the axe handle, there were still five of the townsmen standing in the yard. Wiley stood bent over a body, wiping the blade of his knife on the corpses shirt. Micajah was standing looking at the man who had the axe embedded in his skull. The townsmen grew still as Harpe turned to face them, and suddenly it became deathly quiet in the yard. Harpe's eyes were twin beacons of bright blue flame, blazing like the hottest fires of hell. His mouth was bloody from biting the man's wrist half in two, and as he turned to face them, he let out a roar such as the men had never heard before.

For the first and only time in their lives, the men stood face to face with the devil known as the Wolf, and its rage and power were terrible to see.

Only for a second did the Harpe remain still.

With a fierce sound that was more like a growl than anything else, he leaped across the few feet separating him from the men. His long knife severed the jugular of the first man he reached, and without stopping he buried it in the chest of the next man. Even as Micajah moved, so did Wiley. Wiley grabbed one of the men and plunged his knife into the man's right ear, snarling as the point emerged from the other side. That only left two of the men standing, and they were already in full flight. Not even looking back, both men mounted their horses in flying leaps and pounded away as fast as they could.

Micajah looked at Wiley and made a motion to let them go. Their priority now was to find out about the women and children. Even as they turned and looked at the flames that were consuming the cabin, he heard Susan shouting frantically.

"Micajah," she screamed. "Micajaaaaah. The babies are inside the cabin. We couldn't get them out. Micajah, do something."

Without a word, Micajah leapt into the flames to look for the children. He ran through the roaring furnace to the rear of the cabin where the cribs were, trying desperately to locate them amidst the choking black smoke. The terrible heat was a searing wall that Micajah fought through until at last he stumbled upon the cribs, only to find one was already almost completely consumed by flames, and the baby in the crib literally burning to death. Micajah quickly grabbed up the tiny bundle and saw it was Joshua Benjamin, and that most of his tender skin had already burned away.

Even with lungs that must have been filled with the acrid black smoke, the baby was crying. Little Josh almost never cried, and as the pitiful sound echoed through Micajah's mind there in the burning cabin, he knew he would hear it for the rest of his life. As Micajah stood looking at the tiny face with the flesh burning off it, a single tear dropped from his eye. He knew the baby would only live a few minutes at best, and the women wouldn't be able to stand seeing it in such pain. Bringing the child to his lips, he tenderly kissed the child's forehead, and then with a twist that was as gentle as possible, he snapped the tiny neck, and laid the baby back in the burning crib. He lifted his head and cursed the flames, and in the same breath he cursed the name of Moses Stegall.

"Stegall," he screamed aloud. "Stegall, you'll pay fer this in kind. May God have mercy on whatever family ye hold dear, Stegall. I swar on my child's burning body, I will be yore death and destruction."

Micajah dropped to the floor and quickly moved sideways to the crib that held little William. His crib was farther from the blazing wall and had not yet begun to burn, although the blanket the child was wrapped in had wisps of smoke rising from it. Micajah swiftly grabbed the infant and raced for the door, plunging through the flames to safety.

The wild blue flame that was ignited in Micajah's eyes there in the burning cabin as he held his dying child never again went completely out.

Handing the baby to Susan, he spoke in a voice that was no more than a soft whisper.

"It war Stegall, Susan. Our friend Moses Stegall. He told the men in town about the Cherrykee raid we went on, and thet's why they come out here and burned us out. It war Stegall's fault that er baby is dead. Stegall will pay, Susan. I swear on the Harpe name and by the power of the amulet, he will pay fer whut he's done to us. His family will pay. I made a promise whilst I stood in the flames and held my dead child, and I will keep thet promise, even if it takes ferever."

He raised his head and once again screamed to the heavens.

"Stegall. There is no escape. I will be yore death and destruction."

Susan looked into her husband's eyes and knew he spoke the truth. She had never seen him give in so completely to the Wolf. The flame in his eyes burned brighter than ever before, and there was no trace of humanity there, no trace of the man named Micajah Harpe. The only being living within the flaming blue eyes was the unholy Wolf himself.

"God help us all," Susan whispered, "the Wolf is completely loose."

As Micajah stood in the flames of the burning cabin, he had a vision of the Wolf. It seemed to him he could see deep inside the spirit cave, and he watched as the Wolf slowly gathered himself. Even as Micajah lunged through the doorway out of the flames, the Wolf lunged through the doorway of the spirit world, and into the body of the Harpe. With a quick look through Micajah's eyes, the Wolf saw he would enjoy living in the world of man again. It had been a long time since last he visited here, and he was hungry. Very hungry.

The Harpe brothers wasted no more time at the burned cabin. With hurried instructions to the women to head for the Cumberland Gap and wait for them there, the two men mounted up and rode toward Knoxville.

The first stop was at the blacksmith shop. The rifle Wiley had been using was a fair weapon, but not nearly so good as the one he'd left for the smith to work on. He hoped the stars were already inlaid in the stock, but even if they weren't, he'd still have to take the gun with him tonight. Micajah also wanted to get the twin knives he'd told the smith to hold for him.

They entered the shop and found the old smith taking a late afternoon nap on a cot near the back wall.

"Wake up, old man," Micajah said, shaking the man's arm. "I've come for the twin blades, and my brother wants his rifle. We ain't got much time, so get on with it."

The old smithy rubbed sleep from his eyes and slowly got up from the cot. He hobbled over to his workbench where the knives lay beside the rifle.

"Got the gun finished, Mister, and I think ye'll be likin' it. But I'm sorry bout these knives, I done accepted money from Mister Teil fer 'em. He'll be pickin' up tomorry."

Wiley took the gun from the old man's hand and looked at the inlaid stars. The silver gleamed in the half-light inside the shop and Wiley smiled as he saw the expert craftsmanship.

But Micajah was not smiling as he stepped over to the bench.

"Thought I told ye not to let another man buy these blades, feller," Micajah said.

"Aye, Cap'n, thet ye did, but when ye didn't come back fer 'em, I got the chanct to sell 'em and make a tidy sum, so I jist had to let Mister Teil have em."

Micajah picked up both knives and their matching tooled scabbards. Without a word he removed his belt and threaded it through the scabbards and then replaced it around his waist. He looked at the blacksmith, and for a second seemed undecided about what he intended to do. But the indecision only lasted for a second.

With a motion too fast for the eye to follow, he withdrew one of the knives and swept it viciously across the old mans neck, almost cutting off his head.

"Like I told ye afore, feller, these knives is mine, Mister Teil be damned."

The two of them quit the blacksmith shop and headed toward Hughes tavern, they had a little more unfinished business in Knoxville before they left to rendezvous with the women at the Cumberland Gap.

The Harpes walked into the dim tavern and stopped by the door. There were three men standing by the small counter, and Hughes himself was behind the bar polishing a small glass.

Micajah and Wiley walked over to the counter. "We heerd ye been a'talkin' bout us, Mister Hughes, is thet correct?" Micajah asked, with a sharp edge to his voice.

"No sir. No sir I ain't. I ain't said a word bout the two o' ye boys." Hughes was almost too scared to talk, and his eyes couldn't stop shifting around the room, as if he were frantically hoping to find help.

"I never even knowed ye kilt Mister Johnson thet night ye was in here, so how could I tell anyone bout it?" Hughes was remembering the state that Johnson's body was in when it was found, and had every reason to fear the Harpes.

"How did ye know Johnson's killin' was whut we wanted to talk to ye about, Mister Hughes? I don't recall mentionin' it." Micajah knew the man was lying, and didn't intend to spend much time with him.

Hughes had a pleading look on his face, but the brothers were unaffected by it. Wiley turned to face the other three men at the bar, "It wouldn't do fer any of ye three to be gittin' no ideas now, cause I will surely kill the first man thet moves," he said.

Even before he finished speaking, the man closet to him struck with the speed of a rattlesnake. He lunged at Wiley with a long knife in his hand, and the suddenness of the attack caught Wiley by surprise. The knife struck Wiley just below his left shoulder, cutting a gash all the way under his arm, but somehow missed the bones.

Wiley made a desperate lunge with his rifle, and it was sheer luck the stock happened to strike the man on the side of his face. Seeing that the first blow had injured his opponent, Wiley quickly brought the rifle down upon the man's head, knocking him unconscious to the floor. Wiley didn't know if the man was dead or not, and didn't have time to find out. The other two men had exploded into action as soon as they saw the knife take Wiley in the breast. One of them was moving toward Wiley at a dead run, and it was to this one Wiley first turned his attention.

Bringing his rifle up, Wiley managed to get off a single shot just as the running man crashed headlong into him, causing them both to go crashing to the rough floor. As the man hit him, Wiley dropped his rifle and managed to grab hold of the front of the man's shirt. With a rolling motion Wiley flipped the man over his shoulder as soon as they hit the floor, and completed his own flip on both knees with his long knife already in his hand, ready for any further action that would be needed.

It was soon plain to see no other action was required. Wiley's hastily fired shot had taken the man high in the chest, and he was dead before he had even crashed into Wiley.

He paid no more attention to the dead man, knowing there was still one more man somewhere in the tavern. Wiley scurried to the edge of the bar in time to see the last man crawling on all fours out the door. Wiley jumped to his feet and headed for the door, but heard Micajah talking to Hughes and decided not to give pursuit to the fleeing man. Right now Wiley needed to find Micajah.

The big Harpe wasn't hard to find.

There was a tub of dishwater sitting in the floor behind the bar, and Wiley saw his brother bending over the tub, holding Hughes head under the surface of the dirty, grease filled water. Wiley barely made out Micajah's last words to the drowning bar keeper.

"It's purty dangerous to be gittin' in the water afore ye know how to swim, feller," Micajah said, and then turned and headed toward the door, with only a glance at Wiley.

They had only gone about fifty feet when the man who had crawled out the door appeared, a rifle in his hands, and yelled at them across the narrow dirt road.

"Stop whar ye air, boys," he called, with a trace of panic in his voice. "Yer a'goin' to jail fer whut ye've done this night."

Instead of stopping, as the man had instructed, Micajah dove to the ground to the right, and Wiley to the left. The man got off a shot, which didn't come close to either brother, but Wiley's aim was much better. His one and only shot hit the man just under his left eye and blew away the back of his head. The brother's were up and moving by the time the body had hit the ground.

Their next stop was at the farm of Mister George Teil. Micajah thought he had recognized one of the men who got away from the burning cabin as one of the men who was with Teil the day of the horse race. A Mister William Ballard, he believed the man's name was.

William Ballard was indeed one of the men who had helped burn the Harpe's cabin. However, after he'd seen what had taken place at the cabin, he wished he'd never agreed to ride along. He'd never seen anything like it. The big Harpe was more like a wild animal than he was a human, and Ballard wanted no part of the man.

After helping the mob burn Harpe's cabin, Ballard didn't have a choice. It was already out of his hands, and he'd have to face the Harpes whether he wished to or not.

Ballard took several different trails as he rode back to Teil's place from the Harpe's cabin. He didn't know if he'd been recognized, and if not he would make it as hard as possible for the men to follow him. But he had been recognized, and he wasn't being followed. After leaving Hughes tavern, the Harpes made straight for

Teil's farm, and arrived there just as Ballard finished putting away his horse.

Ballard hastily removed the saddle and threw the blanket in the tack room, and then headed for the main house. But as he rounded the corner of the barn, William Ballard came face to face with the Wolf.

The eyes were on fire and the flames licked at Ballard's soul. He didn't even have a chance to cry out before Micajah killed him. Once again, Harpe's tomahawk sank into bone, and splattered brain matter all about the barnyard. William Ballard never knew what hit him, and that was the only regret the big Harpe had about killing the man so quickly. He'd rather Ballard had suffered the way the baby had.

Wiley had gone into the barn while Micajah waited outside for Ballard, and in a few minutes came walking out leading the great black horse of George Teil. "I'll be a'ridin' this horse from now on Micajah," Wiley said. "Yer horse is faster and has a little more bottom, but I'm a smaller man. I spect we'll both be hard to catch up with now."

Neither of the men looked at the body of William Ballard as they rode past it. They were on their way out of Knoxville and were headed North for the Cumberland Gap.

George Teil found the body of William Ballard lying in front of the barn early the next morning.

"Good God," he exclaimed, "who could have kilt Ballard in this fashion?"

Teil had heard the men discussing the Harpes for the last few days and was afraid the ugly talk would lead to violence, but he didn't think it would come to anything like this.

He called for a few of his hired hands to gather up the body and take it into town for burial, and then walked into the barn to check on his horses. When he discovered his black stallion was missing, he let out an oath that could have been heard for half a mile.

"The dirty scoundrels," he roared. "I'll see them hang fer this. Nobody kin ride on to George Teil's property and kill his friend then steal his best horse. Nobody." He saddled up a small brown mare and headed out on a dead run. He'd organize a posse and track down the killers if it was the last thing he ever did.

It took Teil some four hours to raise nine men who were willing to ride with him after the Harpes. Many of the men in town had seen what the Harpes could do, and most didn't want anything to do with them.

"Nonsense," Teil fumed. "Is Knoxville filled with cowards? Ain't they no men left in our fair town? Come on boys, I need a few stout men to ride with me."

When at last he had managed to raise his posse, the left Knoxville and set out to track down the killers.

Which turned out to be surprisingly easy to do. The Harpes left a wide-open trail that was easy to follow. It didn't even look as if they were trying to cover their tracks. They were headed north, toward the Gap, and it was plain they were alone. Teil guessed they would catch up with the outlaws in about two days.

He was even wrong about that.

They caught up with the brothers early the very next morning. Teil's scout found the men still half asleep, and brought the rest of the posse up quickly. They rushed out of the woods with fierce cries and surrounded the Harpes, and were surprised yet again when the men didn't even put up a fight.

"So these air yer feared killers, boys? Well, whut do ye think of 'em now? They don't look so damned mean to me." George Teil was pleased with him self, but lost most of his good nature when he found the men were on foot. There was not a horse to be seen, and neither of the men was armed. Though he tried to make the men tell where they had left the horses and weapons, neither of them would say a word. Finally resigning himself to losing his horse, Teil gave the order to head back toward Knoxville. At least the men would hang for the murders they'd committed in the past few days, and he allowed himself a grim smile when he thought about the two of them at the end of a rope.

However, Jesse Payton wasn't smiling. Jesse was the last of the men who had taken part in burning the Harpe's cabin, and he knew better than anyone in this group what Micajah was capable of. Try as he may, he couldn't understand why the men gave up without a fight. It just wasn't like them.

The small band had been traveling perhaps three hours when Teil called for a brief rest stop. After several hours in the saddle, his back had begun to ache from a wound he'd received in the battle of King's Mountain.

They were sitting on the ground resting when Micajah broke his silence and spoke to Jesse Payton.

"Ye war thar, weren't ye feller?" Harpe asked Payton. "Ye war the other one thet got away thet night? I didn't know fer shore, not till I seed ye ridin' away from me today, but now I know. It war ye, weren't it?"

"Yes Harpe, it was me," Payton said. "I ain't proud of whut we done out thar thet night, but I ain't ashamed of it neither. I truly believe ye air the white man the injuns call Wolf Spirit, and if ye air, ye deserve everthang ye got. Ye also deserve to be hanged onct we gits ye back to Knoxville, and that's what's bound to happen."

"We ain't a'goin' back to Knoxville with ye and Mister Teil," Micajah said. "But fer yer part in killin' my child, ye air a'goin to hell." The blue spark flared a little brighter in his eyes.

Payton cut the conversation short as Teil gave the order to mount up, and within a minute the southward trek was resumed.

Teil placed four of his men in front of the Harpes, and five behind them as they traveled through the woods. As an extra precaution, he had tightly tied the Harpe's hands and he personally checked their bonds every so often. Jesse Payton was the man closest to the Harpes, because Teil knew Payton would not let down his vigilance for a moment. He was too frightened of the men to take his eyes off them.

After the rest stop, Teil decided he'd try to set a little faster pace. He'd heard what Big Harpe had said to Jesse Payton, and he wanted to get to Knoxville with all possible haste. The faster pace caused his column of men to stretch out a little farther apart, so that meant Teil had to check on his prisoners a little more often. Each time he rode back to take a look, everything was all right, but he still had an uneasy feeling in the pit of his stomach.

In about an hour they came to a place in the trail where the undergrowth was not quite so dense, and the trees were much larger. Teil had been moving at a good pace, and he decided it was time to take another look at his prisoners.

The other men dropped to the grass as Teil rode back to where Jesse Payton sat on his horse. The Harpes had been walking directly behind Payton, and the rest of the men were stretched out behind them.

As Teil approached Payton he saw the man was nodding about in his saddle, as if he were asleep.

Damn the man, Teil thought.

Stopping his horse, he reached over and grabbed Payton by the arm and shook him. But rather than waking up, the man tumbled from the saddle to the ground, and George Teil could see the back of his head had been bashed in. There was no trace of the Harpes.

Although the Harpes had no weapons, Teil had no idea of the destructive force of Micajah big fist. Jesse Payton wasn't the first man to die from one of Harpe's mighty blows, and he wouldn't be the last.

Teil looked at Payton, and shouted for the rest of the men. They came in a rush, each with pistol or blade drawn, and ran out into the forest, hoping to find a trace of the Harpes. But it was as if the men were ghosts. They had vanished into the trees leaving no trace at all. It was as if they had disappeared off the face of the earth. One minute they had been there, tied up and placid, prisoners trudging through the forest in the midst of their captors. The next minute they were gone, and another man was dead.

By piecing together the story, Teil knew Payton was the last of the men who had taken part in burning out the Harpes. He hated the man was dead, but deep in his heart he secretly hoped that by killing Payton the Harpes would be satisfied with their revenge and leave the country. Maybe the killings were over, and Knoxville could get back to some kind of normal life. The Harpes had their vengeance, maybe now the country could rest.

But George Teil didn't know the Wolf. The Wolf was loose, and it was forever hungry.

33

Joseph Ballenger had been in Knoxville on business, and it was only by accident he was in Hughes's tavern the night he'd heard Mister Brown telling the story of the Harpes. As soon as he heard the mention of the Harpe name, he decided to stick around awhile and see what developed. He was glad he had. The events of the last few weeks were enough to start him thinking about another burned cabin, some twelve years ago, and about another man named Harpe.

Ballenger remembered that in the two years following that burning cabin, every man who took part in the raid met an untimely death. He now wondered if all the deaths back then were truly accidental, or were they deliberate acts of revenge. Almost the same thing had happened here in Knoxville. The Harpes had been burned out, their child killed, and this time there was no doubt they were exacting a terrible revenge on the men they held responsible.

Ballenger questioned George Teil, and came to the conclusion the Harpes had allowed themselves to be caught in order to get at Jesse Payton, and had taken their leave as soon as their business was finished. With Payton dead, Ballenger believed the Harpes would move along. There was nothing to keep them in Knoxville, and they'd be looking for another place to try to resume their lives. Ballenger planned on being right behind them. Killers such as them had to be stopped, and it was Ballenger's job to stop them. He didn't know it would be over two years before he caught up with the brothers, or that they would cut a path of blood and violence that would be un-paralleled down through history.

E. DON HARPE

34

It was a hot day near the end of August, about three weeks since the Harpes had escaped from the posse of George Teil.

A young circuit rider of the Methodist Church was riding westward along the Wilderness Road, no doubt thinking about the message he would be giving in the next small community he came to.

By the year 1797, many thousand people headed west had traveled the Wilderness Road. The road had been trampled hard by hundred of horses and wagons, and was by now almost the width of a carriage road.

On either side of the road the trees raised their branches a hundred feet or more into the sunshine and the undergrowth was thick and heavy, and sometimes as high as a man's head.

It was through this dense forest that the young Minister, one William Lambuth by name, rode this fine day.

"Stop whar ye be," came a shout from in front of him, and the young minister looked up to see a man standing in the middle of the road, a rifle in his hand.

The stranger was several inches over six feet tall, and was very muscular and strong looking. He was dressed in deerskin breeches and a leather shirt, and had no hat upon his head. Rough boots and leggings completed his outfit, along with a belt that held a pistol and a gleaming long knife.

There was a strange light shining in the man's blue eyes, almost as if a fire burned deep within them. The man just stood there, not saying a word and not moving, studying the young minister. Then another man, even bigger and more muscular, stepped from the tree and joined the first.

The two men walked over to where Lambuth sat his horse.

"I am a man of God," Lambuth said. "I have no money, and I would pass safely." Most men, even hardened outlaws, had respect for a minister.

"Get down from yore horse," the smaller of the two men said.

When Lambuth had dismounted, the two men went through his pockets and took what silver he had, along with his pistol. They led his horse to the side of the trail and tied it there. Then they took his worn Bible and ruffled the pages, hoping to find paper money. Through it all, neither of the men had spoken another word. The bigger man turned to the title page of the bible and found the owner's name, written near a picture of George Washington.

The big man looked at Lambuth and said.

"That is a brave and good man, but was a mighty rebel against the King. War yer family on the side of the revolution, er did they fight fer England?"

"My family has been ministers of God's word fer generations, Mister," Lambuth replied. "We ministered to Tories as well as to the revolutionaries."

"Is thet a fact? War ye ever up in Caroliny then?"

"Yes sir, my daddy was. He helped to ker fer the men who fit there on Kings Mountain. Were ye thar as well?"

"No sir, not us," the man answered, "but our Daddy fit thar. I reckon as how he might not take too kindly to us harmin' a man of the cloth. Be thankful yer family did not turn its back on the King's soldiers thar on the mountain, feller. It has jist saved yer life here today."

Suddenly from the trees stepped two women and three children. They were clean, though a bit ragged looking. Without haste they walked over to the men. One of the women laid a hand on the big man's arm, and gently took the Bible from his hand. Lambuth noticed the flame in the man's eyes seemed to dim, although it didn't go completely out.

The man knelt in the dirt and laid down the rest of the minister's belongings, and the smaller man handed the reins of the horse back to Lambuth. With nothing more than a deep look, the entire party turned and disappeared back into the trees.

Lambuth breathed a sigh of relief, one that was cut short by the big man's sudden re-appearance.

"Mister, air ye really a preacher?" the man said,

"Yes sir, I am," Lambuth replied.

"Well, if'n ye kin fergive sinners, then would ye say a little prayer fer the likes of us?"

"I'll do it proudly, Mister," Lambuth answered. "Who might ye be?"

"We air the Harpes," the man replied, and once again disappeared into the forest.

Perhaps it was their chance meeting with Reverend Lambuth, or perhaps Micajah had just decided he wanted to finally do something that seemed right. Whatever the reason, on September 5, 1797, the Harpes stopped long enough for Micajah and Susan to be married, and that day may have been the last time anyone heard Micajah humming his mother's song in a moment of happiness.

35

Wiley was more than a little worried about his brother. Micajah hadn't been the same since the day he had walked out of the burning cabin with only one of his children still alive. The Wolf fire never completely faded from his eyes, and he seldom laughed anymore. These days, whenever he hummed their mother's little song, the melody was sad, and held no trace of the simple joy it once had.

It had been almost three months now, and instead of getting better Micajah was growing steadily worse. More and more he was given to spending hours in dark, brooding moods that more often than not led to violence. He killed without reason, and many times now he didn't even rob his victims. The young minister named Lambuth was the only person Micajah had met in the forest and restrained from killing.

Not only that, but Wiley was worried about himself as well. Each murder brought him closer to the state of mind that Micajah was in. Though Wiley didn't wear the Amulet, he knew he was being controlled by it as much as his brother was. Soon that control would be too much for either of them to hold under control.

With the winter coming the men knew they had to find a place of shelter, and it had to be somewhere away from their normal stomping ground. They were too well known in the Knoxville area, and they needed to find a place where they could rest and decide what they intended to do.

After they had met the women at the Cumberland Gap, they had traveled west, going deeper into the Kentucky territory. They had met Lambuth on the Wilderness Road and then headed north for a while, and had spent the last few weeks traveling about the edges of the wilderness. Micajah seemed driven by some inner demon, and seemed to want only to wander about the countryside, preying upon whatever hapless traveler they came upon.

They had considered going to the rock house and staying there for a while, but had decided against it. Micajah wanted to keep it as a safe haven should they have to run quick and hide fast.

There was an old trail that ran from Hartford, crossed Green River at Benton's Ferry and then ran about very near to Caney Station, and the rock house was a mile or so off the trail. There were several hills in that country and they were deeply wooded, but Micajah wanted to head a little farther east, and so they took the lower trail instead. They knew that on the main trail that led past the lick they might find some easy pickings among the travelers who used that road as the main route East and West.

So they headed West.

In early November 1797, the Harpes came to the Ohio river for the first time. They stood on the bank, not knowing what direction to go in, and not really caring. They had heard stories of river pirates, and Micajah thought they might join up with them if they could find the place where they hid.

They decided to head south along the river for a few days and see what they could find.

About four in the afternoon that same day, they came upon a lone woodsman, resting in the shade of a large tree, with a line tied to a long slim tree limb and tossed in the water.

They made little noise as the walked along the banks, and so they came upon the man before he noticed them.

"Howdy feller," Wiley said, "how be ye today?"

Instead of answering, the man made a sudden lunge for a rifle that stood propped against the tree trunk. His right hand had no more than closed around the stock of the gun when he heard a thin whistling sound, and felt a tremendous blow to his right wrist. He stared in disbelief and shock at the tomahawk that had descended upon his arm, cutting the hand completely off at the wrist, and leaving a deep slash in the bark of the tree. The man screamed in pain and his face lost its color and he would have blacked out, except the man holding the tomahawk was shaking him violently and slapping his face to keep him awake.

"Tarnation, Micajah, we need to ask this feller some questions. Ye had no call to go a'tryin' to kill him jist yit." Wiley was upset and didn't care if Micajah liked it or not.

"If'n I aimed to kill him brother, I'd a bashed his skull stead of his arm. Now set him up against the tree so's I kin see him." Micajah didn't allow his brother's anger to affect him at all.

Wiley sat the man upright against the tree and both men squatted down in front of him.

"Ye seed any pirates round here bouts feller?" Micajah asked the half conscious man. The man didn't reply.

"Do ye know whar they might be holed up then?" Wiley tried his luck. There was still no answer from the injured man.

"I believe the cats got his tongue brother," Wiley said to Micajah.

"Pears like it brother," Micajah answered, and then fastened his huge left hand in the man's course hair. He pulled one of his long knives from his belt and looked at Wiley. "If'n the cat ain't got his tongue, brother, it won't be but a few minutes till the cat fishes do," he said, and with these words Micajah plunged his knife into the man's left cheek and jerked it downward, cutting out the man's tongue and part of his jaw. With another motion, he stabbed the bleeding tongue deftly with the point of his knife and flicked it out into the swift current.

Without hesitation, Wiley jammed the barrel of his rifle into the gaping wound of the man's mouth and blew away most of his head.

The force of the rifle shot slammed the man into the tree and then sent his body tumbling to the ground. As Wiley began to reload his rifle, he suddenly noticed the fingers on the severed hand were still contracting.

"Would ye look at thet, Micajah? I don't recall ever seein' one do thet afore." So saying, Wiley used his foot to kick the hand into the river, watching it float for a moment before sinking close to where the tongue had landed.

They didn't bother to go through the man's pockets. Within a few minutes they had filled his belly with rocks and thrown the body into the river to sink. Wiley picked up the man's pack as they walked away down the bank, noticing than the small bobber on the end of the fishing line had disappeared under the water. "Looks like the fellers gittin' a bite Micajah," he said.

"I spect he'll be gittin' a lot of em from now on, brother," Micajah replied, and kept walking.

Billy Blue and his wife Nell were seated near a small spring, dining on fried chicken and biscuits. On the ground nearby, an opened basket of food sat on a ragged old quilt, and 20 year-old Isaiah Crenshaw sat on a rock on the bank of the clear little creek, near enough to the basket he could grab a chicken leg every now and again.

Isaiah was whittling on a stick of wood, and whistling a little tune when Micajah and Wiley walked out of the woods and stopped on the opposite bank of the spring.

Wiley walked to the waters edge and knelt down and to get a drink, then stood and watched as Micajah took his turn at the water.

Isaiah saw the two men and pitched a pebble at Billy, who was laughing at something Nell has just said.

"Howdy, stranger," Isaiah said, "shore is hot today, ain't it?"

Billy and Nell looked up from their food and saw the strangers standing there. Nell smiled at the two men, but Billy just looked at them and didn't say a word.

"You got thet right, boy." Micajah said. "It is a hot 'un."

Micajah looked at the chicken Nell was holding in her hand, then went on.

"How you folks doing today?"

"We're fine mister," Billy said, speaking for the first time. "You folks headed fer Cave In Rock?"

"No sir," Wiley replied, "We'un's is headed fer Tennysee. Heerd they was plenty o' opportunity down that way fer a couple o' young fellers like us."

"Well, be careful as you travel, Billy said. "And stay well away from the cave. They say ole Mason is back up there again."

Micajah once again looked at the chicken Nell was holding, and then directed his gaze toward the food basket. Nell couldn't help but see him looking at the food.

"They say Mason ain't the worst of the lot that hangs out at the cave. They say now and then the Harpes is there."

"Well," Billy said, "everbody hopes that old Joe Ballenger has killed them bastards by now." He smiled at Nell and Isaiah. "But he ain't, and that's a fact."

Micajah shifted his eyes from the food and stared hard at Billy. The wolffire was starting to glow in his eyes as the boy spoke.

Nell once again looked at Micajah.

"Might I offer you boys a drumstick?" she asked. "I'm afraid we've already eaten everything else."

"A drumstick would be just fine, Ma'am. If'n you has one er two ye kin spare."

Micajah waded out into the river, as Wiley sat down on a rock on the other bank.

Billy picked up his rifle and held it at the ready.

"Just a second, feller," he said. "Not that I mean to imply anything, but the boy here will hand you a piece er two of the chicken. There's too many outlaws round here to fer a man to be takin' un-necessary chances."

"True enough, friend. True enough," Micajah said, as he stopped in the middle of the stream. "Don't blame ye a bit. Pays to be safe rather than sorry."

"Ye folks live here bouts," Wiley asked.

"Well, we live . . ." Nell started, and then hushed when Billy interrupted her. "Not too fur from here," he said.

Isaiah walked over and picked up the food basket and took it over to where Micajah stood in the water. Micajah took the basket and stepped back to the other bank and sat down on a rock beside Wiley. Both men helped themselves to a chicken leg and begin to gnaw hungrily.

"You boys got any money, Billy asked? "Maybe a few cents you can spare?"

As he finished the sentence he casually let the rifle point in the direction of the Harpes.

Micajah looked at Wiley and laughed. "I'll be damned. That wouldn't be a threat, now would it? Ye ain't a goin' to rob us, air ye, boy?"

"Well, the thought has crost my mind," Billy said. "That's what we do."

Wiley looked at Micajah and then turns his attention to the young man on the other bank.

"Just who air ye folks, anyway?" he asked.

Billy stood up and puffed out his chest, and smiled as Isaiah walked over and stood beside him. This was obviously something they had done before. "Boys," Billy said in his best bass voice. "You have the misfortune to have met up with the Harpe Brothers. I'm Big Harpe and this is my brother, Little Harpe."

Micajah almost choked as he tried to stop himself from laughing out loud. "Well Big Harpe," he said. "Ye don't look all that much bigger than yer brother. And yer sure as hell an ugly cuss." He paused and looked at Wiley and grinned. "I recall folks sayin' Big Harpe was a mighty handsome man."

This time it was Wiley who almost choked from trying to keep from laughing.

"It ain't the size o' our bodies the names refer to, feller," Billy said, "it's these."

He grabbed his crotch and lifted it, then turned around in a circle and laughed.

Isaiah laughed out loud and looked at Nell. Nell laughed like it was the funniest thing she had ever heard, and Billy paraded around for a moment or so on the bank.

Micajah and Wiley both laughed, and Micajah had to wipe the tears from his eyes.

Billy looked at Nell and then spoke again.

"Ain't that right little darlin'?" he said.

Nell smiled at Micajah and Wiley and then said; "He's right boys. He is the BIG Harpe and I ought to know."

Wiley looked at Micajah and grinned again. "We didn't want to mention it afore now," Wiley said, "but we is outlaws also. We air really on our way to the cave right now to meet up with our women."

Micajah stopped laughing for a minute, then looked at Billy. "We'd kind of take offense should ye try and rob us, seein' as how that's what we do too. And I'll only be tellin' ye the one time."

Suddenly, Billy sensed something about the manner of the two men. He looked over at Isaiah and fingered his rifle nervously, and then swiftly raised it and fired at Micajah.

Micajah had seen the action coming and was already diving across the branch to the bank where the boys were standing. Billy's shot missed Micajah and before the echo had died away Wiley has also leaped across the water.

Isaiah leaped at Wiley and caught him in a headlock and wrestled him to the ground as Billy quickly tried to reload. Billy looked up and saw Micajah standing over him. In Micajah's hand was the biggest long knife Billy had ever seen.

Wiley kneed Isaiah between the legs and scrambled to his feet, then kicked the boy in the head. Isaiah shook his head and tried to rise, and was quickly met by another foot to the face.

Micajah squatted down in front of Billy and began to move the knife around in small circles.

"What's yer true name, Mister?" he asked the boy.

"I told you, I'm Big H . ."

Micajah backhanded Billy across the face with his left hand.

Wiley looked over toward Micajah.

"Kiga, air ye goin to tell this feller where they went wrong, er do ye want me to do it,?" he asked.

Nell looked at Wiley, and suddenly she realized who these two men really are.

"Billy," Nell studdered, "Billy, I think…"

"Shut up, Nell," Billy said. "I told you not to call me my that name."

254

"Billy…" Nell tried again.

"Damnit, Nell, I said shut up," he almost screamed.

Micajah backhanded Billy again.

"Could be the young lady has something ye need to hear, feller," Micajah said. "Maybe ye might want to let her finish."

Nell looked at Billy again, and then looked at Micajah. The blue eyes were flaming by now, and Nell saw the fire there that so many others had seen.

"Billy," she said. "I think these men are the real Harpes." Nell looked at Micajah and smiled. "Ain't that so, Big Harpe?" she asked.

Micajah smiled back at her and winked.

Suddenly, Nell heard the sound of a knife being driven into flesh, and turned her attention from Micajah to Wiley, who had just stabbed Isaiah in the chest.

"Yes ma'am, I reckon yer right," Micajah said. "I got to tell ye, I've enjoyed this little charade, but…" He swiped the blade across Nell's neck, then looked over at the terrified Billy.

"I got to admire yer nerve feller," he said. "I guess if yer gonna pretend to be a bad man, then Big Harpe would be the man to pretend to be."

Micajah wiped the blade of the knife off on Nell's dress, then reached out and grabbed Billy. The last thing the boy who pretended to be Big Harpe saw were the blazing eyes of the true Wolf.

Just as thousands of immigrants were traveling west by land over the Cumberland mountains and down the Wilderness Road, thousands of others were traveling by boat down the Ohio River. Wooden flatboats could be bought in Pittsburgh for about a dollar a foot, and every week found more people anxious to buy one.

The most dangerous stretch of the river lay from the town of Red Bank down to the town of Smithland. The river was filled with sand bars, shoals, and small islands, all of which made the going treacherous for most of the travelers. Most of them were landsmen, and knew little or nothing of piloting a flatboat down such a river as the Ohio, and so they became easy prey for the many outlaws who made the river their home.

One of the first of these outlaws was a man named Wilson.

About sixty miles below Red Bank, Wilson set up shop in a large cave on the Illinois side of the river. On the bank he posted a large sign, which read: "Wilson's Liquor Vault and House of Entertainment." It didn't take long for the cave to become known as the "Cave Inn," which was later changed to "Cave-in-Rock," and it didn't take long for the cave to become a favorite hangout for the many outlaws who plied their ruthless trade on the river.

It was to this cave and to the Ohio River pirates that Micajah and Wiley Harpe and their women and children came in the late fall of 1797.

36

The winter of 1797-98 passed slowly. The Harpes had taken up residence in the cave but were not truly a part of the gang of outlaw pirates already living there. Micajah and Wiley had taken part in three or four raids on the flatboats, but for the most part they kept to themselves at the rear of the large cavern.

The Wolf was growing stronger with every passing day, and the rage inside Micajah grew darker and darker. None of them knew what small act might next set off that rage, but each knew for sure he could not stand to hear the cry of a baby. For some reason a babies cry could drive Micajah into acts of violence quicker than almost anything, and make him even more brutal than what they now thought of as normal.

Even though there was more than enough violence on the river, the Harpe brothers missed the forests and hill country they were accustomed to. After the winter began to fade in March, they began to plan an excursion back to more familiar ground. In the middle of May 1798, Micajah and Wiley left the cave and headed back toward eastern Kentucky. They wanted to see if it was possible that they might bring their families away from the cave and back to the woods to live once again.

At least, that was one of the reasons for the trip.

The other, and more important reason was that the Wolf had been caged all winter and was now demanding to be fed. Both men were by now almost completely under the control of the demon Wolf, and would do anything it required to satisfy the awful hunger.

The pirates secretly wanted the brothers to leave the cave, although they didn't come right out and say so. Had they exclaimed their desires, it would have brought down the wrath of the Harpes against the pirates themselves, and none of them wanted that.

There had been one or two incidents that spring which even the cruelest of the pirates found hard to accept, and if the Harpes wanted to leave, it wouldn't bother the pirates at all.

To start with, the Harpes were strange, silent brutal men, and the pirates didn't understand them in the least. They cared little for the revelry the pirates indulged in after each successful raid, and many times didn't even wait around to receive their share of the booty. They seldom drank whisky with the others, and never sat around the campfire at night telling the tall tales most of the men so dearly loved. The three Harpe children played about the cave, and the women did their share of the chores, but that was about as far as the mingling went.

The first really bad incident was the fight between Wiley and Wilson's second-in-command, a rough and rowdy grizzly of a man named Roscoe Monroe, but commonly known as "Nine Eyes."

One afternoon, Nine Eyes accused little Harpe of stealing a jug of whiskey from him, and Wiley was not about to let such an accusation go un-answered. Wiley didn't even drink whiskey, and would have allowed the man to apologize had he been so inclined, but Nine Eyes wasn't an apologetic person. He made his accusation and then turned and walked toward where his small band of friends stood waiting, intending that Wiley should fight them all if he took up the dare.

Before he'd taken three steps, Wiley had seized a good-sized rock from the floor and thrown it at Nine Eyes back, hitting the man squarely in the back of the head. Even as Nine Eyes roared in pain and fury he turned and charged Wiley at full speed. When he was almost upon him, Wiley brought his right foot up hard into Nine Eyes crotch, but the kick didn't stop the man. It fact, it was hard to tell if it even slowed him down. Nine Eyes grabbed Wiley around the neck and wrestled him to the floor of the cave, shouting at Wiley as they rolled about on the ground.

"Hit me with a rock, will ye," Nine Eyes yelled, as he slammed Wiley's head into the cave wall.

Wiley's right elbow came smashing back and caught Nine Eyes in the face, having about the same effect on the man as had the kick. Again, Nine Eyes lifted Wiley's head and smashed it violently into the rock. All this time Micajah Harpe sat on a small ledge and watched, a little smile on his face.

Wiley managed to loosen Nine Eyes grip upon his neck, and with a great show of strength he slowly pulled Nine Eyes arms apart and held them there. Suddenly turning loose of the man's right arm, Wiley once again slammed his elbow backward into the man's face, this time feeling the man's nose give way as the fragile bones splintered.

It was then that Nine Eyes made a fatal mistake.

He covered his nose with his right hand and picked himself up from the floor. Then in a loud voice he spoke to Wiley:

"Ye put up a fair fight, Harpe, comin' in like a true Kaintuck."

It was plain that Nine Eyes thought the fight was over.

"Them's good words to my ear, Nine Eyes," Wiley said softly, from his position the floor.

Then with blinding speed Wiley grabbed Nine Eyes by his arm and jerked him back down to the floor of the cave, pressing his face into the dust and dirt of the cave floor. Wiley rolled to the side and up on his knees and before Nine Eyes knew what had happened, Wiley was astraddle his back.

Still blinded by the dust and dirt, Nine Eyes felt Wiley lock his hand underneath his chin and began to kick him in the sides with his heels. He was riding the man around the cave floor like a horse or a bull, pulling harder and harder on the man's chin while Nine Eyes bucked about trying to throw him off.

"Yahoo," Micajah yelled, "ride him, Wiley."

Ride him Wiley did.

Nine Eyes hopped about on the floor, jumping and trying to rise to his feet, but being blocked in each attempt by the hard kicks of the man on his back. Wiley began to kick in a pattern, first one leg and then the other, causing Nine Eyes to turn around and around in circles. The other pirates at first thought it was funny, and the fitting end to a good fight. But the end was not at hand just yet.

With two or three last kicks, Wiley had maneuvered Nine Eyes into the position where he wanted him. It was now evident that he had been bringing the man closer and closer to the cooking fire that always burned in the middle of the cave.

Suddenly with one last kick and a shove, Wiley leaped free of Nine Eyes and in so doing shoved him down into the fire. He then jumped directly into the middle of the man's back with both feet, shoving his face and head farther down into the roaring fire. Nine Eyes screamed and jerked about but it was of no use. After the wild fight and the ride, he just didn't have the strength left to throw Wiley off. With one last stomp of his right foot, Wiley broke Nine Eyes neck and leaped free of the smoking body.

Wilson and three or four of the pirates came running over and hastily dragged Nine Eyes body out of the fire, and when they finally had him stretched out on the cool floor of the cave, Wilson turned to Wiley.

"Little Harpe, ye air a dead man. No one kin treat one of Wilson's men in this manner and go on a'livin'." Wilson was clearly of a mind to kill Wiley right there on the spot.

Advancing toward Wiley, Wilson pulled a knife from his belt and began making small circling motions with it. He was about six feet from Wiley when he noticed for the first time the strange blue flame in Wiley's eyes, and saw it was not a reflection from the fire.

Wilson stopped and looked over his shoulder at his two companions. "Stay close, boys," he told them.

Wilson took one more menacing step toward Wiley and then suddenly Micajah came off the ledge in a flying leap. He landed on the cave floor directly between his brother and Wilson and his men. With a gleaming long knife in each hand, he was crouched and ready for action as he landed.

"It war a fair fight, Wilson," Micajah said in a soft voice, "and Wiley beat yore man honest. Now as fer ye and yer men, I'm a'tellin' ye to stand down. And I'll only say it the one time."

Micajah's eyes had the same blue flame as his brothers, but were burning with greater intensity. Wilson looked at the Big Harpe, and then turned to his own men who were standing behind him.

"Aye Harpe," he answered. "T'were a fair fight, thet's true. I jist don't like the way yore brother kilt old Nine Eyes. T'weren't no call to burn him like thet."

Micajah looked at the body of the man lying in the floor, his hair and the skin on his head still smoldering.

"Dead is dead, Wilson," he said, and then pointed at Nine Eyes. "And I'd say thet man is surely dead."

Hearing the wildness barely concealed in the man's voice, Wilson wisely made no further comment. He simply motioned for the other men to remove the body and then walked away.

The Harpes went back into the semi-darkness of the interior of the cave and re-joined their women.

After the fight, the men of the pirate band no longer considered the Harpes as members of their gang, and another incident that happened five weeks later turned the pirates against the Harpes once and for all.

The pirates, being a bit shorthanded that day, asked the Harpes to take part in a raid on a flatboat belonging to a Mister Baylor, and the brothers reluctantly agreed.

There were only three men aboard the boat when the pirates took her over, and two of them were killed outright. When the pirates began looting the boat, Wilson decided on taking the boats owner captive, holding him for ransom until a letter could be sent up river demanding money from the man's family. He entrusted Mister Baylor's care to the Harpe brothers, and then he and his men set about to divide up the booty.

The Harpes were nowhere to be found as the pirates later sat about the campfire talking over the events of the day. It was a chilly spring afternoon and even though it was almost dark there was still plenty of light to see by.

Suddenly the men heard a commotion on the top of the cliff that overlooked the cave. The cliff was over a hundred feet tall and it was impossible for the men below to see what was happening at the top. As the commotion grew louder, most of the men stood up for a better view.

All at once they saw a horse come leaping off the very top of the cliff, and to their horror, there was a rider on the horse's back. With all four legs flying and the rider screaming at the top of his lungs, the two of them plunged headfirst into the rocks that made up the bank of the river, and then tumbled the rest of the way into the water. The horse and rider were swept past the stunned pirates and they could see it was none other than Mister Baylor himself, the captain of the flatboat they had just scuttled, and the man the Harpes had been holding.

They stared in horror as they saw both horse and rider were blindfolded, and Baylor had been tied naked to the horses back with a stout length of rope.

The pirates then heard wild, maniacal laughter echoing out from the top of the cliffs, and when they looked up they saw the Harpe brothers standing at the edge looking down upon them.

This was more than even the wild river pirates could abide. They were mean and vicious men, but none among them would have thought to run man and horse off the cliffs. From that day forth, the pirates secretly discussed ways they may be able to get the

Harpes to leave the cave and not return. The pirates themselves didn't feel entirely safe as long as the Harpes kept up their residence in the cave.

But the pirates didn't have much longer to worry about the brothers. Micajah and Wiley were filled with pent up rage and frustration and were already planning on leaving the cave as soon as the weather permitted.

The third week of May found the brothers headed back toward Kentucky and the Wilderness Road.

And also back toward a county sheriff named Joe Ballenger.

JOSEPH BALLENGER: 1798

Captain Joseph Ballenger was upset and more than a little mad, and all of his anger was directed at himself. He'd been a lawman almost all of his adult life. He'd survived Indian attacks and gunfights, and had captured several of the most notorious highwaymen on the frontier. He had seen men killed and scalped, and was no stranger to pain and suffering. But nothing Captain Ballenger had seen had prepared him for what was about to happen in his territory.

He'd been in Knoxville the year before when the Harpe's cabin had been burned, and felt in his heart at that time trouble was sure to come from the incident. If he was right, and the Harpes were the sons of John Harpe and were the same two men who had taken part in the John Watts Cherokee raid some years ago, they were more terrible than anyone in the territory could imagine.

Ballenger had been trying to capture the Harpes for quite some time now, and that's why he was so beside himself this morning. Last fall, he'd interviewed a minister named William Lambuth who claimed to have met the Harpes in the forest and managed to get away from them with his hide still intact. Ballenger had investigated the incident but had found no trace of the Harpes, and had heard nothing further from them in over six months.

Until this morning.

This morning a man had come into Ballenger's office with a tale so gruesome the only thing the lawman could relate it to was the terrible murders committed by the Harpes in Knoxville after their cabin had been burned.

The witness, a Mister Nathaniel Morton, had been riding along the Wilderness Road when he had noticed several large birds circling a spot some sixty or seventy feet into the trees. Getting off his horse to investigate, Mister Morton had found the bodies of two men who had been horribly killed. He offered to show Ballenger the spot where the bodies lay, and Ballenger had ridden with him into the forest.

The man was right. The men had been shot and then their heads had been split open with some large, sharp instrument. Ballenger's first thought was the weapon could have been an axe, and his second was Micajah Harpe. Ballenger knew the big tomahawk was one of the Harpes favorite means of murder.

That was why he was angry with himself. If the Harpes were back, there was no telling how many lives would be lost before they could be stopped.

Ballenger found a bedroll pack that one of the men had been carrying and in the pack he discovered a letter that told him that the men were named Paca and Bates, and they were headed West from their home in Maryland. Ballenger also found several coins in the pack, and knew whoever had killed them hadn't even taken the time to rob the bodies. It sounded more like the Harpe brothers all the time.

He searched the surrounding trails and could find no evidence at all that told him in what direction the killers had headed, nor any other signs of them for that matter.

To be on the safe side, as he rode back into town, Captain Ballenger stopped at farms and cabins along the way and told everybody to be on the lookout for the Harpes, and to keep their doors locked and their weapons loaded and close at hand. Better to be safe than sorry. He was afraid these two murders would only be the first in his territory, and he was determined to do everything he could to stop the killers before they could run wild among the settlers.

Ballenger's fears only touched upon the reality of what was about to happen in his territory. The truth was that even though Captain Joseph Ballenger was an above average lawman, all the powers he possessed would not be enough to stop the Harpes.

Not even a week had passed before the body of a man named Stanford was found. He had been slaughtered not three miles from where the bodies of Paca and Bates were discovered. Like the first two, Stanford had first been shot and then had his head bashed in.

Once again Joseph Ballenger rode out and investigated the scene, and once again found no clues at all. Again he sent out his warnings to the people, but no one had seen the Harpes.

During June and July there were no more of the savage murders in the territory and Ballenger thought maybe the brothers had moved on, but in August he was called upon to witness yet another pair of bodies.

Two unidentified men had been found floating in the river, heads bashed in and stomachs ripped out. The bodies had been in the water too long to be identified, and Ballenger knew he'd never find out who they were. Worse than that, he was now afraid he'd been wrong about the Harpes leaving the territory. Obviously the men had not stopped their rampage, they had only taken to hiding the bodies a little better.

It wasn't long before Joseph Ballenger was almost terrified to be awakened in the night, fearing someone had found still another victim of the men everyone in the territory was coming to call wild wolves.

In mid-September Ballenger rode out to the edge of the wilderness to look at two more bodies, and these proved to be the most horrendous murders anyone in the territory could ever remember.

The victims were a young man about sixteen named John Coffee, who had been on his way to the gristmill, and another man who was a stranger to Ballenger. Coffee was found lying in pool of dried blood, his throat slashed from ear to ear, and having been stabbed perhaps forty or fifty times. The stranger met the same fate as the previous four victims. A single shot in the back, and his head bashed in by the crushing power of the tomahawk.

Again, Ballenger had no doubt it was the work of the Harpes, for in the strangers pocket he found several dollars of silver, indicating his killers hadn't even taken the time to rob him. They had killed the two of them for the sheer pleasure of killing, and not for any gain of any kind.

Ballenger had no way of knowing the brothers were now almost totally under the control of the Wolf, nor would he have believed such a story had it been explained to him. The fact was the Harpes now could not stop the slaughter, for they were only instruments of destruction, being carried ever forward by the consuming appetite of the Wolf.

Companies of men went abroad armed with guns and knives, and Ballenger organized several posses, but each time it was as though the forest floor had opened and swallowed the prisoners.

October and November passed without further incident and Ballenger once again found himself hoping the Harpes had decided to quit the territory. Although he had vowed to catch them and bring them to justice for their crimes, often he lay awake at night and wished to himself they would just leave his territory. At least then his neighbors and friends would be safe from the fiendish killers, and Ballenger himself could get some much-needed rest.

"The Wilderness" was a stretch of land in central Kentucky some thirty miles wide of wild, Indian infested, un-broken forest territory, with thick undergrowth and torn by ravines and gullies. On the eastern side of the wilderness, small and self-contained, was the settlement of Little Rock Castle, and on the western border stood the town of Crab Orchard.

Before venturing to cross the wilderness, travelers would stop at one or the other of the towns and wait until there were several people assembled. They would then make up a party and cross the wilderness in a body. A man alone stood a very good chance of never reaching the other side.

In Little Rock Castle a man named John Pharris owned and operated a small tavern where travelers could stop and wait a day of so for others before crossing, and most of the time there were one or two people staying there.

On the morning of December 12, 1798, a young man named Thomas Langford had just begun to eat his breakfast when a small party of rough looking people appeared at the inn. There were two men and three women, and Langford counted three small children staying close at hand.

"Set down and have a bite of breakfast," young Langford offered the party.

"I'm afeerd we don't have the money fer to buy food, my friend," the smaller of the two men answered.

"Well, I'll not see anyone go hungry, especially women and children," Langford replied. He also noticed all three of the women were in a family way, and that made him even more determined they should have food.

"Yer a gentleman, ye air," the man said, and the members of his party sat down at the table to have breakfast with this friendly young man.

"Air ye a'headed acrost the wilderness then, feller?" the man then asked Langford.

"Yes sir, I am," Langford said, "just as soon as there is a few more people to travel with. I have no wish to cross the wilderness alone."

"Aye, and ye shouldn't crost it alone, tis true," the man said. "They air a lot of dangerous people out thar, and many redskins. Why, some say the Harpes themselves has been seed in the territory lately. Tell ye what, feller, seein' as how yer been so kind to my kin, and me ye be more than welcome to crost with us. We is headed west to the Ohio River, and maybe beyond."

"You know," Langford said, "I had meant to remain here until there was someone to travel with, but you two look like you can take care of yourselves in a scrap, so maybe I'll just accept your kind invite, and ride along with you." Langford was happy to be able to start across the wilderness this soon. He'd been afraid he might have to wait for days before enough people had gathered to make a safe crossing.

After everyone had finished eating, Langford called to Pharris for the bill, and paid for the food from a wallet fat with cash, not bothering to hide the money from anyone in the room. Under his breath, Pharris cautioned the young man about showing his money in the presence of men he did not know, but Langford was undeterred. With a laugh and a quick step, the young man fell in with his new companions and about seven o'clock that morning they headed out across the great Kentucky wilderness.

That was the last time young Thomas Langford was seen alive.

A week later his body was found in the underbrush at the bottom of a ravine. He had been stripped of his clothes and his head had been split with a stroke of a tomahawk.

This time, the killers had robbed their victim.

Some men had been driving a small herd of cattle through the wilderness when they came upon the body while rounding up a few strays. The body was taken to Pharris' inn where it was identified by Mister Pharris as being that of the young man Thomas Langford.

After the murder of Thomas Langford, Susan called Betsy and Sarah aside for a moment.

"We needs to decide something, and decide it here and now," she told them, and then cast a glance toward the three children who were sitting in the shade of a large oak tree, playing with the acorns scattered about on the ground.

"I'm afeered thet if'n we gits caught, and if'n Kiga and Wiley has to put up a fight, then they is a chanc't the chillun might get hurt, 'er mayhap even kilt. I wants to talk to Kiga about it, and I need the two 'o ye to back me up. Kin ye do it?"

"Shore sister," Betsy said, "ye know ye kin count on us. Whut do ye have in mind?"

"Well, we ain't fur from the rock house, and I would like to go thar fer a few days to rest, and onct we air thar, I want to try and talk Kiga into letting the chillun stay with some of their relatives till this is all over. They is an Uncle of Kiga's living not too fur from here, and also two of his daddy's nephews, and I believe they may take in the chillun if we asks 'em too. We kin ask they raise them as their own, should we not make it through this, and they doesn't has to know who their natural folks air. Thet way they has a chanct at makin' it in this cruel world."

"Aye, Sue," Sarah said, "thet is a good idée, but do ye think Kiga will allow it?'

"I don't know, thet's fer sure. But at the times when the Wolf is not in full control, Kiga wants to do the best fer few the chillun and us. I think he may allow it, because he knows they don't stand a chanct so long as we makes them tag along with us."

269

"Well, we will try it and see whut the Big Harpe has to say, and if'n he is for it we kin start lookin' up the kin folks."

It was less than two weeks later that Micajah walked up to the cabin of his father's brother, William Harpe, and asked if he would be willing to raise one of the boys as his own. He knew William would never reveal the relationship of the boy to his true father, and though it tugged at his heart, he felt it was the only way to be sure his son would live a full and decent life. He also knew if his uncle William raised the boy, he would not be dragged into the half darkness where he must feed the Wolf or die.

William was almost 30 years old and had been married to a good woman named Sally for the past 10 or 12 years, and he recalled the love he had had for his brother and knew he had died too early and for the wrong reasons.

Even though he could not abide the things the young Harpe boys were doing, he knew he could not turn away from taking in Micajah's son.

So it was that William Harpe, the son of Micajah and Betsy, came to live with his namesake, the elder William Harpe, and was never to know his true origin, other than the dreams that came now and then in the night.

Micajah's uncle Thomas Marion lived within walking distance, and he had a grown daughter who was only a year younger than Micajah. Her name was Mourning, and even though Susan did not know it when she named her own daughter, Micajah had recalled the name of his first cousin, and that was one reason why he never objected to the name of his daughter.

Softly and with much regret, later the next week they took little Mourning to the house of Mourning Harp, who, just as William had done, agreed to raise the child as her own. Mourning's husband John agreed with taking in the child, and did not have to tell

Micajah he would look over her just as he would were she his own flesh and blood.

Little Mourning, just as her brother William, would never know who her true parents were, nor anything of them, and in later years would not claim any relationship. However, also like William, she would have troubling nightmares all of her life, never understanding the reason behind them.

Susan never got over being sorry she had allowed the children to be raised in this fashion, but even in her later days she never revealed the truth. It was the only way they could be sure the children would not be treated with hatred over the acts of their fathers.

Micajah did draw the line when it came to James living with anyone else.

Micajah would not allow little James to be placed with any of his kin, and Susan knew when the time came it would be James who would be handed down the Amulet, and the awesome responsibility of carrying on the Harpe name.

"It was them damned Harpe bastards again, shore as I'm standin' here. It had to be."

It was some weeks later and Captain Joseph Ballenger was talking to the men that had assembled at Pharris' Inn after the body of Thomas Langford had been found. Ballenger meant to catch the killers this time, or die in the attempt. He wasn't coming in empty handed again. He had enlisted the aid of two Indian trackers, and thought they had a decent chance of running the killers to ground.

To his surprise, this time he had no trouble at all in finding the Harpe's small party. They were less than ten miles outside town, sitting on a fallen log having a bite to eat when Ballenger and his men came upon them. There were fourteen men in Ballenger's posse, and each man had a rifle or pistol leveled at the Harpes.

All three women were heavy with child, but there was no sign of the three children that had been reported as being with the Harpes. Ballenger wondered where they were, but didn't have the time nor the inclination to try and find out.

"Make just one move, and we'll kill the lot of ye right here," Ballenger called out, before stepping into the clearing and showing himself.

"Ye got us cold, Sheriff," the little Harpe said. "We'll come along peacefully with ye. Have yer men hold their far."

The men warily approached the Harpes and disarmed them, and then four men tied them with stout ropes while the remainder of the posse stood with guns cocked and aimed, ready to fire at the slightest provocation.

As they were being tied, Wiley looked at Ballenger and said, "If'n my brother offered to fight five of yore men at onct, Sheriff, would ye let us go should he win?"

"I got five boys here thet would shorely like to take ye up on thet, Little Harpe," Ballenger answered, "but I plan on seein' the both of ye swingin' at the end of a rope, and it won't be long. Naw, I reckon we'll be takin' ye in." Ballenger would have much preferred to hang the men right then and there, but he'd been a lawman too long. He'd take the Harpes back to stand trial, and then he'd see the bloody bastards hang.

It was Christmas Day, 1798.

37

Ballenger took the Harpes and their women to the jail at Stanford, Kentucky, and instructed the jailer to be sure to reinforce the doors of the jail so as to hold the prisoners.

All three of the women were pregnant and would give birth sometime in the spring, and Ballenger did his best to make them comfortable in the rough jailhouse.

He put his best deputy in charge of watching after the women, and told him to purchase whatever he needed for the women, and once again reminded him to buy whatever materials he needed to make sure the Harpe brothers didn't break out.

On the fifth of January 1799, they transferred all five of the prisoners to the jail in Danville, Kentucky, where they would stand trial in the spring.

On the eighth day of February, 1799, Betsy Harpe, for some reason now calling herself Elizabeth Walker, gave birth to a seven pound, five ounce baby boy which they named Joseph.

On the seventh of March Susan bore a daughter she named Lovie, and on the eighth of April Sarah also gave birth to a daughter, and named her Norah.

On the sixteenth day of March 1799, Micajah and Wiley took their leave of Captain Ballenger's jail. They kicked down a back wall of the wooden structure during the early pre-dawn hours and made their escape without anyone being the wiser.

They had accomplished what they had intended, and saw no reason to remain in the jail any longer. The women were in a safe, warm, dry place where they could bear the children with none of the hardships they would have known had they stayed in the forest. That was the only reason they had allowed Ballenger to capture them in the first place. Micajah was sure the goodhearted townspeople would release the women after the children were born. Everyone knew it was the men the law was after, and there was little chance the women would be put in prison. The women knew to head back to the Cave-in-the rock on the Ohio River once they were released from jail, and Micajah and Wiley would meet them there. If by some chance the women weren't set free, the men would return for them, and God help whoever stood in their way.

On the night of March 15, seeking answers to some questions that had bothered him for years, Joe Ballenger walked back to the small holding room where Micajah and Wiley were locked up. He stood for a long moment staring at the two men, as if he had never seen anybody like them. Maybe he hadn't.

"Big Harpe," Ballenger began. "That's what they call ye, is it?"

Micajah looked at Ballenger but didn't answer.

"Well sir," Ballenger went on, "I got to agree with that. Ye er a big man, and that's a natural fact. Do ye reckon as how ye could've whupped five o' my men if'n I allowed the fight to happen?"

Micajah smiled. "Well, I don't know. Maybe. I might have had to hurt one er two of purty bad if'n I hoped to win."

"Kin I ask ye a question, Harpe?"

"Shore ye kin Ballenger. I got nothing to hide."

"Did ye and yer brother kill the men back in Caroliny that murdered yer Ma and Pa?"

Micajah stood up and moved closer to the door before answering. "Yes sir, I reckon we did. We weren't nothing but lads back then, and them raiders come in the dead o' night, and there wasn't nothing we could do to save our folks. So we jist naturally took ker o' the lot o' 'em soon as we could."

"Well, at least yer honest about it. That clears up a bit of a mystery fer me. Tell me, Harpe, why did ye leave such a mess behind at old Jeremiah Massie's home? He must have done something to really get you mad."

"Massie was the man who killed er Ma, and he bragged about it to me when I went to his cabin. He had Suze and Bet thar, and he was treatin' 'em something awful. I seed whut he was doin', and I'll tell ye right now Ballenger, thet man was more evil than me and little Wiley could ever be."

"Tell me what happened after yer folks was killed, Harpe," Ballenger said. "How did you and Wiley survive?"

"Tweren't hard fer us to survive, Ballenger, not hard a'tall." Micajah looked at Ballenger for a moment, then very slightly shook his head. His eyes closed for a moment and he seemed to be deep in thought.

"The raiders come in with torches, screaming like injuns, and afore we knowed it the cabin was on fire. Pa hollered at us to get us, and then somebody shot Ma and she was dead. Just like that, she was gone. Me and Wiley was jist lads, Joe, just lads, and nobody ought to have to see their Ma killed in such a fashion." He paused.

Ballenger remained silent, not wanting to say anything that might interrupt Harpe.

"Pa made me and Wiley leave the cabin. He wouldn't let us stay and fight. I swore that night that nobody would ever keep me from fightin' again. We stood out in the dark woods and heard er Pa fightin' the raiders, and he took ker o' a bunch o' 'em. They had to take off'n their masks cause it were too hard fer 'em to see to fight, and I seed ' em ever one. Paid 'em back, too. Me'n Wiley lived in the woods like animals fer months, Ballenger, whilst we figured out what to do. We decided to kill 'em all, and then leave the country.

Massie had the two girls, and we took them with us when we left. Reckon as how they don't want to be nowhere else."

Micajah looked at Wiley, and saw that he was also reliving the events.

"We jined up with the Cherrykee and lived with them fer a spell, and saw how the while men treated them. It weren't purty, Ballenger. The whites killed the injuns and made 'em leave their homes, just like they did us. I come to have no sympathy fer no white man. We moved to Knoxville and things was fine fer a spell, then we lost everthang we had on a horse race, and things just kind of went downhill from thar." He stopped, and then stared Ballenger full in the face. Ballenger got a tiny glimpse of the blue flame, and knew what it was that scared the settlers so.

"We never had one person do us a kindness, Ballenger, with but one er two exceptions. We has seen er family killed and er homes burned. We've been accused o' crimes we did not commit, and we ain't seed the good side o' a white man in years. Tis no wonder we has no respect fer any o' the lot. I don't have many regrets, ceptin' I wish the women and chillun didn't have to be a part o' what's comin'. They ain't killed nobody, and truth be told, they has kept us in check better'n ye might think." He paused.

"Me'n little Wiley is gonna git kilt, Ballenger, and hit probably won't be too much longer afore it happens. We knows it, as surely as ye do. But our last hurrah ain't over, not yet. This country has treated us harshly, and we intend to soak the woods in blood afore we is finished."

Ballenger shook his head. "I think yer finished right now, Harpe. Yer locked up, and I have no doubt's that ye'll hang in a matter 'o days. Right here in Danville."

Wiley laughed, and Micajah grinned. It was as if they knew something that Ballenger didn't understand.

"Joe, old son," Micajah said, "I'm a dark wolf, and my brother is a horse alligator. We ain't going to hang here in Danville. The babies is borned, and they is not any reason fer us to linger here. Watch to yer locks, Ballenger, watch to yer locks. We still has a surprise er two up er sleeves."

Micajah walked over to where Wiley sat and laid his hand on his brother's shoulder. "Ain't thet right, Little Harpe, ain't thet right?"

Wiley laughed again, and Ballenger closed the door. That was the last time he saw Micajah Harpe alive.

38

The month of April was a busy month for Micajah and Wiley. After escaping from the Danville jail, they made their way south and their murderous handiwork began showing up again.

Outside the town of Columbia, in Adair County, the Harpes made their first kill since being captured in December. By this time the Wolf had not been fed in over four months, and it was more ravenous than ever before.

Around noon, the two brothers came upon a boy of about fifteen years of age who had been to his neighbors to borrow some flour and some beans. The lads name was John Trabue, and his murder was the most brutal yet. As with their other victims, they had first shot the boy and then split his head. But for some reason they mutilated the boys body with their knives, cutting it into inch long strips of bloody flesh, and leaving it where it lay in the road.

Next they headed southwest, where in Metcalf County they murdered a man named Dooley, again for no apparent reason, and then a man named Stump near Bowling Green.

On April 22nd, 1799, Governor James Garrard of Kentucky issued a proclamation offering a reward of $300.00 for each of the brothers.

When Governor Garrard placed the reward on the heads of the Harpe brothers, it spurred a rash of activity among some of the more adventurous man in the settlements.

Captain Young gathered a group of men he called his Regulators and set out to rid the country of outlaws. His primary target was the Harpes, and he meant to scour the country until he found them, and kill them wherever he came across them.

In the next few weeks, Captain Young and his men succeeded in finding and hanging some fifteen outlaws, and in temporarily clearing out the Cave In Rock safe haven, but he never got close to the Harpes. Young left a string of hanging bodies throughout the woods, but missed the two he wanted most of all.

If Captain Young and his Regulators showed up in Rock Castle, the Harpes were near Knoxville. When Young raided at Cave In Rock, the Harpes were back in Tennessee. After a few weeks of failure, Captain Young disbanded his men, and gave up his chase of the Harpe brothers. Like Ballenger, Captain Young was not there when the chase for the Harpe finally ended.

Meanwhile, in Danville the women had been tried and found not guilty, as Micajah had predicted would happen. They were released from custody and were given a horse and a good stock of provisions and told to go south, away from Kentucky and the Harpe brothers. Under no circumstances were they to attempt to rejoin the men.

Captain Ballenger had stayed in Danville for the trial, and he now followed the women out of town, but soon lost their trail. Soon thereafter they traded the horse for a canoe, and by the next day were on their way down river. They returned to the Cave-in-the-Rock, and there they waited for their men. The women had very little trouble from the pirates in the Cave, and there were two reasons for that. The first reason was the pirates were afraid of what might happen when the men returned, and the second reason was much more immediate.

Susan shot down the first man that approached them once they were back in the cave. What the man intended was plain, but Susan wanted no part of him. She fired the little pistol into the mans chest, killing him instantly, and then turned to the other pirates and said;

"Micajah and Wiley ain't the only people named Harpe in this family, I'll have ye know. Ye men best be keepin' yer distance from us."

Susan turned and grinned at Betsy and Sarah in a little private joke, before speaking again to the pirates.

"And I'll only tell ye the one time," she said, and all three women burst into laughter.

It was mid May before the Harpes struck again.

They went into Russell County on the 18th, intending to visit old man Roberts, the father of Susan and Betsy, and on the way they killed a young girl and boy they found wading in a small branch.

By this time almost every county in southern Kentucky and northern Tennessee had men out looking for the Harpes.

Every man in the territory kept their doors locked and forbade their families to go outside. The men went armed at all times, and took no chances with strangers.

"Hand me my rifle, Annie. Put the children under the bed, and bar the doors" was a common enough statement throughout the territory during those days. It was always followed by the terrifying words; "The Harpes are coming." These four words became the most dreaded sentence a man could speak, and brought chills to everyone who heard them.

Frontier men were not prone to be scared of anything, living or dead, animal or human, but the news the Harpe Brothers might be headed in their direction struck terror to the bravest of hearts.

The entire territory knew the Harpes were the most terrible murderers the frontier had ever known, and none wanted to cross with them.

However, even though the countryside was up in arms, no one was able to capture the brothers again. If a trap was set in a place where they thought the Harpes would appear, they always appeared somewhere else. They were like ghosts, appearing and doing their murderous work, then disappearing back into the oblivion of the forest.

Such was the reputation of the Harpes during this time that once when a heavily armed company of men found themselves face to face with the brothers in a small clearing in the woods, the men did nothing.

Eleven men had banded together a posse and went out looking for the Harpes, intending to bring them in if the came across them. Come across them they did, but as soon as they saw the two Harpes walk out of the trees on the other side of the clearing, the leader of the posse turned to the others and said in a whisper;

"Listen," he said, "If'n they don't start no trouble, then we'll not start any either. Maybe they'll pass us by."

For some reason, with no explanation, that's what they did.

With glowering looks that would have brought a chill to the stoutest heart, the Harpes walked across the clearing and disappeared into the woods on the other side. For the rest of their lives, the men in the posse never lived down the fact they had met the Harpes and hadn't the courage to challenge them.

James and Robert Brassel rode out of Barboursville on a beautiful day in early June and had hardly ridden a mile when they happened to meet with two men traveling the same road.

The men were rough looking and had a fierce countenance and the Brassel brothers were understandably a little nervous when the men stopped them.

"Who might ye be?" the smaller of the men asked the Brassel's.

"We air the Brassel brothers, stranger. My name is James and this is Robert. We just left Barboursville on our way south to visit relatives. Who are the two of ye, if I might ask?"

"We be deputy Sheriff's fer Captain Ballenger, out of Stanford," the bigger man answered. "We air lookin' fer the terrible Harpe brothers. They has kilt many a man around these parts, and we means to stop 'em. They is a big reward on their heads, enough to make a feller rich, were he lucky enough to kill them two rascals."

Then the smaller of the two men spoke.

"We means to stop em'" he said. "And we means to collect thet reward. Has ye seen anything of 'em in yore journey?"

"No sir, we haven't. Ye two are the first people we've run into today," Robert Brassel said.

Neither of the men said anything for a minute, then the big man looked at the smaller one.

"Ye know," he said, "I wouldn't be none too surprised if'n these two men ain't the Harpes themselves."

"I reckon as how they could be," the other answered. "They look suspicious to me. Maybe we oughta take 'em back to old Ballenger"

"Maybe we should at thet," the big one said, as he reached for the pistol at his side.

"Now wait a minute, fellers," Robert Brassel said. "We are not the Harpes, and the two of you have no cause to be takin' us anywhere."

"Hold on brother," James said. "Mayhap the deputies has a reason. Everbody in the countryside has heard of the Harpes, and Ballenger wants 'em terrible bad. Could be we might oughtn ride on back to Stanford with them."

But Robert, who was of a much more suspicious nature than his brother, suddenly leaned over his horses neck and kicked the animal

283

into a run. If he had to meet Captain Ballenger, he'd do it by himself, and not at the hands of two strangers.

Robert had only ridden about half a mile when he came upon a party of men, all acquaintances of his, who were also out looking for the Harpes. He quickly told them what had happened, and all of them together went racing back along the road.

In a matter of minutes the party came to where the strangers had stopped the Brassel brothers, only to find the body of James Brassel lying beside the road, his throat slashed and his head caved in. James' rifle, still loaded, had been smashed to pieces against a tree, and also left by the side of the road.

The posse knew they could not be more than a few minutes behind the killers, but all of their searching was in vain. It was like the many other times when the Harpes had seemingly vanished into thin air.

With so many kills in the past few months, now the Harpe brothers were more like wild wolves than ever. During the next few weeks they appeared in numerous parts of the country, mostly in regions that were sparsely populated, and each time left a broad path of death and destruction behind them when they quit the area.

Two brothers named Tittsworth, along with their families and several slaves were murdered in their sleep near the small settlement called Dromgooles Station. Three Cherokee braves were found nearby, their bodies mutilated and scalped.

In the same vicinity, and in much the same manner, the Harpes murdered John Tully and Thomas Stockton, this time taking their scalps as grisly trophies.

A day or so later the body of a man identified as a Mister Trowbridge was found on the side of the trail. He had been returning from the salt lick when he ran into Micajah and Wiley.

It didn't seem to matter that the entire country was up in arms, nor that the reward was more than a man could earn in a full years work. The Harpes couldn't be caught. They moved around as if they knew where each posse was searching, and by their cunning and stealth eluded even the most diligent hunters.

It was clear they were headed West, but it was anyone's guess as to exactly where in the West the Harpes would turn up.

It was the last week in June when they finally reached their destination.

To the dismay of the pirates at the Cave-in-the-rock, one afternoon two rough looking horsemen touched shore on the Illinois side of the river and the Harpes were once again inhabitants of the cave. All this time they had been en-route to the cave to re-unite with the women and children, and the many ruthless murders had been nothing more than random acts of violence against anyone they happened to come across as they traveled.

But this time the pirates had little to worry about from the Harpes. From the day they came until the day they left was less than a month. The pickings on the river were slim, and the Harpes craved action. More than that, they now lived under a dreadful and constant desire to feed the Wolf.

The last week of July found the Harpes packing their meager belongings and leaving the Cave-in-the-Rock for the green killing fields of southern Kentucky and Middle Tennessee. As they were leaving that part of the country, Micajah had decided it was time to visit their old friend Moses Stegall.

Micajah, even though the rage was black in his mind at all times, had not forgotten the man he held responsible for their downfall. It was time to settle an old debt, once and for all.

39

During the past few days, Susan had noticed Micajah humming the little song, and she wondered if her husband was a little nervous about leaving the safety of the cave.

It wasn't like the Harpe to be nervous about anything, but Susan knew the signs, and she knew there was something on his mind. Something out of the ordinary.

She had never seen her husband more dangerous than he was as that hot, torrid month of July 1799, drew to a close.

A summer storm was whipping the waters of the Ohio, and overhead huge black clouds raced across the sky. La Belle Rivere, as many called the Ohio, was raging, but not anymore so than the storm that was brewing inside the heart of Micajah Harpe.

Micajah stood at the mouth of the cave, staring out across the empty water, but it was plain his mind was elsewhere. There had been no flatboat travelers for almost two weeks, and Harpe was growing tired of the endless boredom of sitting around the damp, hot cave. The Wolf was hungry, and growing more impatient with each day. During the summer the Wolf had become used to feeding well, and even a few days without a kill brought about an anxious feeling that was hard to ignore.

Yes, thought Harpe, as he prowled the riverbank. *It's definitely time to go.*

The voice inside answered:

Yesssssss, Harrrrpe, hunnnngrrrry. Weeee mussst hunnnnt.

Micajah was restless. He could feel the flames inside growing hotter and hotter, and he knew he must release the Wolf lest he himself become consumed by the fire. The hunger demanded blood, and if not the blood of strangers, then the blood of friends.

"Soon," he whispered. "Soon we'll go."

Wiley Harpe lay on a ledge just inside the cave, watching his brother pace the riverbank. He too knew the signs, and he knew that unless a flatboat appeared on the river today, they would be leaving their sanctuary.

We'll be riding back down into Kaintuck fer shore Wiley thought. *Kiga is anxious fer a kill, and Stegall is weighing on his mind something fierce these days. It's apt to be hotter than the fires of hell itself down thar fer us right now, but I don't spect thet'll stop Micajah.*

The truth was that even knowing every man in Kentucky was looking for them, and would hang them without a word was not enough to stop Wiley either. His soul was a twin to his brothers, and burned with the same Wolf fire. Wiley craved the raging thrill of fresh blood as much as his brother did.

As if he could read his brother's thoughts, Micajah stopped his pacing and returned to the cave. His great bushy eyebrows were arched, and his wild blue eyes were turbulent. He stalked around the uneven floor of the cave like a wild animal, caged and wanting to break free.

Very seldom did the big Harpe get this upset. Wiley could only guess it was because he had allowed his mind to dwell for too long on his revenge against Moses Stegall. Micajah hadn't been the same since the man betrayed them, causing the people in Knoxville to burn their cabin and one of their children to die in the flames.

God, thought Wiley, *when he gits this way, he almost even scares me.*

Then Micajah spoke. "Saddle up brother," his voice was a savage whisper, "we got some geese jist a'waitin' fer to be plucked."

"I been ready to go fer nigh on to a week brother," Wiley replied. "We been too long in the cave to suit my taste."

Next Micajah turned to Susan, standing half hidden in the shadows. "Bring little James here to me woman. I think ye know I got something I need to give the boy, and a few things I wish to say to you. Now, I don't want ye to mis-understand me, this time is jist like all the other times we rode out of here. I don't believe they is a man in Kaintuck thet kin kill the Harpe, but this time the whole country is up in arms agin us, and you can't tell when one of the rascals might git lucky. Anyway, if'n somethin' war to happen to me and Wiley, I want all ye women to take the chillun and head down toward the middle Tennyssee territory. They don't know us too well down thar, and I believe ye will be safe. If'n ye has to go, then remember thet we'll catch up with ye. We always has, and we always will. If'n it takes a week, er a year, er a hunnert years, I'll come fer ye. Jist git ye down thar and wait a spell, and don't never doubt my word. I'll come fer ye, Susan, and I'll only tell ye the one time."

Micajah looked at his son and motioned him closer. "James, stand over here. I got something that is now rightfully yore's."

He slowly removed the leather thong that held the amulet from his own neck and showed it to Susan and the boy. The silver star gleamed in the light from the mouth of the cave, and the blood red of its background didn't seem quite so foreboding.

"Ye know what this is Susan, ye've seen it around my neck fer these many years. Tis the Harpe Amulet, the mystical silver star of the Wolf that the Harpes has been chosen to wear. It's been passed down from generation to generation, and now tis time I placed it about the neck of my own firstborn son. Yer a might too young to understand all of this right now, James, but yer Mama kin explain part of it to ye in a few years. Son, they is an awful power locked in this Amulet, one ye kin call on fer help when times is darkest. But the power carries a terrible price. When ye call on it, the Wolf will come, and will do yer biddin'. But the Wolf is always hungry, boy, and it be up to ye to keep him fed. Use the power if ye must, son, but use it wisely. If'n ye don't master the Wolf, the Wolf will master ye. Now, hold out yer right hand."

The boy trustingly put his small hand into the hand of his father, with no sign of fear nor doubt in his eyes. Micajah used the sharp point of the star to make a small cut in the boy's index finger, and solemnly smeared the blood on the face of the amulet. He watched, as the talisman seemed to absorb the blood into itself. From this day forward the boy would be as one with the Amulet, just as surely as each Harpe had been before him.

In an uncharacteristic display of tenderness, Micajah laid his huge hand on his son's head and whispered, almost to himself, "Use it better than I have son, and it will serve ye well."

Turning away from his wife and son, Micajah walked across the cave to where Wiley stood waiting. As he walked he removed one of the great long knives from his belt.

"Wiley, I've sent many a man to his grave with this blade, and I trust it completely. It's never failed me yet. This time I ain't takin' it with me. I'm fixin' to hide it here in the cave, and part of the Wolf power will remain with it. If'n we has to ride back here in a hurry, then it'll be a'waitin' fer me. If'n we don't make it this time, then mayhap another Harpe might need it at a later date."

He turned and walked back into the cave, going deeper and deeper into the darkness until he found just the place he was looking for. About shoulder high he found a small crevice, and it was into the crevice that Micajah placed the knife. Walking outside, he picked up a huge river rock and took it back to the crevice where he'd hidden the knife. Knowing few men would be able to move the rock, he wedged it deeply into the crevice, securely sealing the knife inside. Knowing the knife would be waiting whenever a Harpe had need of a trusted weapon, Micajah said his goodbyes to the women and children, mounted his horse, and he and Wiley rode out of the cave.

Betsy and Sarah moved from where they had been standing and joined Susan at the mouth of the cave. They watched the men until they were out of sight, then Betsy asked; "Do ye think they'll be returnin' this time, Susie?"

"I'm afeerd fer 'em Betsy, this time is different. T'ain't like afore. They is more people around ever day, and since thet Kaintuck Gazette newspaper printed thet story bout the boys, everbody out thar is a'lookin' fer 'em. Old Colonel Trabue has vowed never to rest until he see's Kiga dead fer killin' his boy, and thet infernal Captain Joseph Ballenger and Silas McBee is always a'nosin' round. The boy's is headed fer a showdown with Moses Stegall, and Lord knows he can't be trusted. Naw, Bets, I'm right afeerd fer 'em this time."

"I don't blame Kiga fer huntin' down Stegall, Susie. Stegall deserves killin' fer whut he done to the baby, and the Big Harpe ain't about to let him go free forever."

"I know thet's true sister," Susan said, "but Stegall is a dangerous man. He's afeerd of the Harpe, and thet'll make him even more worse. If'n he gits cornered he'll try and pull one of his tricks like he always does. He's had too many dirty dealin's with the boys to try and turn 'em in to Ballenger, but he will try somethin', ye kin mark my word on thet. And the Harpe ain't wearin' the Amulet this time."

"True enough, sister, true enough. I got me a bad feelin' this time also." There was an air of sadness about Betsy that was out of character and the other two women noticed it.

Susan looked at Betsy and Sarah. Trying to keep the feelings inside her from showing in her voice, she told them, "Girls, pack yer things, it's time we joined the men. If they is to die, I think we need to be close at hand. We was with them at the beginnin' of this mess, and we should be near them at the end. The Harpe said they was headed to Moses Stegall's place, so if we hurry and take the direct trail, we'll likely catch up with them afore they get thar. Get yer stuff together, we got chillun to tend to, and we got to make the best of things."

Susan reached out and patted James Thornton on the head. The boy had just turned nine, and around his neck he wore the Harpe Amulet, the only material legacy of the Harpe family.

Susan held the boy's head with both hands and looked deep into his eyes. In a voice choked with emotion, and without taking her eyes off her son's face, she said:

"I believe this necklace is a cursed thing, and I believe it has brought naught but heartache and hard times to the Harpe men whut has wore it. Mayhap it does have some sorty strange power fer the men, but it wants too much of 'em. It drinks their souls dry and in the end it feeds upon them the same as it feeds upon their enemies. This innocent child is my eldest, and I'll not inflict upon him the eternal damnation of the Harpe."

With these words, Susan removed the Amulet from the child's neck. She placed it in a small leather pouch and put the pouch inside the bodice of her dress. There it would rest until the day Susan Harpe herself decided to pass it along. When she finally did, it would be to a daughter, not a son. It would be available to the Harpe men, should they have a great need of it, but if Susan had her way it would never again claim the heart and soul of a first born Harpe son.

The Harpe was not in a hurry. Knowing a kill was only hours away had aroused the Wolf, and knowing it was Stegall who was to be killed made Micajah want to savor every minute.

But first there was the matter of paying a call to Silas McBee. The man had been a thorn in the Harpe's side since their Pa fought at King's Mountain, and Micajah wanted to take care of him while he was this close to where McBee lived.

The women rejoined the men two days later, near the trail to Stegall's. If Micajah objected, or if he had any thoughts about Susan disobeying his last order, he kept it all to himself. For the rest of the day, he could be heard softly humming his mothers little melody.

When Jim Tompkins heard the knock on his door, he carefully laid his Bible on the table underneath the lamp and went to see who had come calling this late in the afternoon.

When he opened the door, he saw a huge dark man standing there. Although he looked menacing, the man had a smile on his face and was very polite when he spoke.

"Mister Tompkins, we'd shore appreciate it if you'd allow us to come in fer a spell," the big man said. "Silas McBee told us yer name and whar you lived onct a year er so ago, and said we'd be welcome in yer house should we stop by."

"Well, sir," Jim Tompkins replied, "I don't hardly see how I kin turn no strangers away from my door. How many of ye is there?"

"They is me and my brother," the man said, as he stepped inside the cabin. If he noticed the worn and well Bible lying on the small table by a coal oil lamp, he gave no indication of it.

"We has er wives and 2 chillun, and they is a also lady who is travelin' with us up to Greenville,"

"Well, sir," Tompkins said again, "just put yore horses in the barn, and come on in. Yer just in time fer supper. We're having fresh caught catfish, and some sallet greens I picked just this morning. Sorry we ain't got no more'n that, but yer welcome to it, sich as it is."

"We'll be a thankin' ye, sir," the man said. "We ain't eat a set down meal in many a moon. Good home cookin', regardless of what the dish is, will be mighty tasty along about now."

"What kind of work do you and yer brother do, Mister, er, I don't believe I got yer name, young feller." Jim Tompkins looked the question at the big man standing just inside his doorway, and it was plain he wanted an answer.

"My name is Jim Walker and the young man puttin' up the horses is my brother Horace," the man answered. "And we er travelin' ministers o' the Lord. We air headed out across the wilderness to spread the gospel."

With that, the big man reached into a pack that one of the women was carrying and pulled out a weathered Bible. Without hesitation, he then pointed to Tompkins's Bible that was on the table.

"I see ye air God fearin' man, Mister Tompkins," he asked. "And thet makes all the difference in the world to me and my brother. If'n ye don't mind, I'll be wantin' to say a prayer afore we has supper."

"Yessir, Mister Walker," Tompkins said, "yer right about that. I am indeed a God fearin' man, and the prayer'll be more'n appreciated. My wife has been sick, and I run out of powder a week er so ago. Haven't been able to get to town to buy any, and we've been living off'n these cat fish and little old corn dodgers fer a while now."

"You got no powder, you say?" the big man said.

"None a'tall," Tompkins answered, "and it just ain't safe around here with no way to protect yer family."

"No sir, it ain't," the big man said. "Why just yesterday, over near Rock Castle, we heard the Harpes is about. A man has to be careful with them two scoundrels near. They is bad men, and it's wise fer a man to have a loaded rifle handy, just in case."

"Yore surely right about that, Mister Walker," Tompkins said, "And I plan on gittin' to town just as soon as my wife is up and about."

"Well, sir, seein' as how yer so hospitable, and seein' as how I has plenty o' powder, why don't I jist let you have a bit. Do ye have a tea cup I can use?"

"Why, I couldn't take yer powder, Mister Walker, what would you do if you should meet the Harpes?"

"Well, sir, we has plenty o' powder, and we won't miss a bit of it. You need it to protect your family, and besides, we air men o' God, and don't fear the Harpes as much as some men do. Ye know they let that Lambuth minister go a few years ago, and we'll jist trust in the Lord they'll be so kind to us, should we meet up with em'."

The big man said a long and arduous prayer over supper, then retired early and the party slept through an uneventful night.

Jim Tompkins and his wife slept the sleep of the innocent, never knowing the Harpes were only feet away, never knowing the quirk of chance that had caused him to lay his Bible on the table in plain sight had been all that had spared them this night.

They took their time as they rode southward from the river, and down into Kentucky. Micajah silently prayed they would find McBee at home, but knew the true target of this trip was Moses Stegall. McBee would be a tasty victim, but not as important as finding and killing Stegall.

They came to the cabin of Silas McBee about mid afternoon, and watched the cabin for a little over an hour. Micajah saw a pack of large dogs about the cabin, and knew if they decided to attack McBee they'd have the dogs to contend with. It was touch and go for a while, but when two men rode into the clearing and went into McBee's home, Micajah decided to forget McBee and head for Stegall's place. They could catch McBee anytime, and Micajah's thirst for the blood of his old friend Moses Stegall was too strong for him to want to waste time fighting a pack of dogs.

The dogs set up a huge caterwauling as the Harpes silently rode away, but McBee and his guests never got a glimpse of the two men, nor knew how close they had been to a violent death at the hands of the Wolf.

Even moving slowly, they reached the cabin of Moses Stegall in less than two hours.

Shortly before sunset, they rode into the cleared front yard of the cabin and Micajah called out for Stegall.

"Hello the house," he called. "Open up Moses, and greet yore old friends."

From inside the house came the sound of the bar being removed from the door. The door groaned, and a tiny crack appeared. Whoever was opening the door was being very cautious, and wanted to be sure of the identity of the visitors. An eye appeared in the door's crack, followed closely by the barrel of a rifle.

"Who's out there?" a timid female voice asked.

"Friends of Moses Stegall. Open the door and have a look," the big Harpe replied.

The door opened the rest of the way, revealing a pretty but thin faced young woman. She looked to be in her early thirties, and had soft white skin and long thick auburn hair. Her eyes were also dark, and showed tiny sparks of fear when she recognized the two men standing at her door.

"Mister Stegall is not here at the present," she said. "But I do have two house guests." She added this last statement obviously thinking it may deter the Harpes from any violence at the cabin, seeing as how her husband wasn't at home.

She didn't reckon on the fact the Harpes had been too long without a kill, and if Stegall wasn't at home, they would feed the Wolf on whatever hapless souls happened to be in the home of their enemy. Man, woman, or child, it made little difference to the Harpes at this time. The Wolf demanded hot red blood, and the sooner the better.

"We'd like to spend the night, Missus Stegall, if'n we might, and see if'n old Moses might return. Would ye be so kind as to put us up?" Micajah asked. Then, almost as if it were an afterthought, he said, "Whar might yore husband be, Missus Stegall? I'd shorely like to see him."

"I've never yet turned a traveler away from my door, Micajah Harpe, and ye know it," Mrs. Stegall said. "Yer welcome here fer as long as ye need to stay. Mister Stegall has ridden over toward the wilderness to see about sellin' a horse." That wasn't the truth, but she knew if the Harpes found out Moses was only a half-mile away at a neighbors house gambling, they'd be sure to find him there.

"As long as they is others in the house, Missus Stegall, it'd be best if'n ye would not call us by the name of Harpe. It might frighten yore guests, and we don't wish to do thet. Tell 'em we is travelin' ministers, and make arrangements fer each of them to sleep in the room with one of us. We don't wish to wake up in the morning with Captain Ballenger settin' outside the cabin." Micajah held the girls arm as he spoke to her, letting her feel the intensity in his voice as well as hear it.

Mary Stegall did as she was told. Her guests were a surveyor by the name of Major William Love and a nineteen-year-old boy named Hillis Packard. Both men were there to see Moses, and like the Harpes had decided to stay the night. Mary put Wiley in with young Packard for the night, and sent Micajah to sleep in the room with Major Love.

Both men gave their lifeblood to the Wolf during the night. Hillis Packard's throat was slashed from ear to ear, and Michael Love's skull was split open with a single blow from Micajah's tomahawk.

Dawn the next morning found Mary Stegall up and moving about in her kitchen, while she held her five-month-old son. The child made a few crying sounds every now and then, and as she lay it back in it's crib she hushed it as best she could. She had begun rolling out the dough for the biscuits when Micajah and Wiley appeared.

"I hope the crying of my baby didn't disturb yore sleep last night," she said. "The child has a touch of the colic and was awake fer hours. I must hold him almost ever minute to keep him from crying, and tis a tiresome chore."

"Why, Missus Stegall," the big Harpe said, "you know I have babes of my own. I'll be only too happy to hold the child whilst you finish preparin' breakfast."

Partially calmed by the Harpe's words, Mary Stegall walked to the crib, picked up the tiny infant, and placed it in the huge killers arms. As soon the baby felt the absence of his mother, it once again began to cry. "I'll only be a short time with yer food," she said.

Her footsteps back into the kitchen had not died away before Harpe had his knife in his hand. He gently laid the baby back into its crib and without a sound softly drew the razor sharp blade across the throat of the tender child.

The Harpes once again entered the kitchen and sat down for their meal. Thinking the babe asleep, Mary Stegall fussed around the kitchen while they ate, unsure of what the two violent men might do next. For a passing minute she wondered why the other two men were not yet up and about, but was afraid to ask any questions. Finally, seeing the Harpes calmly sitting at the table eating, she decided to look in upon her child. The baby had not made any sounds for quite some time now, and she went to check. Tiptoeing to the side of the crib, she slowly pulled back the covers from the tiny face. Horror seized the young mothers soul when she saw her tender helpless infant lying breathless, it's throat sliced from ear to ear, almost floating in it's own innocent blood. She shrank back in terror from the shocking spectacle and fell against the wall. She uttered a loud and frightful scream as her blood pounded in her veins.

Some sixth sense caused her to look up, and she saw the big Harpe standing over her, holding a long knife that still dripped with her child's blood, wearing a terrible smile upon his face. Worst of all was the raging blue flame that burned in his eyes, and seemed to consume Mary Stegall's soul. She scarcely felt the big hand when it wrapped itself in her long black hair, and she never knew the kiss of the blade as it was slowly pulled across her exposed neck.

Outside the house, her neighbor Elijah Williams was bringing Mrs. Stegall a bucket of cool water from the spring when he heard her chilling scream. Seeing two men walk out of the door, he suspected the worst, and ran back to the spring where he hid in a dense cluster of undergrowth. There he remained for several hours, until Moses Stegall returned home and found the tragedy.

As Mary Stegall slumped against the wall, her lifeblood draining onto the cabin floor, the Harpes returned to the kitchen and finished their meal. Washing down the last bite of the fried egg, Micajah spun around on the bench where he sat. "I told ye we would find a good set down meal here, didn't I brother?"

"Ye shorely did, Kiga, but I reckon it's time we taken our leave. We'll catch up with Stegall in the forest. He won't stray too far from home, seein' as how he knows they's some dangerous men in these woods." Wiley laughed at his little joke.

"Yore right, brother, I reckon," Micajah answered. "But afore we leave I think I'll warm this here cabin up for old Moses."

Laughing, Micajah stood up and kicked the table into the fireplace, scattering the glowing coals over the tiny kitchen area.

"Won't take long fer the cabin to burn, and we'll be well away afore anybody kin catch up with us."

Micajah and Wiley left the burning cabin and headed into the forest, hoping the smoke would attract not only Moses Stegall, but perhaps the good squire McBee as well.

The smoke did attract Squire McBee. He and Jim Tompkins stood in the ashes of the burned cabin, knowing this was the work of the Harpes, and knowing this time they had to find the brothers. With a look of anger and resignation on his face, McBee sent Tompkins to find John Leiper, with instructions to put together a possee and run the Harpes to the ground. Their wild rampage through the countryside had to be stopped, and it had to be stopped now.

The Harpes had lived as wolves, so must they now die as wolves.

40

Captain Joseph Ballenger was not far away. He'd been searching the woods with an almost fanatical fervor since the Harpes had escaped from the jail in Danville. He'd followed their bloody trail across Kentucky for months now, and was determined to bring them to justice once and for all. The fact that he had lost the trail of the women when they'd been released from jail only made him that much more determined. He had known many of the Harpes victims personally, and that also made the situation even worse.

Ballenger was a man with a strong will, and deeply set in his ways. He'd keep after the Harpes till hell froze over if need be, and catch them sooner or later.

Not knowing Stegall and the mysterious "Mister Brown" in Knoxville were one and the same was just another of the small things that seemed to be working against Ballenger. If he had known, he would have watched the cabin of Stegall until the Harpes came to call.

But he didn't know, and he wasn't watching the cabin, and when he heard of the Stegall killings he was almost a full days ride away. He almost killed his horse in pursuit of the company of men Stegall and John Leiper were leading after the fleeing Harpes. He'd get there in time for the kill, damn it. Even if it meant running two horses into the ground.

Neither the Harpes nor Mary Stegall had any way of knowing Moses had actually returned home about an hour before dawn. He'd seen the big black stallion of Micajah Harpe and recognized the animal at once. Knowing what awaited him should the Harpes find him, Moses decided to ride back down the road and enlist the aid of Squire McBee, knowing the man would be eager to catch up with the Harpes.

Stegall didn't think twice about leaving his wife and child in the same house with the savage killers. Moses knew the Harpes might take their revenge on his family, but it never crossed his mind to go inside and confront his two old enemies.

Moses Stegall was not a cowardly man, but he knew better than anyone else the rage of the Harpe brothers, and rather than risk his own life, he elected to go for help, praying he could get back before anything happened to Mary and the baby.

It was not a particularly good risk.

When Moses Stegall next rode into his own yard, the cabin was in flames and the Harpes were nowhere to be found.

MOSES STEGALL

Moses Stegall and Silas McBee rode back to the Stegall cabin about seven-thirty that morning and were still a quarter mile away when they saw the smoke.

Knowing the worst may have happened, McBee galloped off as quickly as his horse could carry him. He had to raise a posse, and he knew John Leiper was visiting at the cabin of Jim Tompkins. He hoped to find them both there and knew they would help him find a few more able riders.

Coming into sight of his cabin, Stegall's worst fears were realized. The cabin was in smoking ruins, and there was no sign of his wife and child, nor of the houseguests that were there when he'd left. Moses rushed forward calling his wife's name.

"Mary. Mary," he shouted. "Come out if you hear me." But he wasn't really surprised when his wife didn't answer. He hadn't actually thought he'd find her hiding in the trees.

Turning his attention to the still smoldering ashes, Moses began frantically searching. Inside the partially burned cabin, he found the remains of his Mary and of their only child, as well as the mutilated bodies of his two guests. Stegall knew without a doubt who it was that had committed this atrocity.

"Micajah. Kiga Harpe," he screamed. With every breath Moses cursed the Harpes. No other people in the country, not even the Indians, were this brutal in their killings.

Moses had thought the brothers to still be down south in Tennessee, but he knew how they liked to travel, and he knew they had never forgiven him for his part in the killing of their own child, back in Knoxville. If he had known they were once again on the prowl, he'd have moved his family around until he could have found a safer place.

Walking outside and laying down his wife's body, Moses Stegall turned his face upward and shouted to the heavens.

"May God place a curse upon ye, ole Kage Harpe, and may he also guide my footsteps until I find ye. I swear ye'll pay fer whut ye've done to my family."

"Stegall. Hello thar, Stegall," he heard someone calling from the trees, and turned to find his neighbor, Elijah Williams, coming out of his place of concealment.

"Elijah, thank God yore here. Kin ye tell me whut happened?" Stegall was almost shouting.

"I was at the spring, drawing water fer Missus Stegall, when all of a sudden I heerd her a'screamin'." Elijah Williams was still very excited also, and his voice was distraught and filled with emotion. "I run back toward the house as quickly as my feet would carry me, and run straight into two of the most fierce men I have ever met. They were huge men, with dark bushy hair, and with scalps at their belts. The biggest of the two had a great, long knife in his hand, and they both had the strangest blue eyes ever I seed. They was on fire, they was. I shouted at them fer to stop, but they paid me no attention. They jist mounted up and rode off."

"Yer a lucky man, Elijah, thet the big Harpe didn't hear ye shout. For if'n he had, you'd likely be as dead as the others. He would have cut ye stem to stern and probably throwed yer body in the spring. I know the man, and when the rage is upon him ten men kin seldom contain him. He kills every man whut gits in his way. Yes, Elijah, yore a lucky man, fer a fact."

Moses looked at the cabin again, and then once again turned his attention to Elijah.

"Tell me whut direction they rode off in, Elijah, and then alert the other neighbors. Find Silas McBee and John Leiper and tell them which direction we air headed in. They're gatherin' a company of good strong boys and ye need to tell 'em to git back here as quickly as possible. If'n we make haste, we might overtake the scoundrels afore they kin find other victims."

Stegall knew John Leiper had a horse that might be able to keep up with the big black horse the Harpe rode. John was a brave man, and though he was quick and strong, Stegall knew he was no match for either of the Harpes, especially Micajah. All Stegall wanted Leiper to do, on his fine horse, was to catch up with the Harpes and leave a good trail. It might take several days, but the rest of the company would catch up in due time, and they'd end this matter once and for all. The Harpe was too dangerous to be allowed to roam the countryside any longer, and Moses Stegall meant to see him dead this time.

As Moses finished patting the last shovel of dirt into the make shift graves of his family, he heard the company of men riding into his yard. There were some 12 or 13 of them, and Stegall knew they would scarce be enough. He took a few more moments to saddle his own horse and explain to John Leiper what he wanted him to do, and the men set off at a gallop.

Stegall thought about the times he had seen Harpe in battle, and prayed the small company of men would be enough. Harpe was an awesome sight to behold when he fought. Fearing neither God nor Devil, man nor beast, the big Harpe was a man perfectly suited for the terrible profession he followed. Some men would argue that a man who would kill helpless women and babies was a cowardly man and would turn tail and back down when confronted by a grown man, armed and also un-afraid. But the true fact was in the past years many full-grown, heavily armed men had died as easily as the women and babies at the hand of either of the Harpe brothers. The Harpes were completely fearless, and had killed more armed and courageous men than they women and children.

Stegall knew the Harpes killed because of the hunger of the savage Wolf that raged inside their souls, and they knew none of the feelings of normal men. When the Wolf was loose, they lost control of all sanity, and killed to appease and satisfy that hunger, and there was no way to stop them.

Stegall also knew there were times they killed women and children, but it was to feed the Wolf, and not because of any special desire on the part of the Harpes. Whoever was closest when the hunger of the Wolf called became a victim, with no regard to anything other than the spilling of blood.

Oh yes, Moses Stegall had seen the Wolf turned loose before, and he knew what lay in store for the little band of men that chased headlong after the Demon. Once again he hoped fourteen would be enough.

The one thing he was sure of was if the Harpe should fall, he himself had to be there. He could not allow the Harpe to live long enough to talk. There were too many things Harpe could tell about Stegall, too many deaths he could speak of. No, if the Harpe were brought down, Stegall must make sure he was dispatched with all

E. DON HARPE

possible haste, and he meant to kill him himself if it was at all possible.

Moses Stegall rode hard in the wake of John Leiper. He had to be on hand when the Harpe fell. If not, he might very well fall himself.

JOHN LEIPER

John Leiper was not a large man, standing only five feet seven inches tall, and weighing perhaps one hundred and sixty pounds, including his clothes and boots, but what he lacked in stature, he more than made up for in courage and valor. Leiper had been known to single handedly attack a band of wild Indians, showing such ferocity the Indians retreated rather than face the wrath of the small warrior. He was known to always champion the cause of the downtrodden, and not a man who knew him could recall his ever showing any apprehension in the face of a fight.

But this time was different. This time he was pursuing Big Harpe, and John Leiper was afraid.

He had heard many horror tales of the Big Harpe, including the ones his family had told of the Indian raid at Nashville. Leiper had an uncle there who had been killed by the Harpes and this gave him a personal interest in the chase, but he knew if the two of them, he and the Big Harpe, should meet face to face the Harpe would surely kill him. For Harpe was not human at all, and there was not a man John Leiper knew who would not quail before the withering blue flame in the eyes of Micajah Harpe. Yes, this was one time in John Leiper's life that he was afraid, and if left a bad taste in his mouth, and an immense emptiness inside him.

Yet, in spite of his fear, or perhaps because of it, Leiper was determined to catch up with the Harpe, and if there was any way possible, he planned to rid the countryside of this menace forever. Harpe was a demon, a monster brought forth from the depths of hell to ravage good people everywhere, and John Leiper intended to do

306

something about it. The wanton destruction by the Harpe brothers had gone on for far too long, and with a great fury John Leiper laid the lash to his horse and spurred him onward.

Absently, he touched the rifle that rested against this saddle. This rifle belonged to Jim Tompkins, and so did the powder that Leiper had in his possession. His own powder had gotten wet in last night's brief rain and was of no use, and to his dismay, he found his ramrod had swollen with the wetness in the air and he could not get his own rifle to load. Tompkins had been kind enough to lend him this fine rifle, but neither of them knew the powder Leiper was using was the very same powder Micajah himself had given Tompkins the night he stayed in his cabin.

While Leiper was ready to go, the others in the small band were not quite so eager, for did they go after the Harpe for the same reason as either John Leiper or Moses Stegall.

Elijah Williams could not rid his pounding brain of the dying screams of Mary Stegall, nor the stench of burning human flesh from his nostrils. In his mind he still cowered in the underbrush, trembling in fear, and thinking each second might be his last. *The others don't know what it's like,* he thought. *They weren't there, and they didn't hear what I heard. They didn't see the Harpe, like I did. If they had, they'd not be so quick to ride out against the monster.*

Williams knew he was riding on the hunt because he had to prove something to himself. He had to find out whether or not he was still a man.

Matthew Christian was riding with the posse because his brother Jesse had been savagely murdered and he had attributed the murder to the Harpes.

Frank Peyton rode for the same reason as Christian. He wanted revenge above all else, even though he didn't really know if the Harpes were guilty of killing his own brother.

William Grissom rode with the posse because he had known the Tittsworth brothers, and wanted to see the Harpes hanged for their murders.

Solomon Trabue was a nephew to Colonel Daniel Trabue and knew the Colonel had lost his only son to the Harpes in a most gruesome manner. The boy was only thirteen, but age didn't matter to monsters such as these. They had killed the boy and cut his body into strips, then stole what meager provisions as he'd had on him at the time. Then they'd left his body in the woods, only to be discovered later by his father. Colonel Trabue never really got over his son's death, and Solomon sought only to stop the same thing from happening ever again.

Neville Lindsey, Buford Swinney and the two Bates brothers were thinking more about the kingly reward that had been issued by Governor James Garrard of Kentucky than they were anything else. Three hundred dollars on the head of each brother. That was a lot of money. A man could buy a farm and several head of cattle with that amount, and it was enough to make men do things they would not ordinarily consider. Fighting the Harpes was one such thing.

Jim Tompkins was riding along because he knew most of the men in the posse, and because he was concerned if the Harpes were allowed to remain at large many more innocent men, women and children would surely be killed.

Moses Stegall and Silas McBee completed the number of men who comprised the posse, and each had his own reasons for wanting to see the Harpes dead.

So it was when John Leiper fired his pistol into the air and called to the others to mount up and ride out, there was little hesitation among the men.

"Rally round, boys," Leiper called. "Every minute we tarry the devil gets farther away. Rally round, rally round and follow me."

With a great shout and a mighty show of bravado, the company of men fell in behind John Leiper, and they pounded off into the hot August afternoon, riding in pursuit of death and destruction.

41

HARPE'S END: PART ONE - MICAJAH

Micajah Harpe stopped his horse on the banks of the Pond River and looked out across the shallows called Free Henry Ford. With a thoughtful look on his face, he lifted his skin canteen to his lips. Taking a sip, he turned to Wiley.

"They's behind us Wiley, I kin feel 'em. Thar's ten er fifteen of 'em, I reckon. Looks like we'll be havin' some fun afore we gits to the settlement. They's fools, little brother, ever one of 'em. They ride after us, a'shoutin' and a'cussin', and none of 'em realize we wishes fer 'em to catch us with us. Lambs, little brother. Thet's whut they er. The posse is made up of lambs and geese jist a'flockin' to the Wolf's lair. Prime yore pistol and loosen yore knife Wiley, fer by mid mornin' tomorry the Wolf will feed agin."

Big Harpe's uncanny ability to sense danger was the reason they had managed to remain free for so long, and were able to roam the countryside at will. His own animal cunning, aided by the mystical power of the Amulet, often allowed him to tell from what direction danger came, and, more often than not, the extent of that danger. Today, even though he was not wearing the Amulet, still Micajah knew about how many men were riding after them, and about how far the men were behind them.

Add to these strange powers and abilities the fact the Harpes knew every cave and hole in the ground in the country that made a good hiding place, and it was plain to see why they were almost impossible to capture. Their reign of terror had many people too afraid to tell anything about them, and there were others they gave small amounts of money to in exchange for their silence. Many of the poor farmers would accept a few dollars even when they knew the reputation of the Harpes. It was a combination of things that made them so elusive. When the Harpes didn't want to be caught up with, they weren't caught up with.

But this time the last thing on their minds was eluding their pursuers. Micajah would pick the time and the place, and then allow the posse to ride into their trap. Then the Wolf would devour the living souls of every last man who rode into the trap.

They had even killed a couple of men near Robertson's Lick, and left their bodies in plain sight, knowing it would keep their pursuers on the right trail. They had to kill two good dogs to get to the men, and Micajah had not wanted to do that. The dogs were only doing what they were born to do. *Come to think of it,* thought Micajah, *That's all me and Little Wiley have been doing for so long.*

The two men, Gilmore and Hodgins, were occasional friends with Stegall, and Micajah didn't waste a moment of thought as he left them lying in their own blood by the side of the trail. He gave more thought to the two dead dogs than he did to the lives of the men.

The one thing Micajah couldn't know about this particular company of men however, was that John Leiper was riding a racehorse that was perhaps a better animal even than the one Harpe himself rode. Leiper's horse was faster than any horse in the territory, and had a bottom that would let him run long after lesser horses had tired. Given the difference in size between Micajah Harpe and John Leiper, this time it would be Harpe's horse that tired first.

Harpe had no way of knowing this. Or of knowing Leiper would come upon them before they were ready.

It was scarcely noon of the second day when John Leiper topped a small rise and saw the Harpes directly below him, sitting on a fallen log having a bite of food.

Quickly and quietly dismounting, Leiper slowly lowered himself to the ground and removed his rifle from his saddle. With his heart pounding and the blood running wildly through his veins, Leiper drew aim and made ready to fire his rifle.

But as his sights held steady on the head of Micajah Harpe, suddenly the man raised his eyes and stared directly at him, meeting his gaze straight on. John Leiper quailed beneath the fearful gaze of the monster. Sensing the danger, Harpe tensed and made ready to move in any direction.

With an oath, Leiper jerked the trigger of his rifle, discharging the weapon in the direction of the Harpe, but knowing even as he fired the shot would not even be close. Even as the rifle sounded, the Harpe was moving. The bullet struck the log some five feet from where he had been sitting, and John Leiper knew he wouldn't get to take another shot.

Micajah, upset because he hadn't realized the danger until it was almost too late, made two additional mistakes. He mistakenly thought the entire company had somehow caught up with them, and immediately shouted for Wiley to mount up. Micajah knew he and Wiley weren't ready to fight them at this place, and decided to make another run for it. His second mistake came when he leaped upon Wiley's horse and not his own. Wiley's horse was a good animal, being the same black stallion they had taken from George Teil, but it was smaller and not as able to carry Micajah's weight as his own horse was. It would not be able to carry him very far without tiring, and Micajah knew it was only a matter of time until the posse once again caught up with them.

As they raced away into the cover of the trees, Micajah shouted at Wiley: "Away with ye, little brother. Head fer the meetin' place. I'll take ker of this posse and then go and fetch the women and chillun. We'll catch up with ye somewhar on the Trace. Away with

313

ye, away with ye now." Saying this, Micajah turned his horse away from Wiley and urged him on to greater speed.

Micajah then turned his attention quickly to the women.

"Stay here, Susan, they will not harm ye. It will be as it was before. They'll take ye in and then release ye. I've never said it afore, but I've loved ye woman, these many years. Now gather in the chillun and hold still. It will be all right. I'll meet ye in Tennysee. Ye go thar, and I'll find ye soon enough."

Without a backward glance he galloped away, leading the posse away from the women as best he could.

He never knew his old enemy Silas McBee broke away from the posse and rode over to take charge of the women and children, but his words of prophecy about the women being set free would prove to be as true as anything he had ever promised them.

Leiper, seeing the Harpes mount up and race off, immediately jumped back on his own horse and raced down the hill, drawing his pistol as he rode, but holding his fire. On his saddle horn he had a rifle old man Tompkins had given him, but he left it where it was hanging. He knew if he caught up with the Harpes he'd need all the firepower he could get.

Suddenly he saw the two men split. The big Harpe continued in the same direction they'd been heading, but the little Harpe veered to the South and raced away into the underbrush. Leiper decided to follow the big Harpe, knowing the man to be the more dangerous of the two and the one who absolutely had to be stopped.

John Leiper screamed at the top of his lungs, whipped his horse into frenzy, and recklessly plunged down the hill in pursuit of Micajah Harpe.

HARPE'S END: PART TWO - WILEY

As soon as Wiley realized which horse he was riding, he knew there was no way the posse could catch up with him. The animal was used to carrying the weight of his brother and could run forever with a man of Wiley's size astride him. Besides, the posse was almost sure to split up and pursue both brothers, and if that was the case, Wiley was more than equal to the task of fighting no more than five or six of them.

Holding a southerly course, Wiley headed directly down toward the Tennessee country. The plan was to go south along the Trace, and on down into Mississippi country. Few people knew the Harpes down there, and it was said their old outlaw friend Samuel Mason had a good thing going for him and his men. Wiley planned to join up with Mason and when Micajah got there it would be no trouble at all to take over the gang. Mason was said to be the toughest and meanest killer the Natchez Trace country had ever seen, but that was subject to change once the Harpes arrived.

HARPE'S END: PART THREE - JOHN LEIPER

Every now and then John Leiper would catch glimpses of the big Harpe as he dodged in and out of the tree line. Trying to elude his pursuer, and knowing his horse could not outdistance the man, Harpe was using every tactic at his command to get away. Leiper was still not shooting, choosing to hold his fire until such time as he could get a clear target.

Both horses were running hard and had been for some time now. Micajah, being on his brother's horse and knowing it would fail soon, had already begun to search the woods for a place to make a stand. Leiper was riding hard, sometimes yelling curses at his foe, and more than once almost coming within firing range, only to see the Harpe find refuge in another grove of trees, or disappear into another of the deep ravines that crisscrossed the countryside.

Coming within firing range once again, Leiper reached for the borrowed rifle, deciding to take one more shot when the opportunity presented itself. He topped a small rise and came into a large clearing in the woods. To his surprise he saw Harpe not more than a hundred yards away, his horse noticeably tiring and moving much slower. Leiper pulled his horse to an abrupt halt and leaped from the saddle. He quickly knelt on one knee and aimed the long rifle at the broad back of the fleeing man. Taking a deep breath, he led the rider by several feet and slowly squeezed the trigger. The rifle barked and suddenly the world seemed to go into slow motion.

Leiper could almost see the ball as it sped toward the Harpe. He still held his breath, not daring to take air, as if the smallest motion might throw the shot off its mark. He could hear nothing except the pounding of his own heart, and scarcely believed his eyes when he saw Harpe jerk erect in the saddle as the round ball took him full in the back. He watched as Harpe then slowly tumbled from the horse and hit the ground with a bounce. Harpe rolled almost to the tree line before his forward motion stopped. Leiper saw the man lurch to his feet and run a few more feet toward the trees, and then fall again. This time he hit the ground on both knees and as he did he raised his great head to the heavens and uttered such a scream as John Leiper had never heard before.

Leiper knew it had been a lucky shot that knocked the outlaw from his horse, and he believed the shot had inflicted quite a lot of damage to the man. But his wasn't about to rush down upon the monster until he knew beyond a shadow of a doubt the bullet had taken its toll. Leiper would keep his distance until he was sure the Harpe wouldn't be able to offer any resistance. A more foolish man than John Leiper might have immediately rushed to the outlaw, and paid for his foolishness with his life. Knowing the posse would be along directly Leiper preferred to exercise caution in this situation. Leiper knew he had plenty of time and all he had to do was stay where he was and watch the outlaw until the others arrived.

Seeing that Harpe had again collapsed upon the ground, Leiper took out his powder and quickly reloaded his rifle. He drew aim once again and fired another shot into the body of the unmoving man, grunting with satisfaction as he saw the bullet strike home. The second shot unleashed feelings inside his breast he had not known he possessed. His chest swelled with pride and self-admiration for bringing down the dreaded monster no one else had been able to stop. He stood up and took another look toward where the man lay, and reloaded the rifle still again.

Still cautious, he moved in fifty yards closer and fired for a third time, hitting the man on the ground again. For the next half hour he fired additional shots at the body, and such was his confidence he believed all his shots were striking home, and he could not miss.

Finally deciding it was safe to stand and move about, Leiper walked to his horse and took down his canteen. He indulged himself in a huge swallow, feeling the cool water wash away the vile taste in his mouth. As the water flowed into his body, relief flooded his mind and he felt himself begin to tremble. The shaking became uncontrollable and he leaned against a tree in order to stay on his feet. The tension of the past few hours had been so great, and he had held it inside so long, that now, as it was finally released he felt large hot teardrops rolling down his cheeks.

Leiper wiped away the tears from his eyes with his shirtsleeve and walked back over to his horse. Replacing the canteen on his saddle, he turned and walked back to where he had left his rifle and picked it up from the ground. He loaded the gun again, and decided to take one last shot at Harpe; just to be sure the man was dead. But when he looked at the spot where the outlaw lay, John Leiper was horrified to discover the man was no longer there. The spot in the meadow was completely empty.

Leiper recoiled in terror. He couldn't believe his eyes.

The Harpe was gone.

The body was not where it should have been. There was no one in sight.

The forest was still, there were no birds singing and no animals moving about, and the breeze lay still across the land. The clearing was frozen in place as if time itself were standing still.

"No, no, no," shouted John Leiper.

But the Harpe was indeed gone. It was as if the forest floor had opened up and swallowed him, leaving no trace behind.

Leiper fell to his belly, and hid his face in the crook of his arm, afraid to look up for fear that Harpe would be standing there, tomahawk in hand, ready to strike at his would be killer.

Several minutes had dragged by, each one seeming to take an eternity, before the disbelieving Leiper could raise his face and once again survey the meadow. Raising himself upon his elbows, Leiper scanned the grass in front of him and inch at a time. Still finding no trace of the big Harpe, John slowly rose to his feet. Letting his eyes roam to the edge of the woods, he saw an old fallen log he had over looked before. "There," he said. "Harpe must be lying behind that log. There is no other place he could be."

Leiper sat down and made a decision. "No more trying to kill the Harpe alone," he reasoned. "This time I'll wait fer the rest of the men and together we'll finish the job. He may not be dead, but he is sorely wounded, and when the posse arrives we'll find the scoundrel and bring this thing to an end." John sank down to the ground and rested his back against a low bush, hoping he wouldn't have to wait long.

HARPE'S END: PART FOUR - JOSEPH BALLENGER

Joseph Ballenger was riding hard. He'd heard from a man on the trail that a company of men had the Harpes on the run, and he was trying his best to be in on the capture.

He'd heard the brothers had burned down a house owned by a man named Moses Stegall, killing the man's wife and child and three or four house guests. Ballenger knew Stegall was a man with a violent temper, and he had some suspicions Stegall had once run with the Harpes. If that was true, then Ballenger knew for sure if they were caught the Harpes didn't stand a chance of being brought to trial.

Ballenger had been after them for so long he would feel cheated if someone else managed to put them in chains. He wanted to see them brought in and hanged for their many crimes, and if that meant killing his horse to get there in time, then so be it.

He brought his heels up sharply into the horse's side, urging it to even greater speed.

HARPES END: PART FIVE - MICAJAH

Micajah knew instantly he had made a mistake. In his haste he had mounted his brother's horse, and though the animal was a good one, it was not strong enough to carry the weight of the big outlaw for any long period of time. There was no time to exchange horses, however, and so the Harpe laid the leather to the one he rode. Shouting hurried instructions to his brother, he reined the horse and headed northward, and slightly to the west.

Plenty of good hiding places out this way, he thought. *I'll jist pick a spot and hole up fer a spell. If'n the company gits too close, then I guess I'll be findin' out what kind of men I have on my tail.*

For several miles, Harpe kept up a mighty pace, hoping to out-distance his pursuers, but every time he troubled himself to look behind, he saw a slender man on a great black horse, doggedly hanging on his every move. Sensing his own horse would not be able to outlast the black, the Harpe began to look for places that would make a likely spot to set up an ambush. As an ambush was nothing new to Harpe, he had little doubt as to the outcome of this chase.

Slowing down a bit as he came to a large meadow, Harpe recognized the spot as one in which his small band had camped on more than one occasion. Spotting a fallen log by the far tree line, he quickly guided the horse in that direction. *This will be as good a' spot as any,* he thought.

Suddenly, Harpe felt a blow to his back like that of a mighty hammer. He felt himself being hurled from the saddle, and turned head over heels as he flew through the air. Even as he landed upon the rolling ground, his mind was rapidly forming a new plan of action.

Curse the luck of the fool behind me, Harpe thought. *Surely this twas the luckiest shot the man has ever made.* Suddenly the blue flame flickered into life in his eyes. "Well, his luck is about to run out." he said to himself, "Come, little man, come and play with the Wolf."

Harpe lay still, thinking to lull the man into believing him dead. Knowing as soon as his pursuer felt safe, he would approach to check upon his handiwork. Suddenly Harpe heard the man's rifle bark and felt another bullet strike his body, this time to his left shoulder blade.

"Damn the man for a coward," he silently shouted to himself, and then braced himself for the onslaught of shots he was sure would come.

He was right. Leiper continued to fire round after round as quickly as he could reload his weapon, but no other lead found the body of the wounded outlaw. Thinking to fool the man, Harpe jerked his body as though he were hit each time the man fired. But Harpe knew he was in trouble. Though the second bulled was only a flesh wound to the shoulder, the first bullet in his back had hit a vital spot, and Micajah had almost no feeling below the waist. His legs seemed to be paralyzed.

When a period of twenty minutes or so had passed with no additional bullets hitting him, Micajah risked a quick look at his attacker. Seeing the man kneeling on the ground, recharging his rifle, Harpe seized the opportunity to roll himself behind the fallen log, and to draw his pistols from his waistband. He checked the load on both weapons, and laid them on the ground beside him. Next he removed the great razor sharp long knife from its holster at his belt.

Reaching again to his waistband, the Harpe withdrew the terrible magical tomahawk. This was the tomahawk he'd won in mortal combat with the renegade Cherokee warrior named Bearkiller, and had served Micajah well over the years. The tomahawk had spilled innocent blood on more than one occasion. It was a killing weapon, as was the long knife, and in the hands of the Harpe either was more than a match for the men who chased him.

The Harpe settled down to wait for his attacker, knowing as soon as the man discovered he was no longer in sight he would certainly come to investigate.

But as the minutes dragged by, it became plain the man intended to wait for the rest of the party before resuming the attack.

So be it, thought Harpe. A smile played around the corners of his mouth as he thought of the words he'd once said to Susan. "If I die today," he'd told her, "then tomorrow the Devil will be looking for a new job. Hell holds no terror for the Harpe. Death is no stranger to me, I have faced it and I do not fear it. I am the un-killable Wolf. I am the Harpe."

He'd made the statement half in jest, but now the words seemed prophetic.

When the brothers had first embarked upon their wild killing crusade, they had come to understand they would die as they lived. Death held no fear for either of them, and with the amulet lending them part of its mysterious power, the brothers knew that perhaps the Death of these bodies would not be final after all, but merely a time to sleep.

Risking another quick look, Harpe saw the rest of the company of mounted men come riding out of the trees, and mill about the man on the ground with the rifle.

Solomon Trabue was the first to see Leiper's great black horse standing alone in the meadow.

"Ho boys," he shouted, as he reined his own mount to a halt. "I believe we've reached the end of our hunt." Dismounting, he walked over to the black horse, which showed no signs of shying away. As he reached for the bridle, he heard a loud whisper.

"Take cover boys, I have the monster at bay. I've wounded him. I believe he's lying behind that big log down by the trees. He may be only hurt and playing possum, and I'm sure he's well armed, so we must be cautious."

Saying this, John Leiper slowly rose to his feet and motioned for the men in the company to fan out across the meadow.

"We must approach him carefully boys," he warned. "Even half dead, the Harpe is still the most dangerous man in the territory." Leiper began to move carefully toward the fallen log, taking a step, then pausing, another step and another pause.

It seemed as though an eternity had passed, and the posse had only advanced a few yards, when Solomon Trabue stood erect and shouted:

"The hell with this creeping about, boys, let's rush the bloody bastard."

At that moment, the Harpe made his terrible presence known with a shot to the head of Solomon Trabue, and another to the body of Frank Payton. Trabue fell, dead instantly with an ugly red hole almost directly centered between eyes that still held an incredulous look. Payton, only wounded, fell to the ground and began frantically crawling for the cover afforded by a small rise. He was desperately seeking a place safe from another shot from the deadly weapons of the outlaw. Several of the men fired at Harpe, but none hit anything other than the log behind which Harpe lay.

"Down boys, down," shouted Leiper. "His pistols are empty, and if we but take our time, we'll have the monster yet."

Even as he spoke, Leiper again began his slow movement toward the log.

Elijah Williams had by this time entered the trees and was making his way to a spot behind Harpe. Still mightily afraid of Harpe, Williams was being extra cautious, and was taking no chances on the outlaw spotting him. He had already moved within firing distance, but was reluctant to fire, lest he miss and give the Harpe have a chance to get off a shot in return. He was sure in a few minutes he would be in position to get off a clear shot.

The two Bates brothers weren't as cautious as Williams however, and were also in position to fire a round. Dropping to one knee, the eldest Bates brother, Henry, fired his long rifle and howled in delight as he saw the ball kick dust from the front of Harpe's buckskin shirt. Rising quickly, Harpe returned the shot with one of his own which struck the younger Bates brother, Jackson, in the neck. Great fountains of blood cascaded from the wound, splattering over the face and hands of the still kneeling Henry Bates. With a loud oath, Henry jumped to his feet and rushed the outlaw, only to be met with the mighty tomahawk as he attempted to leap over the log. He died with a look of amazement on his face that the Harpe, wounded and alone, had killed both Bates brothers, themselves men feared by ordinary folk. Little did he know that Harpe had killed men far meaner and stronger than he and his brother, and without even working up a sweat.

Still, the bullet from Bates rifle had further weakened Harpe, and the loss of blood was beginning to take its toll on the outlaw. His periods of activity were less frequent now, and more and more his movements were offering a better target to the remaining posse members. Already shot three times, the last very serious, and having no more loads left for his pistols, the Harpe was in a bad way. Still, if they were so foolish as to rush him, more of them would die before he drew his last breath.

However, the men were not that foolish just yet. Each time Harpe presented them with a target, they fired a volley. Though they missed more often than they hit, still occasionally one of the rounds found its mark.

Time passed, and as the afternoon sun beat down on the meadow, the heat also began to take its toll on the dwindling strength of the outlaw. When Harpe had lain still for more than two hours, finally John Leiper rose to his feet. Motioning to the rest of the men, he began to advance once again toward the motionless Harpe. As they advanced, the men fired shot after shot into the still body, till there could be no doubt the Harpe was at last truly dead.

Kneeling by the body, Moses Stegall spoke to the two closest men, who happened to be Elijah Williams and Buford Swinney, a hardened man of some forty years who had come along on the chance he might share in the reward.

"You two men lift up the body, and I'll use the bastards own knife on him. The only way to be sure the demon is no more is by cutting off his head." Stegall reached down and with his right hand pried the long, gleaming knife from Harpe's still fingers. He motioned to Williams and Swinney. "C'mon, let's get on with it," he said.

With an oath and a mighty roar that shook the heavens, Big Harpe's wild blue eyes flew open, and his great hands closed around the necks of the two men holding him. His eyes were ablaze with the killing flame of the Wolf, and in his hands was the strength of ten men. His roars echoed through the meadow, and out across the countryside until it seemed as if they could be heard around the entire world. His hands could not be pried from the necks of Williams and Swinney, and his terrible threshing about caused several of the men to empty their bladders. For years afterward, the men would waken from their sleep, the screams running through their minds as fresh as though the bloody deed had happened that day. And each time the nightmares came, they would arise from their beds and gather about them their weapons, and look all around their homes in fear that the Harpe had returned.

Seeing that there was no stopping now, the rest of the men jumped upon the Harpe, and attempted to hold him, as Moses Stegall stabbed him again and again. Later they would have to pry open the hands from the necks of Harpe's last two victims.

Williams and Swinney had met their destruction, their necks snapped as easily as twigs in the hands of the Big Harpe.

As the men finally subdued the struggling outlaw, Moses Stegall wrapped his left hand in the course black hair of Harpe and lifted his head until he was staring full into the eyes of the dying man. With a grim smile, he placed the long knife to the back of Harpe's neck and began to slowly draw it across, deeper and deeper until it struck bone.

The big Harpe vented the full fury of his fiery blue gaze on Stegall, staring him straight in the eye. Stegall shuddered, and withered under such an evil look, and deep in his heart he was afraid. Even now, with the Harpe approaching death, Stegall knew fear of the man. Harpe knew Stegall for what he was, a thief and a killer, and for that reason alone Stegall could not allow Harpe to live. If Harpe ever told anyone all he knew about Stegall, Stegall's life would not be worth the rope it would take to hang him. Yet somehow, in that instant when their eyes met, Stegall knew some day the Harpe would wreak a terrible vengeance upon not only Stegall, but all of his descendants as well.

All of Harpe's mighty muscles were corded, and his terrible blue eyes were still on fire. With his dying breath, the Harpe spoke his final words.

"You're a Goddamned rough butcher, but cut on and be damned. I am the Harpe, Stegall, the Wolf, and I can't be killed. I'll return, for I am your death and destruction."

42

AFTERMATH: PART ONE

The big Harpe was dead. Dead.

The men in the posse were standing staring at the headless body on the ground, yet still they found it hard to believe. Moses Stegall, after hacking off Harpe's head, was holding the grisly trophy high, laughing in fits of uncontrolled laughter that was borderline hysteria. He shook the head in the air, and danced around the body, making sounds like a crowing rooster and a grunting pig all rolled into one.

John Leiper had regained some of his composure, and stood surveying the results of the fight. It had not been a battle easily won, for Harpe had killed five of the men who rode against him that day, and a sixth, Frank Payton, probably wouldn't make it back into town alive. Harpe's shot had struck Payton full in his lower gut and the man had been unconscious for quite some time now. He was still bleeding from the mouth, and his weak shallow breath seemed to be growing farther and farther apart. Still, Leiper considered the six lives a cheap price to pay for the death of the most feared man the territory had ever seen. His only wish was that they had caught both Harpe brothers.

Stegall looked at the six men left standing and without a word viciously threw the head against the ground.

"Well, it's over men. We've finally kilt the bastard. I don't mind telling the lot o' ye I wish we could kill him again. Fer whut he's done to me and mine, I hope his soul burns in hellfire until the end o' time. The only thing left to do is take the head on up to Madisonville where old Newman is the Justice o' the Peace, and have him officially declare the bloody killer dead. And o'course, we gots to go git the women from McBee. They's jist as deservin' of being kilt as the man on the ground."

Stegall was raving now, and the other men could sense it.

"We gots to kill his chillun, too, jist like he did mine. They don't deserve to live. And I serve notice on each o' ye here today thet I intend no rest a'tall fer myself till Wiley Harpe is caught and meets the same end as big Micajah. The Harpes ain't nothin' more than wild wolves that have to be slaughtered. They ain't fit to be around decent folk."

Stegall knew his own life would be in danger as long as even one member of the Harpe clan remained alive, and unless he killed them all, he'd have to sleep with one eye open every night for the rest of his life.

"Who's comin' with me, boys?" Stegall asked. "I need one er two o' ye to ride with me to see Newman, and to relate the facts of whut happened here today. Who's it going to be?"

John Leiper was the first to speak up.

"I am goin' with ye, Stegall, me and Matthew Christian here. The rest o' the boys are fixin' to try to get Payton back to town. He's hit bad, and will likely die before they gits there, but they have to try. He just might turn out to be the last man ever killed by the big Harpe."

But every man there remembered Harpe's last words.

"I am the Harpe," the man had said with his dying breath. "I will be back."

At the remembrance, every one of the men shivered, though the evening was still very hot.

Matthew Christian was some forty years old, and had only been in Kentucky for a few years. He'd started west with his family, but one look at the beautiful Kentucky country was all he needed to know this was where he'd spend the rest of his days. Christian was certainly glad the hunt had ended the way it had. A lot of people would be sleeping better once the news got around the big Harpe was finally dead.

Christian pulled a flour sack out of his saddlebags and handed it to Stegall.

"Here, Moses," he said. "Stick the head in here. I don't enjoy lookin' at thet thing any more than I have to, and not nearly as much as I did just a minute ago. Let's be gettin' it out o' sight now."

The men were mostly quiet on the ride toward Madisonville. Each of them was too preoccupied with his own thoughts to do very much talking. All Stegall could think about was finding the rest of the Harpes and killing them all, and that's all he would think about for the rest of his days.

Matthew Christian was just ready for it to be over so he could get back to his own family. He'd been away from the farm too long already, and the work was piling up at home.

John Leiper was re-living every shot and every sound of the battle. He could see Harpe fall from his horse, and knew it was only a lucky shot that brought him down. In his mind he could still hear the big Harpe's screams, and Leiper knew the screams were not of pain, and certainly not of fear. They were screams of outrage, and frustration at being trapped. Leiper would go over the details of the battle for the rest of his life, and would always wonder what might have happened if the Harpe hadn't been paralyzed when they finally rushed him.

43

AFTERMATH: PART TWO - HARPSHEAD

Squire Newman of Madisonville had been only too happy to certify that the head was indeed that of the outlaw, Big Harpe, and the three men walked out of his office with the head back in the flour sack.

All over the small town people had already heard the news and had begun to gather to view the head of the territories most feared killer, and Stegall had quite a time holding the head aloft and shouting his jubilation to the crowd.

As the three of them prepared to leave town, Stegall suddenly had an idea.

"Let's stop by the smithies shop," he said to his companions.

At the blacksmiths shop, Stegall quickly found what he was looking for. He picked up a sharp iron spike, about a foot long, and asked the smith to borrow a hammer. There was a crossroads just outside town, and that's where Stegall led the little party next.

At the crossroads there was a young oak tree, with a sturdy fork some ten or twelve feet above the ground. Stegall shinnied up the tree to the fork and told Leiper to hand up Harpe's head and the tools.

Placing the head in the forks of the tree, with the face staring downward upon the crossroads, Stegall began to drive the spike through the skull.

THUD. THUD. THUD. THUD.

The hammer pounded home the heavy spike. Bone gave way to the sharp point, and it pierced the brain and drove downward until it emerged from the gaping, bloody neck.

THUD. THUD. THUD. THUD.

Still Stegall pounded the spike, until at last it was embedded deep into the wood of the living tree.

THUD. THUD. THUD. THUD.

None there could see the wild blue flame that had danced in the eyes of the Harpe had not died. It had merely faded into the depths of the blind unseeing eyes, and changed from a roaring fire into a flickering ember, not bright enough to be seen by the gathered crowd.

Somewhere, deep in the cave on the spirit world, the Wolf slipped into his den, and closed his eyes, and slept. One day, when next the Harpe called, the Wolf would awaken, and once again they would hunt the world of man. But for now, he would sleep. He had fed well this day, and he had all the time in the world.

44

AFTERMATH: PART THREE - JOSEPH BALLENGER

Captain Joseph Ballenger had found the headless body lying beside the tree where it had fallen, and knew at once it was the body of Micajah Harpe. From the looks of things, the man had put up a hell of a fight before he was finally slain. There was blood everywhere, too much blood to belong to just one man, and Ballenger knew Harpe had taken at least one, and probably more of his attackers to hell with him.

For Ballenger, it was the end of a long futile chase. With Micajah dead, Ballenger figured there was no use in pursuing Wiley any longer. The little Harpe was a dangerous man, but without the killing instinct of his brother leading him, he was likely to drift out of the territory altogether. Ballenger hoped so. This country had had enough of the Harpes and their murderous ways. Wiley would meet the same fate as Micajah, and Ballenger knew it. Men such as these were destined to find a bloody death waiting wherever they went.

Following the trail of the posse was easy enough for the experienced tracker, and Ballenger arrived at Squire Newman's office only about an hour after Stegall and the rest had left. After a few quick questions, Ballenger climbed back on his tired horse and set off after them. He came upon them just as Stegall was climbing down from the tree.

"Well, Stegall, you bloody lucky bastard, I see you've finally killed your old friend."

"What do ye mean by thet remark, Sheriff? The Harpe t'wern't no friend o' mine."

"Maybe not lately, he warn't," the lawman replied, "but they was a time back in Knoxville town when you were as thick as thieves with the Harpe brothers and their women. Speaking o' the women, just where might they be?"

"I'll be only too happy to tell ye whar the women is, Ballenger, and ye kin go and arrest the lot o' them. Squire McBee has 'em, and that's a fact. He's a takin' 'em in even as we speak. They ain't no better than the men, and deserve to die jist the same as this devil did. I'll be tellin' ye right off thet I intend to kill ever dammed one of 'em myself if'n I gets the chance."

"I'll find McBee and take the women off'n his hands sure enough, Stegall, and I'll take em' in for trial. But let me warn ye thet I'll not stand for the likes o' ye making any threats against any prisoner o' mine. The Harpe women will face up to what they've done, and if ye show up in my town and do any one o' them any harm, I'll kill you just as dead as that there head is, and you can take my word on thet."

Ballenger pointed the index finger on his big left hand at the gruesome object nestled in the forks of the tree, and kept his right hand close to the pistol he wore at his waist. Stegall knew the man meant every word he said. Joseph Ballenger was not a man to take lightly, and every man who heard the words knew it would bad for Stegall if he tried to cause the women any further harm.

Ballenger took one last look at the head of the man he had hunted for so long. The eyes seemed to be staring down upon him as he stood there, and he suddenly realized he would have rather caught up with the Harpe and brought him to trial. Ballenger believed a death as violent as this one sometimes bred more violence, and deep in his heart, Ballenger thought at some point in time the legend of the terrible Harpe's might have another chapter.

45

AFTERMATH: PART FOUR - WILEY

Wiley was in Tennessee, heading South, when Micajah fell. They had agreed to meet along the trace and go down into the Mississippi country. No one knew them there, and the woods would be full of geese ripe for the plucking. They could get word back to the women, and it would only be a matter of time before they were all back together again.

Suddenly, out of nowhere, there came such a pounding in Wiley's head that it drove him to his knees.

THUD. THUD. THUD. THUD.

The pounding boomed like thunder in Wiley's brain. He covered his ears and shook his head, but it was no use.

THUD. THUD. THUD. THUD. The sound came one more time.

Then, as suddenly as it had started, the pounding stopped.

Wiley opened his eyes and looked around, then slowly got to his feet. Something strange was happening, but he wasn't sure exactly what. He raised his eyes to the sky and listened to the whispers inside his head, and for the first time in his life, there was no trace at all of his brother. Micajah wasn't there. But that was impossible. The link the brothers shared was strong enough to reach across the miles that separated them.

"Micajah," Wiley silently screamed. "Kiga, where are you?"

Once again he sent the mental cry ringing out into the void. And once again he touched nothing. Micajah was gone. The presence of his brother was not in his mind anymore.

It's not possible," Wiley thought. *He can't be gone.*

Then the truth came.

There could be only one explanation. If Micajah wasn't in his mind, then he was most certainly dead.

Wiley turned his face back to the trail, and began to ride south.

To the Trace.

There was an emptiness inside him such as he'd never known, but not one tear fell from his eyes. Micajah had told him to go to the Trace and wait, and that's what he intended to do. If it took a day, or a thousand years, when the Wolf called, he'd find little Harpe ready.

As the fact that Micajah was truly dead began to sink in, Wiley picked up his pace. There was nothing in the Tennessee or Kentucky country to hold him, and he had business on the Trace.

46

AFTERMATH: PART FIVE - THE WOMEN

When Micajah galloped off and left them standing them, Susan had a feeling deep in her gut she would never see him alive again. She gathered Betsy and Sarah to her, and they held the children close as Silas McBee came riding in. Whatever followed would be no worse than what they had already lived through, and in some way, each of them was glad this ordeal was about to come to an end.

If they let them go, they would head down into Tennessee, as Micajah had instructed, but none of them held any hopes of life ever being the same as it had been.

They knew if he lived the Harpe would find them, just like he always had. It didn't matter how long it took, the women knew he'd come. Like Wiley, they'd be ready when at last he called.

The women and Silas McBee came to the rock house and were surprised to find Ballenger and his two deputies waiting there for them. The lawman spoke with McBee for a while, and then McBee got on his horse and rode away, leaving the women in the hands of Ballenger.

Ballenger wasted no words as he informed the women Micajah was dead, and the whereabouts of Wiley was still unknown. Although Ballenger wasn't sure how much the women had to do with the killing business their men had been involved in, he still felt obliged to arrest them. They deserved a trial, and Joseph Ballenger intended to see they got one.

Thinking the women deserved proof of Harpe's death, he went several miles out of his way to show them the tree where the skull was impaled. Ballenger had no way of knowing of the amulet Susan had tucked inside the bodice of her dress, nor of any of its strange powers. Although even the powers of the Amulet and the Wolf combined could not bring life back to the mutilated body of Micajah Harpe, its presence in the vicinity of the head would serve to let the Wolf know it had not been lost, and was still in the keeping of the Harpe family.

As Susan came close to the base of the tree and stood looking at the gruesome head of her husband, the wild energy of the amulet reached out across the boundaries deep into the sprit world and touched the sleeping Wolf. In his sleep, the mighty demon slightly stirred. He would slumber for now, but not forever.

The women were brought to trial on October 28th, 1799, at Russellville, Kentucky, with the Honorable Judge James T. Hunter presiding. The trial lasted three days, and throughout that time Stegall strutted and postured about the town, boasting of killing the Big Harpe, and vowing to kill the women should they be acquitted. However, Ballenger was true to his word. He not only protected the women while the trial was in progress, he also enlisted the aid of his old friend William Stewart.

Stewart was a renowned Indian fighter and frontiersman, and he took an oath to personally kill Stegall should he lay one finger on any of the women.

On October 30th, all three women were acquitted and set free.

They never told anyone of the two children that were being raised by Micajah and Wiley's kin, and they never saw the children again, but for some strange reason each of the women took comfort in their knowledge the Harpe bloodline would live on, regardless of what happened to them or to the children they had with them.

John Rice came to Russellville and took his daughter Sarah home with him. Sarah later remarried, and she and her new husband moved to a small new settlement on Wolf River in Northern Middle Tennessee. Although no longer married to Wiley, she still felt the need to live in Tennessee, thereby heeding the final instructions of Micajah.

Betsy also remarried, and she and her children moved to a small settlement in Illinois, wanting nothing else to do with anything that may happen in Kentucky or Tennessee. She raised her children with no knowledge of Micajah and Wiley, for fear that should the neighbors learn her true identity they would band together and drive the family from the community as had happened before.

Susan intended to follow Micajah's final instructions and go with Betsy to Tennessee, but instead she came down sick that first winter in Russellville, and went to live with a man named Butler.

Colonel Butler had a fine farm in Russellville, and vowed to keep Susan safe from the wrath of the family and friends of any of the victims of the Harpe's bloody rampage. Butler offered Susan a good home where she could raise the two children in peace, and Susan agreed to live with him until such time as she could carry out the final wishes of her husband.

For several years, Susan maintained the dream of moving to Tennessee, but her health failed even more as the years passed, and she remained in Kentucky for the rest of her days.

But it was not an easy existence.

The good townspeople of Russellville could never forgive her the fact she had been married to the big Harpe, and they never missed an opportunity to call her ugly names and speak harshly to her. Although Susan was a strong willed woman, eventually she grew tired of the whispers and finger pointing. There was nothing she could do to change her past, and she felt a deep sadness that the townspeople could not forgive her.

She endured the abuse for years, always telling herself some day she would leave Kentucky and go to Tennessee to await the time when Micajah would return. But as her children grew older they began to ask questions Susan found harder and harder to answer. The day finally came when she could take no more.

Her son James had started farming a few acres of his own, just a couple of miles from Colonel Butler's place, and Susan knew it was only a matter of time until some busybody of a neighbor decided to tell him the truth about his father. Susan had told James much of what had happened, but she knew there was no way he would listen to the people of the town speak ill of his father. James was a Harpe, and Susan knew all too well what would happen should he ever become possessed of any portion of the rage that consumed Micajah and Wiley.

At times, when the townspeople were the harshest, Susan entertained the idea of placing the amulet about the neck of James, and finding out if the Wolf still hungered. It was at these times she remembered the hell they had lived through and determined that even though she may die from the pain that ate at her heart, she would never give in to the temptation. She had no desire to see her son turn into the monster the amulet had made of her husband.

In the end, Susan decided to end the gossip once and for all. One Sunday afternoon, she and Lovie went to visit James and they sat into motion a plan that freed them from the prying eyes and ears of the good people of Russellville, and from the emotional hurt she had endured for years.

Colonel Butler had told Susan she could move onto a small piece of land he owned just outside town, and that's what she decided to do. Though she longed for Tennessee, she knew the stories would follow her there as well. And although she wasn't actually going to Tennessee, she knew Micajah would find her. She would wait, if it took forever, and she knew he would come.

In town one afternoon, she made a big to do about moving to Tennessee, and told several of the people she met she would be leaving the next day. Early the next morning, a wagon driven by Susan came rolling through the middle of the small town, supposedly headed for Tennessee.

Lovie sat on the wagon seat by her mother's side, defiantly looking each and every person they met squarely in the eye. James rode along beside them, head held high, daring anyone to make so much as a sound. After stopping at the general store, they continued out of town. The stop was necessary for two reasons. They needed a few supplies, and of course they wanted to spread the story about where they were moving too. Which was Tennessee, as they told everyone they talked to.

Late Saturday night, the wagon pulled into the yard of a small farmhouse in a bottom on the south side of Russellville, and there, the next day, a lady named "Fannie White" sat up housekeeping.

Monday morning came and James was back hard at work on his own farm, and Susan Harpe was no longer a resident of Russellville.

The mysterious Fannie White and her daughter lived alone and kept to themselves, with Colonel Butler visiting them every now and then, bringing them supplies from town.

Fannie continued living at her small bottomland farm for many years, alone with her memories of Micajah Harpe and times she sometimes wished she could forget. Shut off from people, with almost no friends, one night Susan passed away in her sleep.

Colonel Butler's daughter, Dolly, spent many long days sitting with Susan, talking about the days when Micajah and Wiley roamed the countryside, and knew the women better than perhaps anyone else ever had. Susan taught Dolly the little melody she had learned so long ago, and told her it was a special song, handed down in the Harpe family.

It was Dolly that found Susan the day after she passed away, and Dolly that buried her in the meadow beside the house. From then on the Butlers kept the small gravesite and the tombstone well tended in memory of a woman that had seen too much heartache in her life. In death, Susan Harpe was finally freed from the hardship the people of the town had heaped upon her.

Dolly often found herself humming the haunting little melody in times when she needed strength, and taught it to her own daughter when the time came.

For years afterward, the people said when the wind was right you could walk out into the meadow around Fannie's abandoned cabin and hear someone humming the tune. And sometimes at night, in the dark of the moon, they said you might catch a glimpse of Fannie herself, standing in the window, waiting for the time when her man returned for her.

Lovie Marie took up with Colonel Anthony butler, and followed him to Texas, where they lived for a few years. But as time passed she grew lonely for home, and finally she moved to the small town of Lafayette, Tennessee and there found a new home for herself. She had made it to Tennessee, even though her mother had died in Kentucky, and Lovie knew somehow things would work out as her father had intended. Inside her dress, nestled close against her bosom, Lovie kept the small leather pouch that held the Harpe Amulet. The beautiful silver star her mother had cherished so much. Lovie knew better than to wear the necklace, for Susan had told her some of its history. She knew it was an heirloom of the Harpe family, and held strange mysterious powers, which could only be awakened when the amulet was placed around the neck of a first-born Harpe son.

Although Lovie never married, she gave birth to four children, three girls and a boy. She gave them the name Roberts, though they were entitled to wear the Harpe name should they so desire. As they grew older and learned the story of their grandfather, her only son, whom she had named James Daniel, chose to be called Harp. He never moved from Macon County, Tennessee, where he eventually married and raised a family of his own.

The daughters kept the name Roberts, as Lovie had, and it was to her eldest daughter Elizabeth she passed on the necklace.

Elizabeth never married, and like her mother kept the name Roberts, which started a tradition that would continue through the years. Each eldest daughter would always go by the name Roberts, and each became the keeper of the amulet, though the story of its powers became lost as time wore on. Each succeeding generation of eldest daughters neither married, nor ever took another family name.

Along with the amulet, it also came down through the years that a Robert's girl should never, under any circumstances, marry a Harp man. It was strictly forbidden, and always adhered to, even though the reason was lost somewhere with the passing of time, much as the story of the amulet's powers.

47

AFTERMATH: PART SIX - STEGALL: CURSE OF THE LONG KNIFE

In the days that followed, Moses Stegall made many idle boasts about what he intended to do to the Harpe women, but never carried through on any of them. To begin with, Stegall didn't want a set-to with William Stewart, and secondly, Stegall wasn't sure exactly what had become of Wiley Harpe. Moses knew his life wouldn't be worth dime if he harmed the women and Wiley learned of it.

After the trial, Stegall rebuilt his cabin and early the next year married a young girl named Nannie Mattlock. They had two sons, the eldest of which they named Andrew. It was to Andrew that Moses gave the long knife of Micajah Harpe.

Moses fashioned a strong box of seasoned oak, and lined it with a piece of dark red velvet cut from an old dress that belonged to the mother of his wife. He secured the knife inside the box, and fastened it with a heavy lock. The key he placed on a leather thong and kept if around his neck at all times.

The knife, in its wooden casket, was handed down through the Stegall family from father to son, and each generation heard the same exhortation.

"This was the knife that was used to kill Micajah Harpe, the man known as the Wolf. It is the duty of the Stegall family to keep the knife, guard it well, and never let its blade become dull. With his dying breath, Big Harpe cursed the Stegall family, and swore he would return from the grave to bring upon us death and destruction. This knife killed the monster once, it may be the only power in the world that can stand against him should he find some way of keeping the curse. Guard the knife well, for when the hammer pounds in your head like thunder, know that the Harpe has returned, and the knife may mean the difference between life and death."

So it was that each Stegall son that guarded the knife, came to spend long hours watching the night sky, and dreading the thought that one day they may hear the thunder of the hammer pounding inside their head.

48

AFTERMATH: PART SEVEN - WILEY

After finally accepting the fact Micajah was really dead, Wiley slowly made his way down through Tennessee and into Mississippi along the route that came to be known as the Natchez Trace. He joined forces with a band of outlaws under the leadership of a man named Mason, known as the most terrible and feared murderer on the Trace.

The Harpes had known Mason back at the Cave In The Rock, and Wiley knew he would be in the company of men who were of a like mind as he was.

Wiley, using the name John Setton, became Mason's right hand, and together they robbed and killed many unwary travelers during the next five years.

In January of 1804, the Governor of Mississippi placed a reward of some $900.00 dollars upon Mason's head, dead or alive. When Wiley learned of the reward, it was only a matter of days before the "most terrible murderer on the Trace" came face to face with the man who was the most terrible murderer in the entire land. Mason himself soon became a victim, meeting his end under the knife of Wiley Harpe. The ferocity of the Wolf knew no equal, and Mason, terrible though he was, was nothing more than another sheep to the man who had been known as Little Harpe.

Wiley, still using the name Setton, and one of his companions, a man called Mays, took the head of the outlaw, wrapped it in blue clay to preserve it, and then presented it to the circuit court in Greenville, Mississippi, claiming the reward. The fact that Mason's upper front teeth were exceptionally long and fang like made identifying the outlaw's head quite easy.

But in the courtroom that day was a man named John Bowman, lately from Knoxville, Tennessee. When "Setton" and "Mays" walked into the court with the head, Bowman was there and recognized 'Setton' as Wiley Harpe.

"Why that man there," Bowman exclaimed, pointing directly at 'Setton', "is none other than Wiley Harpe. That man is Little Harpe, one of the brothers that terrorized the settlements in Kentucky and Tennessee a few years back."

"Nonsense," cried Wiley. My name is John Setton, and I defy any man to prove different."

"Tis not hard to prove a'tall," Bowman replied. "A few years back, I heard about a fight in Knoxville in old man Hughes tavern, between the Harpes and some customers. They say Wiley was stabbed in the fight, and if you'll just make old Setton thar remove his shirt I think you'll find I'm right. If'n he truly be Harpe, he'll have a scar under his left breast, compliments of whar the blade struck home."

It took eight men to hold Wiley while two others ripped off his shirt.

Under his left breast, exactly as Bowman had described it, was a long ragged knife scar, for which all there took as proof of the mans true identity. Wiley didn't bother to protest any further, and he was brought to trial in less than three weeks.

Wiley was quickly found guilty of murder and other crimes, and on the eighth day of February 1804, he was hanged by the neck until he was dead.

Two days later his body was removed from the makeshift gallows and taken to a fallen tree trunk, where the head was unceremoniously cut off.

In a field outside Greenville, Mississippi, the head of Wiley Harpe was nailed to a tall post, where it remained for several years, a grisly reminder of the horrors of the outlaws who stalked the Natchez Trace.

49

THE DARKWOLF

The last rampage of the Terrible Harpes was over, and there the saga should have ended.

With the head of William Micajah "Big" Harpe spiked to the forks of a tree outside Greenville, Kentucky, and the head of Joshua Wiley "Little" Harpe nailed to a post outside Greenville, Mississippi, the story should have been over for all time.

The demon wolves were dead. The Terrible Wolf was no more, and the countryside could once again sleep at night.

Yet even after death, deep inside both of the grotesquely grinning skulls, a tiny blue flame faintly glimmered.

The mystic talisman known as the Harpe Amulet was safe, its power intact, and still in the possession of its rightful owners.

The Wolf himself had slipped inside the cave on the spirit world, and once more fell asleep. There would he remain, until such time as the Harpe should have need of him. Well knew the Wolf the time would come when the Harpe would call, and the next time he awakened he would be stronger, more fierce, more powerful. In his slumber, the Wolf would be transformed into the DarkWolf, and when he awoke again the world would tremble.

The Harpe would call, the DarkWolf would awaken, and once again would they hunt.

The terrible hunger that dwelled within the soul of the DarkWolf could be abided.

Until then.

# # # #

AVAILABLE FROM E. DON HARPE

DARK WOLF

RESURRECTION

BOOK TWO IN THE HARPE SERIES

In 1804, some five years after the death of Micajah Harpe, Wiley Harpe was recognized and arrested in Greenville, Mississippi, where he stood trial for his crimes. He was found guilty and sentenced to be hanged. Not only did the citizens of Greenville hang Little Harpe, after a couple of days on the gallows the body was taken town and the head was cut off. The nailed the head to a stout pole in a field at the edge of town, where it remained for many years.

A few miles outside Greenville, Kentucky, in the forks of a tree rested the head of Big Harpe, and a few miles from Greenville, Mississippi, on the pole in the field rested the head of Little Harpe, and the legend of two of the most violent killers in the history of the country came to an end.

Or did it?

In the shadows of the cave in the spirit world, the DarkWolf slumbered, waiting only for a call from the Harpe to awaken.

Throughout the settlements the cry went.

"The Big Harpe is dead. Tis true I say. They've killed the Big Harpe, and his head is nailed in a tree. I've seen in myself. Have ye heard the news, the Big Harpe is dead."

All along the frontier the settlers were passing the word. The most feared killer of all had been caught and killed, and his head had been nailed in the forks of a sturdy oak tree.

A sigh of relief could be heard as each new person learned the Harpe was dead. The men knew they no longer had to worry about a monster such as the Harpe coming to their cabin and killing their women and children. The women were happy that once again their men could walk the forest trails in relative safety, and would more than likely reach their destination without running into the vicious wild wolf they called Harpe.

Throughout much of Kentucky, Tennessee and Southern Illinois, it was as though a violent storm had passed. Even if it had left behind a legacy of terror and bloodshed, with the Harpe dead the storm was over. The Harpes were a force of nature that touched the lives of every man, woman and child in the territory, and now they were gone.

As the word spread, the lives of the settlers began to return to normal, and many of the more courageous of them traveled to the cross roads to view the head of the man they had feared so much.

The community near the cross roads eventually came to be called "Harpshead," and the road called "Harpshead Road." There were few in the country that could not tell a stranger how to find Harpshead, and most were more than happy to spend a moment of two relating the adventures of the outlaw and his brother and their women to any travelers who didn't already know the story.

To those who came to see the head, there was no doubt the Harpe was dead. There was no mistaking that awful countenance. The spike that held the head had already begun to rust, but for years there remained faint traces of a reddish substance on it, and many thought it was the blood of the outlaw that stained the iron. Eventually the hair fell out and the flesh rotted away as the birds and the elements took their toll.

Still, deep in the vacant eye sockets, it appeared as if the skull were watching, waiting for something, keeping vigilance over the crossroads and the people who visited there. More than one traveler swore he felt a burning gaze from the skull as he rode beneath the tree.

Even in broad daylight, strong men felt the bumps arise on their necks as they walked the trail, and almost everyone avoided the crossroads after night had fallen.

The men who took part in the killing of Micajah Harpe stayed clear of the spot. They remembered all too well the promise made by the Harpe to return.

"Yer a goddamned rough butcher, but cut on and be damned," the Harpe had said, as Moses Stegall drew the knife around his neck. "I am the Harpe, the Wolf, and I can't be killed. I'll return, for I am yer death and destruction."

These words haunted John Leiper. They kept him awake at night, and he heard them rustling through the leaves in the trees as he road in the forest. He collected his gold, but he would never go near the crossroads again.

The words came stealing into the cabin of Matthew Christian in the middle of the night, waking him in a cold sweat, and causing him to arm himself and sit at the door of his cabin staring out into the darkness.

But most of all the last words of the Harpe whispered in the mind of Moses Stegall. Stegall knew much more than the others about the Harpe, and about the Wolf. He knew it was not a question of if the Harpe was coming back, but when. Stegall knew the Wolf could not die, and he was only waiting for the time to be right to return.

Stegall took Harpe's long knife home with him, and spent countless hours sitting at his tiny kitchen table, staring at the knife and reflecting on the ghastly deeds of his past. He whiled away the hours sharpening the knife until it was keen as a razor, and the blade gleamed and shimmered in the light of the oil lamp Stegall kept burning at all times, night and day.

He fashioned a case for the knife from seasoned oak, and lined it with two thicknesses of blood red velvet. He locked the cast with a sturdy padlock, and placed the key on a leather thong he wore around his neck until the day he died.

Stegall passed the story of the Harpes down to his son, along with the key to the casket, and bade him to pass it along to his first-born son. He recited the admonition over and over the Harpe would return, until his son was caught up in the same terror that lived in Moses' heart.

"Listen," he told his son. "Listen well to this story for there may come a day when these words will save your life. Till this day I recall the words of the Harpe, and I recall the sound the nail made as I pounded it into his dead and bloody skull. Thud. Thud. Thud. Thud. The nail sounded as I struck it with the hammer and drove it through flesh and bone. Remember well that sound, for when ye hear it onct again, t'will mean the monster has come back. Remember the sound, and understand one day it will sound in yer mind even as it now sounds in mine. On that fateful day when ye hears the sound, the Wolf will be back, and will onct again be hunting men to feed upon. No man will be safe, and certainly not one that bears the name Stegall."

Moses Stegall could be seen at times riding about the tree where the skull still rested, staring at the head and mumbling to himself. All too well he knew the Harpe, and all too much he feared the Wolf.

During the time when the Wolf and Micajah Harpe were one and the same, the Wolf knew the day would come when Harpe would lose his battle with one or another of his enemies. Not even the power of the spirit world could hold off the power of Fate. The body of the Harpe would die, and the Wolf would have to retreat back into his own world. Knowing this, the Wolf laid his plans well.

The Wolf knew the power of the Amulet could awaken him, and all that had to be done was for the Amulet to be placed about the neck of a first-born Harpe son. Once this happened, the doorway between the two worlds would open, and the Wolf would be free to hunt once again.

Being the most wise of the forest spirits, the Wolf decided he would devise a secondary plan as well, just in case anything went wrong with the first. He sent a bit of energy into one of the great knives the Harpe carried, and caused Micajah to hide the knife in a crevice deep inside Cave In Rock. If a Harpe child should find the knife, the spiritual energy of Micajah Harpe would be released into that child, and once again the forces of the two worlds would be united.

The plan of the Wolf was twofold, and was well prepared. When the time came that Micajah fought his final battle, the Wolf was ready. The day the Harpe fell, the Wolf gathered the energy of the dying man and enclosed it within a circle of the scared blue flame. So it was that even as the body of Micajah Harpe died, the energy of the being known as The Harpe lived on. With a final curse at the murderers of Micajah Harpe, the Wolf withdrew into the spirit world; there to remain until one or the other of his well laid plans come to fruition.

For countless years the Wolf slumbered deep inside the spirit world's chilly cave. He slept the deep peaceful sleep of an innocent child, restful and unencumbered by dreams. Time meant nothing to the Wolf, and only the growing hunger within told him years were passing by in the world of man.

Occasionally some small thing would bridge the gap between the human world and the place where the Wolf slept, and at those times one eye would open slightly and a blue flame would flicker for a few moments. But there never came a call from the Harpe, and the Wolf never fully awakened.

In 1849, Micajah's first grandson was born. James named him Thornton, and when the midwife slapped him on the behind and he uttered his first cry, the eyes of the Wolf slowly opened. He looked around the cave and saw only darkness, and let his vision shift to the eyes in Micajah's skull. Though the physical skull had long since disappeared, the spiritual skull was still in place. The Wolf looked out across the road and saw nothing on interest, not even one single traveler. He listened for a few moments but when the Harpe child did not call out to him, he once again closed his eyes and continued with his sleep.

More and more settlers came down into Kentucky and Tennessee, and the land changed. Trees gave way to houses, and more and more roads began to crisscross the wilderness.

In 1861 the Wolf's eyes suddenly snapped open. Even deep within the confines of the spirit world, he could feel the awful tension that wracked the world of men. Yet, even though the next few years were the worst the young country had ever seen, not once did the Harpe call upon the Wolf.

Thornton's firstborn male child came in 1901, and was named James after his father. Once again the Wolf waited, and again was not summoned. The blue flames flickered briefly and the hunger grew.

Odell Harp was born in 1940, and with his first cry the Wolf felt more intensity than he had felt in a generation. He yawned, opened his eyes, and once again peered through the eyes of the skull. He was not prepared for what he saw. There were houses and people everywhere, and strange machines roared along paved roads. With a low growl, the Wolf prepared himself for one more short nap.

In 1968, two hundred years to the day from the day Micajah Harpe was born, another firstborn Harpe child drew his first breath. He was Odell's child, and they named him James William Harp, and called him Billy. When he was born the eyes of the Wolf snapped wide open. The blue flame danced in all its wild fury, and the hunger inside his belly grew to gigantic proportions. The Wolf had no doubts. This child was the one. He was the Harpe, the chosen, and he was back. Soon would he hunger, as the Wolf had hungered for so long.

As Billy grew, now and then the Wolf would open his eyes and watch for a moment or so. He watched for any sign of weakness in the boy, ready to breach the line between the two worlds and send part of his spirit to reinforce the boy's resolve, but not once did he find a single chink in the boy's armor. Occasionally, when Billy would injure himself, the Wolf would send the energy through the gate to aid in his healing, and more than once he sent tiny fingerlings of wildness slithering through the darkness between the two worlds and into the boys mind.

Billy grew strong and brave, ready to face anything life threw at him, never once suspecting the presence of the Wolf.

Billy was eleven the first time the Wolf touched him with the rage.

Billy had a brand new pocketknife his father had given him just a few weeks before. He had sharpened in until he could shave the soft hair on his arm with it, and had practiced getting it out of his pocket and opening it as quickly as possible. He was very fast with it, never knowing it was a talent he was born to.

It was Halloween, and Billy had collected a large bag of candy on his trick or treat rounds of the neighborhood. He had told the last of his friends' goodnight and continued home alone, never once thinking to be afraid of the bigger kids that lived nearby.

As Billy passed the last street light before he reached his own home, he heard a voice softly call to him from the darkness.

"Hey, Harp," the voice said. "Come over here for a minute."

Billy walked over to the tall hedge where the words had come from.

"Who's there?" he asked.

"It's just me and Tommy," he heard a rough voice say, and recognized it as belonging to Buck Hendricks, one of the biggest bullies in school.

"What do you want, Tommy," Billy asked, his own voice sounding loud in his ears. He realized the two of them were probably going to try and beat him up, and though he wasn't afraid of them, he'd really just as soon pass on fighting them both.

Tommy and Buck stepped out from behind the hedge and stood staring at Billy in the pale yellow glow of the small streetlight.

"Don't worry, Harp, we just want to talk to you. And maybe eat a little bit of that trick or treat candy you got in the bag. We ain't going to hurt you."

Stepping back a step, Billy slowly eased his hand into his pocket where the knife rested.

Deep in the cave on the sprit world, as Billy's hand touched the knife, the eyes of the DarkWolf snapped open. The Wolf peered through Billy's eyes and saw the two bigger boys, and without a thought he sent a small hunger pang through the gate and into Billy's mind.

"Yeah, I know," Billy breathed, and his voice was quieter now. For some reason he had suddenly become very calm.

The steel of the knife was warm from the heat of Billy's hand, and as he opened it, something strange happened. A feeling came over Billy that he had never felt before, and a small flue flame began to flicker in his eyes.

"No, I know you're not going to hurt me," Billy said, whipping the knife open and holding it in front of him. The blade caught a tiny ray of light from the overhead street light and gleamed yellow in the darkness.

"I've got a sharp knife and a short temper, boys, and I'll cut you if I have to. And I'll only tell you the one time."

Perhaps it was the knife in Billy's hand, or perhaps they heard something in his voice that told them he was deadly serious. They may have even seen the faint glow in his eyes and recognized something that struck fear in their hearts, but whatever it was, it was enough to convince them to leave him alone. Turning away from Billy, the two bullies began to step back through the hedge.

"Just a minute," Billy said. "You'll be wanting to know the next time I hear of you two beating up one of the little kids, you'll have to answer to me. And I won't be playing any games with you." Without another word, Billy left the two boys standing by the hedge and walked on down the street toward his house.

He was almost home before he noticed that he still held the open knife in his hand, and only then was the urge in his heart to use the blade beginning to fade.

The Wolf smiled and closed his eyes. Yes, the Harpe was back. Soon would they hunt. Hhurry Harpe, I hunggggerrrrrrrr…

During the next few years the Wolf visited Billy Harp several times, each time bringing Billy closer to the day when he would be ready once again to become as one with the Wolf. Ready to take up the mantle of the Harpe and resume the hunt.

The Wolf knew it was only a matter of time before Billy found either the Amulet or the Blade. Either would do, and there was no doubt in the mind of the Wolf the Harpe had returned, and the world would once again tremble.

# # # #

Award winning author E. DON HARPE is a direct decendant of the Harpes, and his branch of the family is the only one that can be found that never denied their connection to the brothers.

E. DON HARPE has had a varied career, from military service in the 60's to years spent as an industrial engineer for a major appliance firm. Harpe is a Nashville songwriter who has had many recorded, and who for years ran his own music publishing company. While in Nashville Harpe was the office manager of a publishing company that had several number one country music hits, and was also the Creative Director for one of the most successful syndicated radio programs of the early 90's. During this time he won the coveted Silver Pen Award from the Nashville Banner daily newspaper.

Since retiring from public work in 2004, Harpe has concentrated on writing novels, and currently has more new books in the works. In all, he has nearly 40 short stories available on line, including two in an anthology called Twisted Tails II, published by Double Dragon Publishing, which won the *EPPIE AWARD* for best science fiction ebook anthology of 2007.

His memoir, *THE LAST OF THE SOUTH TOWN RINKY DINKS* was an instant success with readers everywhere. The stories are touching, down to earth tales of small town America, which bring tears and laughter to all who can remember when the world was a kinder, simpler place. It's the kind of book that you can't put down, and one that you will re-read many times over the years.

Now retired and living in Georgia, Harpe devotes his time to Helen, his wife of more than 50 years, to his children, grandchildren, great grandchildren, and to his writing.

"I'm pretty satisfied in my own skin right now," Harpe says, *"and I just want to continue to write things that will entertain and hold the readers interest."*

Connect with Harpe on the Internet at his website, as well as on Facebook and other social media.

website - http://www.donharpe.com/
http://www.flintriverpress.com/
Facebook - http://www.facebook.com/home.php?
Books and shorts available on Amazon, Createspace, and Smashwords
Follow Harpe on Twitter at @harpe

ALSO BY E. DON HARPE

RESURRECTION: REBIRTH OF THE TERRIBLE HARPES
THE LAST OF THE SOUTH TOWN RINKY DINKS
REDNECK UNIVERSE
MUSIC CITY MYTH
UNDER THE INFLUENCE OF A FULL MOON
BOLWING BETTER – LESS PAIN ON THE LANES
SUNDOWN TWO with PHIL WHITLEY
JAGGED EDGE OF OTHER WHEN with EUGEN BACON

SHORT STORIES

THE HARPE'S LAST RAMPAGE
FIRE FROM HEAVEN
REDNECK RIVIERA - A REDNECK RIVIERA STORY
TALLEDEGA TWOSTEP - A REDNECK RIVIERA STORY
COTTONDALE CONFIRMATION - A REDNECK RIVIERA STORY
MUSIC CITY MOJO - A REDNECK RIVIERA STORY
STUBIAN SWAMPDEVILS - A REDNECK RIVIERA STORY
FLAMINGO FIASCO - A REDNECK RIVIERA STORY
REDNECK RASSLIN' - A REDNECK RIVIERA STORY
ANGEL IN AMBER
KILLING FROST
THE DEMON REGISTRATION ACT

CYPHONS
THE TROPICAL TABOO CAPER
MILLER'S LUCK
THE EDGE
THE SKY IS FALLING
WHAT GOES AROUND
THE BIG PICTURE
FEBRUARY
THE WEDDING HELMET
SLUGGER
REST
THE FLAT ROCK KID - ABILENE

www.ingramcontent.com/pod-product-compliance
Lightning Source LLC
Chambersburg PA
CBHW050919030726
47503CB00007BB/2365